The Complete Short Stories

'A wholly original presence in modern literature' Andrew Motion

'My admiration for Spark's contribution to world literature knows no bounds. She was peerless, sparkling, inventive and intelligent – the crème de la crème' Ian Rankin

'One of this [20th] century's finest creators of the comic-metaphysical entertainment' *New York Times*

'Muriel Spark's novels linger in the mind as brilliant shards, decisive as a smashed glass is decisive' John Updike, *New Yorker*

'She can be compared to Evelyn Waugh . . . but there's Chekhov here, and a tincture of Stevie Smith . . . polished . . . individual . . . exacting' *Daily Telegraph*

'Spark is a natural, a paradigm of that rare sort of artist from whom work of the highest quality flows as elementally as current through a circuit: hook her to a pen and the juice purls out of her' *New Yorker*

'It is perhaps her short stories that demonstrate her gifts best: wit, perception, acute characterisation, elegance and precision. They mark her out as one of the finest writers of her generation' *Observer*

'Muriel Spark has made herself a mistress at writing stories which seem to trip blithely and bitchily along life's way until the reader is suddenly pulled up with a shock recognition of death and judgment, heaven and hell' *London Review of Books*

'All [the stories] are hallmarked with those instantly identifiable Sparkian qualities; brevity, detachment and a sly, sinister wit' *Literary Review*

'Dullness is as alien to her as inelegance' *New Statesman & Society*

Also by Muriel Spark

FICTION

The Comforters
Robinson
The Go-Away Bird and Other Stories
Memento Mori
The Ballad of Peckham Rye
The Bachelors
Voices at Play
The Prime of Miss Jean Brodie
The Girls of Slender Means
The Mandelbaum Gate
The Public Image
The Driver's Seat
Not to Disturb
The Hothouse by the East River
The Abbess of Crewe
The Takeover
Territorial Rights
Loitering with Intent
Bang-bang You're Dead and Other Stories
The Only Problem
The Stories of Muriel Spark
A Far Cry From Kensington
Symposium
Reality and Dreams
Aiding and Abetting
The Finishing School

CHILDREN'S FICTION

The French Window
The Small Telephone
The Very Fine Clock

PLAYS

Doctors of Philosophy

POETRY

Going Up to Sotheby's

AUTOBIOGRAPHY

Curriculum Vitae

ESSAYS

The Essence of the Brontës

the canons 2

MURIEL SPARK

The Complete Short Stories

Introduction by
Janice Galloway

CANONGATE
Edinburgh · London · New York · Melbourne

This edition published in Great Britain in 2011 by Canongate Books,
14 High Street, Edinburgh, EH1 1TE

First published in Great Britain in 2001 by
Viking, Penguin Books Ltd, 80 Strand,
London WC2R ORL

www.canongate.tv

1

British Library Cataloguing-in-Publication Data
A catalogue record for this book is available on
request from the British Library

ISBN 978 0 85786 227 3

Typeset in Goudy by Palimpsest Book Production Ltd,
Falkirk, Stirlingshire

Printed and bound in Great Britain by CPI Mackays, Chatham ME5 8TD

CONTENTS

THE SMALLER BIGGER PICTURE

by Janice Galloway

They are my own secret rules but they arise from deep conviction. They cannot be formulated, they are as sincere and indescribable as are the primary colours; they are not of a science, but of an art.

The voice of Lucy, 'The Fortune Teller', Muriel Spark

I met Mrs Spark for the first time in specious surroundings. The place was a television studio where a pilot chat show in the guise of a dinner party hosted by the comedienne Ruby Wax was about to be filmed. I was first to arrive, and nervous. Jeremy Hardy and Dr Jonathan Miller were next, and Mrs Spark, five foot one and not small at all, joined us to make the full quartet. Our job was to chat and 'be natural' whilst poking rocket leaves about with our forks, all the while ignoring the cameras and crew as they lurked and tiptoed under quasi-intimate low lighting. Everything was odd. Ms Wax looked unsettled, Dr Miller began to assume the manner of someone suffering from status anxiety and Mr Hardy was, despite his best attempts, too frequently sidelined to bring us together. Only Mrs Spark, her hair subtly curled, was unruffled. She looked coolmaxed. Even amused.

Maybe that's what years and reputation do for you, I thought; maybe she's senior enough and fêted enough not to give much of a toss. The more I watched, however, the more I realised that that wasn't it. Dame Muriel was *comfortable,* not bored. The work I knew and loved came to mind as I focussed on her expression, her mannerisms: all those tales fraught with tripwires and trapdoors, spies, eavesdroppers and voices offstage; those inexplicably discomfited atmospheres in which banalities and non sequiturs filled in for conversation. And I got it. The great writer, a watcher since childhood, was enjoying watching us struggle to be *normal.* In terms of her literary preoccupations, this was *terra* entirely *cognita.* She was, almost, at home.

If writing came naturally to Muriel Spark – and she insists it did – so did her material. She specialises in paradox, danger, assumption, the Great Unseen. In her stories and novels, even in her biographies of Mary Shelley and Emily Brontë, the air crawls with treachery and half-truths. Characters pilfer, conceal and betray. Wrong ends of sticks poke out at you from thickets and something, somewhere, is on the prowl, keen to shiver your spine as it walks across your grave. Is it a monster, bad luck or simple comeuppance? Is it the residue of God's relentless wrath against the unfortunate Job? That, dear reader, is up to you. Reading Muriel Spark's stories demands a little reading between their lines. Furthermore, though much has been made of her Catholic conversion (most of it useful as a herring in a box of fireworks), no ecclesiastical empathy or insight is required to love her keen eye for human frailty or her near-Calvinist skepticism – even from those who tell you to question everything. 'Beware of writers', she asserts. 'Beware of me.'

Muriel Camberg was born in 1918 in Edinburgh, the daughter of Jewish and English Anglican parents. Her background was, in her own words, 'humble' – it sounds nicer than 'working class' in the douce Scottish capital – and her relatives were 'plain'. Isolated, curious, Muriel found much entertainment in her mother's English idioms, and an early preoccupation with listening and detecting nuance honed what would become her fine ear for dialogue in later life. To add further spice, the gentile jewess enjoyed a sound Presbyterian education at James Gillespie's School and read the bloody, crow-picked Scots–English Border ballads – one of the cornerstones of Scottish literature – for pleasure. After a brief secretarial course at Heriot-Watt College, she dispensed with formal education altogether as 'dull'. After a few years of office work, she turned refugee by marrying Oswald Spark (as much for his tickets to Rhodesia as anything else) and shipping off to Africa, where things went from bad to potentially fatal. Her near-miraculous escape after Mr Spark threatened to shoot her brought her home, thankful and in desperate need of a living wage. Handing over her baby to the grandparents in Bruntsfield allowed her to hare off to the safety of the biggest city on offer, where concealment was not only possible but easy. In London, and in poverty, she let poetry, the hallucinogenic side-effects of Dexedrine and the Catholic Church provide both her break and her fresh, new start with quite literal blessings.

Keeping her husband's name as a souvenir and a metaphor, Mrs Spark began her writing life in earnest in her early thirties. Her first novel, *The Comforters* – a book about writing a book, a talking typewriter, delusion and overcoming crisis – set it on course. Her autobiography, *Curriculum Vitae*, covers these events as though consigning them to a bonfire before swiftly moving on: 'I only made it about those days because after that, everybody knew what I was doing. I was writing.'

She was writing a lot. In London, New York and Italy, while constantly moving to avoid 'enemies', crowds and constricting cliques, she produced twenty-two novels, a sheaf of poems, one play and two brace of stories in a non-stop career that lasted four and a half decades. In all of her work her voice is unmistakable: flexible, shrewd, crackling with life. That voice could have been pared back as the years went by, but she started as she meant to go on, and refused to settle into any one tradition. Her work takes what it needs from crime stories, ghost stories, parody, camp and kitchen-sink realism and weaves it all together in a way that is both clipped and free-wheeling, saturnine and light, allusive, direct, playful, serious and straight to the point. Even in the slighter pieces of word-play (now and then she opts for simply amusing herself), fewer words are always more. 'I sometimes think,' she confessed, 'that a novel is a kind of lazy way of writing a short story, a short story a lazy way of writing a poem. The longer they become, the more they seem to lose value.'

Concision matters because human life is short and, indeed, only part of the picture. Wonder, pity, cruelty, the eternal (for which one need not read a religious meaning, but the sweep of history that was there before us and will be there after we are gone) and the frankly ludicrous must be made room for too (as in a Breughel painting), and no one dimension can dominate the alleged meaning of the story. She has ground to cover, Mrs Spark. Her pace, perforce, must be fleet.

Now, mixing these insights is not to everyone's taste. Malcolm Bradbury is on record as reading Mrs Spark's essence as 'hardness'. Others – mostly chaps – sum her up as 'steely', 'aloof', 'brusque', 'capricious' and 'queer'. I mention such commentary only because it astonishes me. How can they *not see* her playfulness, the shapeliness of her language, the luxury of her best aphorisms? Why deny the arch, even flirtatious, tone she adopts at her wittiest, or the catch in the heart when a character's vulnerability is peeled, helpless as a clam, from its carapace? 'My work is not easy to classify,' she used to confide in conversation, not just one-to-one but with whole audiences. 'It bothers people. Makes them nettlesome.'

Could it be the case, as she suggests, that her detractors feel forced to squash her entire *oeuvre* into one mean adjective precisely *because* of her diversity? Is that knowing, deeply womanly tone cheek by jowl with a resistance to conventional surrender what 'bothers' them most? Maybe, keen on single-trajectory arousal, they feel snubbed? Who knows? I am as certain as I can be that this resistance to classification is not coquetry or anything like. It is something much more useful.

Her two biographies, do not forget, researched writers who experienced critical censure much focussed on their sex: Mary Shelley, the author of *Frankenstein*, had variously been called a 'mere sponge who absorbed the ideas of the great men who surrounded her', a cypher of her talented husband and a hysteric, while Emily Brontë hid behind a male pseudonym (as did her sisters) to avoid the double dismissal of her work as not only tragically girly but also unwomanly in her immodest desire to parade it shamelessly before the public. The literary London in which Mrs Spark earned a pittance as a poetry magazine editor was not wildly supportive, made up as it was of a rather self-regarding and heavily male in-crowd (she had unhappy affairs with more than one member of it) quick to classify female aspirants to their number as neurotics, bluestockings (unfeminine, unprepossessing and sex-starved in one) or scribblers of something inconsequential called 'women's books'.* That Mrs Spark's literary intuition picked resistance to classification as its hallmark seems an astute subconscious choice and no surprise. What makes one prickle with delight is how seductively she accomplishes it; how naturally, in the disguise of character, she is able to assume aplomb.

As for subject matter, what surer to stand on than one's own two feet? 'She had all these years of really great experience,' says her fan the crime-writer Ian Rankin, 'from wartime London, Edinburgh, breakdowns, Africa, her Jewish heritage, marriages going bad – and it's all there, laid out on the page for people to explore, book by book.'

It's also not there, of course. This writing is not autobiographical reportage or police-report detail. Instead, it uses her small place in the scheme of things as a conduit, and attends to the transformations of Art. 'I don't see what else you can draw on for fiction but your life,' she said. 'Not only your own life but what you've learned or grasped about other people's. It's one's own experience after all. What else can it be? All writers do this.' Of course they do. It's just that some have more bother acknowledging it than others. As befits a writer with a clear understanding of her own mortality, Mrs Spark grasps her own life and those of her characters with the same hands. Often, in a wonderful gesture of self-implication, her narrator is 'I'. Far from being 'harsh' or 'aloof', Mrs S is there too, at the heart of the crowd, as both observer and observed.

Though much of Muriel Spark's fame rests in her novels (*The Ballad of Peckham Rye, Memento Mori, Loitering with Intent* and *The Driver's Seat* are my list of stand-outs), the lady herself felt happier with her shorter work: the bigger picture in fewer words. You may recognise some themes. Five are set in Africa, a country where the near-tangible, menacing pervasiveness of heat can turn milk and men's minds with equal ease. Colonial life is full of drink, careless social divisions and latent sexual violence. In this jungle, the unexpected is guaranteed. 'The blacks look happy enough,' says one complacent onlooker in 'Bang-Bang You're Dead'. '"Did you have any trouble with them in those days?" "No," said Sybil. "Only with the whites."' World-weary Sybil knows more than she says.

'The Go-Away Bird', a more traditionally structured tale, weaves signs and portents, misreadings and an ominous sense of growing tension towards its ghastly end. Mrs Van der Merwe ('A Curtain Blown by the Wind') can change her surroundings and even her expectations, but not her dreadful, almost pre-destined, vulnerability. Most of us, Spark implies, see what we want to see and what we want to see is not necessarily what's there.

Ghosts are everywhere, some on buses or in office-blocks, some (the catching kind) in doctors' surgeries, and others wave innocuous hellos on the Portobello Road. Angels and demons (further explorations of the plausible Edinburgh time-

and-motion demon from the novel *The Ballad of Peckham Rye*) drift back and forth carrying fags and parcels; they manifest as cranky uncles and irritable, drug-wary cooks. Do not be surprised if you laugh even as death surrounds you – some tales (like 'The Executor', which makes fun of golf, fishing, the moral high ground and the Edinburgh stereotype), provoke it all too well.

You will encounter protagonists who have been corrupted, sucked dry of purpose and wired to the moon. Some are from the moon. Mrs Spark, famously Catholic and somewhat nervous, has fun even with the religious and the 'highly strung'. 'Come Along Marjorie', a glimpse of life in a religious retreat, details the (first person) author and other 'neurotics' with such relentless plain-speaking, I smiled all the way through. Till the end of course. 'The Black Madonna' carries everything a stage further into near-unsayable black farce. Bugger hushed reverence: Mrs Spark speaks as she finds. A master blender of the lightest lights with dreadful dark, Spark went her own way for over forty years, and that dogged originality is what I hope you enjoy most. Remember we are dust, by all means. But look out for the primary colours. Rejoice. Take in the Art.

* In 2004, I recall the estimable Gerard Carruthers of Glasgow University confiding, in a taped interview, that a friend of his father's, on finding he was interested in the work of Spark, asked him if he was 'still reading those women's books' – perhaps it still goes on.

The Complete Short Stories

THE GO-AWAY BIRD

1

All over the Colony it was possible to hear the subtle voice of the grey-crested lourie, commonly known as the go-away bird by its call, "go'way, go'way". It was possible to hear the bird, but very few did, for it was part of the background to everything, a choir of birds and beasts, the crackle of vegetation in the great prevalent sunlight, and the soft rhythmic pad of natives, as they went barefoot and in single-file, from kraal to kraal.

Out shooting with her uncle and her young friends, happy under her wide-brimmed hat, Daphne du Toit would sometimes hear the go-away bird. Sometimes, during the school holidays, her aunt and uncle would have the young neighbours over from farms thirty miles distant. They would scrounge a lift into the nearest township – "the dorp" they called it, for it was no more than a sandy main street in a valley, frequently cut off in the rainy season, when the rivers would swell above the bridges.

As they rumbled down the hill in the Ford V8 the uneven line of corrugated iron roofs would rise to meet them, and presently the car would stop outside the post office which was also the headquarters of the Native Commissioner. They would spill out to receive calls and glances of recognition from the white population. Natives would appear from nowhere to group themselves a few yards from the car, grinning with a kind of interest. They would amble past the general European store, two or three native stores and a dozen haphazard houses with voices of women scolding their servants rising from behind the torn mosquito-wire around the dark stoeps. Though it was a British colony, most of the people who lived in the dorp and its vicinity were Afrikaners, or Dutch as they were simply called. Daphne's father had been Dutch, but her mother had been a Patterson from England, and since their death she had lived with her mother's relations, the Chakata Pattersons, who understood, but preferred not to speak Afrikaans. Chakata was sixty, he had been very much older than Daphne's mother, and his own children were married, were farming in other colonies. Chakata nourished a passionate love for the natives. No one had called him James for thirty-odd years; he went by the natives' name for him, Chakata. He loved the natives as much as he hated the Dutch.

Daphne had come into his household when she was six, both parents then being dead. That year Chakata was awarded an OBE for his model native villages. Daphne remembered the great creaky motor-vans and horse-drawn, sometimes ox-drawn, covered wagons pouring into the farm from far distances, thirty miles or five hundred miles away, neighbours come to congratulate Chakata. The empty bottles piled up in the yard. The native boys ran about all day to attend to the guests, some of whom slept in the house, most of whom bedded down in their wagons. Some were Dutch, and these, when they dismounted from their wagons, would kneel to thank God for a safe arrival. They would then shout their orders to their servants and go to greet Old Tuys who had come out to welcome them. Chakata always fell back a little behind Old Tuys when Dutch visitors came to the farm. This was out of courtesy and tact for Old Tuys, the tobacco manager on Chakata's farm who was Dutch, and Chakata felt that these Afrikaners would want to linger first with him, and exchange something sociable in Afrikaans. As for Chakata, although he spoke at least twenty native dialects, he would no more think of speaking Afrikaans than he would think of speaking French. The Dutch visitors would have to congratulate Chakata on his OBE in the English tongue, however poorly managed, if they really wished to show they meant him well. Everyone knew that Old Tuys was a constant irritant to Chakata, addressing him usually in Dutch, to which Chakata invariably replied in English.

During those weeks following Chakata's return from Government House with the Order, when he kept open house, Daphne would loiter around the farmhouse, waiting for the arrival of the cars and wagons, in the hope that they might bring a child for her to play with. Her only playmate was the cook's piccanin, Moses, a year older than Daphne, but frequently he was called away to draw water, sweep the yard, or fetch wood. He would trot across the yard with a pile of wood pressed against his chest and rising up to his eyes, clutching it officiously in his black arms which themselves resembled the faggots he bore. When Daphne scampered after Moses to the well or the wood-pile one of the older natives would interfere. "No, Missy Daphne, you do no piccanin's work. You go make play." She would wander off barefoot to the paddock beyond the guava bushes, or to the verging plantation of oranges, anywhere except the tobacco sheds, for there she might bump into Old Tuys who would then stop what he was doing, stand straight and, folding his arms, look at her with his blue eyes and sandy face. She would stare at him for a frightened moment and then run for it.

Once when she had been following a dry river-bed which cut through Chakata's land she nearly trod on a snake, and screaming, ran blindly to the nearest farm buildings, the tobacco sheds. Round the corner of one of the sheds came Old Tuys, and in her panic and relief at seeing a human face, Daphne ran up to him. "A snake! There's a snake down the river-bed!" He straightened up, folded his arms, and looked at her until she turned and ran from him, too.

Old Tuys was not yet sixty. He had been called Young Tuys until his wife was known definitely to have committed adultery, not once, but a number of times. After her death it was at first a matter of some surprise among the farmers that Old Tuys did not leave Chakata's, for with his sound health and experience of tobacco, he could have been anyone's manager in or beyond the Colony. But word got round why Tuys remained with Chakata, and the subject was no more mentioned, save as passed on from fathers to sons, mothers to daughters, like the local genealogies, the infallible methods of shooting to kill, and the facts of life.

Daphne was only half conscious of the go-away bird, even while she heard it, during the first twelve years of her life. In fact she learnt about it at school during Natural History, and immediately recognized the fact that she had been hearing this bird calling all her life. She began to go out specially to hear it, and staring into the dry river-bed, or brushing round the orange trees, she would strain for its call; and sometimes at sundowner time, drinking her lemonade between Chakata and his wife on the stoep, she would say, "Listen to the go-away bird."

"No," said Chakata one evening, "it's too late. They aren't about as late as this."

"It *was* the Bird," she said, for it had assumed for her sufficient importance to be called simply this, like the biblical Dove, or the zodiacal Ram.

"Look yere, Daphne, ma girl," said Mrs Chakata, between two loud sucks of whisky and water, "chuck up this conversation about the blerry bird. If that's all they teach you at the blerry boarding-school –"

"It's Natural History," Chakata put in. "It's a very good thing that she's interested in the wild life around us."

Mrs Chakata had been born in the Colony. She spoke English with the African Dutch accent, although her extraction was English. Some said, however, that there was a touch of colour, but this was not sufficiently proved by her crinkled brown skin: many women in the Colony were shrivelled in complexion, though they were never hatless, nor for long in the sun. It was partly the dry atmosphere of the long hot season and partly the continual whisky drinking that dried most of them up. Mrs Chakata spent nearly all day in her kimono dressing-gown lying on the bed, smoking to ease the pains in her limbs the nature of which no doctor had yet been able to diagnose over a period of six years.

Since ever Daphne could remember, when Mrs Chakata lay on her bed in the daytime she had a revolver on a table by her side. And sometimes, when Chakata had to spend days and nights away from the farm, Daphne had slept in Mrs Chakata's room, while outside the bedroom door, on a makeshift pallet, lay Ticky Talbot, the freckled Englishman who trained Chakata's racers. He lay with a gun by his side, treating it all as rather a joke.

From time to time Daphne had inquired the reasons for these precautions. "You can't trust the munts," said Mrs Chakata, using the local word for the natives. Daphne never understood this, for Chakata's men were the finest in the Colony, that was an axiom. She vaguely thought it must be a surviving custom of general practice, dating from the Pioneer days, when white men and women were frequently murdered in their beds. This was within living history, and tales of these past massacres and retributions were part of daily life in the great rural districts of the Colony. But the old warrior chiefs were long since dead, and the warriors disbanded, all differences now being settled by the Native Commissioners. As she grew older Daphne thought Mrs Chakata and her kind very foolish to take such elaborate precautions against something so remote as a native rising on the farm. But it was not until the Coates family moved in to the neighbouring farm thirty-five miles away that Daphne discovered Mrs Chakata's precautionary habits were not generally shared by the grown-up females of the Colony. Daphne was twelve when the Coates family, which included two younger girls and two older boys, came to the district. During the first school holidays after their arrival she was invited over to stay with them. Mr Coates had gone on safari, leaving his wife and children on the farm. The only other European there was a young married student of agriculture who lived on their land two miles from the farmhouse.

Daphne was put up on a camp bed in Mrs Coates's bedroom. She noticed that her hostess had no revolver by her side, nor was anyone on sentry duty outside the door.

"Aren't you afraid of the munts?" said Daphne.

"Good gracious, why? Our boys are marvellous."

"Auntie Chakata always sleeps with a pistol by her side."

"Is she afraid of rape, then?" said Mrs Coates. All the children in the Colony understood the term; rape was a capital offence, and on very remote occasions the Colony would be astir about a case of rape, whether the accused was a white man or a black.

It was a new thought to Daphne that Mrs Chakata might fear rape, not murder as she had supposed. She looked at Mrs Coates with wonder. "There isn't anyone, is there, would rape Auntie Chakata?" Mrs Coates was smiling to herself.

Often, when she was out with the Coates children, Daphne would hear the go-away bird. One day when the children were walking through a field of maize, the older Coates boy, John, said to Daphne,

"Why do you suddenly stop still like that?"

"I'm listening to the go-away bird," she said.

Her face was shaded under the wide brim of her hat, and the maize rose all round her, taller than herself. John Coates, who was sixteen, folded his arms and looked at her, for it was an odd thing for a little girl to notice the go-away bird.

"What are you looking at?" she said.

He didn't answer. The maize reached to his shoulder. He was put into a dither, and so he continued to look at her, arms folded, as if he felt confident.

"Don't stand like that," Daphne said. "You remind me of Old Tuys."

John immediately laughed. He took his opportunity to gain a point, to alleviate his awkwardness and support his pose. "You got a handful there with Old Tuys," he said.

"Old Tuys is the best tobacco baas in the country," she said defiantly. "Uncle Chakata likes Old Tuys."

"No, he does not like him," said John.

"Yes, he does so, or he wouldn't keep him on."

"My girl," said John, "I know why Chakata keeps on Old Tuys. *You* know. Everyone knows. It isn't because he likes him."

They moved on to join the other children. Daphne wondered why Chakata kept on Old Tuys.

They scrounged a lift to the dorp. The Coates family were uninhibited about speaking Afrikaans, chatting in rapid gutturals to people they met while Daphne stood by, shyly following what she could of the conversation.

They were to return to the car at five ôclock, and it was now only half-past three. Daphne took her chance and slipped away from the group through the post office and out at the back yard where the natives were squatting round their mealie-pot. They watched her with their childish interest as she made her way past the native huts and the privies and out on the sanitary lane at the foot of the yard.

Daphne nipped across a field and up the steep track of Donald Cloete's kopje. It bore this name, because Donald

Cloete was the only person who lived on the hill, although there were several empty shacks surrounding his.

Donald Cloete had been to Cambridge. Indoors, he had two photographs on the wall. One was Donald in the cricket team, not easily recognizable behind his wide, curly moustache and among the other young men who looked so like him and stood in the same stiff, self-assured manner that Daphne had observed in pictures of the Pioneer heroes. The picture was dated 1898. Another group showed Donald in uniform among his comrades of the Royal Flying Corps. It was dated 1918, but Donald behind his moustache did not look much older than he appeared in the Cambridge picture.

Daphne looked round the open door and saw Donald seated in his dilapidated cane chair. His white shirt was stained with beetroot.

"Are you drunk, Donald," she inquired politely, "or are you sober?"

Donald always told the truth. "I'm sober," he said. "Come in."

At fifty-six his appearance now had very little in common with the young Cambridge cricketer or the RFC pilot. He had been in hundreds of jobs, had married and lost his wife to a younger and more energetic man. The past eight years had been the most settled in his life, for he was Town Clerk of the dorp, a job which made few demands on punctuality, industry, smartness of appearance, and concentration, which qualities Donald lacked. Sometimes when the Council held its monthly meeting, and Donald happened to stagger in late and drunk, the Chairman would ask Donald to leave the meeting, and in his absence propose his dismissal. Sometimes they unanimously dismissed him and after the meeting he was informed of the decision. However, next day Donald would dress himself cleanly and call in to see the butcher with a yarn about the RFC; he would call on the headmaster who had been to Cambridge some years later than Donald; and after doing a round of the Council members he would busy himself in the district, would ride for miles on his bicycle seeing that fences were up where they should be, and sign-posts which had fallen in the rains set upright and prominent. Within a week, Donald's dismissal would be ignored by everyone. He would relax then, and if he entered up a birth or a death during the week, it was a good week's work.

"Who brought you from the farm?" said Donald.

"Ticky Talbot," said Daphne.

"Nice to see you," said Donald. And he called to his servant for tea.

"Five more years and then I go to England," said Daphne, for this was the usual subject between them, and she did not feel it right to come to the real purpose of her visit so soon.

"That will be the time," said Donald. "When you go to England, that will be the time." And he told her all over again about the water meadows at Cambridge, the country pubs, the hedging and ditching, the pink-coated riders.

Donald's ragged native brought in tea in two big cups, holding one in each hand. One he gave to Daphne and the other to Donald.

How small, Donald said, were the English streams which never dried up. How small the fields, little bits of acreage, and none of the cottage women bitchy for they did their own house-work and had no time to bitch. And then, of course, the better classes taking tea in their long galleries throughout the land, in springtime, with the pale sunlight dripping through the mullioned windows on to the mellow Old Windsor chairs, and the smell of hyacinths . . .

"Oh, I see. Now tell me about London, Donald. Tell me about the theatres and bioscopes."

"They don't say 'bioscope' there, they say 'cinema' or 'the pictures'."

"I say, Donald," she said, for she noticed it was twenty-past four, "I want you to tell me something straight."

"Fire ahead," said Donald.

"Why does Uncle Chakata keep on Old Tuys?"

"I don't want to lose my job," he said.

"Upon my honour," she said, "if you tell me about Old Tuys I shan't betray you."

"The whole Colony knows the story," said Donald, "but the first one to tell it to you is bound to come up against Chakata."

"May I drop dead on this floor," she said, "if I tell my Uncle Chakata on you."

"How old are you, now?" Donald said.

"Nearly thirteen."

"It was two years before you were born – that would make it fifteen years ago, when Old Tuys . . ."

Old Tuys had already been married for some time to a Dutch girl from Pretoria. Long before he took the job at Chakata's he knew of her infidelities. They had one peculiarity: her taste was exclusively for Englishmen. The young English settlers whom she met in the various establishments where Tuys was employed were, guilty or not, invariably accosted by Tuys: "You committed adultery with my wife, you swine." There might be a fight, or Tuys would threaten his gun. However it might be, and whether or not these young men were his wife's lovers, Tuys was usually turned off the job.

It was said he was going to shoot his wife and arrange it to look like an accident. Simply because this intention was widely reported, he could not have carried out the plan successfully, even if he did, in fact, contemplate the deed. Certainly he beat her up from time to time.

Tuys hoped eventually to get a farm of his own. Chakata, who knew of his troubles, took Tuys on to learn the tobacco sheds. Tuys and his wife moved into a small house on Chakata's land. "Any trouble with the lady, Tuys," said Chakata, "come to me, for in a young country like this, with four white men to every one white woman, there is bound to be trouble."

There was trouble the first week with a trooper.

"Look here, Tuys," said Chakata, "I'll talk to her." He had frequently in his life had the painful duty of giving his servants a talking-to on sex. At the Pattersons' home in England it had been a routine affair.

Hatty Tuys was not beautiful: in fact she was dark and scraggy. However, Chakata not only failed to reform her, he succumbed to her. She wept. She said she hated Tuys.

Donald paused in his story to remark to Daphne, "Mind you, this sort of thing doesn't happen in England."

"Doesn't it?" said Daphne.

"Oh well, there are love affairs but they take time. You have to sort of build them up with a woman. In England, a man of Chakata's importance might feel sorry for a slut if she started to cry, but he wouldn't just make love to her on the spot. The climate's cooler there, you see, and there are a lot more girls."

"Oh, I see," said Daphne. "What did Uncle Chakata do next?"

"Well, as soon as he had played the fool with Mrs Tuys he felt sorry. He told her it was a moment of weakness and it would never occur again. But it did."

"Did Tuys find out?"

"Tuys found out. He went to Mrs Chakata and tried to rape her."

"Didn't it come off?"

"No, it didn't come off."

"It must have been the whisky in her breath. It must have put him off," said Daphne.

"In England," said Donald, "girls your age don't know very much about these things."

"Oh, I see," said Daphne.

"It's all different there. Well, Mrs Chakata complained to Chakata, and wanted him to shoot Tuys. He refused, of course, and he gave Tuys a rise and made him manager. And from that day he wouldn't look at Mrs Tuys, wouldn't even look at her. Whenever he caught sight of her about the farm, he looked the other way. In the end she wrote to Chakata to say she was mad in love with him and if she couldn't have him she would shoot herself. The note was written in block letters, in Afrikaans."

"Chakata would never answer it, then," Daphne said.

"You are right," said Donald. "And Mrs Tuys shot herself. Old Tuys has sworn to be revenged on Chakata some day.

That's why Mrs Chakata has a gun at her bedside. She has implored Chakata to get rid of Old Tuys. So he should, of course."

"He can't, very well, when you think of it," said Daphne.

"It's only his remorse," said Donald, "and his English honour. If Old Tuys was an Englishman, Daphne, he would have cleared off the farm long ago. But no, he remains, he has sworn on the Bible to be revenged."

"It must be our climate," said Daphne. "I have never liked the way Old Tuys looks at me."

"The Colony is a savage place," he said. He rose and poured himself a whisky. "I grant you," he said, "we have the natives under control. I grant you we have the leopards under control –"

"Oh, remember Moses," said Daphne. Her former playmate, Moses, had been got by a leopard two years ago.

"That was exceptional. We are getting control over malaria. But we haven't got the *savage in ourselves* under control. This place brings out *the savage in ourselves*." He finished his drink and poured another. "If you go to England," he said, "don't come back."

"Oh, I see," said Daphne.

She was ten minutes late when she arrived at the car. The party had been anxious about her.

"Where did you get to? You slipped away . . . we asked everywhere . . ."

John Coates said in a mock-girlish tone, "Oh, she's been listening to the go-away bird out on the lone wide veldt."

"Five more years and then I go to England. Four years . . . three . . ."

Meanwhile, life in the Colony seemed to become more exciting every year. In fact, it went on as usual, but Daphne's capacity for excitement developed as she grew into her teens.

She had a trip to Kenya to stay with a married cousin, another trip to Johannesburg with Mrs Coates to buy clothes.

"Typical English beauty Daphne's turning out to be," said Chakata. In reality she was too blonde to be typically English; she took after her father's family, the Cape du Toits, who were a mixture of Dutch and Huguenot stock.

At sixteen she passed her matric and her name was entered for a teachers' training college in the Capital. During the holidays she flirted with John Coates, who would drive her round the countryside in the little German Volkswagen which his father had obtained for him. They would go on Sunday afternoons to the Williams Hotel on the great main road for tea and a swim in the bathing-pool with all the district who converged there weekly from farms and towns.

"In England," Daphne would tell him, "you can bathe in the rivers. No bilharzia there, no crocs."

"There's going to be a war in Europe," said John.

Daphne would sit on the hotel stoep in her smart new linen slacks, sipping her gin and lime, delighted and amazed to be grown-up, to be greeted by her farming neighbours.

"'Lo, Daphne, how are your mealies?"

"Not too bad, how are yours?"

"Hallo, Daphne, how's the tobacco?"

"Rotten, Old Tuys says."

"I hear Chakata's sold La Flèche."

"Well, he's had an offer, actually."

She had been twice to a dance at Williams Hotel. Young

Billy Williams, who was studying medicine at Cape Town, proposed marriage to her, but as everyone knew, she was to go to college in the Capital and then to England to stay with the English Pattersons for a couple of years before she could decide about marriage.

War broke out at the beginning of her first term at the training college. All her old young men, as well as her new, became important and interesting in their uniforms and brief appearances on leave.

She took up golf. Sometimes, after a hole, when she was following her companions to the next tee, she would lag behind or even stop in her tracks.

"Feeling all right, Daphne?"

"Oh, I was only listening to the go-away bird."

"Interested in ornithology?"

"Oh yes, fairly, you know."

When she returned to the farm after her first term at the college Chakata gave her a revolver.

"Keep it beside your bed," he said.

She took it without comment.

Next day, he said, "Where did you go yesterday afternoon?"

"Oh, for a trek across the veldt, you know."

"Anywhere special?"

"Only to Makata's kraal. He's quite determined to hang on to that land the Beresfords are after. He's got a wife for his son, he paid five head." Makata was the local chief. Daphne enjoyed squatting in the shade of his great mud hut drinking the tea specially prepared for her, and though the rest of the Colony looked with disfavour on such visits, it was something which Chakata and his children had always done, and no one felt inclined to take up the question with Chakata. Chakata wasn't just anyone.

"I suppose," said Chakata to Daphne, "you always carry a gun?"

"Well, yesterday," said Daphne, "I didn't actually."

"*Always*," said Chakata, "take a gun when you go out on the veldt. It's a golden rule. There's nothing more exasperating than to see a buck dancing about in the bush and to find yourself standing like a fool without a gun."

Since she was eight and had first learnt to shoot, this had been a golden rule of Chakata's. Many a time she had been out on her own, weighed down with the gun, and had seen dozens of buck and simply had not bothered to shoot. She hated venison, in any case. Tinned salmon was her favourite dish.

He seemed to know her thoughts. "We're always short of buck for the dogs. Remember there's a war on. Remember *always*," said Chakata, "to take a gun. I hear on the wireless," he added, "that there's a leopard over in the Temwe valley. The mate has young. It's got two men, so far."

"Uncle Chakata, that's a long way off," Daphne said explosively.

"Leopards can travel," said Chakata. He looked horribly put out.

"Oh, I see," said Daphne.

"And you ought to ride more," he said, "it's far better exercise than walking."

She saw that he was not really afraid of her meeting the leopard, nor did he need meat for the dogs; and she thought of how, yesterday afternoon, she had been followed all the way to the kraal by Old Tuys. He had kept to the bush, and seemed not to know he had been observed. She had been glad that several parties of natives had passed her on the way. Afterwards, when she was taking leave of Makata, he had offered to send his nephew to accompany her home. This was a customary offer: she usually declined it. This time, however, she had accepted the escort, who plodded along behind her until she dismissed him at the edge of the farm. Daphne did not mention this incident to Chakata.

That afternoon when she set off for tea at the Mission, she was armed.

Next day Chakata gave her the old Mercedes for herself. "You walk too much," he said.

It was no use now, checking off the years before she should go to England. She climbed Donald Cloete's kopje: "Are you sober, Donald, or –?"

"I'm drunk, go away."

Towards the end of her course at the training college, when she was home for the Christmas holidays, she rode her horse along the main wide road to the dorp. She did some shopping; she stopped to talk to the Cypriot tailor who supplied the district with drill shorts, and to the Sephardic Jew who kept the largest Kaffir store.

"Live and let live," said Chakata. But these people were never at the farm, and this was Daphne's only chance of telling them of her college life.

She called in at the Indian laundry to leave a bottle of hair oil which, for some unfathomable reason, Chakata had promised to give to the Indian.

She had tea with the chemist's wife, then returned to the police station where she had left the horse. Here she stopped for about an hour chatting with two troopers whom she had known since her childhood. It was late when she set off up the steep main road, keeping well to the side of the tarmac strips on which an occasional car would pass, or a native on a bicycle. She knew all the occupants of the cars and as they slowed down to pass her they would call a greeting. She had gone about five miles when she came to a winding section of the road with dense bush on either side. This part was notorious for accidents. The light was failing rapidly, and as she heard a car approaching round the bend ahead of her she reined in to the side. Immediately the car appeared its lights were switched on, but before they dazzled her she had recognized Old Tuys at the wheel of the shooting-brake. As he approached he gave no sign of slowing down. Not only did Old Tuys keep up his speed, he brought the car off the strips and passed within a few inches of the animal.

Daphne had once heard a trooper say that for a human being to fall in the bush at sundown or after was like a naked man appearing in class at a girl's school. As she landed in the dark thicket every living thing screeched, rustled, fled, and flapped in a feminine sort of panic. The horse was away along the road, its hooves beating frantic diminishing signals in the dusk. Daphne's right shin was giving her intense pain. She was fairly sure Old Tuys had stopped the car. She rose and limped a few steps, pushing her way through the vegetation and branches, to the verge of the road. Here she stopped, for she heard footsteps on the road a few feet away. Old Tuys was waiting for her. She looked round her and quickly saw there was no chance of penetrating further into the bush with safety. The sky was nearly dark now, and the pain in her leg was threatening to overcome her. Daphne had never fainted, even when, once, she had wanted to, during an emergency operation for a snake-bite, the sharp blade cutting into her unanaesthetized flesh. Now, it seemed that she would faint, and this alarmed her, for she could hear Old Tuys among the crackling branches at the side of the road, and presently could discern his outline. The sound of a native shouting farther up the road intruded upon her desire to faint, and, to resist closing her eyes in oblivion she opened them wide, wider, staring into the darkness.

Old Tuys got hold of her. He did not speak, but he gripped her arm and dragged her out of the bush and threw her on the ground at the side of the road out of the glare of the headlamps. Daphne screamed and kicked out with her good leg. Old Tuys stood up, listening. A horse was approaching. Suddenly round the bend came a native leading Daphne's horse. It shied at the sight of the van's headlights, but the native held it firmly while Old Tuys went to take it.

"Clear off," said Tuys to the boy in kitchen Kaffir.

"Don't go," shouted Daphne. The native stood where he was.

"I'll get you home in the van," said Old Tuys. He bent to lift Daphne. She screamed. The native came and stood a little closer.

Daphne lifted herself to her feet. She was hysterical. "Knock him down," she ordered the native. He did not move. She realized he would not touch Old Tuys. The Europeans had a name of sticking together, and, whatever the circumstances, to hit a white man would probably lead to prison. However, the native was evidently prepared to wait, and when Old Tuys swore at him and ordered him off, he merely moved a few feet away.

"Get into the van," shouted Tuys to Daphne. "You been hurt in an accident. I got to take you home."

A car came round the bend, and seeing the group by the standing car, stopped. It was Mr Parker the headmaster.

Old Tuys started the tale about the accident, but Mr Parker was listening to Daphne who limped across to him.

"Take me back to the farm, Mr Parker, for God's sake."

He helped her in and drove off. The native followed with the horse. Old Tuys got into the van and made off in the opposite direction.

"I won't go into details," said Chakata to Daphne next day, "but I can't dismiss Tuys. It goes back to an incident which occurred before you were born. I owe him a debt of honour. Something between men."

"Oh, I see," said Daphne.

Old Tuys had returned to the farm in the early hours of the morning. Daphne knew that Chakata had waited up for him. She had heard the indeterminate barking of a row between them.

She sat up in bed with her leg in splints.

"We could be raped and murdered," said Mrs Chakata, "but Chakata still won't get rid of the bastard. Chakata would kick his backside out of it if he was a proper man."

"He says it's because of a debt of honour," said Daphne.

"That's all you get from Chakata. Whatever you do," said Mrs Chakata, "don't marry a blerry Englishman. They got no thought for their wives and kids, they only got thought for their blerry honour."

It had always been understood that she was to go to England in 1940, when she was eighteen. But now there was no question of going overseas till the war should end. Daphne had been to see a Colonel, a Judge and a Bishop: she wanted to go to England to join one of the women's services. They told her there was no hope of an exit permit for England being granted to a civilian. Besides, she was under age: would Chakata give his permission?

At twenty she took a teaching job in the Capital rather than join any of the women's services in the Colony, for these seemed to her feeble organizations compared with the real thing.

She was attracted by the vast new RAF training camps which were being set up. One of them lay just outside the Capital, and most of her free time was spent at sundowners and dances in the mess, or week-end tennis parties at outlying farms where she met dozens of young fighter pilots with their Battle of Britain DFCs. She was in love with them collectively. They were England. Her childhood neighbour, John Coates, was a pilot. He was drafted to England, but his ship and convoy were mined outside the Cape. News of his death reached Daphne just after her twenty-first birthday.

She drove out to the camp with one of her new English friends to attend a memorial service for John at the RAF chapel. On the way the tyre burst. The car came to a dangerous screeching stop five yards off the road. The young man set about changing the tyre. Daphne stood by.

He said to her for the third time, "OK. All *set*, Daphne." She was craning her head absently.

"Oh," she said, bringing her attention back to him. "I was listening to the go-away bird."

"What bird?"

"The grey-crested lourie. You can hear it all over the Colony. You hardly ever see it. It says 'Go'way'."

He stood listening. "I can't hear a thing."

"It's stopped now," she said.

"Are there any yellow-hammers here?" he said.

"No, I don't think so."

"They say 'a little bit of bread and *no* cheese'," he said.

"D'you find them all over England?"

"I think so. Anyway, there are millions in Hertfordshire."

She engaged herself to marry a flight-lieutenant instructor. He was killed the following week in a flying accident. He had said, describing his home near Henley, "Ghastly place really. The river simply walks over the garden. Father's been doubled with rheumatism, but won't move." These words had somehow enchanted her. "The river simply walks over the garden," and she knew that the river was the Thames and that the garden was full of English bushes and all the year round was green. At his funeral she felt that the garden had gone under the sea. His family lived not far away from the English Pattersons. "No," he had said, "I don't think we know them." It seemed incredible that he did not know his neighbours of only fifteen miles distant. "No," wrote the English Pattersons, "we don't know the people. Are they Londoners come down since the war? There are a lot of Londoners . . ."

In the Christmas holidays after her twenty-first birthday

she said to Chakata, "I'm giving a term's notice. I'm going to Cape Town."

"Have you had more trouble with Tuys?" he said.

"No. It's just that I want a change. I should like to see the sea."

"Because, if you have had trouble with Tuys, I shall speak to him."

"Are you at all thinking of getting rid of Old Tuys?" said Daphne.

"No," he said.

He tried to persuade her to go to Durban instead of Cape Town. "Durban is more English." He did not like the idea of her staying with her father's people, the du Toits, in Cape Town.

Cape Town made her hanker all the more for England. There was just enough of the European touch – old sedate Dutch houses, cottage gardens, green meadows, a symphony orchestra, a modern art gallery – to whet her appetite for the real thing. The fact that the servants were paler than those of the Colony, and more European in feature, suggested to her a proximity to England where servants were white. "We have no one left," wrote the English Pattersons, "but Clara, and half the time *we* have to wait on *her*. She has lost her memory and she keeps thinking you are your mother. She thinks Toad is Uncle Pooh-bah. Aunt Sarah is a trial. *She* thinks we pinch her sweet coupons."

Daphne longed to be waiting on Clara, to be accused by Aunt Sarah of stealing the coupons, to be washing up the dishes and climbing over stiles with the cousins whom she had never seen. Some of her relations were nicknamed after characters in *The Wind in the Willows*, Rat, Mole, Toad, others named from as yet unaccountable sources – her uncles Pooh-bah and The Dong, for instance. The du Toits could not quite follow the drift of Daphne's letters from England when she read them aloud, herself carried away by the poetry of the thing. "Rat,' she would explain, "is Henry Middleton, Molly's husband. He's in the navy . . ."

"Doesn't he treat her right, then?"

"He adores her actually," said Daphne, using the infectious phraseology of the letters from England.

"Why does she call him a rat, then?"

Chakata was right, thought Daphne, you simply can't explain the English sense of humour.

She went to night-clubs in Cape Town, keeping steadily in her thoughts the fact, of which she was convinced, that these were but tawdry versions of the London variety.

The du Toits were members of an Afrikaner élite. They tolerated but did not cultivate the English. One of their cousins, an Oxford graduate now fighting in North Africa, came home on leave and made a bid for Daphne. Just at that moment she became attached to a naval officer who had arrived a fortnight ago in a corvette which had been badly hit. Ronald was the most typical, Daphne thought, Englishman she had ever met, and the most unaffected. The ship, he whispered confidentially, for no one was supposed to know it, would be in port for six weeks. Meanwhile, might they consider themselves engaged? Daphne said, oh really, all right. And regardless of anything the du Toits might speculate, she spent a night with him at a sea-front hotel. With the utmost indifference Ronald mentioned that, before the war, he had captained the village cricket team – "The squire usually does." Daphne saw, in a vision, numerous long white-flannelled legs, the shadowy elms, pretty sisters in pastel dresses, the mothers in old-fashioned florals and the fathers in boaters, all cool and mellow as the lemonade being served, under the marquee by the lake, on trays borne by pale-faced, black-frocked, white-frilled maids. Daphne thought of the heat and glare of Chakata's farm, the smell of the natives, and immediately felt bloated and gross.

A few days later, while she was dancing cheek-to-cheek with Ronald, at the tea-dance provided by the hotel on the sea-front, to the strains of

> The fundamental things apply
> As time goes by

– at the same moment young Jan du Toit was informing the assembled family that Daphne's fiancé was a married man.

Her Aunt Sonji spoke to Daphne next morning.

Daphne said, "He's the captain of his local cricket team."

"He could still be a married man," said Sonji.

By lunch-time the information was confirmed, and by sundown the corvette had sailed.

Daphne felt irrationally that it was just the sort of thing one would expect to happen while living with the du Toits. She removed to Durban, treating the English ships with rather more caution than hitherto. She eschewed altogether the American navy which had begun to put in frequent appearances.

Among her colleagues at the school where she taught in

Durban was a middle-aged art master who had emigrated from Bristol some years before the war. He saw England as the Barbarian State which had condemned him to be an art master instead of an artist. He spoke often to Daphne on these sad lines, but she was not listening. Or rather, what she was listening to were the accidentals of this discourse. "Take a fashionable portrait painter," he would say. "He is prepared to flatter his wealthy patrons – or more often patronesses. He's willing to turn 'em out pretty on the canvas. He can then afford to take a Queen Anne house in Kensington, Chelsea, or Hampstead, somewhere like that. He turns the attic into a studio, a great window frontage. A man I know was at college with me, he's a fashionable portrait painter now, has a studio overlooking the Regent's Canal, gives parties, goes everywhere, Henley, Ascot, titled people, dress designers, film people. That's the sort of successful artist England produces today."

Daphne's mind played like the sun over the words "Queen Anne house", "Kensington", "Chelsea", "Studio", "Regent's Canal", "Henley". She had ears for nothing else.

"Now take another fellow," continued the art master, "I knew at college. He hadn't much talent, rather ultra-modern, but he wanted to be an artist and he wouldn't be anything else. What has he got for it? The last time I saw him he hadn't the price of a tube of paint. He was sharing a Soho attic with another artist – who's since become famous as a theatrical designer incidentally – name G.T. Marvell. Heard of him?"

"No," Daphne said.

"Well, he's famous now."

"Oh, I see."

"But the artist he was living with in Soho never got

anywhere. They used to partition the room with blankets and clothes hung on a piece of rope. That's the sort of thing you get in Soho. The native in the bush is better off than the artist in England."

Daphne took home all such speeches of discouragement, and pondered them with delight: "Soho", "poet", "attic", "artist".

In 1946, at last, she got a place on a boat. She went to say goodbye to Chakata. She sat with the ageing man on the stoep.

"Why did *you* never go back to England for a visit?" she said.

"There has always been too much to do on the farm," he said. "I could never leave it." But his head inclined towards the room at the back of the stoep, where Mrs Chakata lay on her bed, the whisky and the revolver by her side. Daphne understood how Chakata, having made a mistake in marriage, could never have taken Mrs Chakata home to the English Pattersons, nor could he ever have left her in the Colony, even with friends, for he was a man of honour.

"I suppose," said Daphne, "the Pattersons will be thrilled to hear about our life out here."

He looked worried. "Remember," he said, "that Auntie Chakata is an invalid. At home they don't understand tropical conditions, and—"

"Oh, I shall explain about Auntie Chakata," she said, meaning she would hush it up.

"I know you will," he said admiringly.

She walked over to Makata's kraal to say goodbye. There

was a new Makata; the old chief was dead. The new chief had been educated at the Mission, he wore navy blue shorts and a white shirt. Whereas old Makata used to speak of his tribe as "the men", this one called them "my people". She had used to squat with old Makata on the ground outside his large rondavel. Now a grey army blanket was spread, on which two kitchen chairs were placed for the chief and his visitor. Daphne sat on her kitchen chair and remembered how strongly old Makata used to smell; it was the unwashed native smell. Young Makata smelt of carbolic soap. "My people will pray for you," he said. He did not offer to send a man to escort her to the farm, as old Makata had always done.

She knew Old Tuys had followed her to the kraal, and she was aware that he was awaiting her return. Her arms were swinging freely, but she had a small revolver in the pocket of her shorts.

A mile from the farm Old Tuys walked openly over the veldt towards her. He was carrying a gun. Daphne doubled as casually as possible into the bush. It was sparse at this point, and so she was easily visible. She picked her way through the low brushwood, moving towards the farm. She heard Old Tuys crackling through the dry wood behind her.

"Stop there," she heard him say, "or I shoot."

Her hand was on her revolver, and it was her intention to wheel round and shoot before he could aim his gun. But as she turned she heard a shot from behind him and saw him fall. Daphne heard his assailant retreating in the bush behind him, and then on the veldt track the fading sound of bicycle wheels.

Old Tuys was still conscious. He had been hit in the base of the neck. Daphne looked down at him.

"I'll send them to fetch you," she said.

The following week the police made half-hearted raids on the native dwellings in the district. No firearms were discovered. In any case, Daphne had called in at the police station, and told her old friend, Johnnie Ferreira, that if any man black *or* white was brought to trial for shooting Old Tuys, she would give evidence for the assailant.

"Old Tuys was after you, then?"

"He was. I had a revolver and I intended to use it. Only the other got him first."

"Quite *sure* you didn't see who shot him?"

"No. Why?"

"Because you say 'black or white'. We have been more or less assuming it was a native since we understand the man had a bicycle."

"Black or white," said Daphne, "it makes no difference. He was only doing his duty."

"Oh, I know," said Johnnie, "but we like to know the facts. If we got the man, you see, there are good grounds for having the charge against him dismissed, then we should bring Old Tuys on a charge when he comes out of hospital. It's about time Chakata was rid of that slug."

"Well, you haven't got the man," said Daphne, "have you?"

"No," he said. "But if you have any ideas, come and let's know. Think it over."

Daphne parked the car at the foot of Donald Cloete's kopje and climbed slowly, stopping frequently to look at the wide land below, the little dorp, the winding main road, and faintly, the farm roofs in the distance. She took in the details like a camera, and as if for the first time, for soon she would be gone to England.

She sat on a stone. A lizard slid swiftly between her feet and disappeared among the grasses.

"Go'way. Go'way."

The sound darted forth and vanished. Two or three times she had seen the go-away bird. It was quite colourless, insignificant. She rose and plodded on.

"D or S, Donald?"

"So-so. Come in."

"Johnnie Ferreira wants to bring a charge against Old Tuys," she said, "for his attempt on me the other day."

"I know," he said, "Johnnie's boys have been here."

"What did you say?"

"I told them to try elsewhere."

There were few white men in the Colony who rode bicycles, and only one in the district. Bicycles were used mostly by natives and a few schoolboys. All the children were away at school. Daphne's unknown protector was therefore either a passing native or Donald doing his rounds. Moreover, there was the question of the gun. Few natives, if they owned firearms, would be likely to risk betraying this illicit fact. And few natives, however gallant, would risk the penalty for shooting a white man.

"Why not let them put Old Tuys on charge?" said Daphne.

"I don't prevent them," he said. "They can go ahead."

"They need a witness," she said. "Otherwise it's his word against mine. Old Tuys would probably be acquitted on appeal."

"Nothing doing," he said. "I don't like the law-courts."

"Well, it *was* very nice of you, Donald," she said. "I'm grateful."

"Then don't talk to me about law cases."

"All right, I won't."

"You see," he said, "how it is. Chakata wouldn't like the scandal. All the past might come out. You never know what might come out if they start questioning Old Tuys in the courts. Old Chakata wouldn't like it."

"I think he knows what you did, Donald. He's very grateful."

"He'd be more grateful if Old Tuys had been killed."

"Did you catch Old Tuys on purpose or did you just happen to be there when Old Tuys came after me?" she inquired.

"Don't know what you mean. I was putting up the Foot and Mouth notices that day. I was busy. I've got more to do than keep Old Tuys in sight."

"I'm going away next week," she said, "for about two years."

"So I hear. You have no conception of the greenness of the fields. It rains quite often . . . Go to see the Tower . . . Don't return."

2

Linda Patterson, aged twenty-eight, was highly discontented. Daphne could not see why. She herself adored Uncle Pooh-bah with his rheumatism and long woollen combies. Only his constant threats to sell the damp old house and go to live in some hotel alarmed Daphne at the same time as the idea gave hope to her cousin Linda. Linda's husband had been killed in a motor accident. She longed to be free to take a job in London.

"How could you leave that lovely climate and come to this dismal place?" Linda would say.

"But," Daphne said happily, "this at least is England."

Not long after she arrived Aunt Sarah, who was eighty-two, said to Daphne, "My dear, it isn't done."

"What isn't done?"

Aunt Sarah sighed, "You know very well what I mean. My nightdresses, dear, the rayon ones. There were three in my drawer, a green, a peach, and a pink. I only discovered this morning that they were gone. Now there is no one else in this house who could have taken them but you. Clara is above reproach, and besides, she can't climb the stairs, how could she? Linda has lots of nighties left over from her trousseau, poor gel –"

"What are you saying?" said Daphne. "What are you saying?"

Aunt Sarah took a pin out of her needle-box and pricked Daphne on the arm. "That's for stealing my nighties," she said.

"She'll have to go to a home," said Linda. "We can't keep a daily woman for more than a week because of Aunt Sarah's accusing them of stealing."

Pooh-bah said, "D'you know, apart from *that one thing* she's quite normal, really. Wonderful for her age. If we could only somehow get her to realize how utterly foolish she is over *that one thing* –"

"She'll have to go to a home."

Pooh-bah went out to look at the barometer and did not return.

"I don't mind, really," said Daphne.

"Look at the work she causes," said Linda. "Look at the trouble!"

Next day, when Daphne was scrubbing the kitchen floor Aunt Sarah came and stood in a puddle before her. "My Friar's Balsam," she said. "I left a full bottle in the bathroom, and it's gone."

"I know," said Daphne, scrubbing away, "I took it in a weak moment, but now I've put it back."

"Very well," said Aunt Sarah, trotting off and dragging the puddle with her. "But don't do it again. Pilfering was always a great weakness in your mother, I recall."

The winter temperature lasted well into April. Linda and Daphne had to sit by a one-bar electric fire in the library if they wanted to smoke; Pooh-bah's asthma was affected by cigarette smoke.

Linda was conducting a weekend liaison with a barrister in London, and with Daphne in the house she found it easier to disappear for longer weekends, and then, sometimes, a week. "Daphne," she would say on the phone, "you don't mind holding the fort, honestly? This is so important to me."

Daphne went for walks with Uncle Pooh-bah. She had to take short steps, for he was slow. They walked on the well-laid paths to the river which Daphne always referred to as "the Thames", which indeed, of course, it was.

"We went as far as the Thames," Daphne would tell Linda on their return. They ventured no further than the local lock, a walk bordered with green meadows and wonderful sheep.

Relations of some friends in the Colony invited her to London. She accepted, then told Linda when she would be away.

"But," said Linda, "*I* shall be in London next week. It's important, you know. Someone's got to look after Pooh-bah and Aunt Sarah."

"Oh, I see," said Daphne.

Linda cheered up. "Perhaps you could go the week after?"

"No, next week," said Daphne patiently, "that's when I'm going."

"*Someone's* got to look after Pooh-bah and Aunt Sarah."

"Oh, I see."

Linda started to cry. Daphne said, "I'll write to my friends, and explain."

Linda dried her eyes and said, "You can't imagine how deadly it is living in this awful house year after year with a couple of selfish old people and that helpless Clara."

Next weekend, while Linda was away, several Patterson relations arrived. Molly, Rat, Mole and an infant called Pod. Mole was an unattached male cousin. Daphne expressed a desire to see Cambridge. He said it would be arranged. She said she would probably be in London soon. He said he hoped to see her there. Aunt Sarah stuck a pin in the baby's arm, whereupon Molly and Rat took Daphne aside and advised her to clear out of the house as soon as possible. "It's unhealthy."

"Oh," said Daphne, "but it's typically English."

"Good gracious me!" said Rat.

At last she had her week in London with the relations of her friends in the Colony. Daphne had been told they were wealthy, and was surprised when the taxi drove her to a narrow house in a mean little side street which was otherwise lined with garages.

"Are you sure this is the right place?" she asked the driver.

"Twenty-five Champion Mews," he said.

"That's right," said Daphne. "This must be it."

Before Daphne had left the country Linda had remarked, "A house in Champion Mews. They must be rather rich. How I would adore a mews house." Daphne remembered this.

The interior of the house was very winning. She readjusted her ideas, and at dinner was able to say to her hostess, "What an adorable mews house."

"Isn't it? We were so lucky – literally *everyone* was after it."

Mrs Pridham was middle-aged, and smart. Mr Pridham was a plastic surgeon.

"I shan't make the mistake," he said to Daphne, "of asking you about all the dangers you encountered in darkest Africa."

Daphne laughed.

"You must have a Season of course," said Mrs Pridham. "Have you arranged anything?"

"I'm here for two years at least." Then she remembered about the London Season, and said, "No, I have nothing arranged. But my uncle has written to various friends."

"It's getting a little late in the year," said Mrs Pridham.

"Really," said Daphne, "I just want to see England. I'd like to see London. I'd like to see the Tower, and Uncle Chakata's friends."

"I shall take you to the Tower tomorrow afternoon," said Mr Pridham.

He did, and afterwards they went for a spin round Richmond and Kingston. He pulled up at a pleasant spot. "Daphne," he said, "I love you." And he pressed his lips of sixty summers to hers.

As soon as she could disengage herself, she casually wiped her mouth with her handkerchief – casually, for she did not want to hurt his feelings. However, she told him she was engaged to be married to someone in the Colony.

"Oh dear, I've done the wrong thing. Have I done the wrong thing?"

"Daphne is engaged to a lucky fellow in Africa," he said at dinner that night. Mole was present. He looked at Daphne. She looked back helplessly. Mrs Pridham looked at her husband, and said to Daphne, "Before you do anything, you must have your London Season. Stay six weeks with us, do. I've brought out girls before. It's too late of course to do anything much but –"

"Do stay with us," said Mr Pridham.

Later, when Daphne explained the tale of her "engagement" to Mole, he said, "You can't stay with the Pridhams. I know someone else you can stay with, the mother of a friend of mine."

Mrs Pridham looked sad when Daphne told her she could not prolong her visit. For the rest of the week she unmistakably cast Daphne into her husband's way, frequently left them alone together, and often arranged to be picked up somewhere in the car, so that Daphne was obliged to dine with Mr Pridham alone.

Daphne mentioned to Mole, "She hasn't the least suspicion of what he's like. In fact, she seems to throw the man at me."

"She wants to hot him up," said Mole. "There are plenty of women who behave like that. They get young girls to the house simply in order to give the old man ideas. Then they get rid of the girls."

"Oh, I see."

She went to stay as a paying guest with the mother of Mole's friend, Michael. It was arranged by letter.

Michael Casse was thin and gangling with an upturned nose. He had been put to stockbroking with an uncle, but without success. He giggled a great deal. His mother, with whom he lived, took a perverse pride in his stupidity. "Michael's hopelessness," she told Daphne, "is really . . ." During the war, his mother told her, she had been living in Berkshire. Michael came home on leave. She sent him out with the ration book one day after lunch to buy a packet of tea. He did not return until next morning. He handed his mother the tea, explaining that he had been held up by the connections.

"What connections?" said his mother.

"Oh, the trains, London, you know."

And it transpired that he had gone all the way to Fortnum's for the tea, it never having occurred to him that tea could be bought in the village, nor indeed anywhere else but Fortnum's. Daphne thought that *very* English.

Michael now lived with his mother in her flat in Regent's Park. Greta Casse was as gangling as her son, but she gangled effectively and always put her slender five foot ten into agreeable poses, so that even her stooping shoulders and hollow chest, her bony elbows akimbo, were becoming. She spoke with a nasal drawl. She lived on alimony and the rewards of keeping PGs.

She took vastly too much money from Daphne, who suspected as much, but merely surmised that Greta Casse was, like her son, stupid, living in an unreal world where money hardly existed, and so one might easily charge one's PGs too much. Daphne frequently slipped out to Lyons for a sandwich, so hungry did she go. She assumed at first that society women were simply not brought up to the food idea, but when she saw Greta Casse tucking in at anyone else's expense, she amended her opinion, and put Greta's domestic parsimony down to her vagueness about materialistic things. This was a notion which Greta fostered in various ways, such as always forgetting to give Daphne the change of a pound, or going off for the day and leaving nothing in the house for lunch.

That she was, however, a society woman, in a sense that Daphne's relations were not, was without doubt. Molly and Linda had been presented, it was true. And Daphne had seen photographs of her mother and Aunt Sarah beplumed and robed, in the days when these things were done properly. But they were decidedly not society women. Daphne mused often on Greta Casse, niece of a bishop and cousin of an earl, her distinctive qualities. She went to see Pooh-bah one weekend, and mentioned Greta Casse to a Miss Barrow, a notable spinster of the district who had come to tea. Daphne was surprised to learn that this woman, in her old mannish Burberry, her hands cracked with gardening, her face cracked with the weather, had been a contemporary of Greta's. They had been to various schools together, had been presented the same year.

"How odd," Daphne remarked to Pooh-bah later, "that two such different people as Mrs Casse and Miss Barrow should have been brought up in the same way."

He gave a verbal assent, "I suppose so, yes," but clearly he did not understand what she meant about it being odd.

Back she went to Regent's Park. Greta Casse arranged a dinner party for Daphne at a West End restaurant, followed by an all-night session in a night-club. About twenty young people were invited, most of them in their early teens, which made Daphne feel old, and she was not compensated by the presence of a few elders of Greta's generation. Michael came, of course. Englishman though he was, Daphne could not take him very seriously.

The party was followed by another, and that by another. "Can't we invite Mole?" Daphne said.

"Well," said Greta, "the whole idea is for you to meet *new* people. But of course, if you like . . ."

The bill for these parties used up half of Daphne's annual allowance. Luncheons, at which she met numerous women friends of Greta's, used up the other half. Daphne longed to explain to Mrs Casse that she had not understood what was involved by becoming her lodger. She did not want to be entertained, for she had merely counted on somewhere jolly to stay. Daphne had not the courage to put this to Greta who was so uncertain, precarious, slippery, indefinite and cold. She wrote to Chakata for money. "Of course," she wrote, "when I've had my fun I'll take a job."

"I hope you are seeing something of England," he replied when he sent his cheque. "My advice to you is to go on a coach tour. I hear they are excellent, and a great advance on my time, when there was nothing of that sort." She rarely took much notice of Chakata's advice, for so much of it was inapplicable. "Do introduce yourself to Merrivale at the bank," he had written. "He will give you sherry in the parlour, as he used to do me when I was your age." On inquiring for Mr Merrivale at the bank, Daphne was unsuccessful. "Ever heard of a chap called Merrivale?" the clerks asked each other. "Sure it's this branch?" they asked Daphne.

"Oh yes. He used to be the manager."

"Sorry, madam, no one's heard of him here. Must have been a way back."

"Oh, I see."

Daphne got into the habit of ignoring Chakata's questions, "Have you been to Hampton Court?" "Did you call on Merrivale at the bank? He will give you sherry . . ." "Have you booked for a tour of England and Wales? I trust you are planning to see something of the English countryside?"

"I couldn't find that bootmaker in St Paul's Churchyard," she wrote to him, "because it is all bombed. Better stick to the usual place in Johannesburg. Anyway, I might not order the right boots."

Soon, then, she made no reply to his specific requests and suggestions, but merely gave him an account of her parties, pepping them up for his benefit. He seemed not to read her letters properly, for he never referred to the parties.

Greta came back to the flat one afternoon with a toy poodle. "He's yours," she said to Daphne.

"How utterly perfect!" said Daphne, thinking it was a gift, and wanting to express her appreciation as near as possible in the vernacular.

"I *had* to have him for you," said Greta, and went on to demand a hundred and ten guineas. Daphne ducked her face affectionately in the pet's curly coat to hide her dismay.

"We were so terribly lucky to get him," Greta was saying. "You see, he's not just a miniature – they're slightly bigger – he's a *toy*."

Daphne gave her a cheque, and wrote to Chakata to say how expensive London was. She decided to take a job in the autumn, and to cut out the fortnight's motoring tour of the north with Molly, Rat, and Mole which she had arranged to share with them.

Chakata sent her the money as an advance on her next quarterly allowance. "Sorry can't do more. Fly has had a go at the horses, and you will have read about the tobacco crops." She had not read about the blight, but a bad year was not an uncommon occurrence. She was surprised at Chakata's attitude, for she believed him to be fairly wealthy. Shortly after this she heard from friends in the Colony that Chakata's daughter and her husband who had gone to farm in Kenya, had been murdered by the Mau Mau. "Chakata implored us not to tell you," wrote her friend, "but we thought you should know. Chakata is educating the two boys."

It was the middle of May. Daphne had engaged to be Mrs Casse's lodger till the end of June. However, she telephoned to Linda that she was returning to the country. Greta was out. Daphne packed and sat down courageously with Popcorn (the poodle) on her lap to await her return, and explain her financial predicament.

Michael came in first. He was carrying an empty birdcage and a cardboard box with holes in it. On opening the box a bird flew out in a panic.

"A budgerigar," said Michael. "I expect they fly about

wild where you've come from. They talk, you know. It's frightened at the moment, but when they get used to you, they talk." He giggled.

The bird was perched on a lampshade. Daphne caught it and put it in the cage. It had a lavender breast.

"It's for you," Michael said. "Mummy sent me home with it. She bought it for you. It says 'Come here, darling' and 'Go to hell', and things like that."

"I really don't want it," said Daphne in despair.

"Peep, peep, peep," said Michael to the bird, "say hallo, say hallo. Say come here darling."

It sat on the floor of the cage and moved only its head from side to side.

"Really," said Daphne, "I have no money. I'm hard up. I can't afford your mother's birds. I'm just waiting to say goodbye to her."

"No," said Michael.

"Yes," said Daphne.

"Listen," he said. "Take my advice and clear out now before she comes back. If you tell her this to her face there's bound to be hell." He giggled weakly, poured himself a drink of brandy which his mother had watered, and said, "Shall I get you a taxi now? She'll be back in half an hour."

"No, I'll wait," said Daphne, and ran her hand nervously through the poodle's curls.

"There was nearly a court action one time," said Michael, "about another girl. Mummy was supposed to have given two balls for her, but she didn't or something, and the girl's people got worked up. I think Mummy spent the money on something else, or something." He giggled.

"Oh, I see." Daphne went and telephoned to Mole and asked him to call for her when he left his office.

Greta arrived, and when she had taken in the situation she sent Michael from the room.

"I must tell you," said Greta to Daphne, "that what you are proposing is illegal. You realize that, don't you?"

"I can give you a week's money in lieu of notice," Daphne said, "and a little extra."

"You agreed to stay till the end of June, my dear. I have it in black and white." This was true. Daphne realized how deliberately her letter of confirmation from the country had been extracted from her.

"My uncle has had some unforeseen expenses. My cousins were murdered by the Mau Mau, and their sons –"

"I'm sorry, my dear, but one just can't be sentimental. It's not like taking in ordinary lodgers. A Season is a Season, and one can't get another girl at this time of the year. Look what I've done for you. Parties, the races, meeting important people . . . No, sorry, I can't consider releasing you from the obligation. I've arranged a cocktail party at Claridge's for you next week. After all, I don't make anything out of it. Mercy Slater charges fifteen hundred to bring a girl out."

This put Daphne off her stroke, it prompted her to haggle: "Lady Slater gives balls for her debs."

Greta rapidly got in: "You surely didn't expect the full deb process in your position?"

"Mole is calling for me," Daphne said.

"I don't want to keep you against your will, Daphne. But if you leave now you must compensate me fully. Then, if you want to go away, go away."

"Go'way. Go'way, go to hell," said the budgerigar, which had now risen to its perch.

"And then there's the bird," said she. "I bought it for you this afternoon. I thought you'd be thrilled." She began to weep.

"I don't want it," said Daphne.

"All my girls have adored their pets," Greta said.

"Come here darling," said the bird. "Go'way, go to hell."

Greta was doing a sum. "The bird is twenty guineas. Then there's the extra clothes I've ordered –"

"Go'way. Go'way," said the bird.

Mole arrived. Daphne placed a cheque for twenty pounds on the hall table and slipped down to his car, leaving him to cope with her bags. "You will hear from my solicitors," Greta called after her.

Michael was hanging about in the hall. He took the scene calmly. He giggled at Daphne, then went to help Mole with the luggage.

They had been driving for ten minutes before they had to stop for a traffic light. Then, when the engine stopped, Daphne heard the budgerigar chirping at the back of the car.

"You've brought the bird!" she said.

"Yes. Isn't it yours? Michael told me it was yours."

"I'll ring the pet shop," she said, "and ask them to take it back. Do you think Greta Casse will sue me?"

"She hasn't a hope," said Mole. "Forget it."

Daphne rang the pet shop next morning from the country.

"This is Mrs Casse speaking," she said with a nasal voice. "I bought a budgerigar from you yesterday. So silly of me, I've forgotten what I paid you, and I'd like to know, just for my records."

"Mrs Greta Casse?"

"That's right."

"I don't think we sold a budgie yesterday, Mrs Casse. Just a moment, I'll inquire."

After a pause another, more authoritative, person came on the line. "You're inquiring about a budgerigar, Mrs Casse?"

"Yes, I bought it yesterday," said Daphne through her nose.

"Not from us, Mrs Casse – oh, and by the way, Mrs Casse . . ."

"Yes," twanged Daphne.

"While you're on the phone, I'd like to mention the account."

"Of course. How much is it? I'll send a cheque."

"Eighty guineas – that's of course including the toy poodle."

"Ah, yes. What exactly was the sum for the poodle? I'm so scatty about these things."

"The poodle was sixty. Then there was an amount last October –"

"Thanks. I'm sure it's quite correct. I'll send a cheque."

"You have stolen that bird, *I* know," said Aunt Sarah that afternoon, giving the cage a shove.

"No," said Daphne, "I paid for it."

In the spring of 1947 Linda died of a disease of the blood. At the funeral a short man of about forty-five introduced himself to Daphne. He was Martin Grindy, the barrister who had been Linda's lover.

He gave Daphne his card. "Would you come some time and talk about Linda?"

"Yes, of course."

"Next week?"

"Well, I'm teaching. But when school breaks up I'll write to you."

She wrote during the Easter holidays, and met him for lunch a few days later.

He said, "I miss Linda."

"Yes, I'm sure you must."

"The trouble is, you see, I'm a married man."

She thought him attractive and understood why Linda had always felt urgently about keeping her appointments with him.

In the summer she started to replace Linda as Martin's lover. They met in London at weekends and more frequently in the summer holidays.

Daphne was teaching at a private school in Henley. She lived with Pooh-bah and a middle-aged housekeeper whom they had persuaded into service, the old servant, Clara, having died, and Aunt Sarah having been removed to a nursing home.

Mole had married, and Daphne missed his frequent visits, and the long drives in his car. Until she met Martin Grindy her life was enlivened only by the visiting art master at the school, who came down twice a week.

Martin's wife, several years older than he, lived in Surrey and was always ill with a nervous complaint.

"There's no question of a divorce," Martin said. "My wife's against it on religious grounds, and though I myself don't share these principles I feel a personal obligation towards her."

"Oh, I see."

They spent their time in his flat in Kensington. There was a heatwave. They bathed in the Serpentine.

Sometimes, if his wife was specially ill, he would be summoned to the country. Daphne stayed alone in the flat or wandered round the shops.

"This year," said Martin, "she has been more ill than usual. But next year, if she's better, I hope to take you to Austria."

"Next year," she said, "I am supposed to be returning to Africa."

Earlier Chakata had written, "Old Tuys has had a stroke. He is up now, but very feeble in his mind." Since then, he had seemed less keen on Daphne's return. Daphne thought this odd, for previously he had been wont to write when sending her news of the farm, "You will see many changes when you return," or, when mentioning affairs at the dorp, "There's a new doctor. You'll like him." But in his last letter he said, "There have been changes in the educational system. You will find many changes if you return." Sometimes she thought Chakata was merely becoming forgetful. "I'm trying to make the most of my stay in England," she wrote, "but travelling is very expensive. I doubt if I shall see anything of Europe before my return." Chakata, in his next letter, did not touch on the question. He said, "Old Tuys just sits about on the stoep. Poor old chap, he is incapable of harm now. He is rather pathetic on the whole."

At the end of the summer Daphne's lover took his wife to Torquay. Daphne wandered about Kensington alone for a few days, then went back to Pooh-bah. She took him for walks. She asked him to lend her some money so that she might spend a week in Paris. He replied that he didn't really see the necessity. Next day the housekeeper told her of a man in the village who would give her thirty pounds for the poodle. Daphne had grown fond of the dog. She refused the offer, then wrote to her lover in Torquay to ask him to lend her the money to go to Paris. She received a postcard from Martin, with no mention of her request. "Will be back in London 1st week October," he wrote on the card.

Term started at the beginning of October. That week Martin's wife turned up and demanded of Pooh-bah Daphne's whereabouts. She was directed to the school, and on confronting Daphne there, made a scene.

Later, the headmistress was highly offensive to Daphne, who straight-way resigned. The headmistress relented, for she was short of staff. "I am only thinking of the girls," she explained. Hugh, the visiting art master, suggested to Daphne that she might find a better job in London. She left that night. Pooh-bah was furious. "Who's going to attend to things on Mrs Vesey's day off?" Daphne realized why he had not wished her to go to Paris.

"You could marry her," Daphne suggested. "Then she'd be on duty all the time."

He did this in fact, within a month. Daphne settled in a room in Bayswater, poorly furnished for the price; but on the other hand the landlady was willing to take the poodle.

Martin Grindy traced her to that place.

"I don't like your wife," she said.

"I'm afraid she got hold of your letter. What can I give you? What can I do for you? What can I possibly say?"

*　*　*

Besides teaching art to schoolchildren, Hugh Fuller painted. He took Daphne to his studio in Earl's Court, where she sat and reflectively pulled the stuffing even further out of the torn upholstery of the armchair.

Quite decidedly, she said, she would not come and live with him, but she hoped they would always be friends.

He thought he had made a mistake in putting the proposition to her before making love, so he made moves to repair his error.

Daphne screamed. He looked surprised.

"You see," she explained, "I've got nerves, frightfully, at the moment."

He took her frequently to Soho, and sometimes to parties where, for the first time, she entered a world in the existence of which she had previously disbelieved. Here the poets *did* have long hair, and painters wore beards, and what was more, two of the men wore bracelets and earrings. One group of four girls lived all together in two rooms with a huge old negress. Among Hugh's acquaintance were those who looked upon him with scorn for his art teaching, those who considered this activity harmless in view of his lack of talent, and those who admired him for his industry as much as his generosity.

Daphne found this company very relaxing to her nerves.

No one asked her the usual questions about Africa, and what was more surprising, no one made advances to her, not even Hugh. Daphne was teaching at a Council school. On half-holidays in spring she would sometimes meet Hugh and his friends, and regardless of the staring streets, would straggle with them along the pavements, leap on and off buses, to the current art show. There, it was clear to Daphne that Hugh's friends occupied a world which she could never penetrate. But she came to be more knowing about pictures. It may have been the art master in Hugh, as one of his friends suggested, but he loved to inform Daphne as to form, line, light, masses, pigments.

Her cousin Mole looked her up one day. He told her that Michael, the silly son of that Greta Casse at Regent's Park, had married a woman ten years his senior, and was emigrating to the Colony. Daphne was affected with an attack of longing for the Colony, more dire than any of those bouts of homesickness which she had yet experienced.

"I shall have to go back there soon," she said to Mole. "I've saved enough for the fare. It's a good thought to know I can go any time I please."

One night Daphne and Hugh were drinking in a pub in Soho with his friends, when suddenly there fell a hush. Daphne looked round to see why everyone's eyes were on a slight very dark man in his early forties, who had just entered the bar. After a moment, everyone started talking again, some giggled, and continued to glance at the man who had come in.

"That's Ralph Mercer," one of Hugh's friends whispered to Daphne.

"Who?"

"Ralph Mercer, the novelist. He was at school with Hugh, I believe. Rather a *popular* writer."

"Oh, I see," said Daphne, "he looks as if he might be popular."

Hugh was collecting drinks at the bar. The novelist saw him, and they spoke together for a while. Presently Hugh brought him to be introduced. The novelist sat next to Daphne. "You remind me of someone I used to know from Africa," he said.

"I come from Africa," said Daphne.

Hugh asked him, "Often come here?"

"No, it was just, you know, I was passing . . ."

One of the girls chuckled, a deep masculine sound. "A whim," she said.

When he had gone Hugh said, "He's rather sweet, isn't he, considering how famous . . ."

"Did you hear him," said an oldish man, "when he said, 'Speaking as an artist . . .' Rather funny, that, I thought."

"Well, he *is* an artist in the sense," said Hugh, "that –" But his words were obliterated by the others' derision.

A few days later Hugh said to Daphne, "I've heard from Ralph Mercer."

"Who?"

"That novelist we met in the pub. He writes to know if I'll give him your address."

"Why's that, do you think?"

"He likes you, I suppose."

"Is he married?"

"No. He lives with his mother. Actually I've sent him your address. Do you mind?"

"Yes, I do. I'm not a name and address to be passed round. I'm afraid I don't wish to see you again."

"You know," said Hugh, "I'm glad it never came to an affair between us. You see, Daphne, I'm not entirely a woman's man."

"I don't know what to say," she said.

"I hope you will like Ralph Mercer. He's very well-off. Very interesting, too."

"I shall refuse to see him," said Daphne.

* * *

Her association with Ralph Mercer lasted two years. Her infatuation was as gluttonous as her status as his mistress was high among the few writers and numerous film people who kept him company. She had a grey-carpeted flat in Hampstead, with the best and latest Swedish furniture. Ralph's male friends wooed her, telephoned all day, came with flowers and theatre tickets.

For the first three months Ralph was with her constantly. She told him of her childhood, of Chakata, the farm, the dorp, Donald Cloete, the affair of Old Tuys. He demanded more and more. "I need to know your entire background, every detail. Love is an expedition of discovery into unexplored territory." To Daphne this approach had such force of originality that it sharpened her memory. She remembered incidents which had been latent for fifteen years or more. She sensed the sort of thing that delighted him; the feud, for instance, between Old Tuys and Chakata; revenge and honour. One day after receiving a letter from Chakata she was able to tell him the last sentence of Donald Cloete's story: he had died of drink. She offered him this humble contribution with pride, for it showed that she, too, though no novelist, possessed a sense of character and destiny. "Always," she said, "I would ask him was he drunk or sober, and he always told the truth." Later in the day, when the thought of Donald's death came suddenly to her mind, she cried for a space.

News came that Mrs Chakata had followed Donald to the grave, and for the same cause. Daphne laid this information on the altar. The novelist was less impressed than on the former occasion. "Old Tuys has been done out of his revenge," Daphne added for good measure, although she was aware that Old Tuys had been silly and senile since his stroke. One of her friends in the Colony had written to say that Mrs Chakata had long since ceased to have the pistol by her side: "Old Tuys takes no notice of her. He's forgotten what it was all about."

"Death has cheated Old Tuys," said Daphne.

"Very melodramatic," he commented.

Ralph began to disappear for days and weeks without warning. In a panic, Daphne would telephone to his mother. "I don't know where he is," Mrs Mercer would say. "Really, dear, he's like that. It's very trying."

Much later, his mother was to tell Daphne, "I love my son, but quite honestly I don't *like* him." Mrs Mercer was an intensely religious woman. Ralph loved his mother but did not like her. He was frequently seized by nervy compulsions and superstitions.

"I must," said Ralph, "write. I need solitude to write. That is why I go away."

"Oh, I see," said Daphne.

"If you say that again I'll hit you." And though she did not repeat the words, he did, just then, hit her.

Afterwards she said, "If only you would say goodbye before you leave I wouldn't mind so much. It's the suddenness that upsets me."

"All right then. I'm going away tonight."

"Where are you going? Where?"

"Why," he said, "don't you go back to Africa?"

"I don't want to." Her obsession with Ralph had made Africa seem a remote completed thing.

His next book was more successful than any he had written. The film was in preparation. He told Daphne he adored her really, and he quite saw that he led her a hell of a life. That was what it meant to be tied up with an artist, he was afraid.

"It's worth it," Daphne said, "and I think I can help you in some ways."

He thought so too just at that moment, for it occurred to him that his latest book was all of it written during his association with Daphne. "I think we should get married," he said.

Next day he left the flat and went abroad. Now, after two years her passion for him was not diminished, neither were her misery and dread.

Three weeks later he wrote from his mother's address to suggest that she moved out of the flat. He would make a settlement.

She telephoned to his mother's house. "He won't speak to you," his mother said. "I'm ashamed of him, to tell the truth."

Daphne took a taxi to the house.

"He's upstairs writing," his mother said. "He's going away somewhere else tomorrow. I hope he stays away, to tell the truth."

"I must see him," said Daphne.

His mother said, "He makes me literally ill. I'm too old for this sort of thing, my dear. God bless you."

She went and called upstairs, "Ralph, come down a moment, please." She waited till she heard his footsteps on the stairs, then she disappeared quickly.

"Go away," said Ralph to Daphne. "Go away and leave me in peace."

3

Daphne arrived in the Colony during the rainy season. The rains made Chakata's rheumatism bad. He talked a lot about his rheumatism, would question her about England without listening to her replies.

"The West End is badly bombed," she said.

"It gets me in the groin when I turn in bed," he answered.

Various neighbours looked in to see Daphne. The young had married, and some who called were new to her.

"There's a chap out from England farming over at the south, says he knows you," said Chakata. "Name Cash, I think."

"Casse," said Daphne, "Michael Casse. Is that the name?"

"This stuff the doctor gives me's no good. In fact it makes me worse."

Another tobacco manager was living in the house Old Tuys had occupied. Old Tuys was at the farmhouse with Chakata. He sat in his corner of the stoep, talking nonsense to himself, or ambled about the farm. Chakata was annoyed when Old Tuys walked about, for he himself could barely hobble. "A pathetic case," he would say as Old Tuys strolled by, "he's got his limbs, but he hasn't got his faculties. I at least have my faculties." He preferred to see Old Tuys in his chair on the stoep. Then Chakata would say, "You know, after all these years, I have a soft spot for Old Tuys."

Old Tuys ate noisily. Chakata did not seem to mind. It struck Daphne that she was useless to Chakata now that she was no longer a goad for Old Tuys. She decided to stay at the farm no longer than a month. She would get a job in the Capital.

The third day after her arrival there was a break in the

rains. She wandered round the sunny farm all morning, and after lunch set off northward for Makata's kraal. The new tobacco manager agreed very happily to come with his car and fetch her later on.

She had become unused to trekking any distance. Her energy ebbed after the first mile. A cloud of locusts caught her attention and automatically she stopped to watch anxiously whether the swarm would settle on Chakata's mealies or miss them. It passed over. She sat to rest on a stone, disturbing a baby lizard. "Go'way. Go'way," she heard.

Daphne called aloud, "God help me. Life is unbearable."

A house-boy came running to Chakata who was round by the tobacco shed resting on two sticks.

"Baas Tuys is gone to shoot buck. The piccanin say he take a gun to shoot buck."

"Who? What?"

"Baas Tuys with gun."

"Where? Which way?"

"Is gone by north. The piccanin have seen him. Was after lunch piccanin say, he talk that he go to shoot buck."

A few more natives had gathered round.

"Run, quick, all of you. Get that gun off Old Tuys. Fetch him back."

They looked at him hesitantly. It was not every day that a native was instructed to wrest a gun from the hands of a white man.

"Go, you fools. Run."

They returned slowly and fearfully half an hour later. Chakata had hobbled to the end of the paddock to meet them.

"Where's Tuys? Did you get him?"

They did not answer at first. Then one of them pointed to the path through the maize where Old Tuys was staggering home, exhausted, dragging something behind him.

"Go and pick her up," ordered Chakata.

"I got me a buck," said Old Tuys, looking with pride at the company. "Man, there's life in the old dog yet. I got us a buck."

He looked closely at Chakata. He could not understand why Chakata was not impressed.

"We have buck for dinner, man Chakata," he said.

Burials follow quickly after death in the Colony, for the temperature does not allow of delay. The inquest was held and Daphne was buried next day. Michael Casse came over for the funeral to the cemetery outside the dorp.

"I knew her quite well, you know. She stayed with my mother," he said to Chakata. "My mother gave her a bird, or something like that." He giggled. Chakata looked at him curiously and saw that the man was not smiling.

Chakata was being helped into the car. "I must see a specialist," he said.

Ralph Mercer was moved when he heard the news. It was like the confirmation of something one knew already. Daphne had begun to live when he had first met her, and when she had gone she had been in a sense dead. He tried to explain this to his mother.

"Like flowers, you know, in the garden. One can't say they really *exist* unless one's looking at them. Or take –"

"Flowers, garden . . . You are talking of a human soul."

* * *

It was a year later that Ralph felt a crisis in his work. His books were selling, but on the other hand they were not taken seriously enough by serious people. All his novels had ended happily. He decided to write a tragedy.

He ranged his experience for a tragedy. He thought of, and rejected as too banal, the domestic ruptures of his friends past and present. He rejected the story of his mother, widowed young, disappointed in her son, but still pushing on: that was too personal. He thought of Daphne. That might lead to something both exotic and tragic. He recalled her stories of Old Tuys and Chakata, the theme of the lifelong feud. He took a ticket on a plane to the Colony in order to obtain background material at first hand.

Almost immediately he arrived in the Colony he found himself beset by admirers. He had never before been so celebrated and popular in his person. He was invited to Government House. Dinners were given in his honour, and people drove in through swollen rivers from outlying districts to attend them. He had to pick and choose amongst the invitations he received. Everyone with a white skin had heard of, if they had not read, Ralph Mercer. Moreover, seated among this company on wide verandas after dinner he could look round without catching the cool eye of some critic, some frightful man whom the public hardly ever heard of, but who, at home, was always present at parties of this sort, and who put Ralph out. He began to think he had vastly underrated the intelligence of his public.

"I have been thinking of changing my style. I've been thinking of writing a tragedy."

"Good Lord," said the retired brigadier whom he had addressed, "you don't want to do that."

Everyone said the same.

Another thing everyone said was, "Why don't you settle here?" or "Why don't you take a place and live here for part of the year? It's the only way to avoid the heavy taxes."

At the Club he had met Michael Casse who had come up to the Capital to see the Land Bank about a loan.

"My wife adores your books," said Michael. He giggled. Ralph wondered for a moment if Michael was a critic.

"We have a mutual friend," said Michael, "or rather *had*. Daphne du Toit. I went to her funeral." He giggled.

"The reason I've come out here is to see her grave," said Ralph defensively. "And to talk to her uncle."

"Got a car?" said Michael. "If not I'll drive you down. I live near them." Ralph realized that Michael's giggle was a nervous tic.

"I might settle in the Colony – seven months in the year, you know," he confided.

"There's a nice place near us," said Michael. "It's coming up for sale soon."

Ralph had been two months in the Colony, had toured the country, had been shown all the interesting spots, and met the enjoyable people, when at last he accepted Michael's invitation to stay at his farm.

"Are you writing anything at the moment?" said Michael's wife.

"No, but I'm collecting material."

"Oh, will it be about the Colony?"

"It's difficult to say."

He was not sure now that the Daphne idea would be as appealing as he had thought. He could not envisage his public, especially that section which he had recently met at close quarters, appreciating such a theme.

Michael showed him over the farm which was up for sale. Ralph said he would almost certainly take it.

They went to see Chakata and Ralph spoke of Daphne. Chakata said, "Why didn't she settle down in England? Why did she come back?"

"I suppose she wanted to," said Michael, and giggled.

Chakata spoke of his rheumatism. He hobbled out on the stoep and called for drinks. As they followed, Ralph noticed a lanky old man seated in the corner, muttering to himself.

He inquired of Chakata. "Is that Mr Tuys? Daphne told me about Mr Tuys."

Chakata said, "Bad year for maize. I shan't live long."

Michael drove Ralph down to the cemetery. His wife had suggested: "Leave him alone for a while in the cemetery. I think he was in love with the girl." Michael respected his wife's delicacy. He giggled, left Ralph at the graveside, and explaining that he had some errands to do in the village, said he would be back by and by.

"You won't be long," said Ralph, "will you?"

"Oh no," said Michael.

"There seem to be a lot of mosquitoes about here. Is it a fever area?"

"Oh no." He giggled and went.

After Ralph had looked at the inscription, "Daphne du Toit, 1922–1950", he walked up and down. He looked blankly at the gravestones and noticed one inscribed "Donald Cloete". This name seemed familiar, but he could not remember in what way. Perhaps it was someone Daphne had talked about.

"Go'way, go'way."

That was the bird, just behind Daphne's grave. She had often mentioned the bird.

"It says go'way, go'way."

"Well, what about it?" he had said to her irritably, for sometimes she had appeared to him, as in a revelation, a personified Stupidity.

She would tell him, "There's a bird that says 'Go'way, go'way'," without connecting the information with any particular event; she would expect him to be interested, as if he were an ornithologist, not an author.

"Go'way, go'way," said the bird behind Daphne's grave.

He heard the bird at some time during each day for the next six weeks while he was completing his tour of the rural spaces. He was glad to return to the Capital, and to be free of its voice. Relaxing in the Club, it was as though the bird had never existed.

However, he went with the Governor for a round of golf:

"Go'way. Go'way . . ."

He booked a seat on the plane to England for the following week. He met Michael once more by chance at Williams Hotel.

"That farm," said Michael "– someone else has made an offer. You'd better settle right away."

"I don't want it," said Ralph. "I don't want to stay here."

They sat on the stoep drinking highballs. Beyond the mosquito netting was the bird.

"Can you hear that go-away bird?" said Ralph.

Michael listened obediently.

"No, I can't say I can." He giggled, and Ralph wanted to hit him.

"I hear it everywhere," said Ralph. "I don't like it. That's why I'm going."

"Good Lord. Keen on bird life, are you?"

"No, not particularly."

"Ralph Mercer isn't going to buy the farm," Michael told his wife that evening.

"I thought it was settled."

"No, he's going home. He isn't coming back. He says he doesn't like the birds here."

"I wish you could cure that giggle, Michael. What did you say he doesn't like?"

"The birds."

"*Birds*. Is he an ornithologist then?"

"No, I think he's RC."

"A *man*, darling, who studies birds."

"Oh! Well, no, he said no, he's not particularly interested in birds."

"How extraordinary," she said.

THE CURTAIN BLOWN BY THE BREEZE

It is always when a curtain at an open window flutters in the breeze that I think of that frail white curtain, a piece of fine gauze, which was drawn across the bedroom windows of Mrs Van der Merwe. I never saw the original curtains, which were so carelessly arranged as to leave a gap through which that piccanin of twelve had peeped, one night three years before, and had watched Mrs Van der Merwe suckle her child, and been caught and shot dead by Jannie, her husband. The original curtains had now been replaced by this more delicate stuff, and the husband's sentence still had five years to run, and meanwhile Mrs Van der Merwe was changing her character.

She stopped slouching; she lost the lanky, sullen look of a smallholder's wife; she cleared the old petrol cans out of the yard, and that was only a start; she became a tall lighthouse sending out kindly beams which some took for welcome instead of warnings against the rocks. She bought the best china, stopped keeping pound notes stuffed in a stocking, called herself Sonia instead of Sonji, and entertained.

* * *

This was a territory where you could not bathe in the gentlest stream but a germ from the water entered your kidneys and blighted your body for life; where you could not go for a walk before six in the evening without returning crazed by the sun; and in this remote part of the territory, largely occupied by poor whites amidst the overwhelming natural growth of natives, a young spinster could not keep a cat for a pet but it would be one day captured and pitifully shaved by the local white bachelors for fun; it was a place where the tall grass was dangerous from snakes and the floors dangerous from scorpions. The white people seized on the slightest word, Nature took the lightest footfall, with fanatical seriousness. The English nurses discovered that they could not sit next a man at dinner and be agreeable – perhaps asking him, so as to slice up the boredom, to tell them all the story of his life – without his taking it for a great flirtation and turning up next day after breakfast for the love affair; it was a place where there was never a breath of breeze except in the season of storms and where the curtains in the windows never moved in the breeze unless a storm was to follow.

The English nurses were often advised to put in for transfers to another district.

"It's so much brighter in the north. Towns, life. Civilization, shops. Much cooler – you see, it's high up there in the north. The races."

"You would like it in the east – those orange-planters. Everything is greener, there's a huge valley. Shooting."

"Why did they send you nurses to this unhealthy spot? You should go to a healthy spot."

Some of the nurses left Fort Beit. But those of us who were doing tropical diseases had to stay on, because our clinic, the largest in the Colony, was also a research centre for tropical diseases. Those of us who had to stay on used sometimes to say to each other, "Isn't it wonderful here? Heaps of servants. Cheap drinks. Birds, beasts, flowers."

The place was not without its strange marvels. I never got used to its travel-film colours except in the dry season when the dust made everything real. The dust was thick in the great yard behind the clinic where the natives squatted and stood about, shouting or laughing – it came to the same thing – cooking and eating, while they awaited treatment, or the results of X-rays, or the results of an X-ray of a distant relative. They gave off a fierce smell and kicked up the dust. The sore eyes of the babies were always beset by flies, but the babies slept on regardless, slung on their mothers' backs, and when they woke and cried the women suckled them.

The poor whites of Fort Beit and its area had a reception room of their own inside the building, and here they ate the food they had brought, and lolled about in long silences, sometimes working up to a fight in a corner. The remainder of the society of Fort Beit did not visit the clinic.

The remainder comprised the chemist, the clergyman, the veterinary surgeon, the police and their families. These enjoyed a social life of a small and remote quality, only coming into contact with the poor white small-farmers for business purposes. They were anxious to entertain the clinic staff who mostly spent its free time elsewhere – miles and miles away, driving at weekends to the Capital, the north, or to one of the big dams on which it was possible to set up for a sailor. But sometimes the nurses and medical officers would, for a change, spend an evening in the village at the house of the chemist, the clergyman, the vet, or at the police quarters.

Into this society came Sonia Van der Merwe when her husband had been three years in prison. There was a certain slur attached to his sentence since it was generally felt he had gone too far in the heat of the moment, this sort of thing undermining the prestige of the Colony at Whitehall. But nobody held the incident against Sonia. The main difficulty she had to face in her efforts towards the company of the vet, the chemist and the clergyman was the fact that she had never yet been in their company.

The Van der Merwes' farm lay a few miles outside Fort Beit. It was one of the few farms in the district, for this was an area which had only been developed for the mines, and these had lately closed down. The Van der Merwes had lived the makeshift, toiling lives of Afrikaner settlers who had trekked up from the Union. I do not think it had ever before occurred to Sonia that her days could be spent otherwise than in rising and washing her face at the tub outside, baking bread, scrappily feeding her children, yelling at the natives, and retiring at night to her feather bed with Jannie. Her only outings had been to the Dutch Reformed gathering at Easter when the Afrikaners came in along the main street in their covered wagons and settled there for a week.

It was not till the lawyer came to arrange some affair between the farm and the Land Bank that she learned she could actually handle the fortune her father had left her, for she had imagined that only the pound notes she kept stuffed in the stocking were of real spending worth; her father in his time had never spent his money on visible things, but had invested it, and Sonia thought that money paid into the bank was a sort of tribute-money to the bank people which patriarchal farmers like her father were obliged to pay under the strict ethic of the Dutch Reformed Church. She now understood her cash value, and felt fiercely against her husband for failing to reveal it to her. She wrote a letter to him, which was a difficult course. I saw the final draft, about which she called a conference of nurses from the clinic. We were wicked enough to let it go, but in fact I don't think we gave it much thought. I recall that on this occasion we talked far into the night about her possibilities – her tennis court, her two bathrooms, her black-and-white bedroom – all of which were as yet only a glimmer at the end of a tunnel. In any case, I do not think we could have succeeded in changing her mind about the letter which subsequently enjoyed a few inches in the local press as part of Jannie's evidence. It was as follows:

> *Dear Jannie there is going to be some changes I found out what pa left is cash to spend I only got to sine my name do you think I like to go on like this work work work counting the mealies in the field By God like poor whites when did I get a dress you did not say a word that is your shame and you have landed in jale with your bad temper you shoud of amed at the legs. Mr Little came here to bring the papers to sine he said you get good cooking in jale the kids are well but Hannah got a bite but I will take them away from there now and send them to the convent and pay money. Your Loving Wife, S. Van der Merwe*

There must have been many occasions on which I lay on my bed on summer afternoons in Worcestershire, because at that time I was convalescent. My schooldays had come to an end. My training as a radiotherapist was not to begin till the autumn.

I do not know how many afternoons I lay on my bed listening to a litany of tennis noises from where my two brothers played on the court a little to the right below my window. Sometimes, to tell me it was time to get up, my elder brother Richard would send a tennis ball through the open window. The net curtain would stir and part very suddenly and somewhere in the room the ball would thud and then roll. I always thought one day he would break the glass of the window, or that he would land the ball on my face or break something in the room, but he never did. Perhaps my memory exaggerates the number of these occasions and really they only occurred once or twice.

But I am sure the curtains must have moved in the breeze as I lay taking in the calls and the to and fro of tennis on those unconcerned afternoons, and I suppose the sight was a pleasurable one. That a slight movement of the curtains should be the sign of a summer breeze seems somewhere near to truth, for to me truth has airy properties with buoyant and lyrical effects; and when anything drastic starts up from some light cause it only proves to me that something false has got into the world.

I do not actually remember the curtains of my room being touched by the summer wind although I am sure they were; whenever I try to bring to mind this detail of the afternoon sensations it disappears, and I have knowledge of the image only as one who has swallowed some fruit of the Tree of

Knowledge – its memory is usurped by the window of Mrs Van der Merwe's house and by the curtains disturbed, in the rainy season, by a trifling wind, unreasonably meaning a storm.

Sometimes, on those restful afternoons, I was anxious. There was some doubt about my acceptance for training as a radiotherapist because of my interrupted schooling. One day the letter of acceptance came by the late post. I read the letter with relief and delight, and at that same moment decided to turn down the offer. It was enough that I had received it. I am given to this sort of thing, and the reason that I am drawn to moderate and tranquil motives is that I lack them. I decided instead to become a hospital nurse and later to follow my brother Richard, who was then a medical student, to Africa, and specialize, with him, in tropical diseases.

It was about a year after my arrival at Fort Beit that I came across Sonji Van der Merwe and, together with the other nurses, read the letter which was about to be sent to her husband four hundred miles away in the Colony's prison. She posted the letter ritualistically the next afternoon, putting on her church-going gloves to do so. She did not expect, nor did she receive, a reply. Three weeks later she started calling herself Sonia.

Our visits to the farm began to take the place of evenings spent at the vet's, the chemist's and the clergyman's, to whose society Sonia now had good hopes of access. And every time we turned up something new had taken place. Sonia knew, or discovered as if by bush-telegraph, where to begin. She did not yet know how to travel by train and would have been afraid to make any excursion by herself far from the area, but through one nurse or another she obtained furnishings from the Union, catalogues, books about interior decoration and fashion magazines. Travel-stained furniture vans began to arrive at her bidding and our instigation. Her first move, however, was to join the Church of England, abandoning the Dutch Reformed persuasion of her forefathers; we had to hand it to her that she had thought this up for herself.

We egged her on from week to week. We taught her how not to be mean with her drinks, for she had ordered an exotic supply. At first she had locked the bottles in the pantry and poured them into glasses in the kitchen and watered them before getting the house-boy to serve them to her guests. We stopped all that. A contractor already had the extensions to the house in hand, and the rooms were being decorated and furnished one by one. It was I who had told her to have two bathrooms, not merely one, installed. She took time getting used to the indoor lavatories and we had to keep reminding her to pull the chain. One of us brought back from the Capital a book of etiquette which was twenty-eight years old but which she read assiduously, following the words with her forefinger. I think it was I who had suggested the black-and-white bedroom, being a bit drunk at the time, and now it was a wonder to see it taking shape; it was done within a month – she had managed to obtain black wallpaper, and to put it up, although wallpaper was a thing unheard of in the Colony and she was warned by everyone that it would never stick to the walls. There was in this bedroom a white carpet and a chaise-longue covered with black-and-white candy-striped satin. It was less than a year before she got round to adding the Beardsley reproductions, but by that time she was entertaining, and had the benefit of the vet's counsel, he having once been a young man in London.

She told us one day – lying on the chaise-longue and looking very dramatic with her lanky hair newly piled up and her black chiffon dressing-gown – the story of the piccanin, which we already knew:

"It was through that window he was looking. Yere I was sitting yere on the bed feeding the baby and I look up at the window and so help me God it was a blerry nig standing outside with his face at the window. You should of heard me scream. So Jannie got the gun and caught the pic and I hear the bang. So he went too far in his blerry temper so what can you expect? Now I won't have no more trouble from them boys. That's the very window, I was careless to leave the curtain aside. So we show them what's what and we get a new set of boys. We didn't have no boys on the farm, they all run away."

There was a slight warm breeze floating in little gusts through the window. "We'd better be getting back," said one of the girls. "There's going to be a storm."

A storm in the Colony was such that before it broke the whole place was spasmodic like an exposed nerve, and after it was over the body of the world from horizon to horizon moved in a slow daze back into its place. Before it broke there was the little wind, then a pearly light, then an earthen smell; the birds screamed and suddenly stopped, and the insects disappeared. Afterwards the flying ants wriggled in a drugged condition out of the cracks in the walls, found their wings, and flew off in crazy directions, the more extreme colours of the storm faded out of the sky in a defeated sort of way, and the furniture felt clammy from the ordeal. One day I was caught at Sonia's house when a storm broke. This was when she had already settled in to her status, and the extensions to the house were completed, and the furniture all in place. Night fell soon after the storm was over, and we sat in her very Europeanized drawing-room – for she had done away with the stoep – sipping pink gins; the drinks were served by a native with huge ape-like hands clutching the tray, his hands emerging from the cuffs of the green-and-white uniform which had lately glared in the light of the storm. Sonia kept saying, "I feel I've made a corner of civilization for myself in doing up this house." It was a version of one of the clergyman's chance compliments on one of his visits; she had seized on it as a verity, and made it known to all her visitors. "I feel I must live up to it, man," she said. I was always amazed at her rapid acquisition of new words and highly useful sayings.

Outside, the night sounds were coming back. One could hear the beasts finding each other again by their calls whenever Sonia stopped talking, and even further in the distance, the drum business, with news of which kraals had been swamped and wrecked, or perhaps no news, for all we understood of their purpose. Just outside the window there was an occasional squelch of bare feet on the wet gravel drive which Sonia had constructed. She rose and adjusted the light window curtains, then drew the big ones. She was better now. During the storm she had squatted with hunched shoulders on the carpet like a native in his but, letting the waves of sound and light break over her. It was generally thought she had some coloured blood. But this, now that she had begun to reveal such visible proof of her glamorous fortune and character, was no bar to the society of the vet, the chemist and the clergyman. Many of the doctors from the clinic visited her and were enchanted by her eccentric grandeur, and much preferred her company to that of the tropical-skinned vet's wife and the watery-blonde chemist's wife and the music-loving clergyman's wife, at sultry sundowner times in the rainy season. My brother Richard was fascinated by Sonia.

We nurses were astonished that the men were so dazzled. She was our creature, our folly, our lark. We had lavished our imagination upon her eager mind and had ourselves designed the long voile "afternoon" dresses, and had ourselves put it to her that she must have a path leading down to the river and a punt on the little river and a pink parasol to go with the punt. There was something in the air of the place that affected the men, even those newly out from England, with an overturn of discrimination. One of the research workers at the clinic had already married a brassy barmaid from Johannesburg, another had married a neurotic dressmaker from the Cape who seemed to have dozens of elbows, so much did she throw her long bony arms about. We too were subject to the influence of the place but we did not think of this when we were engrossed in our bizarre cultivation of Sonia and our dressing her up to kill. At the time, we only saw the men taking our fantasy in earnest, and looked at each other, smiled and looked away.

In the year before Jannie Van der Merwe was due to be released from prison I spent much of my free time at Sonia's with my brother Richard. Her house was by now a general meeting-place for the district and she conducted quite a salon every late afternoon. About this time I became engaged to marry a research worker at the clinic.

I do not know if Richard slept with Sonia. He was very enamoured of her and would not let anyone make fun of her in his hearing.

She said one day: "Why d'you want to marry that Frank? Man, he looks like your brother, you want to catch a fellow that doesn't look like one of the family. I could get you a fellow more your type."

I was irritated by this. I kept Frank from seeing her as much as possible; but it was not possible; all our lives outside the clinic seemed to revolve round Sonia. When Frank began to ridicule Sonia I knew he was in some way, which he was afraid to admit, attracted by her.

She chattered incessantly, her voice accented in the Afrikaans way. I had to admire her quick grasp of every situation, for now she was acquainted with the inner politics of the clinic, and managed to put in effective words here and there with visiting Government officials who took it for granted she had ruled the district for years and, being above the common run, pleased herself how she dressed and what she did.

I heard her discussing our disagreeable chief radiologist with an important member of the Medical Board: "Man, he got high spirits I tell you, man. I see him dig the spurs into the horse when he pass my house every morning, he goes riding to work off those high spirits. But I tell one thing, he's good at his job. Man, he's first rate at the job." Soon after this our ill-tempered radiologist, who did not ride very frequently, was transferred to another district. It was only when I heard that the important man from the Medical Board was a fanatical horse-lover that I realized the full force of Sonia's abilities.

"God, what have we done?" I said to my best friend.

She said, "Leave well alone. She's getting us a new wing."

Sonia made plans to obtain for Richard the job of Chief Medical Officer in the north. I suspected that Sonia meant to follow him to the north if he should be established there, for she had remarked one day that she would have to get used to travel; it must be easy: "Man, everyone does it. Drink up. Cheerio."

Frank had also applied for the job. He said – looking at the distance with his short-sighted eyes, which gave to his utterances a suggestion of disinterestedness – "I've got better qualifications for it than Richard." So he had. "Richard is the better research worker," Frank said. This was true. "Richard should stay here and I should go up north," Frank said. "You would like it up there," he said. All this was undeniable.

It became apparent very soon that Frank was competing with Richard for Sonia's attention. He did this without appearing to notice it himself, as if it were some routine performance in the clinic, not the method but the results of which interested him. I could hardly believe the ridiculous carry-on of these two men.

"Do they think she will really have any influence in the question of that job?"

"Yes," my best friend said, "and so she will."

That important member of the Medical Board – he who was passionate about horses – was in the district again. He had come for a long weekend's fishing. It was all mad. There was no big fishing at Fort Beit.

I began to want Richard to get the job. I cooled off where Frank was concerned; he did not notice, but I cooled off.

Richard had become highly nervous. As soon as he had free time he raced off in his car to Sonia's. Frank, who was less scrupulous about taking free time, was usually there first.

I was at the tea-party when the ageing, loose-mouthed, keen-eyed chief of the Medical Board turned up. Richard and Frank sat at opposite ends of a sofa. Richard looked embarrassed; I knew he was thinking of the job, and trying not to seem to be exploiting his attachment to Sonia. I sat near them. Sonia, reciting a long formula from her book of etiquette, introduced us to the important man. As she did so it struck me that this recitation might to some ears sound like a charming gesture against the encroaching slackness of the times. She sat the man between Richard and Frank, and clearly she meant business.

She stood by. She had a beautiful shape; we nurses had not provided that, we had only called it forth from the peasant slouch. She said to the old man, "Richard yere wants to talk to you, Basil, man," and touched Richard's shoulder. Frank was peering into the abstract distance. It occurred to me that Frank was the administrative type; none of the research workers I had known were dispassionate, they were vulnerable and nervous.

Richard was nervous. He did not look at the man, he was looking up at Sonia's face with its West End make-up.

"Applied for the job up north?" said this Basil to Richard.

"Yes," Richard said, and smiled with relief.

"Want it?" said the man, casually, in his great importance.

"Oh, rather," Richard said.

"Well, have it," said the man, flicking away the invisible job with his forefinger as lightly as if it were a ping-pong ball.

"Well," Richard said, "no thank you."

"What did you say?" said the man.

"What that you say?" said Sonia.

My brother and I are very unlike in most ways, but there are a few radical points of similarity between us. It must be something in the blood.

"No thank you," Richard was saying. "After all, I feel I ought to go on with research in tropical diseases."

Sonia's fury only made a passing pattern on her face. Her first thought was for the old man, fussed and suddenly groundless as he was. "Basil, man," she said, bending over him with her breasts about his ears, "you got the wrong chap. This yere Frank is the boy I was talking of to you. Frank, may I have the honour to introduce to you this yere distinguished –"

"Yes, we've met," said the man, turning to Frank.

Frank returned from the middle distance. "I've applied for the job," he said, "and my qualifications are, I think –"

"Married?"

"No, but hoping to be." He turned duly to me and I smiled back most nastily.

"Want the job?"

"Oh, rather."

"Sure?"

"Oh yes, quite sure."

The old man was not going to be caught again. "I hope you really want the job. There are a good many excellent applicants and we want a keen –"

"Yes, I want the job."

Sonia said, "Well, have it," and I thought, then, she had really done for the whole thing and outrun her influence.

But the old man beamed up at her, took both her prettily restored hands in his, and I nearly saw his slack mouth water.

Other people were pressing round for a word with this Medical Board man. Sonia was treating Richard with ostentatious neglect. Frank was leaning against the wall, now, talking to her. Suddenly I did not want to lose Frank. I looked round the company and wondered what I was doing there, and said to Richard, "Let's go."

Richard was looking at Sonia's back. "Why do you want to go?" Richard said. "It's early yet. Why?"

Because the curtain was fluttering at the open window, letting in wafts of the savage territory beyond the absurd drawing-room. The people were getting excited; I thought soon they might scream, once or twice like the birds, and then be silent. I thought, even, that Richard might change his mind again about the job, and tell Sonia so, and leave it to her to sort it out for him. It was the pull of Sonia that made him reluctant to leave. She was adjusting Frank's tie and telling him he needed looking after, for all the world as if she had been brought up to that old line; we must tell her, I thought, not to do that sort of thing in public. And I would gladly have stayed on till sundowner time in order to jerk Frank back into a sense of my personality; but there was a storm coming, and it was no fun driving home through a storm.

Richard is stronger-willed than I am. After this party he kept away from Sonia's and stuck in to his work. I broke off my engagement. It was impossible to know whether Frank was relieved or not. There were still three months before he was to take up his appointment in the north. He spent most of his time with Sonia. I was not sure how things stood between them. I still drove over to Sonia's sometimes and found Frank there. I was dissatisfied and attracted by both of them and by their situation. In the dry spells they would often be down the river in the punt when I arrived, and I would wait for the sight of the returning pink parasol, and be glad of the sight. Once or twice when we met at the clinic Frank said to me, factually, "We could still be married." Once he said, "Old Sonia's only a joke, you know." But I thought he was afraid I might take him at his word, or might do so too soon.

Sonia spoke again of travelling. She was learning to study road maps. She told one of the nurses, "When Frank's settled up at the north I'll go up and settle him down nicer." She told another of the nurses, "My old husband's coming from gaol this month, next month, I don't know, man. He'll see some changes. He get used to them."

One afternoon I drove over to the farm; I had not seen Sonia for six weeks because her children had been home for the holidays and I loathed her children. I had missed her, she was never boring. The house-boy said she was down the river with Dr Frank. I wandered down the path, but they were not in sight. I waited for about eight minutes and walked back. All the natives except the house-boy had gone to sleep in their huts. I did not see the house-boy for some time, and when I did I was frightened by the fear on his face.

I was coming round by the old ox-stalls, now deserted – since Sonia had abandoned farming, even with a tractor, far less a span of oxen. The house-boy appeared then, and whispered to me. "Baas Van der Merwe is come. He looking in the window."

I walked quietly round the stalls till I had a view of the house, and saw a man of about fifty, undernourished-looking, in khaki shorts and shirt. He was standing on a box by the drawing-room window. He had his hand on the curtain, parting it, and was looking steadily into the empty room.

"Go down to the river and warn them," I said to the boy.

He turned to go, but "Boy!" shouted the man. The house-boy in his green-and-white clothes rapidly went towards the voice.

I got down to the river just as they were landing. Sonia was dressed in pale blue. Her new parasol was blue. She looked specially fabulous and I noticed her very white teeth, her round brown eyes and her story-book pose, as she stood dressed up in the middle of Africa under the blazing sun with the thick-leaved plants at her feet. Frank, looking nice in tropical suiting, was tying up the punt. "Your husband has returned," I said, and ran fearfully back to my car. I started it up and made off, and as I sped past the house over the gravel I saw Jannie Van der Merwe about to enter the house, followed by the servant. He turned to watch my car and spoke to the native, evidently asking who I was.

Afterwards the native deposed that Jannie went all through the house examining the changes and the new furniture. He used the lavatory and pulled the chain. He tried the taps in both bathrooms. In Sonia's room he put straight a pair of her shoes which were lying askew. He then tested all the furniture for dust, all through the house, touching the furniture with the middle finger of his right hand and turning up his finger to see if it showed any dust. The house-boy followed, and when Jannie came to an old oak Dutch chest which was set away in a corner of one of the children's rooms – since Sonia had taken against all her father's old furniture – he found a little dust on it. He ordered the native to fetch a duster and remove the dust. When this was done Jannie proceeded on his tour, and when he had tried everything for dust he went out and down the path towards the river. He found Sonia and Frank at the ox-stalls arguing about what to do and where to go, and taking a revolver from his pocket, shot them. Sonia died immediately. Frank lingered for ten hours. This was a serious crime and Jannie was hanged.

I waited all the weeks ahead for Richard to make the first suggestion that we should move away. I was afraid to suggest it first lest he should resent the move all his life. Our long leave was not due for another year. Our annual leave was not due for some months. At last he said, "I can't stand it here."

I wanted to return to England. I had been thinking of nothing else.

"We can't stay here," I said, as if it were a part in a play.

"Shall we pack up and go?" he said, and I felt a huge relief.

"No," I said.

He said, "It would be a pity to pack it all in when we've both gone so far in tropical diseases."

In fact I left the following week. Since then, Richard has gone far in tropical diseases. "It's a pity," he said before I left, "to let what's happened come between us."

I packed up my things and departed for dear life, before the dry season should set in, and the rainy season should follow, and all things be predictable.

BANG-BANG YOU'RE DEAD

At that time many of the men looked like Rupert Brooke, whose portrait still hung in everyone's imagination. It was that clear-cut, "typically English" face which is seldom seen on the actual soil of England but proliferates in the African Colonies.

"I must say," said Sybil's hostess, "the men look charming."

These men were all charming, Sybil had decided at the time, until you got to know them. She sat in the dark room watching the eighteen-year-old film unrolling on the screen as if the particular memory had solidified under the effect of some intense heat coming out of the projector. She told herself, I was young, I demanded nothing short of perfection. But then, she thought, that is not quite the case. But it comes to the same thing; to me, the men were not charming for long.

The first reel came to an end. Someone switched on the light. Her host picked the next film out of its tropical packing.

"It must be an interesting experience," said her hostess, "seeing yourself after all those years."

"Hasn't Sybil seen these films before?" said a latecomer.

"No, never – have you, Sybil?"

"No, never."

"If they had been my films," said her hostess, "my curiosity could not have waited eighteen years."

The Kodachrome reels had lain in their boxes in the dark of Sybil's cabin trunk. Why bother, when one's memory was clear?

"Sybil didn't know anyone who had a projector," said her hostess, "until we got ours."

"It was delightful," said the latecomer, an elderly lady, "what I saw of it. Are the others as good?"

Sybil thought for a moment. "The photography is probably good," she said. "There was a cook behind the camera."

"A cook! How priceless; whatever do you mean?" said her hostess.

"The cook-boy," said Sybil, "was trained up to use the camera."

"He managed it well," said her host, who was adjusting the new reel.

"Wonderful colours," said her hostess. "Oh, I'm so glad you dug them out. How healthy and tanned and open-necked everyone looks. And those adorable shiny natives all over the place."

The elderly lady said, "I liked the bit where you came out on the veranda in your shorts carrying the gun."

"Ready?" said Sybil's host. The new reel was fixed. "Put out the lights," he said.

It was the stoep again. Through the French windows came a dark girl in shorts followed by a frisky young Alsatian.

"Lovely dog," commented Sybil's host. "He seems to be asking Sybil for a game."

"That is someone else," Sybil said very quickly.

"The girl there, with the dog?"

"Yes, of course. Don't you see me walking across the lawn by the trees?"

"Oh, of course, of course. She did look like you, Sybil, that girl with the dog. Wasn't she like Sybil? I mean, just as she came out on the veranda."

"Yes, *I* thought it was Sybil for a moment until I saw Sybil in the background. But you can see the difference now. See, as she turns round. That girl isn't really like Sybil, it must be the shorts."

"There was a slight resemblance between us," Sybil remarked.

The projector purred on.

"Look, there's a little girl rather like you, Sybil." Sybil, walking between her mother and father, one hand in each, had already craned round. The other child, likewise being walked along, had looked back too.

The other child wore a black velour hat turned up all round, a fawn coat of covert-coating, and at her neck a narrow white ermine tie. She wore white silk gloves. Sybil was dressed identically, and though this in itself was nothing to marvel at, since numerous small girls wore this ensemble when they were walked out in the parks and public gardens of cathedral towns in 1923, it did fortify the striking resemblance in features, build, and height, between the two children. Sybil suddenly felt she was walking past her own reflection in the long looking-glass. There was her peak chin, her black bobbed hair under her hat, with its fringe almost touching her eyebrows. Her wide-spaced eyes, her nose very small like a cat's. "Stop staring,

Sybil," whispered her mother. Sybil had time to snatch the gleam of white socks and black patent leather button shoes. Her own socks were white but her shoes were brown, with laces. At first she felt this one discrepancy was wrong, in the sense that it was wrong to step on one of the cracks in the pavement. Then she felt it was right that there should be a difference.

"The Colemans," Sybil's mother remarked to her father. "They keep that hotel at Hillend. The child must be about Sybil's age. Very alike, aren't they? And I suppose," she continued for Sybil's benefit, "she's a good little girl like Sybil." Quick-witted Sybil thought poorly of the last remark with its subtle counsel of perfection.

On other occasions, too, they passed the Coleman child on a Sunday walk. In summer time the children wore panama hats and tussore silk frocks discreetly adorned with drawn-thread work. Sometimes the Coleman child was accompanied by a young maid-servant in grey dress and black stockings. Sybil noted this one difference between her own entourage and the other girl's. "Don't turn round and stare," whispered her mother.

It was not till she went to school that she found Désirée Coleman to be a year older than herself. Désirée was in a higher class but sometimes, when the whole school was assembled on the lawn or in the gym, Sybil would be, for a few moments, mistaken for Désirée. In the late warm spring the classes sat in separate groups under the plane trees until, as by simultaneous instinct, the teachers would indicate time for break. The groups would mingle, and "Sybil, dear, your shoelace," a teacher might call out; and then, as Sybil regarded her neat-laced shoes, "Oh no, not Sybil, I mean Désirée." In the percussion band Sybil banged her triangle triumphantly when the teacher declared, "*Much* better than yesterday, Sybil." But she added, "I mean Désirée."

Only the grown-ups mistook one child for another at odd moments. None of her small companions made this mistake. After the school concert Sybil's mother said, "For a second I thought you were Désirée in the choir. It's strange you are so alike. I'm not a bit like Mrs Coleman and your daddy doesn't resemble *him* in the least."

Sybil found Désirée unsatisfactory as a playmate. Sybil was precocious, her brain was like a blade. She had discovered that dull children were apt to be spiteful. Désirée would sit innocently cross-legged beside you at a party, watching the conjurer, then suddenly, for no apparent reason, jab at you viciously with her elbow.

By the time Sybil was eight and Désirée nine it was seldom that anyone, even strangers and new teachers, mixed them up. Sybil's nose became more sharp and pronounced while Désirée's seemed to sink into her plump cheeks like a painted-on nose. Only on a few occasions, and only on dark winter afternoons between the last of three o'clock daylight and the coming on of lights all over the school, was Sybil mistaken for Désirée.

Between Sybil's ninth year and her tenth Désirée's family came to live in her square. The residents' children were taken to the gardens of the square after school by mothers and nursemaids, and were bidden to play with each other nicely. Sybil regarded the intrusion of Désirée sulkily, and said she preferred her book. She cheered up, however, when a few weeks later the Dobell boys came to live in the square. The two Dobells had dusky-rose skins and fine dark eyes. It appeared the father was half Indian.

How Sybil adored the Dobells! They were a new type of playmate in her experience, so jumping and agile, and yet so gentle, so unusually courteous. Their dark skins were never dirty, a fact which Sybil obscurely approved. She did not then mind Désirée joining in their games; the Dobell boys were a kind of charm against despair, for they did not understand stupidity and so did not notice Désirée's.

The girl lacked mental stamina, could not keep up an imaginative game for long, was shrill and apt to kick her playmates unaccountably and on the sly; the Dobells reacted to this with a simple resignation. Perhaps the lack of opposition was the reason that Désirée continually shot Sybil dead, contrary to the rules, whenever she felt like it.

Sybil resented with the utmost passion the repeated daily massacre of herself before the time was ripe. It was useless for Jon Dobell to explain, "Not yet, Désirée. Wait, wait, Désirée. She's not to be shot down yet. She hasn't crossed the bridge yet, and you can't shoot her from there, anyway – there's a big boulder between you and her. You have to creep round it, and Hugh has a shot at you first, and he thinks he's got you, but only your hat. And . . ."

It was no use. Each day before the game started the four sat in conference on the short dry prickly grass. The proceedings were agreed. The game was on. "Got it all clear, Désirée?" "Yes," she said, every day. Désirée shouted and got herself excited, she made foolish sounds even when supposed to be stalking the bandits through the silent forest. A few high screams and then, "Bang-bang," she yelled, aiming at Sybil, "you're dead." Sybil obediently rolled over, protesting none the less that the game had only begun, while the Dobells sighed, "Oh, *Désirée!*"

Sybil vowed to herself each night, I will do the same to her. Next time – tomorrow if it isn't raining – I will bang-bang her before she has a chance to hang her panama on the bough as a decoy. I will say bang-bang on her out of turn, and I will do her dead before her time.

But on no succeeding tomorrow did Sybil bring herself to do this. Her pride before the Dobells was more valuable than the success of the game. Instead, with her cleverness, Sybil set herself to avoid Désirée's range for as long as possible. She dodged behind the laurels and threw out a running commentary as if to a mental defective, such as, "I'm in disguise, all in green, and no one can see me among the trees." But still Désirée saw her. Désirée's eyes insisted on penetrating solid mountains. "I'm half a mile away from everyone," Sybil cried as Désirée's gun swivelled relentlessly upon her.

I shall refuse to be dead, Sybil promised herself. I'll break the rule. If it doesn't count with her why should it count with me? I won't roll over any more when she bangs you're dead to me. Next time, tomorrow if it isn't raining . . .

But Sybil simply did roll over. When Jon and Hugh Dobell called out to her that Désirée's bang-bang did not count she started hopefully to resurrect herself; but "It does count, it *does*. That's the rule," Désirée counter-screeched. And Sybil dropped back flat, knowing utterly that this was final.

And so the girl continued to deal premature death to Sybil, losing her head, but never so much that she aimed at one of the boys. For some reason which Sybil did not consider until she was years and years older, it was always herself who had to die.

One day, when Désirée was late in arriving for play, Sybil put it to the boys that Désirée should be left out of the game in future. "She only spoils it."

"But," said Jon, "you need four people for the game."

"You need four," said Hugh.

"No, you can do it with three." As she spoke she was inventing the game with three. She explained to them what was in her mind's eye. But neither boy could grasp the idea, having got used to Bandits and Riders with two on each side. "I am the lone Rider, you see," said Sybil. "Or," she wheedled, "the cherry tree can be a Rider." She was talking to stone, inoffensive but uncomprehending. All at once she realized, without articulating the idea, that her intelligence was superior to theirs, and she felt lonely.

"Could we play rounders instead?" ventured Jon.

Sybil brought a book every day after that, and sat reading beside her mother, who was glad, on the whole, that Sybil had grown tired of rowdy games.

"They were preparing," said Sybil, "to go on a shoot."

Sybil's host was changing the reel.

"I get quite a new vision of Sybil," said her hostess, "seeing her in such a . . . such a *social* environment. Were any of these people intellectuals, Sybil?"

"No, but lots of poets."

"Oh, *no*. Did they all write poetry?"

"Quite a lot of them," said Sybil, "did."

"Who *were* they all? Who was that blond fellow who was standing by the van with you?"

"He was the manager of the estate. They grew passion-fruit and manufactured the juice."

"Passion-fruit – how killing. Did *he* write poetry?"

"Oh, yes."

"And who was the girl, the one I thought was you?"

"Oh, I had known her as a child and we met again in the Colony. The short man was her husband."

"And were you all off on safari that morning? I simply can't imagine you shooting anything, Sybil, somehow."

"On this occasion," said Sybil, "I didn't go. I just held the gun for effect."

Everyone laughed.

"Do you still keep up with these people? I've heard that colonials are great letter-writers, it keeps them in touch with –"

"No." And she added, "Three of them are dead. The girl and her husband, and the fair fellow."

"Really? What happened to them? Don't tell me *they* were mixed up in shooting affairs."

"They were mixed up in shooting affairs," said Sybil.

"Oh, these colonials," said the elderly woman, "and their shooting affairs!"

"Number three," said Sybil's host. "Ready? Lights out, please."

"Don't get eaten by lions. I say, Sybil, don't get mixed up in a shooting affair." The party at the railway station were unaware of the noise they were making for they were inside the noise. As the time of departure drew near Donald's relatives tended to herd themselves apart while Sybil's clustered round the couple.

"Two years – it will be an interesting experience for them."

"Mind out for the shooting affairs. Don't let Donald have a gun."

There had been an outbreak of popular headlines about the shooting affairs in the Colony. Much had been blared forth about the effect, on the minds of young settlers, of the climate, the hard drinking, the shortage of white women. The Colony was a place where lovers shot husbands, or shot themselves, where husbands shot natives who spied through bedroom windows. Letters to *The Times* arrived belatedly from respectable colonists, refuting the scandals with sober statistics. The recent incidents, they said, did not represent the habits of the peaceable majority. The Governor told the press that everything had been highly exaggerated. By the time Sybil and Donald left for the Colony the music-hall comics had already exhausted the entertainment value of colonial shooting affairs.

"Don't make pets of snakes or crocs. Mind out for the lions. Don't forget to write."

It was almost a surprise to them to find that shooting affairs in the Colony were not entirely a music-hall myth. They occurred in waves. For three months at a time the gun-murders and suicides were reported weekly. The old colonists with their very blue eyes sat beside their whisky bottles and remarked that another young rotter had shot himself. Then the rains would break and the shootings would cease for a long season.

Eighteen months after their marriage Donald was mauled

by a lioness and died on the long stretcher journey back to the station. He was one of a party of eight. No one could really say how it happened; it was done in a flash. The natives had lost their wits, and, instead of shooting the beast, had come calling "Ah-ah-ah," and pointing to the spot. A few strides, shouldering the grass aside, and Donald's friends got the lioness as she reared from his body.

His friends in the archaeological team to which he belonged urged Sybil to remain in the Colony for the remaining six months, and return to England with them. Still undecided, she went on a sight-seeing tour. But before their time was up the archaeologists had been recalled. War had been declared. Civilians were not permitted to leave the continent, and Sybil was caught, like Donald under the lioness.

She wished he had lived to enjoy a life of his own, as she intended to do. It was plain to her that they must have separated had he lived. There had been no disagreement but, thought Sybil, given another two years there would have been disagreements. Donald had shown signs of becoming a bore. By the last, the twenty-seventh, year of his life, his mind had ceased to inquire. Archaeology, that thrilling subject, had become Donald's job, merely. He began to talk as if all archaeological methods and theories had ceased to evolve on the day he obtained his degree; it was now only a matter of applying his knowledge to field-work for a limited period. Archaeological papers came out from England. The usual crank literature on roneo foolscap followed them from one postal address to another. "Donald, aren't you going to look through them?" Sybil said, as the journals and papers piled up. "No, really, I don't see it's necessary." It was not necessary because his future was fixed; two years in the field and then a lectureship. If it were my subject, she thought, these papers would be necessary to me. Even the crackpot ones, rightly read, would be, to me, enlarging.

Sybil lay in bed in the mornings reading the translation of Kierkegaard's *Journals*, newly arrived from England in their first, revelatory month of publication. She felt like a desert which had not realized its own aridity till the rain began to fall upon it. When Donald came home in the late afternoons she had less and less to say to him.

"There has been another shooting affair," Donald said, "across the valley. The chap came home unexpectedly and found his wife with another man. He shot them both."

"In this place, one is never far from the jungle," Sybil said.

"What are you talking about? We are eight hundred miles from the jungle."

When he had gone on his first big shoot, eight hundred miles away in the jungle, she had reflected, there is no sign of a living mind in him, it is like a landed fish which has ceased to palpitate. But, she thought, another woman would never notice it. Other women do not wish to be married to a Mind. Yet I do, she thought, and I am a freak and should not have married. In fact I am not the marrying type. Perhaps that is why he does not explore my personality, any more than he reads the journals. It might make him think, and that would be hurtful.

After his death she wished he had lived to enjoy a life of his own, whatever that might have been. She took a job in a private school for girls and cultivated a few friends for diversion until the war should be over. Charming friends need not possess minds.

Their motor launch was rocking up the Zambezi. Sybil was leaning over the rail mouthing something to a startled native in a canoe. Now Sybil was pointing across the river.

"I think I was asking him," Sybil commented to her friends in the darkness, "about the hippo. There was a school of hippo some distance away, and we wanted to see them better. But the native said we shouldn't go too near – that's why he's looking so frightened – because the hippo often upset a boat, and then the crocs quickly slither into the water. There, look! We got a long shot of the hippo – those bumps in the water, like submarines, those are the snouts of hippo."

The film rocked with the boat as it proceeded up the river. The screen went white.

"Something's happened," said Sybil's hostess.

"Put on the light," said Sybil's host. He fiddled with the projector and a young man, their lodger from upstairs, went to help him.

"I loved those tiny monkeys on the island," said her hostess. "Do hurry, Ted. What's gone wrong?"

"Shut up a minute," he said.

"Sybil, you know you haven't changed much since you were a girl."

"Thank you, Ella." I haven't changed at all so far as I still think charming friends need not possess minds.

"I expect this will revive your memories, Sybil. The details, I mean. One is bound to forget so much."

"Oh yes," Sybil said, and she added, "but I recall quite a lot of details, you know."

"Do you *really*, Sybil?"

I wish, she thought, they wouldn't cling to my least word.

The young man turned from the projector with several feet of the film-strip looped between his widespread hands. "Is the fair chap your husband, Mrs Greeves?" he said to Sybil.

"Sybil lost her husband very early on," her hostess informed him in a low and sacred voice.

"Oh, I *am* sorry."

Sybil's hostess replenished the drinks of her three guests. Her host turned from the projector, finished his drink, and passed his glass to be refilled, all in one movement. Everything they do seems large and important, thought Sybil, but I must not let it be so. We are only looking at old films.

She overheard a sibilant "Whish-sh-sh?" from the elderly woman in which she discerned, "Who is she?"

"Sybil Greeves," her hostess breathed back, "a distant cousin of Ted's through marriage."

"Oh yes?" The low tones were puzzled as if all had not been explained.

"She's quite famous, of course."

"Oh, I didn't know that."

"Very few people know it," said Sybil's hostess with a little arrogance.

"OK," said Ted, "lights out."

"I must say," said his wife, "the colours are marvellous."

All the time she was in the Colony Sybil longed for the inexplicable colourings of her native land. The flamboyants were too rowdy, the birds, the native women with their heads bound in cloth of piercing pink, their blinding black skin and white teeth, the baskets full of bright tough flowers or oranges on their heads, the sight of which everyone else admired ("How I wish I could paint all this!") distressed Sybil, it bored her.

She rented a house, sharing it with a girl whose husband was fighting in the north. She was twenty-two. To safeguard her privacy absolutely, she had a plywood partition put up in the sitting-room, for it was another ten years before she had learnt those arts of leading a double life and listening to people ambiguously, which enabled her to mix without losing identity, and to listen without boredom.

On the other side of the partition Ariadne Lewis decorously entertained her friends, most of whom were men on leave. On a few occasions Sybil attended these parties, working herself, as in a frenzy of self-discipline, into a state of carnal excitement over the men. She managed to do this only by an effortful sealing-off of all her critical faculties except those which assessed a good male voice and appearance. The hangovers were frightful.

The scarcity of white girls made it easy for any one of them to keep a number of men in perpetual attendance. Ariadne had many boyfriends but no love affairs. Sybil had three affairs in the space of two years, to put herself to the test. They started at private dances, in the magnolia-filled gardens that smelt like a scent factory, under the Milky Way which looked like an overcrowded jeweller's window. The affairs ended when she succumbed to one of her attacks of tropical flu, and lay in a twilight of the senses on a bed which had been set on the stone stoep and overhung with a white mosquito net like something bridal. With damp shaky hands she would write a final letter to the man and give it to her half-caste maid to post. He would telephone next morning, and would be put off by the house-boy, who was quite intelligent.

For some years she had been thinking she was not much inclined towards sex. After the third affair, this dawned and rose within her as a whole realization, as if in the past, when she had told herself, "I am not predominantly a sexual being," or "I'm rather a frigid freak, I suppose," these were the sayings of an illiterate, never quite rational and known until now, but after the third affair the notion was so intensely conceived as to be almost new. It appalled her. She lay on the shady stoep, her fever subsiding, and examined her relations with men. She thought, what if I married again? She shivered under the hot sheet. Can it be, she thought, that I have a suppressed tendency towards women? She lay still and let the idea probe round in imagination. She surveyed, with a stony inward eye, all the women she had known, prim little academicians with cream peter-pan collars on their dresses, large dominant women, a number of beauties, conventional nitwits like Ariadne. No, really, she thought; neither men nor women. It is a not caring for sexual relations. It is not merely a lack of pleasure in sex, it is dislike of the excitement. And it is not merely dislike, it is worse, it is boredom.

She felt a lonely emotion near to guilt. The three love affairs took on heroic aspects in her mind. They were an attempt, thought Sybil, to do the normal thing. Perhaps I may try again. Perhaps, if I should meet the right man . . . But at the idea "right man" she felt a sense of intolerable desolation and could not stop shivering. She raised the mosquito net and reached for the lemon juice, splashing it jerkily into the glass. She sipped. The juice had grown warm and had been made too sweet, but she let it linger on her sore throat and peered through the net at the backs of houses and the yellow veldt beyond them.

Ariadne said one morning, "I met a girl last night, it was funny. I thought it was you at first and called over to her. But she wasn't really like you close up, it was just an impression. As a matter of fact, she knows you. I've asked her to tea. I forget her name."

"I don't," said Sybil.

But when Désirée arrived they greeted each other with exaggerated warmth, wholly felt at the time, as acquaintances do when they meet in another hemisphere. Sybil had last seen Désirée at a dance in Hampstead, and there had merely said, "Oh, hallo."

"We were at our first school together," Désirés explained to Ariadne, still holding Sybil's hand.

Already Sybil wished to withdraw. "It's strange," she remarked, "how, sooner or later, everyone in the Colony meets someone they have known, or their parents knew, at home."

Désirée and her husband, Barry Weston, were settled in a remote part of the Colony. Sybil had heard of Weston, unaware that Désirée was his wife. He was much talked of as an enterprising planter. Some years ago he had got the idea of manufacturing passion-fruit juice, had planted orchards and set up a factory. The business was now expanding wonderfully. Barry Weston also wrote poetry, a volume of which, entitled

Home Thoughts, he had published and sold with great success within the confines of the Colony. His first wife had died of blackwater fever. On one of his visits to England he had met and married Désirée, who was twelve years his junior.

"You *must* come and see us," said Désirée to Sybil; and to Ariadne she explained again, "We were at our first little private school together." And she said, "Oh, Sybil, do you remember Trotsky? Do you remember Minnie Mouse, what a hell of a life we gave her? I shall never forget that day when . . ."

The school where Sybil taught was shortly to break up for holidays; Ariadne was to visit her husband in Cairo at that time. Sybil promised a visit to the Westons. When Désirée, beautifully dressed in linen suiting, had departed, Ariadne said, "I'm so glad you're going to stay with them. I hated the thought of your being all alone for the next few weeks."

"Do you know," Sybil said, "I don't think I shall go to stay with them after all. I'll make an excuse."

"Oh, why not? Oh, Sybil, it's such a lovely place, and it will be fun for you. He's a poet, too." Sybil could sense exasperation, could hear Ariadne telling her friends, "There's something wrong with Sybil. You never know a person till you live with them. Now Sybil will say one thing one minute, and the next . . . Something wrong with her sex-life, perhaps . . . odd . . ."

At home, thought Sybil, it would not be such a slur. Her final appeal for a permit to travel to England had just been dismissed. The environment mauled her weakness. "I think I'm going to have a cold," she said, shivering.

"Go straight to bed, dear." Ariadne called for black Elijah

and bade him prepare some lemon juice. But the cold did not materialize.

She returned with flu, however, from her first visit to the Westons. Her 1936 Ford V8 had broken down on the road and she had waited three chilly hours before another car had appeared.

"You must get a decent car," said the chemist's wife, who came to console her. "These old crocks simply won't stand up to the roads out here."

Sybil shivered and held her peace. Nevertheless, she returned to the Westons at mid-term.

Désirée's invitations were pressing, almost desperate. Again and again Sybil went in obedience to them. The Westons were a magnetic field.

There was a routine attached to her arrival. The elegant wicker chair was always set for her in the same position on the stoep. The same cushions, it seemed, were always piled in exactly the same way.

"What will you drink, Sybil? Are you comfy there, Sybil? We're going to give you a wonderful time, Sybil." She was their little orphan, she supposed. She sat, with very dark glasses, contemplating the couple. "We've planned – haven't we, Barry? – a surprise for you, Sybil." "We've planned – haven't we, Désirée? – a marvellous trip . . . a croc hunt . . . hippo . . ."

Sybil sips her gin and lime. Facing her on the wicker sofa, Désirée and her husband sit side by side. They gaze at Sybil affectionately, "Take off your smoked glasses, Sybil, the sun's nearly gone." Sybil takes them off. The couple hold hands. They peck kisses at each other, and presently, outrageously, they are entwined in a long erotic embrace in the course of which Barry once or twice regards Sybil from the corner of his eye. Barry disengages himself and sits with his arm about his wife; she snuggles up to him. Why, thinks Sybil, is this performance being staged? "Sybil is shocked," Barry remarks. She sips her drink, and reflects that a public display between man and wife somehow is more shocking than are courting couples in parks and doorways. "We're very much in love with each other," Barry explains, squeezing his wife. And Sybil wonders what is wrong with their marriage since obviously something is wrong. The couple kiss again. Am I dreaming this? Sybil asks herself.

Even on her first visit Sybil knew definitely there was something wrong with the marriage. She thought of herself, at first, as an objective observer, and was even amused when she understood they had chosen her to be their sort of Victim of Expiation. On occasions when other guests were present she noted that the love scenes did not take place. Instead, the couple tended to snub Sybil before their friends. "Poor little Sybil, she lives all alone and is a teacher, and hasn't many friends. We have her here to stay as often as possible." The people would look uneasily at Sybil, and would smile. "But you must have *heaps* of friends," they would say politely. Sybil came to realize she was an object of the Westons' resentment, and that, nevertheless, they found her indispensable.

Ariadne returned from Cairo. "You always look washed out when you've been staying at the Westons'," she told Sybil eventually. "I suppose it's due to the late parties and lots of drinks."

"I suppose so."

Désirée wrote continually. "Do come, Barry needs you. He needs your advice about some sonnets." Sybil tore up these letters quickly, but usually went. Not because her discomfort was necessary to their wellbeing, but because it was somehow necessary to her own. The act of visiting the Westons alleviated her sense of guilt.

I believe, she thought, they must discern my abnormality. How could they have guessed? She was always cautious when they dropped questions about her private life. But one's closest secrets have a subtle way of communicating themselves to the resentful vigilance of opposite types. I do believe, she thought, that heart speaks unto heart, and deep calleth unto deep. But rarely in clear language. There is a misunderstanding here. They imagine their demonstrations of erotic bliss will torment my frigid soul, and so far they are right. But the reason for my pain is not envy. Really, it is boredom.

Her Ford V8 rattled across country. How bored, she thought, I am going to be by their married tableau! How pleased, exultant, they will be! These thoughts consoled her, they were an offering to the gods.

"Are you comfy, Sybil?"

She sipped her gin and lime. "Yes, thanks."

His pet name for Désirée was Dearie. "Kiss me, Dearie," he said.

"There, Baddy," his wife said to Barry, snuggling close to him and squinting at Sybil.

"I say, Sybil," Barry said as he smoothed down his hair, "you ought to get married again. You're missing such a lot."

"Yes, Sybil," said Désirée, "you should either marry or enter a convent, one or the other."

"I don't see why," Sybil said, "I should fit into a tidy category."

"Well, you're neither one thing nor another – is she, honeybunch?"

True enough, thought Sybil, and that is why I'm laid out on the altar of boredom.

"Or get yourself a boyfriend," said Désirée. "It would be good for you."

"You're wasting your best years," said Barry.

"Are you comfy there, Sybil? . . . We want you to enjoy yourself here. Any time you want to bring a boyfriend, we're broadminded – aren't we, Baddy?"

"Kiss me, Dearie," he said.

Désirée took his handkerchief from his pocket and rubbed lipstick from his mouth. He jerked his head away and said to Sybil, "Pass your glass."

Désirée looked at her reflection in the glass of the French windows and said, "Sybil's too intellectual, that's her trouble." She patted her hair, then looked at Sybil with an old childish enmity.

After dinner Barry would read his poems. Usually, he said, "I'm not going to be an egotist tonight. I'm not going to read my poems." And usually Désirée would cry. "Oh do, Barry, do." Always, eventually, he did. "Marvellous." Désirée would comment, "wonderful." By the third night of her visits, the farcical aspect of it all would lose its fascination for Sybil, and boredom would fill her near to bursting point, like gas in a balloon. To relieve the strain, she would sigh deeply from time to time. Barry was too engrossed in his own voice to notice this, but Désirée was watching. At first Sybil worded her comments tactfully. "I think you should devote more of your time to your verses," she said. And, since he looked puzzled, added, "You owe it to poetry if you write it."

"Nonsense," said Désirée, "he often writes a marvellous sonnet before shaving in the morning."

"Sybil may be right," said Barry. "I owe poetry all the time I can give."

"Are you tired, Sybil?" said Désirée. "Why are you sighing like that; are you all right?"

Later, Sybil gave up the struggle and wearily said, "Very good," or "Nice rhythm" after each poem. And even the guilt of condoning Désirée's "marvellous . . . wonderful" was less than the guilt of her isolated mind. She did not know then that the price of allowing false opinions was the gradual loss of one's capacity for forming true ones.

Not every morning, but at least twice during each visit Sybil would wake to hear the row in progress. The nanny, who brought her early tea, made large eyes and tiptoed warily. Sybil would have her bath, splashing a lot to drown the noise of the quarrel. Downstairs, the battle of voices descended, filled every room and corridor. When, on the worst occasions, the sound of shattering glass broke through the storm, Sybil would know that Barry was smashing up Désirée's dressing-table; and would wonder how Désirée always managed to replace her crystal bowls, since goods of that type were now scarce, and why she bothered to do so. Sybil would always find the two girls of Barry's former marriage standing side by side on the lawn frankly gazing up at the violent bedroom window. The nanny would cart off Désirée's baby for a faraway walk. Sybil would likewise disappear for the morning.

The first time this happened, Désirée told her later, "I'm afraid you unsettle Barry."

"What do you mean?" said Sybil.

Désirée dabbed her watery eyes and blew her nose. "Well, of *course*, it stands to reason, Sybil, you're out to attract Barry. And he's only a man. I know you do it *unconsciously*, but . . ."

"I can't stand this sort of thing. I shall leave right away," Sybil said.

"No, Sybil, no. Don't make a *thing* of it. Barry needs you. You're the only person in the Colony who can really talk to him about his poetry."

"Understand," said Sybil on that first occasion, "I am not at all interested in your husband. I think he's an all-round third-rater. That is my opinion."

Désirée looked savage. "Barry," she shouted, "has made a fortune out of passion-fruit juice in eight years. He has sold four thousand copies of *Home Thoughts* on his own initiative."

It was like a game for three players. According to the rules, she was to be in love, unconsciously, with Barry, and tortured by the contemplation of Désirée's married bliss. She felt too old to join in, just at that moment.

Barry came to her room while she was packing. "Don't go," he said. "We need you. And after all, we are only human. What's a row? These quarrels only happen in the best marriages. And I can't for the life of me think how it started."

"What a beautiful house. What a magnificent estate," said Sybil's hostess.

"Yes," said Sybil, "it was the grandest in the Colony."

"Were the owners frightfully grand?"

"Well, they were rich, of course."

"I can see that. What a beautiful interior. I adore those lovely old oil lamps. I suppose you didn't have electricity?"

"Yes, there was electric light in all the rooms. But my friends preferred the oil-lamp tradition for the dining-room. You see, it was a copy of an old Dutch house."

"Absolutely charming."

The reel came to an end. The lights went up and everyone shifted in their chairs.

"What were those large red flowers?" said the elderly lady.

"Flamboyants."

"Magnificent," said her hostess. "Don't you miss the colours, Sybil?"

"No, I don't, actually. There was too much of it for me."

"You didn't care for the bright colours?" said the young man, leaning forward eagerly.

Sybil smiled at him.

"I liked the bit where those little lizards were playing among the stones. That was an excellent shot," said her host. He was adjusting the last spool.

"I rather *liked* that handsome blond fellow," said her hostess, as if the point had been in debate. "Was he the passion-fruiter?"

"He was the manager," said Sybil.

"Oh yes, you told me. He was in a shooting affair, did you say?"

"Yes, it was unfortunate."

"Poor young man. It sounds quite a dangerous place. I suppose the sun and everything . . ."

"It was dangerous for some people. It depended."

"The blacks look happy enough. Did you have any trouble with them in those days?"

"No," said Sybil, "only with the whites."

Everyone laughed.

"Right," said her host. "Lights out, please."

Sybil soon perceived the real cause of the Westons' quarrels. It differed from their explanations: they were both, they said, so much in love, so jealous of each other's relations with the opposite sex.

"Barry was furious," said Désirée one day, "– weren't you, Barry? – because I smiled, merely smiled, at Carter."

"I'll have it out with Carter," muttered Barry. "He's always hanging round Désirée."

David Carter was their manager. Sybil was so foolish as once to say, "Oh surely David wouldn't –"

"Oh wouldn't he?" said Désirée.

"Oh wouldn't he?" said Barry.

Possibly they did not themselves know the real cause of their quarrels. These occurred on mornings when Barry had decided to lounge in bed and write poetry. Désirée, anxious that the passion-fruit business should continue to expand, longed for him to be at his office in the factory at eight o'clock each morning, by which time all other enterprising men in the Colony were at work. But Barry spoke more and more of retiring and devoting his time to his poems. When he lay abed, pen in hand, worrying a sonnet, Désirée would sulk and bang doors. The household knew that the row was on. "Quiet! Don't you see I'm trying to think," he would shout. "*I* suggest," she would reply, "you go to the library if you want to write." It was evident that her greed and his vanity, facing each other in growling antipathy, were too terrible for either to face. Instead, the names of David Carter and Sybil would fly between them, consoling them, pepping-up and propagating the myth of their mutual attraction.

"Rolling your eyes at Carter in the orchard. Don't think I didn't notice."

"Carter? That's funny. I can easily keep Carter in his place. But while we're on the subject, what about you with Sybil? You sat up late enough with her last night after I'd gone to bed."

Sometimes he not only smashed the crystal bowls, he hurled them through the window.

In the exhausted afternoon Barry would explain, "Désirée was upset – weren't you, Désirée? – because of you, Sybil. It's understandable. We shouldn't stay up late talking after Désirée has gone to bed. You're a little devil in your way, Sybil."

"Oh well," said Sybil obligingly, "that's how it is."

She became tired of the game. When, in the evenings, Barry's voice boomed forth with sonorous significance as befits a hallowed subject, she no longer thought of herself as an objective observer. She had tired of the game because she was now more than nominally committed to it. She ceased to be bored by the Westons; she began to hate them.

"What I don't understand," said Barry, "is why my poems are ignored back in England. I've sold over four thousand of the book out here. Feature articles about me have appeared in all the papers out here; remind me to show you them. But

I can't get a single notice in London. When I send a poem to any of the magazines I don't even get a reply."

"They are engaged in a war," Sybil said.

"But they still publish poetry. Poetry so-called. Utter rubbish, all of it. You can't understand the stuff."

"Yours is too good for them," said Sybil. To a delicate ear her tone might have resembled the stab of a pin stuck into a waxen image.

"That's a fact, between ourselves," said Barry. "I shouldn't say it, but that's the answer."

Barry was overweight, square and dark. His face had lines, as of anxiety or stomach trouble. David Carter, when he passed, cool and fair through the house, was quite a change.

"England is finished," said Barry. "It's degenerate."

"I wonder," said Sybil, "you have the heart to go on writing so cheerily about the English towns and countryside." Now, now, Sybil, she thought; business is business, and the nostalgic English scene is what the colonists want. This visit must be my last. I shall not come again.

"Ah, that," Barry was saying, "was the England I remember. The good old country. But now, I'm afraid, it's decadent. After the war it will be no more than . . ."

Désirée would have the servants into the drawing-room every morning to give them their orders for the day. "I believe in keeping up home standards," said Désirée, whose parents were hotel managers. Sybil was not sure where Désirée had got the idea of herding all the domestics into her presence each morning. Perhaps it was some family-prayer assembly in her ancestral memory, or possibly it had been some hotel-staff custom which prompted her to "have in the servants" and instruct them beyond their capacity. These half-domesticated peasants and erstwhile small-farmers stood, bare-footed and woolly-cropped, in clumsy postures on Désirée's carpet. In pidgin dialect which they largely failed to comprehend, she enunciated the duties of each one. Only Sybil and David Carter knew that the natives' name for Désirée was, translated, "Bad Hen". Désirée complained much about their stupidity, but she enjoyed this morning palaver as Barry relished his poetry.

"Carter writes poetry too," said Barry with a laugh one day.

Désirée shrieked. "Poetry! Oh, Barry, you can't call that stuff *poetry*."

"It is frightful," Barry said, "but the poor fellow doesn't know it."

"I should like to see it," Sybil said.

"You aren't interested in Carter by any chance, Sybil?" said Désirée.

"How do you mean?"

"Personally, I mean."

"Well, I think he's all right."

"Be honest, Sybil," said Barry. Sybil felt extremely irritated. He so often appealed for frankness in others, as if by right; was so dishonest with himself. "Be honest, Sybil – you're after David Carter."

"He's handsome," Sybil said.

"You haven't a chance," said Barry. "He's mad keen on Désirée. And anyway, Sybil, you don't want a beginner."

"You want a mature man in a good position," said Désirée.

"The life you're living isn't natural for a girl. I've been noticing," she said, "you and Carter being matey together out on the farm."

Towards the end of her stay David Carter produced his verses for Sybil to read. She thought them interesting but unpractised. She told him so, and was disappointed that he did not take this as a reasonable criticism. He was very angry. "Of course," she said, "your poetry is far better than Barry's." This failed to appease David. After a while, when she was meeting him in the town where she lived, she began to praise his poems, persuading herself that he was fairly talented.

She met him whenever he could get away. She sent excuses in answer to Désirée's pressing invitations. For different reasons, both Sybil and David were anxious to keep their meetings secret from the Westons. Sybil did not want the affair mythologized and gossiped about. For David's part, he valued his job in the flourishing passion-fruit concern. He had confided to Sybil his hope, one day, to have the whole business under his control. He might even buy Barry out. "I know far more about it than he does. He's getting more and more bound up with his poetry, and paying next to no attention to the business. I'm just waiting." He is, Sybil remarked to herself on hearing this, a true poet all right.

David reported that the quarrels between Désirée and Barry were becoming more violent, that the possibility of Barry's resigning from business to devote his time to poetry was haunting Désirée. "Why don't you come," Désirée wrote, "and talk to Barry about his poetry? Why don't you come and see us now? What have we done? Poor Sybil, all alone in the world, you ought to be married. David Carter follows me all over the place, it's most embarrassing, you know how furious Barry gets. Well, I suppose that's the cost of having a devoted husband." Perhaps, thought Sybil, she senses that David is my lover.

One day she went down with flu. David turned up unexpectedly and proposed marriage. He clung to her with violent, large hands. She alone, he said, understood his ambitions, his art, himself. Within a year or two they could, together, take over the passion-fruit plantation.

"Sh-sh, Ariadne will hear you." Ariadne was out, in fact. David looked at her somewhat wildly. "We must be married," he said.

Sybil's affair with David Carter was over, from her point of view, almost before it had started. She had engaged in it as an act of virtue done against the grain, and for a brief time it had absolved her from the reproach of her sexlessness.

"I'm waiting for an answer." By his tone, he seemed to suspect what the answer would be.

"Oh, David, I was just about to write to you. We really must put an end to this. As for marriage, well, I'm not cut out for it at all."

He stooped over her bed and clung to her. "You'll catch my flu," she said. "I'll think about it," she said, to get rid of him.

When he had gone she wrote him her letter, sipping lemon juice to ease her throat. She noticed he had brought for her, and left on the floor of the stoep, six bottles of Weston's Passion-fruit Juice. He will soon get over the affair, she thought, he has still got his obsession with the passion-fruit business.

But in response to her letter David forced his way into

the house. Sybil was alarmed. None of her previous lovers had persisted in this way.

"It's your duty to marry me."

"Really, what next?"

"It's your duty to me as a man and a poet." She did not like his eyes.

"As a poet," she said, "I think you're a third-rater." She felt relieved to hear her own voice uttering the words.

He stiffened up in a comical melodramatic style, looking such a clean-cut settler with his golden hair and tropical suiting.

"David Carter," wrote Désirée, "has gone on the bottle. I think he's bats, myself. It's because I keep giving him the brush-off. Isn't it all silly? The estate will go to ruin if Barry doesn't get rid of him. Barry has sent him away on leave for a month, but if he hasn't improved on his return we shall have to make a change. When are you coming? Barry needs to talk to you."

Sybil went the following week, urged on by her old self-despising; driving her Ford V8 against the current of pleasure, yet compelled to expiate her abnormal nature by contact with the Westons' sexuality, which she knew, none the less, would bore her.

They twisted the knife within an hour of her arrival.

"Haven't you found a man yet?" said Barry.

"You ought to try a love affair," said Désirée. "We've been saying – haven't we, Barry? – you ought to, Sybil. It would be good for you. It isn't healthy, the life you lead. That's why you get flu so often. It's psychological."

"Come out on the lawn," Barry had said when she first

arrived. "We've got the ciné camera out. Come and be filmed."

Désirée said, "Carter came back this morning."

"Oh, is he here? I thought he was away for a month."

"So did we. But he turned up this morning."

"He's moping," Barry said, "about Désirée. She snubs him so badly."

"He's psychological," said Désirée.

"I love that striped awning," said Sybil's hostess. "It puts the finishing touch on the whole scene. How carefree you all look – don't they, Ted?"

"*That* chap looks miserable," Ted observed. He referred to a shot of David Carter who had just ambled within range of the camera.

Everyone laughed, for David looked exceedingly grim.

"He was caught in an off-moment there," said Sybil's hostess. "Oh, there goes Sybil. I thought you looked a little sad just then, Sybil. There's that other girl again, and the lovely dog."

"Was this a *typical* afternoon in the Colony?" inquired the young man.

"It was and it wasn't," Sybil said.

Whenever they had the camera out life changed at the Westons'. Everyone, including the children, had to look very happy. The house natives were arranged to appear in the background wearing their best whites. Sometimes Barry would have everyone dancing in a ring with the children, and the natives had to clap time.

Or, as on the last occasion, he would stage an effect of gracious living. The head cook-boy, who had a good knowledge of photography, was placed at his post.

"Ready," said Barry to the cook, "shoot."

Désirée came out, followed by the dog.

"Look frisky, Barker," said Barry. The Alsatian looked frisky.

Barry put one arm round Désirée and his other arm through Sybil's that late afternoon, walking them slowly across the camera range. He chatted with amiability and with an actor's lift of the head. He would accentuate his laughter, tossing back his head. A sound track would, however, have reproduced the words, "Smile, Sybil. Walk slowly. Look as if you're enjoying it. You'll be able to see yourself in later years, having the time of your life."

Sybil giggled.

Just then David was seen to be securing the little lake boat between the trees. "He must have come across the lake," said Barry. "I wonder if he's been drinking again?"

But David's walk was quite steady. He did not realize he was being photographed as he crossed the long lawn. He stood for a moment staring at Sybil. She said, "Oh, hallo, David." He turned and walked aimlessly face-on towards the camera.

"Hold it a minute," Barry called out to the cook.

The boy obeyed at the moment David realized he had been filmed.

"OK," shouted Barry, when David was out of range. "Fire ahead."

It was then Barry said to Sybil, "Haven't you found a

man yet . . . ?" and Désirée said, "You ought to try a love affair . . ."

"We've made Sybil unhappy," said Désirée.

"Oh, I'm quite happy."

"Well, cheer up in front of the camera," said Barry.

The sun was setting fast, the camera was folded away, and everyone had gone to change. Sybil came down and sat on the stoep outside the open French windows of the dining-room. Presently, Désirée was indoors behind her, adjusting the oil lamps which one of the house-boys had set too high. Désirée put her head round the glass door and remarked to Sybil, "That Benjamin's a fool, I shall speak to him in the morning. He simply will not take care with these lamps. One day we'll have a real smoke-out."

Sybil said, "Oh, I expect they are all so used to electricity these days . . ."

"That's the trouble," said Désirée, and turned back into the room.

Sybil was feeling disturbed by David's presence in the place. She wondered if he would come in to dinner. Thinking of his sullen staring at her on the lawn, she felt he might make a scene. She heard a gasp from the dining-room behind her.

She looked round, but in the same second it was over. A deafening crack from the pistol and Désirée crumpled up. A movement by the inner door and David held the gun to his head. Sybil screamed, and was aware of running footsteps upstairs. The gun exploded again and David's body dropped sideways.

With Barry and the natives she went round to the dining-room. Désirée was dead. David lingered a moment enough to roll his eyes in Sybil's direction as she rose from Désirée's body. He knows, thought Sybil quite lucidly, that he got the wrong woman.

"What I can't understand," said Barry when he called on Sybil a few weeks later, "is why he did it."

"He was mad," said Sybil.

"Not all that mad," said Barry. "And everyone thinks, of course, that there was an affair between them. That's what I can't bear."

"Quite," said Sybil. "But of course he was keen on Désirée. You always said so. Those rows you used to have . . . You always made out you were jealous of David."

"Do you know," he said, "I wasn't, really. It was a sort of . . . a sort of . . ."

"Play-act," said Sybil.

"Sort of. You see, there was nothing between them," he said. "And honestly, Carter wasn't a bit interested in Désirée. And the question is *why* he did it. I can't bear people to think . . ."

The damage to his pride, Sybil saw, outweighed his grief. The sun was setting and she rose to put on the stoep light.

"Stop!" he said. "Turn round. My God, you did look like Désirée for a moment."

"You're nervy," she said, and switched on the light.

"In some ways you *do* look a little like Désirée," he said. "In some lights," he said reflectively.

I must say something, thought Sybil, to blot this notion

from his mind. I must make this occasion unmemorable, distasteful to him.

"At all events," she said, "you've still got your poetry."

"That's the great thing," he said, "I've still got that. It means everything to me, a great consolation. I'm selling up the estate and joining up. The kids are going into a convent and I'm going up north. What we need is some good war poetry. There hasn't been any war poetry."

"You'll make a better soldier," she said, "than a poet."

"What do you say?"

She repeated her words fairly slowly, and with a sense of relief, almost of absolution. The season of falsity had formed a scab, soon to fall away altogether. There is no health, she thought, for me, outside of honesty.

"You've always," he said, "thought my poetry was wonderful."

"I have said so," she said, "but it was a sort of play-act. Of course, it's only my opinion, but I think you're a third-rater poet."

"You're upset, my dear," he said.

He sent her the four reels of film from Cairo a month before he was killed in action. "It will be nice in later years," he wrote, "for you to recall those good times we used to have."

"It has been delightful," said her hostess. "You haven't changed a bit. Do you *feel* any different?"

"Well yes, I feel rather differently about everything, of course." One learns to accept oneself.

"A hundred feet of one's past life!" said the young man.

"If they were mine, I'm sure I should be shattered. I should be calling 'Lights! Lights!' like Hamlet's uncle."

Sybil smiled at him. He looked back, suddenly solemn and shrewd.

"How tragic, those people being killed in shooting affairs," said the elderly woman.

"The last reel was the best," said her hostess. "The garden was entrancing. I should like to see that one again; what about you, Ted?"

"Yes, I liked those nature-study shots. I feel I missed a lot of it," said her husband.

"Hark at him – nature-study shots!"

"Well, those close-ups of tropical plants."

Everyone wanted the last one again.

"How about you, Sybil?"

Am I a woman, she thought calmly, or an intellectual monster? She was so accustomed to this question within herself that it needed no answer. She said, "Yes, I should like to see it again. It's an interesting experience."

THE SERAPH AND THE ZAMBEZI

You may have heard of Samuel Cramer, half poet, half journalist, who had to do with a dancer called the Fanfarlo. But, as you will see, it doesn't matter if you have not. He was said to be going strong in Paris early in the nineteenth century, and when I met him in 1946 he was still going strong, but this time in a different way. He was the same man, but modified. For instance, in those days, more than a hundred years ago, Cramer had persisted for several decades, and without affectation, in being about twenty-five years old. But when I knew him he was clearly undergoing his forty-two-year-old phase.

At this time he was keeping a petrol pump some four miles south of the Zambezi River where it crashes over a precipice at the Victoria Falls. Cramer had some spare rooms where he put up visitors to the Falls when the hotel was full. I was sent to him because it was Christmas week and there was no room in the hotel.

I found him trying the starter of a large, lumpy Mercedes outside his corrugated-iron garage, and at first sight I judged him to be a Belgian from the Congo. He had the look of north and south, light hair with canvas-coloured skin. Later, however, he told me that his father was German and his mother Chilean. It was this information rather than the "S. Cramer" above the garage door which made me think I had heard of him.

The rains had been very poor and that December was fiercely hot. On the third night before Christmas I sat on the stoep outside my room, looking through the broken mosquito-wire network at the lightning in the distance. When an atmosphere maintains an excessive temperature for a long spell something seems to happen to the natural noises of life. Sound fails to carry in its usual quantity, but comes as if bound and gagged. That night the Christmas beetles, which fall on their backs on every stoep with a high tic-tac, seemed to be shock-absorbed. I saw one fall and the little bump reached my ears a fraction behind time. The noises of minor wild beasts from the bush were all hushed-up, too. In fact it wasn't until the bush noises all stopped simultaneously, as they frequently do when a leopard is about, that I knew there had been any sound at all.

Overlying this general muted hum, Cramer's sundowner party progressed farther up the stoep. The heat distorted every word. The glasses made a tinkle that was not of the substance of glass, but of bottles wrapped in tissue paper. Sometimes, for a moment, a shriek or a cackle would hang torpidly in space, but these were unreal sounds, as if projected from a distant country, as if they were pocket-torches seen through a London fog.

Cramer came over to my end of the stoep and asked me to join his party. I said I would be glad to, and meant it, even though I had been glad to sit alone. Heat so persistent and so intense sucks up the will.

Five people sat in wicker armchairs drinking highballs and chewing salted peanuts. I recognized a red-haired trooper from Livingstone, just out from England, and two of Cramer's lodgers, a tobacco planter and his wife from Bulawayo. In the custom of those parts, the other two were introduced by their first names. Mannie, a short dark man of square face and build, I thought might be a Portuguese from the east coast. The woman, Fanny, was picking bits out of the frayed wicker chair and as she lifted her glass her hand shook a little, making her bracelets chime. She would be about fifty, a well-tended woman, very neat. Her grey hair, tinted with blue, was done in a fringe above a face puckered with malaria.

In the general way of passing the time with strangers in that countryside, I exchanged with the tobacco people the names of acquaintances who lived within a six-hundred-mile radius of where we sat, reducing this list to names mutually known to us. The trooper contributed his news from the region between Lusaka and Livingstone. Meanwhile an argument was in process between Cramer, Fanny and Mannie, of which Fanny seemed to be getting the better. It appeared there was to be a play or concert on Christmas Eve in which the three were taking part. I several times heard the words "troupe of angels", "shepherds", "ridiculous price" and "my girls" which seemed to be key words in the argument. Suddenly, on hearing the trooper mention a name, Fanny broke off her talk and turned to us.

"She was one of my girls," she said, "I gave her lessons for three years."

Mannie rose to leave, and before Fanny followed him she picked a card from her handbag and held it out to me between her fingernails.

"If any of your friends are interested . . ." said Fanny hazily.

I looked at this as she drove off with the man, and above an address about four miles up the river I read:

Mme La Fanfarlo (Paris, London)
Dancing Instructress. Ballet. Ballroom.
Transport provided By Arrangement

Next day I came across Cramer still trying to locate the trouble with the Mercedes.

"Are you the man Baudelaire wrote about?" I asked him.

He stared past me at the open waste veldt with a look of tried patience.

"Yes," he replied. "What made you think of it?"

"The name Fanfarlo on Fanny's card," I said. "Didn't you know her in Paris?"

"Oh, yes," said Cramer, "but those days are finished. She married Manuela de Monteverde – that's Mannie. They settled here about twenty years ago. He keeps a Kaffir store."

I remembered then that in the Romantic age it had pleased Cramer to fluctuate between the practice of verse and that of belles-lettres, together with the living up to such practices.

I asked him, "Have you given up your literary career?"

"As a career, yes," he answered. "It was an obsession I was glad to get rid of."

He stroked the blunt bonnet of the Mercedes and added, "The greatest literature is the occasional kind, a mere afterthought."

Again he looked across the veldt where, unseen, a grey-crested lourie was piping "go'way, go'way".

"Life," Cramer continued, "is the important thing."

"And do you write occasional verses?" I inquired.

"When occasion demands it," he said. "In fact I've just written a Nativity Masque. We're giving a performance on Christmas Eve in there." He pointed to his garage, where a few natives were already beginning to shift petrol cans and tyres. Being members neither of the cast nor the audience, they were taking their time. A pile of folded seats had been dumped alongside.

Late on the morning of Christmas Eve I returned from the Falls to find a crowd of natives quarrelling outside the garage, with Cramer swearing loud and heavy in the middle. He held a sulky man by the shirt-sleeve, while with the other hand he described his vituperation on the hot air. Some mission natives had been sent over to give a hand with laying the stage, and these, with their standard-three school English, washed faces and white drill shorts, had innocently provoked Cramer's raw rag-dressed boys. Cramer's method, which ended with the word "police", succeeded in sending them back to work, still uttering drum-like gutturals at each other.

The stage, made of packing-cases with planks nailed across, was being put at the back of the building, where a door led to the yard, the privy and the native huts. The space between this door and the stage was closed off by a row of black Government blankets hung on a line; this was to be the dressing-room. I agreed to come round there that evening to help with the lighting, the make-up, and the pinning on of angels' wings. The Fanfarlo's dancing pupils were to make an angel chorus with carols and dancing, while she herself, as the Virgin, was to give a representative ballet performance. Owing to her husband's very broken English, he had been given a silent role as a shepherd, supported by three other shepherds chosen for like reasons. Cramer's part was the most prominent, for he had the longest speeches, being the First Seraph. It had been agreed that, since he had written the masque, he could best deliver most of it; but I gathered there had been some trouble at rehearsals over the cost of the production, with Fanny wanting elaborate scenery as being due to her girls.

The performance was set to begin at eight. I arrived behind the stage at seven-fifteen to find the angels assembled in ballet dresses with wings of crinkled paper in various shades. The Fanfarlo wore a long white transparent skirt with a sequin top. I was helping to fix on the Wise Men's beards when I saw Cramer. He had on a toga-like garment made up of several thicknesses of mosquito-net, but not thick enough to hide his white shorts underneath. He had put on his make-up early, and this was melting on his face in the rising heat.

"I always get nerves at this point," he said. "I'm going to practise my opening speech."

I heard him mount the stage and begin reciting. Above the voices of excited children I could only hear the rhythm of his voice; and I was intent on helping the Fanfarlo to paint her girls' faces. It seemed impossible. As fast as we lifted the sticks of paint they turned liquid. It was really getting abnormally hot.

"Open that door," yelled the Fanfarlo. The back door was opened and a crowd of curious natives pressed round the entrance. I left the Fanfarlo ordering them off, for I was determined to get to the front of the building for some air. I mounted the stage and began to cross it when I was aware of a powerful radiation of heat coming from my right. Looking round, I saw Cramer apparently shouting at someone, in the attitude of his dealings with the natives that morning. But he could not advance because of this current of heat. And because of the heat I could not at first make out who Cramer was rowing with; this was the sort of heat that goes for the eyes. But as I got farther towards the front of the stage I saw what was standing there.

This was a living body. The most noticeable thing was its constancy; it seemed not to conform to the law of perspective, but remained the same size when I approached as when I withdrew. And altogether unlike other forms of life, it had a completed look. No part was undergoing a process; the outline lacked the signs of confusion and ferment which commonly indicate living things, and this was also the principle of its beauty. The eyes took up nearly the whole of the head, extending far over the cheekbones. From the back of the head came two muscular wings which from time to time folded themselves over the eyes, making a draught of scorching air. There was hardly any neck. Another pair of wings, tough and supple, spread from below the shoulders, and a third pair extended from the calves of the legs, appearing to sustain the body. The feet looked too fragile to bear up such a concentrated degree of being.

European residents of Africa are often irresistibly prompted to speak kitchen kaffir to anything strange.

"*Hamba!*" shouted Cramer, meaning "Go away".

"Now get off the stage and stop your noise," said the living body peaceably.

"Who in hell are you?" said Cramer, gasping through the heat.

"The same as in Heaven," came the reply, "a Seraph, that's to say."

"Tell that to someone else," Cramer panted. "Do I look like a fool?"

"I will. No, nor a Seraph either," said the Seraph.

The place was filling with heat from the Seraph. Cramer's paint was running into his eyes and he wiped them on his net robe. Walking backward to a less hot place he cried, "Once and for all –"

"That's correct," said the Seraph.

"– this is my show," continued Cramer.

"Since when?" the Seraph said.

"Right from the start," Cramer breathed at him.

"Well, it's been mine from the Beginning," said the Seraph, "and the Beginning began first."

Climbing down from the hot stage, Cramer caught his seraphic robe on a nail and tore it. "Listen here," he said, "I can't conceive of an abnormality like you being a true Seraph."

"True," said the Seraph.

By this time I had been driven by the heat to the front entrance. Cramer joined me there. A number of natives had assembled. The audience had begun to arrive in cars and the rest of the cast had come round the building from the back. It was impossible to see far inside the building owing to the Seraph's heat, and impossible to re-enter.

Cramer was still haranguing the Seraph from the door,

and there was much speculation among the new arrivals as to which of the three familiar categories the present trouble came under, namely, the natives, Whitehall, or leopards.

"This is my property," cried Cramer, "and these people have paid for their seats. They've come to see a masque."

"In that case," said the Seraph, "I'll cool down and they can come and see a masque."

"My masque," said Cramer.

"Ah, no, *mine*," said the Seraph. "Yours won't do."

"Will you go, or shall I call the police?" said Cramer with finality.

"I have no alternative," said the Seraph more finally still.

Word had gone round that a mad leopard was in the garage. People got back into their cars and parked at a safe distance; the tobacco planter went to fetch a gun. A number of young troopers had the idea of blinding the mad leopard with petrol and ganged up some natives to fill petrol cans from the pump and pass them chainwise to the garage.

"This'll fix him," said a trooper.

"That's right, let him have it," said Cramer from his place by the door.

"I shouldn't do that," said the Seraph. "You'll cause a fire."

The first lot of petrol to be flung into the heat flared up. The seats caught alight first, then the air itself began to burn within the metal walls till the whole interior was flame feeding on flame. Another car-load of troopers arrived just then and promptly got a gang of natives to fill petrol cans with water. Slowly they drenched the fire. The Fanfarlo mustered her angels a little way up the road. She was trying to reassure their parents and see what was happening at the same time, furious at losing her opportunity to dance. She aimed a hard poke at the back of one of the angels whose parents were in England.

It was some hours before the fire was put out. While the corrugated metal walls still glowed, twisted and furled, it was impossible to see what had happened to the Seraph, and after they had ceased to glow it was too dark and hot to see far into the wreck.

"Are you insured?" one of Cramer's friends asked him.

"Oh yes," Cramer replied, "my policy covers everything except Acts of God – that means lightning or flood."

"He's fully covered," said Cramer's friend to another friend.

Many people had gone home and the rest were going. The troopers drove off singing "Good King Wenceslas", and the mission boys ran down the road singing "Good Christian Men, Rejoice".

It was about midnight, and still very hot. The tobacco planters suggested a drive to the Falls, where it was cool. Cramer and the Fanfarlo joined us, and we bumped along the rough path from Cramer's to the main highway. There the road is tarred only in two strips to take car-wheels. The thunder of the Falls reached us about two miles before we reached them.

"After all my work on the masque and everything!" Cramer was saying.

"Oh, shut up," said the Fanfarlo.

Just then, by the glare of our headlights I saw the Seraph again, going at about seventy miles an hour and skimming the tarmac strips with two of his six wings in swift motion, two folded over his face, and two covering his feet.

"That's him!" said Cramer. "We'll get him yet."

We left the car near the hotel and followed a track through the dense vegetation of the Rain Forest, where the spray from the Falls descends perpetually. It was like a convalescence after fever, that frail rain after the heat. The Seraph was far ahead of us and through the trees I could see where his heat was making steam of the spray.

We came to the cliff's edge, where opposite us and from the same level the full weight of the river came blasting into the gorge between. There was no sign of the Seraph. Was he far below in the heaving pit, or where?

Then I noticed that along the whole mile of the waterfall's crest the spray was rising higher than usual. This I took to be steam from the Seraph's heat. I was right, for presently, by the mute flashes of summer lightning, we watched him ride the Zambezi away from us, among the rocks that look like crocodiles and the crocodiles that look like rocks.

THE PAWNBROKER'S WIFE

At Sea Point, on the coast of the Cape of Good Hope, in 1942, there was everywhere the sight of rejoicing, there was the sound of hilarity, and the sea washed up each day one or two bodies of servicemen in all kinds of uniform. The waters round the Cape were heavily mined. The people flocked to bring in the survivors. The girls of the seashore and harbour waited two by two for the troops on shore-leave from ships which had managed to enter the bay safely.

I was waiting for a ship to take me to England, and lived on the sea-front in the house of Mrs Jan Cloote, a pawnbroker's wife. From her window where, in the cool evenings, she sat knitting khaki socks till her eyes ached, Mrs Jan Cloote took note of these happenings, and whenever I came in or went out she would open her door a little, and, standing in the narrow aperture, would tell me the latest.

She was a small woman of about forty-three, a native of Somerset. Her husband, Jan Cloote, had long ago disappeared into the Transvaal, where he was living, it was understood, with a native woman. With his wife, he had left three daughters, the house on the sea-front, and, at the back of the house which opened on to a little mean street, a pawnshop.

Mrs Jan Cloote had more or less built up everything that her husband had left half-finished. The house was in better repair than it ever had been, and she let off most of the rooms. The pawnshop had so far flourished that Mrs Jan Cloote was able to take a shop next door where she sold a second-hand miscellany, unredeemed from the pawnshop. The three daughters had likewise flourished. From all accounts, they had gone barefoot to school at the time of their father's residence at home, because all his profit had gone on his two opulent passions, yellow advocaat and black girls. As I saw the daughters now, I could hardly credit their unfortunate past life. The youngest, Isa, was a schoolgirl with long yellow plaits, and she was quite a voluptuary in her manner. The other two, in their late teens, were more like the mother, small, shy, quiet, ladylike, secretarial and discreet. Greta and Maida, they were called.

It was seldom that Mrs Jan Cloote opened the door of her own apartment wide enough for anyone to see inside. This was a habit of the whole family, but they had nothing really to hide, that one could see. And there Mrs Jan Cloote would stand, with one of the girls, perhaps, looking over her shoulder, wedged in the narrow doorway, and the door not twelve inches open. The hall was very dark, and being a frugal woman, she did not keep a bulb in the hall light, which therefore did not function.

One day, as I came in, I saw her little shape, the thin profile and knobbly bun, outlined against the light within her rooms.

"Sh-sh-sh," she said.

"Can you come in tonight for a *little* cup of tea with the

others?" she said in a hushed breath. And I understood, as I accepted, that the need for the hush had something to do with the modesty of the proposed party, conveyed in the words, "a *little* cup . . ."

I knocked on her door after dinner. Maida opened it just wide enough for me to enter, then closed it again quickly. Some of the other lodgers were there: a young man who worked in an office on the docks, and a retired insurance agent and his wife.

Isa, the schoolgirl, arrived presently. I was surprised to see that she was heavily made up on the mouth and eyes.

"Another troopship gone down," stated Isa.

"Hush, dear," said her mother; "we are not supposed to talk about the shipping."

Mrs Jan Cloote winked at me as she said this. It struck me then that she was very proud of Isa.

"An Argentine boat in," said Isa.

"Really?" said Mrs Jan Cloote. "Any nice chaps?"

The old couple looked at each other. The young man, who was new to many things, looked puzzled but said nothing. Maida and Greta, like their mother, seemed agog for news.

"A lot of nice ones, eh?" said Maida. She had the local habit of placing the word "eh" at the end of her remarks, questions and answers alike.

"I'll say, man," said Isa, for she also used the common currency, adding "man" to most of the statements she addressed to man and woman alike.

"You'll be going to the Stardust!" said Mrs Jan Cloote. "Won't you now, Isa?"

"The Stardust?" said Mrs Marais, the insurance agent's wife. "You surely don't mean the nightclub, man?"

"Why, yes," said Mrs Jan Cloote in her precise voice. She alone of the family did not use the local idiom, and in fact her speech had improved since her Somerset days. "Why, yes," she said, "she enjoys herself, why not?"

"Only young once, eh?" said the young man, putting ash in his saucer as Mrs Jan Cloote frowned at him.

Mrs Jan Cloote sent Maida upstairs to fetch some of Isa's presents, things she had been given by men; evening bags, brooches, silk stockings. It was rather awkward. What could one say?

"They are very nice," I said.

"This is nothing, nothing," said Mrs Jan Cloote, "nothing to the things she could get. But she only goes with the nice fellows."

"And do you dance too?" I inquired of Greta.

"No, man," she said. "Isa does it for us, eh. Isa dances lovely."

"You said it, man," said Maida.

"Ah yes," sighed Mrs Jan Cloote, "we're quiet folk. We would have a dull life of it, if it wasn't for Isa."

"She needs taking care of, that child," said Mrs Marais.

"Isa!" said her mother. "Do you hear Mrs Marais, what she says?"

"I do, man," said Isa. "I do, eh."

From my room it was impossible not to overhear all that was going on in the pawnshop, just beneath my window.

"I hope it doesn't disturb you," said Mrs Jan Cloote, with a sideways glance at her two elder daughters.

"No," I thought it best to say, "I don't hear a thing."

"I always tell the girls," said Mrs Jan Cloote, "that there is nothing to be ashamed of, being a PB."

"PB?" asked the young clerk, who had a friend who played the drums in the Police Band.

Mrs Jan Cloote lowered her voice. "A *pawnbroker*," she informed him rapidly.

"That's right," said the young man.

"There's nothing to be ashamed of in it," said Mrs Jan Cloote. "And of course I'm only down as a PB's *wife*, not a PB."

"We keep the shop beautiful, man," said Maida.

"Have you seen it?" Mrs Jan Cloote asked me.

"No," I said.

"Well, there's nothing to see inside, really," she said; "but some PB shops are a sight enough. You should see some of the English ones. The dirt!"

"Or so I'm told," she added.

"They *are* very rough-and-tumble in England," I admitted.

"Why," said Mrs Jan Cloote, "have you been inside one?"

"Oh, yes, quite a few," I said, pausing to recollect; ". . . in London, of course, and then there was one in Manchester, and –"

"But what for, man?" said Greta.

"To pawn things," I said, glad to impress them with my knowledge of their trade. "There was my compass," I said, "but I never saw *that* again. Not that I ever used the thing."

Mrs Jan Cloote put down her cup and looked round the room to see if everyone had unfortunately heard me. She was afraid they had.

"Thank God," she said; "touch wood I have never had to do it."

"I can't say that I've ever popped anything, myself," said Mrs Marais.

"My poor mother used to take things now and again," said Mr Marais.

"I dare say," said Mrs Marais.

"We get some terrible scum coming in," said the pawnbroker's wife.

"I'm going to the PB's dinner-dance," said Isa. "What'll I way?" she added, meaning what would she wear. The girls did not pronounce the final "r" in certain words.

"You can way your midnight blue," said Greta.

"No," said her mother, "no, no, no. She'll have to get a new dress."

"I'm going to get my hay cut short," announced Isa, indicating her yellow pigtails.

Her mother squirmed with excitement at the prospect. Greta and Maida blushed, with a strange and greedy look.

At last the door was opened a few inches and we were allowed to file out, one by one.

Next morning as usual I heard Mrs Jan Cloote opening up the pawnshop. She dealt expertly with the customers who, as usual, waited on the doorstep. Once the first rush was over, business generally became easier as the day progressed. But for the first half-hour the bell tinkled incessantly as sailors and other troops arrived, anxious to deposit cameras, cigarette cases, watches, suits of clothes, and other things which, like my compass, would never be redeemed. Though I could not see her, it was easy to visualize what actions accompanied the words I could hear so well; Mrs Jan Cloote would, I supposed, examine the proffered article for about three minutes (this would account for a silence which followed her opening "Well?"). The examination would be conducted with utter intensity, seeming to have its sensitive point, its assessing faculty, in her long nose. (I had already seen her perform this feat with Isa's treasures.) She would not smell the thing, actually; but it would appear to be her nose which calculated and finally judged. Then she would sharply name her figure. If this evoked a protest, she would become really eloquent; though never unreasonable, at this stage. A list of the object's defects would proceed like ticker tape from the mouth of Mrs Jan Cloote; its depreciating market value was known to her; this suit of clothes would never fit another man; that ring was not worth the melting. Usually, the pawners accepted her offer, after she ceased. If not, the pawnbroker's wife turned to the next customer without further comment. "Well?" she would say to the next one. Should the first-comer still linger, hesitant, perplexed, it was then that Mrs Jan Cloote became unreasonable in tone. "Haven't you made up your mind yet?" she would demand. "What are you waiting for, what are you waiting for?" The effect of this shock treatment was either the swift disappearance of the customer, or his swift clinching of the bargain.

Like most establishments in those parts, Mrs Jan Cloote's pawnshop was partitioned off into sections, rather like a public house with its saloon, public and private bars. These compartments separated white customers from black, and black from those known as coloured – the Indians, Malays and half-castes.

Whenever someone with a tanned face came in at the

white entrance, Mrs Jan Cloote always gave the customer the benefit of the doubt. But she would complain wearily of this to Maida and Greta as she rushed back and forth.

"Did you see that coloured girl that went out?" she would say. "Came in the white way. Oh, coloured, of course she was coloured but you daren't say anything. We'd be up for slander."

This particular morning, trade was pressing. A troopship had come in.

"Now *that* was a coloured," said Mrs Jan Cloote in a lull between shop bells. "He came in the white way."

"I'd have kicked his behind," said Isa.

"Listen to Isa, eh!" giggled Maida.

"Isa's the one!" said the mother, as she rushed away again, summoned by the bell.

This time the voices came from another part of the shop set aside from the rest. I had noticed, from the outside, that it was marked OFFICE-PRIVATE.

"Oh, it's you?" said Mrs Jan Cloote.

"That picture," said the voice. "Here's the ticket."

"A month late," she said. "You've lost it."

"Here's the fifteen bob," said the man.

"No, no," she said. "It's too late. You haven't paid up the interest; it's gone."

"I'll pay up the interest now," he said. "Come now," he said, "we're old friends and you promised to keep it for me.

"My grandfather painted that picture," he said.

"You promised to keep it for me," he said.

"Not for a month," she said at last. "Not for a whole month. It was only worth the price of the frame."

"It's a good picture," he said.

"A terrible picture," she said. "Who would want a picture like that? It might bring us bad luck. I've thrown it away."

"Listen, old dear –" he began.

"Out!" she said. "Outside!"

"I'm staying here," he said, "till I get my picture."

"Maida! Greta!" she called.

"All right," he said, hopeless and lost. "I'm going."

A week later Mrs Jan Cloote caught me in the hall again. "A *little* cup of tea," she whispered. "Come in for a chat, just with ourselves and young Mr Fleming, tonight."

It was imperative to attend these periodic tea sittings. Those of Mrs Jan Cloote's lodgers who did not attend suffered many discomforts; rooms were not cleaned nor beds made; morning tea was brought up cold and newspapers not at all. It was difficult to find rooms at that time. "Thank you," I said.

I joined the family that night. The Marais couple had left, but I found the young clerk there. Isa came in, painted up as before.

There was one addition to the room; a picture on the wall. It was dreadful as a piece of work, at the same time as it was fascinating on account of the period it stood for. The date of this period would be about the mid-1890s. It represented a girl bound to a railway line. Her blue sash fluttered across her body, and her hands were raised in anguish to her head, where the hair, yellow and abundant, was spreading over the rails around her. Twenty yards away was a bend on the rail-track. A train approached this bend, full-steam. The driver could not see the girl. As you know, the case was hopeless. A moment, and she would be pulp. But wait! A motor car, one of the first of its kind, was approaching a level crossing nearby. A group of young men, out for a joy-ride, were loaded into this high, bright vehicle. One of them had seen the girl's plight. This Johnnie was standing on the seat, waving his motoring cap high above his head and pointing to her. His companions were just on the point of realizing what had happened. Would they be in time to rescue her? – to stop the onrushing train? Of course not. The perspective of the picture told me this clearly enough. There was not a chance for the girl. And anyhow, I reflected, she lies there for as long as the picture lasts; the train approaches; the young mashers in their brand-new automobile – they are always on the point of seeing before them the girl tied to the rails, her hair spread around her, the ridiculous sash waving about, and her hands uplifted to her head.

On the whole, I liked the picture. It was the prototype of so many other paintings of its kind; and the prototype, the really typical object, is something I rarely have a chance of seeing.

"You're looking at Isa's picture," said Mrs Jan Cloote.

"It's a very wonderful picture," she declared. "A very famous English artist flew out on a Sunderland on purpose to paint Isa. The RAF let him have the plane and all the crew so that he could come. As soon as they saw Isa's photo at the RAF Headquarters in London, they told the artist to take the Sunderland.

"He put Isa in that pose, doing her hair," Mrs Jan Cloote continued, gazing fondly at the picture.

I said nothing. Nor did the young clerk. I tried looking at the picture with my head on one side, and, indeed, the girl bore a slight resemblance to Isa; the distracted hands around her head did look rather as if she were doing her hair. Of course, to get this effect, one had to ignore the train, and the motor car, and the other details. I decided that the picture would be about fifty years old. Undoubtedly, it was not recent.

"What do you think of it?" said Mrs Jan Cloote.

"Very nice," I said.

The young clerk was silent.

"You're very quiet tonight, Mr Fleming," said Maida.

He gave a jerky laugh which nearly knocked over his cup.

"I saw Mrs Marais today," he ventured.

"Oh, her," said Mrs Jan Cloote. "Did you speak?"

"Certainly not," he said; "I just passed her by."

"Quite right," said Mrs Jan Cloote.

"I gave them notice," she explained to me. "Mr wasn't so bad, but Mrs was the worst tenant I've ever had."

"The things she said!" Greta added.

"I showed her every consideration," said the pawnbroker's wife, "and all I got was insults."

"Insults," Mr Fleming said.

"Mr Fleming was here when it happened," said Mrs Jan Cloote.

"We were showing her Isa's picture," she continued, "and do you believe it, she said it wasn't Isa at all. To my face she as good as called me a liar, didn't she, Mr Fleming?"

"That's true," said Mr Fleming, examining a tea-leaf on his spoon.

"Mr Marais, of course, was in an awkward position," said Mrs Jan Cloote. "You see, he's right under his wife's thumb, and he didn't dare contradict her. He only said there might be some mistake. But she sat on him at once. '*That's* not Isa,' she said."

"Poor Mr Marais!" said Greta.

"I'm sorry for Mr Marais," said Maida.

"He's soft in the head, man," said Isa.

"Isa's a real scream," said her mother when she had recovered from her gust of laughter. "And she's right. Old Marais isn't all there."

"What was it again?" she inquired of the young clerk. "What was it again, that old Marais told you afterwards, about Isa's picture?"

The young clerk looked at me, and quickly looked away.

"What did Mr Marais say about the picture?" I said insistently.

"Well," said Mr Fleming, "I don't really remember."

"Now, you remember all right," said Mrs Jan Cloote. "Come on, give us a laugh."

"Oh, he only said," Mr Fleming replied, gazing manfully at the painting, "he only said there were railway lines and a train in the picture."

"*Only* said!" Mrs Jan Cloote put in.

"Well, poor thing," said Mr Fleming; "he can't help it, I suppose. He's mad."

"And didn't he say there was an old-fashioned car in the picture, man?" said Greta. "That's what you told us, man."

"Yes," said the clerk, with a giggle, "he said that too."

"So you see," said Mrs Jan Cloote. "The man's out of his mind. A railway in Isa's picture! I laugh every time I think of it."

"As for Mrs Marais," she added; "as for *her*, I never trusted the woman from the start. 'Mrs Marais,' said I, 'you'll take a week's notice.' And they left the next day."

"Good riddance to the old bitch," said Isa.

"She was jealous of Isa's picture, eh," chuckled Greta.

"We had a nice time with the artist, though, when he was painting Isa," said Mrs Jan Cloote.

"I'll say, man," said Maida, "and the crew as well."

"We often have famous artists here," said the mother, "don't we?"

"We do, man," said Greta. "They come after Isa."

"And the crew," said Maida. "They was nice. But the pilot did a real man's trick on Isa."

"Yes, the swine," said the mother. "But never mind, Isa's got other boys. Isa could go on the films."

"Isa would be great on the films," said Greta.

"All the famous actors come here," said Mrs Jan Cloote. "We get all the actors. They want Isa for the films. But we wouldn't let her go on the films."

"She'd be a star, man," said Greta.

"But we wouldn't let her go on the films," Maida said.

"She'll do what she likes," said the mother, "when she leaves school."

"Bloody right," said Isa.

"You know Max Melville?" said Mrs Jan Cloote to me.

"I've *heard* the name . . ." I said warily.

"Heard the *name*! Why, Max Melville's a top-ranking star! He was here after Isa the other day. Isn't that right, Greta?"

"Sure," said Greta.

And Mrs Jan Cloote took up the story again. "I told him

there was too much publicity on the films for Isa. 'We're quiet folk, Max,' I said. *Max*, I called him, just like that."

"Max was a rare guy," said Maida.

"He gave Isa a wonderful present," said Mrs Jan Cloote. "Not that it's worth much, but it belonged to his family and it's got the sentimental value, and he wouldn't have parted with it to anyone else but Isa. Run upstairs and fetch it, Maida."

Maida hesitated. "Was it that brooch . . . ?" she began.

"No," said her mother sorrowfully and slowly. "Isa got the brooch from the artist. I'm surprised at you forgetting what Max Melville gave to Isa."

"I'll get it," said Greta, jumping up.

She returned presently, with a small compass in her hand.

"It isn't worth much," Mrs Jan Cloote was saying as she handed it round. "But Max's great-grandfather was an explorer, and he had this very compass on him when he crossed the Himalayas. He never came back, but the compass was found on his body. So it was very very precious to Maxie, but he parted with it to Isa."

I had been given the compass when I was fourteen; it was new then; I recognized it immediately, and while Mrs Jan Cloote was talking, I recognized it more and more. The scratches and dents which I made on my own possessions are always familiar to me, like my own signature . . .

"A very old antique compass," said the pawnbroker's wife, passing her hand over its face appraisingly. "It was nice of Max Melville to give it away. But of course he wanted Isa for the films, and that may have been the reason."

"What do you think of it?" she asked me.

"Very interesting," I said.

What voyager had fetched it over the seas? How many hands had it passed through in its passage from the pawnshop where I had pledged it, to the pawnshop of Mrs Jan Cloote? I wondered these things, and also, why it was that I didn't really mind seeing my compass caressed by the hands of this pawnbroker's wife – seeing it made to serve her pleasure. I didn't care. Her nose pointed towards it, as to a North . . .

"We shall never part with this," Mrs Jan Cloote was saying; "because of the sentimental reason, you know. It wouldn't fetch a price, of course."

I had, for a few years, kept the compass lying about amongst my things, until the day came to pawn it. That was how it had got scratched and knocked about. It was knocked about in the drawer, thrown aside always, because I was looking for something else. I had never used the compass, never taken my bearings by it. Perhaps, it had never been very much used at all. The marks of wear upon it were mainly those I had made. Whoever had pledged it at Mrs Jan Cloote's pawnshop did not think enough of it to redeem it. The pawnbroker's wife was welcome to the compass, for it was truly hers.

"It wouldn't fetch a price," said Mrs Jan Cloote. "Not that we think of the price; it's the thought that matters."

"It's Isa's lucky mascot," said Maida. "You'll have to take it with you when you go to Hollywood, Isa, man."

"Hollywood!" said Mrs Jan Cloote. "Oh, no, no. If Isa goes on the pictures she'll go to an English studio. There's too much publicity in Hollywood. Do you see our Isa in Hollywood, Mr Fleming?"

"Not exactly," said the young man.

"I'd be great in Hollywood, man," said young Isa.

"Well, maybe . . ." said the mother.

"Yes, maybe," said Mr Fleming.

"But there's too much show in Hollywood," said Isa.

"You see," said Mrs Jan Cloote, turning to me, "we're quiet people. We keep ourselves to ourselves, and as Mr Fleming was saying the other day, we live in quite a world of our own, don't we, Mr Fleming?"

They opened the door and let me sidle through, into the dark hall.

THE SNOBS

"Snob: A person who sets too much value on social standing, wishing to be associated with the upper class and their mores, and treating those viewed as inferior with condescension and contempt" – *Chambers Dictionary*.

I feel bound to quote the above definition, it so well fits the Ringer-Smith couple whom I knew in the nineteen-fifties and of whom I have since met variations and versions enough to fill me with wonder. Snobs are really amazing. They mainly err in failing to fool the very set of people they are hoping to be accepted by, and above all, to seem to belong to, to be taken for. They may live in a democratic society – it does nothing to help, Nothing.

Of the Ringer-Smith couple, he, Jake, was the more snobbish. She, at least, had a certain natural serenity of behaviour which she herself never questioned. She was in fact rather smug. Her background was of small land-owning farmers and minor civil servants. She, Marion, was stingy, stingy as hell. Jake also had a civil service background and, on the mother's side, a family of fruit export-import affairs which had not left her very well off, the inheritance having been absorbed by the male members of the family. Jake and Marion were a fairly suitable match. He was slightly the shorter of the two. Both were skinny. They had no children. Skeletons in the family cupboard do nothing to daunt the true snob, in fact they provoke a certain arrogance, and this was the case with Jake. A family scandal on a national scale had grown to an international one. A spectacular bank robbery with murder on the part of a brother had resulted in the family name being reduced to a byword in every household. The delinquent Ringer-Smith and his associates had escaped to a safe exile in South America leaving Jake and his ageing mother to face the music of the press and TV reporters. Nobody would have taken it out on them in the normal way if it had not been for the contempt with which they treated police, journalists, interrogators, functionaries of the law and the public in general. They put on airs suggesting that they were untouchably "good family", and they generally carried on as if they were earls and marquises instead of ordinary middle-class people. No earl, no marquis at present alive would in fact be so haughty unless he were completely out of his mind or perhaps an unfortunate drug addict or losing gambler.

I was staying with some friends at a château near Dijon when the Ringer-Smiths turned up. This was in the nineties. I hardly recognized them. The Ringer-Smiths had not just turned up at the château, they were found by Anne, bewildered, outside the village shop, puzzling over a map, uncertain of their way to anywhere. Warming towards their plight as she always would towards those in trouble, Anne invited these lost English people for a cup of tea at the château where they could work out their route.

Anne and Monty, English themselves, had lived in the

château for the last eight years. It was a totally unexpected inheritance from the last member of a distant branch of Monty's family. The house and small fortune that went with it came to him in his early fifties as an enormous surprise. He had been a shoe salesman and a bus driver, among other things. Anne had been a stockbroker's secretary. Their two children, both girls, were married and away. The "fairy tale" story of their inheritance was in the newspapers for a day, but it wasn't everybody who read the passing news.

Monty was out when Anne brought home the Ringer-Smiths. I was watching the television – some programme which now escapes me for ever due to the shock of seeing those people. Anne, tall, merry, blonded-up and carrying her sixties well, took herself off to the kitchen to put on the kettle. She had made the sitting room as much like England as possible.

"Who does this place belong to?" Jake inquired of me as soon as Anne was out of the room. Obviously, he had not recognized me in the present context, although I felt Marion's eyes upon me in a penetrating stare of puzzlement, of quasi-remembrance.

"It belongs," I said, "to the lady who invited you to tea."

"Oh!" he said.

"Haven't we met?" Marion was speaking to me.

"Yes, you have." I made myself known.

"What brings you here?" said Jake outright.

"The same as brings you here. I was invited."

Anne returned with the tea, served with a silver tea service and pretty china cups. She carried the tray while a young girl who was helping in the house followed with hot water and a plate of biscuits.

"You speak English very well," Jake said.

"Oh, we are English," said Anne. "But we live in France now. My husband inherited the château from his family on his mother's side, the Martineaus."

"Oh, of course," said Jake.

The factor came in from the farm and took a cup of tea standing up. He addressed Anne as "Madame".

Anne was already regretting her impulse in asking the couple to tea. They said very little but just sat on. She was afraid they would miss the last bus to the station. Looking at me, she said, "The last bus goes at six, doesn't it?"

I said to Marion, "You don't want to miss the last bus."

"Could we see round the château?" said Marion. "The guidebook says it's fourteenth century."

"Well, not all of it is," said Anne. "But today is a bit difficult. We don't, you know, open the house to the public. We live in it."

"I'm sure we've met," said Marion to Anne, as if this took care of their catching the last bus – a point which was not lost on Anne. Kindly though she was I knew she hated to have to ferry people by car to the station and take on other chores she was not prepared for. I could see, already in Anne's mind, the thought: "I have to get rid of these people or they'll stay for dinner and then all night. They are château-grabbers."

Anne had often lamented to me about the château-grabbers of her later life. People who didn't want to know her when she was obscure and a bus driver's wife now wanted to know her intimately. Monty didn't care much about this, one way or another. But then the work of organizing meals and entertaining in style fell more on Anne than on Monty, who mostly spent his time helping the factor in the grounds, game-keeping and forest-clearing.

Anne could see that the English couple she had invited in "for a cup of tea" were clingers, climbers, general nuisances, and she especially cast a look of desperation at me when Marion Ringer-Smith said, "I'm sure we've met."

"You think so?" Anne said. She had got up and was leading the way to the back door. "This is the *Cour des Adieus*," she said; "it leads quicker to your bus stop." Marion stooped and took a cake as if it was her last chance of ever eating a cake again.

I was at this moment coming to the end of a novel I was writing. Anne had offered me the peace and quiet of French château life and the informality of her own life-style which made it an ideal arrangement. She had also undertaken to type out the novel from any handwritten manuscripts on to a word-processor. But now at a quarter to six, I could see the rest of our afternoon's plans slipping away.

I doubted that Marion had indeed seen Anne before. It was by some mental process of transferance that she had picked on Anne. The one she had actually met was myself, but she wasn't very much aware of it. After a gap of forty years, she remembered very little of me.

Jake Ringer-Smith asked if he could use the bathroom. Oh, you bore, I thought. Why don't you *go*? There are trees and thick bushes all the way down the drive for you to pee on. But no, he had to be shown the bathroom. It was nearly ten minutes to their bus time. Jake kicked his backpack over to his wife and said, "Take this, will you?"

"I would really like to see round the château," Marion said, "while we're here and since we've come all this way."

I had come across this situation before. There are people who will hold up a party of tired and worn fellow travellers just because *they* have to see a pulpit. There are people who will arrive an hour late for dinner with the excuse that they *had* to see over some art gallery on the way. Marion was very much one of those. If challenged she would have thought nothing of pointing out that, after all, she had paid a plane fare to arrive at where she was. I remember Marion's shapeless cheesecloth dress and her worn sandals and Jake's baggy, ostentatiously patched, grubby trousers, their avidity to get on intimate terms with the lady of the house, to be invited to supper and, no doubt, to spend the night. I was really sorry for Anne who, I was aware, was sorry for herself and most of all regretting her own impulsive invitation to a cup of tea in her house.

Anne kept a soup kitchen in a building some way from the house, beyond a vegetable garden. She was pledged, I knew, to be there and help whenever possible, at six-thirty every evening. Laboriously, she explained this to the Ringer-Smiths. ". . . otherwise I'd have been glad to show you the house, not that there's much to see."

"Soup kitchen!" said Jake. "May we join it for a bowl of soup? Then perhaps we can stretch out our sleeping-bag for the night under one of your charming archways and see the house tomorrow."

Does this sound like a nightmare? It was a nightmare. Nothing could throw off these people.

Down at the soup kitchen that evening, dispensing slabs of bread and cheese with bowls of tomato soup, I was not surprised to see the Ringer-Smiths appear.

"We belong to the lower orders," he said to me with an exaggeratedly self-effacing grin that meant "We do not belong to any lower orders and just see how grand we really are – *we* don't care what we look like or what company we keep. We are Us."

In fact they looked positively shifty among the genuine skin-and-bone tramps and hairy drop-outs and bulging bag-ladies. I dished out their portions to them without a smile. They had missed the last bus. Somehow, Anne and Monty had to arrange for them to have a bedroom for the night. "We stayed at the Château Leclaire de Martineau at Dijon" I could hear them telling their friends.

Before breakfast I advised Anne and Monty to make themselves scarce. "Otherwise," I said, "you'll never get rid of them. Leave them to me."

"I'm sure," said Marion, "I've met Anne before. But I can't tell where."

"She has been a cook in many houses," I said. "And Monty has been a butler."

"A cook and a butler?" said Jake.

"Yes, the master and mistress are away from home at present."

"But she *told me she was the owner*," Marion said, indicating the dining-room door with her head.

"Oh no, you must be mistaken."

"But I'm sure she said –"

"Not at all," I said. "What a pity you can't see over the château. Such lovely pictures. But the Comtesse will be here at any moment. I don't know how you will explain yourselves. So far as I know you haven't been invited."

"Oh we have," said Jake. "The servants begged us to stay. So typical, posing as the lord and lady of the manor! But it's getting late, we'll miss the bus."

They were off within four minutes, tramping down the drive with their bulging packs.

Anne and Monty were delighted when I told them how it was done. Anne was sure, judging from a previous experience, that the intruders had planned to stay for a week.

"What else can you do with people like that?" said Anne.

"Put them in a story if you are me," I said. "And sell the story."

"Can they sue?"

"Let them sue," I said. "Let them go ahead, stand up, and say Yes, that was Us."

"An eccentric couple. They took the soap with them," said Anne.

Monty went off about his business with a smile. So did Anne. And I, too. Or so I thought.

It was eleven-thirty, two hours later that morning, when, looking out of the window of my room as I often do when I am working on a novel, I saw them again under one of the trees bordering a lawn. They were looking up towards the house.

I had no idea where Monty and Anne were at that moment, nor could I think how to locate the factor, Raoul, or his wife, Marie-Louise. This was a disturbance in the rhythm of my morning's work, but I decided to go down and see what was the matter. As soon as they saw me Marion said, "Oh hallo. We decided it was uncivil of us to leave without seeing the lady of the house and paying our respects."

"We'll wait till the Comtesse arrives," Jake stated.

"Well, you're unlucky," I said. "I believe there's word come through that she'll be away for a week."

"That's all right," said Marion. "We can spare a week."

"Only civil . . ." said Jake.

I managed to alert Anne before she saw them. They were very cool to her when she did at last appear before them. "The Comtesse would, I'm sure, be offended if we left without a word of thanks," said Jake.

"Not at all," said Anne. "In fact, you *have to go*."

"Not so," said Marion.

Raoul tackled them, joined by Monty. Marion had already reclaimed their bedroom. "As the beds had to be changed anyway," she said, "we may as well stay on. We don't mind eating down at the shed." By this she meant the soup kitchen. "We are not above eating with the proletariat," said Jake.

Raoul and I searched the house, every drawer, for a key to the door of their bedroom. Eventually we found one that fitted and succeeded in locking them out. Monty took their packs and dumped them outside the gates of the château. These operations took place while they were feeding in the soup kitchen. We all five (Marie-Louise had joined us) confronted them and told them what we had done.

What happened to them after that none of us quite knows. We do know that they went to retrieve their bags and found themselves locked out by the factor. Anne received a letter, correctly addressed to her as the Comtesse, from Jake, indignantly complaining about the treatment they had received at the hands of the "staff".

"Something," wrote Jake, "told me not to accept their invitation. I knew instinctively that they were not one of us. I should have listened to my instincts. People like them are such frightful snobs."

A MEMBER OF THE FAMILY

"You must," said Richard, suddenly, one day in November, "come and meet my mother."

Trudy, who had been waiting for a long time for this invitation, after all was amazed.

"I should like you," said Richard, "to meet my mother. She's looking forward to it."

"Oh, does she know about me?"

"Rather," Richard said.

"Oh!"

"No need to be nervous," Richard said. "She's awfully sweet."

"Oh, I'm sure she is. Yes, of course, I'd love –"

"Come to tea on Sunday," he said.

They had met the previous June in a lake town in Southern Austria. Trudy had gone with a young woman who had a bed-sitting-room in Kensington just below Trudy's room. This young woman could speak German, whereas Trudy couldn't.

Bleilach was one of the cheaper lake towns; in fact, cheaper was a way of putting it: it was cheap.

"Gwen, I didn't realize it ever rained here," Trudy said

on their third day. "It's all rather like Wales," she said, standing by the closed double windows of their room regarding the downpour and imagining the mountains which indeed were there, but invisible.

"You said that yesterday," Gwen said, "and it was quite fine yesterday. Yesterday you said it was like Wales."

"Well, it rained a bit yesterday."

"But the sun was shining when you said it was like Wales."

"Well, so it is."

"On a much larger scale, I should say," Gwen said.

"I didn't realize it would be so wet." Then Trudy could almost hear Gwen counting twenty.

"You have to take your chance," Gwen said. "This is an unfortunate summer."

The pelting of the rain increased as if in confirmation.

Trudy thought, I'd better shut up. But suicidally: "Wouldn't it be better if we moved to a slightly more expensive place?" she said.

"The rain falls on the expensive places too. It falls on the just and the unjust alike."

Gwen was thirty-five, a schoolteacher. She wore her hair and her clothes and her bit of lipstick in such a way that, standing by the window looking out at the rain, it occurred to Trudy like a revelation that Gwen had given up all thoughts of marriage. "On the just and the unjust alike," said Gwen, turning her maddening imperturbable eyes upon Trudy, as if to say, you are the unjust and I'm the just.

Next day was fine. They swam in the lake. They sat drinking apple juice under the red-and-yellow awnings on the terrace of their guesthouse and gazed at the innocent smiling mountain. They paraded – Gwen in her navy blue shorts and Trudy in her puffy sunsuit – along the lake-side where marched also the lean brown camping youths from all over the globe, the fat print-frocked mothers and double-chinned fathers from Germany followed by their blonde sedate young, and the English women with their perms.

"There aren't any men about," Trudy said.

"There are hundreds of men," Gwen said, in a voice which meant, whatever do you mean?

"I really must try out my phrasebook," Trudy said, for she had the feeling that if she were independent of Gwen as interpreter she might, as she expressed it to herself, have more of a chance.

"You might have more of a chance of meeting someone interesting that way," Gwen said, for their close confinement by the rain had seemed to make her psychic, and she was continually putting Trudy's thoughts into words.

"Oh, I'm not here for that. I only wanted a rest, as I told you. I'm not –"

"Goodness, Richard!"

Gwen was actually speaking English to a man who was not apparently accompanied by a wife or aunt or sister.

He kissed Gwen on the cheek. She laughed and so did he. "Well, well," he said. He was not much taller than Gwen. He had dark crinkly hair and a small moustache of a light brown. He wore bathing trunks and his large chest was impressively bronze. "What brings you here?" he said to Gwen, looking meanwhile at Trudy.

He was staying at an hotel on the other side of the lake. Each day for the rest of the fortnight he rowed over to meet them at ten in the morning, sometimes spending the whole day with them. Trudy was charmed, she could hardly believe in Gwen's friendly indifference to him, notwithstanding he was a teacher at the same grammar school as Gwen, who therefore saw him every day.

Every time he met them he kissed Gwen on the cheek.

"You seem to be on very good terms with him," Trudy said.

"Oh. Richard's an old friend. I've known him for years."

The second week, Gwen went off on various expeditions of her own and left them together.

"This is quite a connoisseur's place," Richard informed Trudy, and he pointed out why, and in what choice way, it was so, and Trudy, charmed, saw in the peeling pastel stucco of the little town, the unnecessary floral balconies, the bulbous Slovene spires, something special after all. She felt she saw, through his eyes, a precious rightness in the women with their grey skirts and well-filled blouses who trod beside their husbands and their clean children.

"Are they all Austrians?" Trudy asked.

"No, some of them are German and French. But this place attracts the same type."

Richard's eyes rested with appreciation on the young noisy campers whose tents were pitched in the lake-side field. The campers were long-limbed and animal, brightly and briefly dressed. They romped like galvanized goats, yet looked surprisingly virtuous.

"What are they saying to each other?" she inquired of Richard when a group of them passed by, shouting some words and laughing at each other through glistening red lips and very white teeth.

"They are talking about their fast MG racing cars."

"Oh, have they got racing cars?"

"No, the racing cars they are talking about don't exist. Sometimes they talk about their film contracts which don't exist. That's why they laugh."

"Not much of a sense of humour, have they?"

"They are of mixed nationalities, so they have to limit their humour to jokes which everyone can understand, and so they talk about racing cars which aren't there."

Trudy giggled a little, to show willing. Richard told her he was thirty-five, which she thought feasible. She volunteered that she was not quite twenty-two. Whereupon Richard looked at her and looked away, and looked again and took her hand. For, as he told Gwen afterwards, this remarkable statement was almost an invitation to a love affair.

Their love affair began that afternoon, in a boat on the lake, when, barefoot, they had a game of placing sole to sole, heel to heel. Trudy squealed, and leaned back hard, pressing her feet against Richard's.

She squealed at Gwen when they met in their room later on. "I'm having a heavenly time with Richard. I do so much like an older man."

Gwen sat on her bed and gave Trudy a look of wonder. Then she said, "He's not much older than you."

"I've knocked a bit off my age," Trudy said. "Do you mind not letting on?"

"How much have you knocked off?"

"Seven years."

"Very courageous," Gwen said.

"What do you mean?"

"That you are brave."

"Don't you think you're being a bit nasty?"

"No. It takes courage to start again and again. That's all I mean. Some women would find it boring."

"Oh, I'm not an experienced girl at all," Trudy said. "Whatever made you think I was experienced?"

"It's true," Gwen said, "you show no signs of having profited by experience. Have you ever found it a successful tactic to remain twenty-two?"

"I believe you're jealous," Trudy said. "One expects this sort of thing from most older women, but somehow I didn't expect it from you."

"One is always learning," Gwen said.

Trudy fingered her curls. "Yes, I have got a lot to learn from life," she said, looking out of the window.

"God," said Gwen, "you haven't begun to believe that you're still twenty-two, have you?"

"Not quite twenty-two is how I put it to Richard," Trudy said, "and yes, I do feel it. That's my point. I don't feel a day older."

The last day of their holidays Richard took Trudy rowing on the lake, which reflected a grey low sky.

"It looks like Windermere today, doesn't it?" he said.

Trudy had not seen Windermere, but she said, yes it did, and gazed at him with shining twenty-two-year-old eyes.

"Sometimes this place," he said, "is very like Yorkshire, but only when the weather's bad. Or, over on the mountain side, Wales."

"Exactly what I told Gwen," Trudy said. "I said Wales, I said, it's like Wales."

"Well, of course, there's quite a difference, really. It –"

"But Gwen simply squashed the idea. You see, she's an older woman, and being a schoolmistress – it's so much different when a man's a teacher – being a woman teacher, she feels she can treat me like a kid. I suppose I must expect it."

"Oh well –"

"How long have you known Gwen?"

"Several years," he said. "Gwen's all right, darling. A great friend of my mother, is Gwen. Quite a member of the family."

Trudy wanted to move her lodgings in London but she was prevented from doing so by a desire to be near Gwen, who saw Richard daily at school, and who knew his mother so well. And therefore Gwen's experience of Richard filled in the gaps in his life which were unknown to Trudy and which intrigued her.

She would fling herself into Gwen's room. "Gwen, what d'you think? There he was waiting outside the office and he drove me home, and he's calling for me at seven, and next week-end . . ."

Gwen frequently replied, "You are out of breath. Have you got heart trouble?" – for Gwen's room was only on the first floor. And Trudy was furious with Gwen on these occasions for seeming not to understand that the breathlessness was all part of her only being twenty-two, and excited by the boyfriend.

"I think Richard's so exciting," Trudy said. "It's difficult to believe I've only known him a month."

"Has he invited you home to meet his mother?" Gwen inquired.

"No – not yet. Oh, do you think he will?"

"Yes, I think so. One day I'm sure he will."

"Oh, do you mean it?" Trudy flung her arms girlishly round Gwen's impassive neck.

"When is your father coming up?" Gwen said.

"Not for ages, if at all. He can't leave Leicester just now, and he hates London."

"You must get him to come and ask Richard what his intentions are. A young girl like you needs protection."

"Gwen, don't be silly."

Often Trudy would question Gwen about Richard and his mother.

"Are they well off? Is she a well-bred woman? What's the house like? How long have you known Richard? Why hasn't he married before? The mother, is she –"

"Lucy is a marvel in her way," Gwen said.

"Oh, do you call her Lucy? You must know her awfully well."

"I'm quite," said Gwen, "a member of the family in my way."

"Richard has often told me that. Do you go there *every* Sunday?"

"Most Sundays," Gwen said. "It is often very amusing, and one sometimes sees a fresh face."

"Why," Trudy said, as the summer passed and she had already been away for several weekends with Richard, "doesn't he ask me to meet his mother? If my mother were alive and living in London I know I would have asked him home to meet her."

Trudy threw out hints to Richard. "How I wish you could meet my father. You simply must come up to Leicester in the Christmas holidays and stay with him. He's rather tied up in Leicester and never leaves it. He's an insurance manager. The successful kind."

"I can't very well leave Mother at Christmas," Richard said, "but I'd love to meet your father some other time." His tan had worn off, and Trudy thought him more distinguished and at the same time more unattainable than ever.

"I think it only right," Trudy said in her young way, "that one should introduce the man one loves to one's parents" – for it was agreed between them that they were in love.

But still, by the end of October, Richard had not asked her to meet his mother.

"Does it matter all that much?" Gwen said.

"Well, it would be a definite step forward," Trudy said. "We can't go on being just friends like this. I'd like to know where I stand with him. After all, we're in love and we're both free. Do you know, I'm beginning to think he hasn't any serious intentions after all. But if he asked me to meet his mother it would be a sort of sign, wouldn't it?"

"It certainly would," Gwen said.

"I don't even feel I can ring him up at home until I've met his mother. I'd feel shy of talking to her on the phone. I must meet her. It's becoming a sort of obsession."

"It certainly is," Gwen said. "Why don't you just say to him, 'I'd like to meet your mother'?"

"Well, Gwen, there are some things a girl can't say."

"No, but a woman can."

"Are you going on about my age again? I tell you, Gwen,

I feel twenty-two. I think twenty-two. I am twenty-two so far as Richard's concerned. I don't think really you can help me much. After all, you haven't been successful with men yourself, have you?"

"No," Gwen said, "I haven't. I've always been on the old side."

"That's just my point. It doesn't get you anywhere to feel old and think old. If you want to be successful with men you have to hang on to your youth."

"It wouldn't be worth it at the price," Gwen said, "to judge by the state you're in."

Trudy started to cry and ran to her room, presently returning to ask Gwen questions about Richard's mother. She could rarely keep away from Gwen when she was not out with Richard.

"What's his mother really like? Do you think I'd get on with her?"

"If you wish I'll take you to see his mother one Sunday."

"No, no," Trudy said. "It's got to come from him if it has any meaning. The invitation must come from Richard."

Trudy had almost lost her confidence, and in fact had come to wonder if Richard was getting tired of her, since he had less and less time to spare for her, when unexpectedly and yet so inevitably, in November, he said, "You must come and meet my mother."

"Oh!" Trudy said.

"I should like you to meet my mother. She's looking forward to it."

"Oh, does she know about me?"

"Rather."

"Oh!"

"It's happened. Everything's all right," Trudy said breathlessly.

"He has asked you home to meet his mother," Gwen said without looking up from the exercise book she was correcting.

"It's important to me, Gwen."

"Yes, yes," Gwen said.

"I'm going on Sunday afternoon," Trudy said. "Will you be there?"

"Not till supper time," Gwen said. "Don't worry."

"He said, 'I want you to meet Mother. I've told her all about you.'"

"All about you?"

"That's what he said, and it means so much to me, Gwen. So much."

Gwen said, "It's a beginning."

"Oh, it's the beginning of everything. I'm sure of that."

Richard picked her up in his Singer at four on Sunday. He seemed preoccupied. He did not, as usual, open the car door for her, but slid into the driver's seat and waited for her to get in beside him. She fancied he was perhaps nervous about her meeting his mother for the first time.

The house on Campion Hill was delightful. They must be very *comfortable*, Trudy thought. Mrs Seeton was a tall, stooping woman, well dressed and preserved, with thick steel-grey hair and large light eyes. "I hope you'll call me Lucy," she said. "Do you smoke?"

"I don't," said Trudy.

"Helps the nerves," said Mrs Seeton, "when one is getting on in life. You don't need to smoke yet awhile."

"No," Trudy said. "What a lovely room, Mrs Seeton."

"*Lucy*," said Mrs Seeton.

"Lucy," Trudy said, very shyly, and looked at Richard for support. But he was drinking the last of his tea and looking out of the window as if to see whether the sky had cleared.

"Richard has to go out for supper," Mrs Seeton said, waving her cigarette holder very prettily. "Don't forget to watch the time, Richard. But Trudy will stay to supper with me, I *hope*. Trudy and I have a lot to talk about, I'm sure." She looked at Trudy and very faintly, with no more than a butterfly-flick, winked.

Trudy accepted the invitation with a conspiratorial nod and a slight squirm in her chair. She looked at Richard to see if he would say where he was going for supper, but he was gazing up at the top pane of the window, his fingers tapping on the arm of the shining Old Windsor chair on which he sat.

Richard left at half-past six, very much more cheerful in his going than he had been in his coming.

"Richard gets restless on a Sunday," said his mother.

"Yes, so I've noticed," Trudy said, so that there should be no mistake about who had been occupying his recent Sundays.

"I dare say now you want to hear all about Richard," said his mother in a secretive whisper, although no one was in earshot. Mrs Seeton giggled through her nose and raised her shoulders all the way up her long neck till they almost touched her earrings.

Trudy vaguely copied her gesture. "Oh, yes," she said, "Mrs Seeton."

"Lucy. You must call me Lucy, now, you know. I want you and me to be friends. I want you to feel like a member of the family. Would you like to see the house?"

She led the way upstairs and displayed her affluent bedroom, one wall of which was entirely covered by mirror, so that, for every photograph on her dressing-table of Richard and Richard's late father, there were virtually two photographs in the room.

"This is Richard on his pony, Lob. He adored Lob. We all adored Lob. Of course, we were in the country then. This is Richard with Nana. And this is Richard's father at the outbreak of war. What did you do in the war, dear?"

"I was at school," Trudy said, quite truthfully.

"Oh, then you're a teacher, too?"

"No, I'm a secretary. I didn't leave school till after the war."

Mrs Seeton said, looking at Trudy from two angles, "Good gracious me, how deceiving. I thought you were about Richard's age, like Gwen. Gwen is such a dear. This is Richard as a graduate. Why he went into schoolmastering I don't know. Still, he's a very good master. Gwen always says so, quite definitely. Don't you adore Gwen?"

"Gwen is a good bit older than me," Trudy said, being still upset on the subject of age.

"She ought to be here any moment. She usually comes for supper. Now I'll show you the other rooms and Richard's room."

When they came to Richard's room his mother stood on the threshold and, with her finger to her lips for no apparent reason, swung the door open. Compared with the rest of the house this was a bleak, untidy, almost schoolboy's room.

Richard's green pyjama trousers lay on the floor where he had stepped out of them. This was a sight familiar to Trudy from her several weekend excursions with Richard, of late months, to hotels up the Thames valley.

"So untidy," said Richard's mother, shaking her head woefully. "So untidy. One day, Trudy, dear, we must have a real chat."

Gwen arrived presently, and made herself plainly at home by going straight into the kitchen to prepare a salad. Mrs Seeton carved slices of cold meat while Trudy stood and watched them both, listening to a conversation between them which indicated a long intimacy. Richard's mother seemed anxious to please Gwen.

"Expecting Grace tonight?" Gwen said.

"No, darling, I thought perhaps *not tonight*. Was I right?"

"Oh, of course, yes. Expecting Joanna?"

"Well, as it's Trudy's *first* visit, I thought perhaps not –"

"Would you," Gwen said to Trudy, "lay the table, my dear. Here are the knives and forks."

Trudy bore these knives and forks into the dining-room with a sense of having been got rid of with a view to being talked about.

At supper, Mrs Seeton said, "It seems a bit odd, there only being the three of us. We usually have such jolly Sunday suppers. Next week, Trudy, you must come and meet the whole crowd – mustn't she, Gwen?"

"Oh yes," Gwen said, "Trudy must do that."

Towards half past ten Richard's mother said, "I doubt if Richard will be back in time to run you home. Naughty boy, I daren't think what he gets up to."

On the way to the bus stop Gwen said, "Are you happy now that you've met Lucy?"

"Yes, I think so. But I think Richard might have stayed. It would have been nice. I dare say he wanted me to get to know his mother by myself. But in fact I felt the need of his support."

"Didn't you have a talk with Lucy?"

"Well yes, but not much really. Richard probably didn't realize you were coming to supper. Richard probably thought his mother and I could have a heart-to-heart –"

"I usually go to Lucy's on Sunday," Gwen said.

"Why?"

"Well, she's a friend of mine. I know her ways. She amuses me."

During the week Trudy saw Richard only once, for a quick drink.

"Exams," he said. "I'm rather busy, darling."

"Exams in November? I thought they started in December."

"Preparation for exams," he said. "Preliminaries. Lots of work." He took her home, kissed her on the cheek and drove off.

She looked after the car, and for a moment hated his moustache. But she pulled herself together and, recalling her youthfulness, decided she was too young really to judge the fine shades and moods of a man like Richard.

He picked her up at four o'clock on Sunday.

"Mother's looking forward to seeing you," he said. "She hopes you will stay for supper."

"You won't have to go out, will you, Richard?"

"Not tonight, no."

But he did have to go out to keep an appointment of which his mother reminded him immediately after tea. He had smiled at his mother and said, "Thanks."

Trudy saw the photograph album, then she heard how Mrs Seeton had met Richard's father in Switzerland, and what Mrs Seeton had been wearing at the time.

At half-past six the supper party arrived. These were three women, including Gwen. The one called Grace was quite pretty, with a bewildered air. The one called Iris was well over forty and rather loud in her manner.

"Where's Richard tonight, the old cad?" said Iris.

"How do I know?" said his mother. "Who am I to ask?"

"Well, at least he's a hard worker during the week. A brilliant teacher," said doe-eyed Grace.

"Middling as a schoolmaster," Gwen said.

"Oh, Gwen! Look how long he's held down the job," his mother said.

"I should think," Grace said, "he's wonderful with the boys."

"Those Shakespearian productions at the end of the summer term are really magnificent," Iris bawled. "I'll hand him that, the old devil."

"Magnificent," said his mother. "You must admit, Gwen –"

"Very middling performances," Gwen said.

"I suppose you are right, but, after all, they are only schoolboys. You can't do much with untrained actors, Gwen," said Mrs Seeton very sadly.

"I adore Richard," Iris said, "when he's in his busy, occupied mood. He's so –"

"Oh yes," Grace said, "Richard is wonderful when he's got a lot on his mind."

"I know," said his mother. "There was one time when Richard had just started teaching – I must tell you this story – he . . ."

Before they left Mrs Seeton said to Trudy, "You will come with Gwen next week, won't you? I want you to regard yourself as one of us. There are two other friends of Richard's I do want you to meet. Old friends."

On the way to the bus Trudy said to Gwen, "Don't you find it dull going to Mrs Seeton's every Sunday?"

"Well, yes, my dear young thing, and no. From time to time one sees a fresh face, and then it's quite amusing."

"Doesn't Richard ever stay at home on a Sunday evening?"

"No, I can't say he does. In fact, he's very often away for the whole weekend. As you know."

"Who are these women?" Trudy said, stopping in the street.

"Oh, just old friends of Richard's."

"Do they see him often?"

"Not now. They've become members of the family."

THE FORTUNE-TELLER

The château lay among woodlands in a wide valley in the heart of the old Troubadour country of France. It was about ten years ago at the end of summer.

We were a party of three, Raymond, his wife Sylvia, and me, Lucy. The marriage between Raymond and Sylvia was already going bad, which made me very uncomfortable. I had already decided after the third day of our travels that I would never again go on holiday alone with a married couple, and I never have since.

I had begun to wonder why they had asked me to join them and I fairly guessed that they were trying to prove, by the evidence of my single state, that they were truly a couple. We arrived at the château after a week in France, by which time I was on the point of getting on a train to the nearest airport and so back to London.

But I changed my mind precisely at the château. Sylvia asked for rooms. Mme Dessain, thin, tall, work-worn and elegant, who had come round the side of the house with a bucket of pigswill in her hand to greet us, declined to answer Sylvia. She addressed me, saying very politely that yes, she had a double room for me and my husband and a small room for Mlle on the maids' floor at the top of the house. Raymond intervened to explain the relationships aright. She gave the sort of smile by which it was plain she had understood perfectly well. I supposed that Sylvia, who spoke French better than I did, had nevertheless lacked the required respect; she had taken Mme Dessain for one of the hired hands, and had selected her tone accordingly. This was a habit of Sylvia's; I always marvelled at the trouble she must have put into harbouring such a range of initial attitudes as she had for different people, when one alone would serve for all. She was, of course, a follower of Lenin who was class-conscious by profession. Raymond was fairly neutral about the incident. He was big and bearded, a television producer; and he was intelligent. But he was vain enough, and perhaps sufficiently at the point of exasperation with his marriage to show himself pleased with the proprietor's mistake, if mistake it was. Madame did not apologize; she merely told us the price of the rooms and asked if we wanted demipension. Sylvia, when angry, had a leer. Her teeth protruded and for some reason she dyed her hair bright red. In spite of this she had a handsome look. But, leering, she looked, to me, morally low, very low, and stupid although in fact she was a rodent-biologist of some distinction.

Mme Dessain put down the bucket and again addressed me. She asked me if I would like to see the rooms. Plainly, she was not too grand to be catty and she had taken against Sylvia.

"Have we decided to stay?" Sylvia said to Raymond. "Do you like the place?" "It looks lovely," he said, "I would like to see the room anyway, because I would like to stay."

Mme Dessain led the way upstairs. I followed with my two clever friends behind me. The rooms were fine and we all decided to stay. Strangely enough I wasn't put in a maid's room upstairs, but in a large room on the same floor as my friends. Madame – it turned out that she was in fact a marquise – ran down to get on with her jobs, leaving us to cope with our luggage. I thought she looked well over fifty when I had first seen her but watching her trip so easily downstairs I could see she was younger, not much over forty. She had obviously taken a dislike to Sylvia, but I didn't care. Already I felt free of the embarrassing couple. In a curious way Mme Dessain had released me. She had held out a straw. I clutched it and miraculously it held me up. It struck me she was highly intuitive, as indeed are so many in the hotel business.

I was delighted with my room. It had windows on two sides. The furniture was French Provincial, plainly belonging to the eighteenth-century château and by no means brought in for hotel guests. It was much the same all over the house. There were two drawing-rooms, the yellow one and the green, and these were by no means rustic, but in the great high style of eighteenth-century France. There was an Oriental room with a Chinese part and an Egyptian part, full of those furnishings and treasures brought back from the travels of nineteenth century ancestors, which are too good for the use of ordinary tourists yet not too rare for everyday accommodation. It was a satisfaction to feel we had been taken in as guests, since plainly Mme Dessain had to be discriminate.

Few of the guests used the Oriental room, or the other priceless-seeming rooms with their Sèvres ornaments and plates behind glass cabinets. There was a more serviceable library in general use, with a television set, tables, and plenty of worn, cretonne-covered sofas and chairs.

It was there that a few evenings later I offered to tell Mme Dessain's fortune by cards. People were grouped around, after dinner, some just talking, others playing various card games and a couple in a far corner were playing chess. Outside it was pelting with heavy thick rain; it had been raining all day. A small, stout, elderly man was Mme Dessain's husband; a surprising couple. He sat by her side while I told her fortune. Sylvia and Raymond, bored with my fortune-telling, had moved away.

I must explain that when I find myself in a country or seaside establishment of the residential sort on any of my many travels, if I see someone lonely or ill at ease, and obviously not enjoying their stay, I always offer to tell their fortune by my cards. I've never been refused. On the contrary, it tends to have a hypnotic effect on the other guests, and candidates for my fortune-telling are never wanting; they even come up to me and ask me what I charge, and when I explain that I do it for free, they are slightly embarrassed, but want their fortune just the same, and politely accept being put off when I've had too much or for some good reason don't want to do it.

My peculiar method of fortune-telling follows no tradition of occult sciences; I follow rules, but they are my own secret ones, varying quite a lot in their application to each individual. They are my own secret rules but they arise from deep conviction. They cannot be formulated, they are as sincere and indescribable as are the primary colours; they are not of a science but of an art. Very often I make a mistake, but I know it; at such moments I'm thinking my way, talking through a dense fog, shining the torch of my intuition here and there until it hits on some object which may or may not prove to be what I say it is. Sometimes my predictions are wildly astray as they pertain to the present time and environment, but I have known them to become surprisingly true much later in life, in a different place, and presume that this may happen, too, in some of the cases where I lose sight of the person whose fortune I have told.

For the actual selection of the cards I have a precise system. I should never reveal it in detail, except to say that it is based on sevens and fives. Sevens and fives; and if you should ask me any more about this initial stage of the proceedings I should tell you a falsehood; indeed the whole of the process is most precious-fragile to me, and I wouldn't give it away lest I should lose my powers. I mean what Yeats meant:

> I have spread my dreams under your feet;
> Tread softly because you tread on my dreams.

To tell the cards I begin by asking my client to shuffle them. Then I deal according to my seven and five system; a varying number of cards which emerge from this process are set apart and I ask my client to shuffle again. Again I deal and set apart, and a third time, three cycles in all. The client then shuffles the cards which have been set aside; these are the cards of his fortune. At the same time the client is asked to make a silent wish, and mightily concentrate upon it.

Now, I take these cards and again deal them. You mustn't think that because I take my gifts seriously, I take them solemnly. It is all an airy dream of mine, unsinkable because it is light. I don't play the eerie fortune-teller at all; I don't play anything when I tell the cards; I am simply myself.

Well, I take the cards that have fallen to my client's lot and deal them under the following headings: (1) the secret self; (2) the known self (by which I mean, the more limited aspect of the person as he is observable by others); (3) the client's hopes; (4) the client's degree of self-ignorance; (5) his present destination (I don't say his "destiny" for this reason, that any destiny I might take from the cards would be prematurely conceived and would fail to allow for a client's probable divergence from his present destination. Circumstances change. There can be a change of heart. Human nature is essentially unpredictable in the long run. But "destination" none the less often answers for destiny. No clairvoyant, believe me, can say more); (6) affairs of the heart, which means the prevailing love; that is, of any object, including, from time to time, that of money; (7) the wish – will it or won't it come true?

Again I see Mme Dessain in the friendly library of her house leaning over the table, those many years ago, with her husband by her side as I began to tell her cards.

While she was shuffling I saw that she was extremely punctilious about the performance. While I dealt and discarded according to my secret method she watched me with an intensity that meant, to me, a decided confidence in my powers. Her wish was evidently of critical importance. She seemed absorbed by the cards that fell to constitute her fortune, but I advised her light-heartedly not to give weight to them herself, to concentrate hard on the wish, and to leave the interpretation in due time to me.

"There are many spades," observed Mme Dessain. "And there is an ace of spades, Madame." I was puzzled as to why she insisted on addressing me as "Madame" when I was plainly "Mademoiselle". I was dealing the third cycle. In my conjuring out of the meaning of cards I never go by the tradition. It is true that no one is delighted by the ace of spades but it does not necessarily mean a personal death. It might mean the death of a hope, or the end of a fear. Everything depends on the combination. Anyway, I was dealing the third cycle. I said, "Leave it to me," and finished.

Now I gathered up Mme Dessain's cards.

"Will the rain never stop?" said Mme Dessain, her eyes wandering to the enormous French windows. She was putting this on, this absent air as if she didn't care in the least about her fortune.

"Concentrate on your wish, Madame," I said.

"Oh, I am concentrating. The rain is a tourist attraction if they like the flooded fields, very beautiful." So she laughed off her fortune-telling, but I could see she was eager, even a little agitated. Her husband, too, watched with care. I wanted to remind them it was only a game, but I refrained; I didn't want to bring their nervousness to light.

I dealt the cards under their seven headings, which naturally I didn't pronounce. Thirteen cards had emerged from the process of selection. I noticed the high proportion of court cards in Mme Dessain's set.

Now, in the first round to her secret self, came up the eight of spades, to her known self the six of spades.

"Spades in my wish!" said Mme Dessain immediately.

"Have patience," I said, still setting forth the cards. It was obvious to me now that she was trying to penetrate my method for when I put down the king of hearts she said, "a fair, handsome lover." But I gave no sign, although I felt annoyed at the interruption.

Her cards finally came out as follows:

Secret self: eight of spades and six of clubs
Known self: six of spades and nine of diamonds
Things hoped for: king of hearts and ace of spades
Self-ignorance: five of hearts and king of clubs
Present destination: queen of hearts and three of hearts
Affairs of the heart: queen of clubs and three of diamonds
The wish: knave of hearts.

Mme Dessain was really perplexed. She saw all seven sets of cards placed out before her, but she had no way of guessing the private headings I had placed them under. Her eyes were bright upon the cards as if she were telling my fortune, not me hers.

"You have got your wish," I said at once, seeing that she had come in for one card only, the knave of hearts, under that heading, and there was no opposition. "However, it is a wish that you should not have made."

"Which cards represent my wish?" she asked, almost in a panic, strange for such a grand lady.

I wouldn't tell her. I smiled at her and said, "This is only a game, after all."

She put on an air that she was pacified, pulled together. But I could see that she was not.

Altogether, from this moment what her cards told me

was one thing and what I told her was another. I had reason to be cautious. As I looked at the whole picture that was formed by the seven groups of cards it was at first a coloured mass, changing into a tableau of patterns until one idea protruded larger and more brilliantly than the others. And so, it appeared to me all in a quick moment that Mme Dessain was herself a natural clairvoyant; she was able to read my mind perhaps better than I was able to read her cards. What had been to me a laughing matter, a game, seemed now to veer rather dangerously towards myself, and I knew that her wish had been in some way connected with me. I say connected with me, not directed at me, because there was something indirect about it; at the same time it was distinctly malevolent.

I braved out the performance. I told her a certain amount of nonsense, but as I spoke I could see she discerned that I wasn't as frank as I might have been. More specifically than before I could now see under the heading of the secret self that she was clairvoyant.

Now, for instance, I looked at the known self in a special way. I felt that her very attractive, haggard and aristocratic appeal was by no means as artless as it had seemed when she was working around the outhouses or busy with the vast baronial pans in the great stone kitchen. She looked airily up at the beautiful windows, now, those tall windows with leaded corners. I was aware of her husband's attention upon her and thought he seemed jealous, wondering what had been her wish and looking for her reaction to everything I said.

I continued to say many sweet things with a grain of what seemed probable. "You are hoping," I said, "for a visit from a tall bearded man, I should imagine an Englishman, who has an interest in gardening –" Indeed I received from Mme Dessain's cards a very strong premonition concerning the garden.

"That's Camillo, our odd-job man," said the anxious husband. "He's been away for five days, and he's overdue. But he's Italian."

"Alain!" rebuked Mme Dessain. "Let Mme Lucy continue."

I continued. It did seem to me very plainly that Mme Dessain had set her heart on a visitor. He would be about her age, probably an American or an Englishman (he could have been a German but for the fact it was extremely unlikely that a woman of Mme Dessain's age and ethos would have a German lover). She was, however, moving towards this love affair full tilt. I was sure he had been a guest at the château, certainly married then, if not now, and decidedly rich. It was a disastrous enough attachment for her house and family.

All this I saw, and Mme Dessain knew that I saw it. What she was unaware of, or was bound by her infatuation to ignore, was the vast amount of bother and anxiety this course was leading her to. Her husband, though not in the least faithful to her, would make nothing but bitterness of the affair.

"You may be unaware that certain benefits will come to the house as a result of your visitor's appearance," I said. And I told her the visitor would be poor, and warned her against unforeseen expenditure. The husband rejoiced to hear these words, and I wound up, "Tomorrow you will receive a very important family letter," – one of the few honest comments on Mme Dessain's cards that I chose to make. Indeed, I thought it was harmless, for the husband said, "That will be from our son, Charles," and Mme Dessain once more cried out "Alain! You interrupt."

I said, "I've finished."

Mme Dessain was looking beyond me. "Here comes Madame's husband," she said ambiguously; anyway, I looked round and saw Raymond approaching. I guessed he had quarrelled with Sylvia who, leaving the room, looked round smiling with that deplorable angry leer of hers, which quite ruined her appearance.

I left next day. The tense atmosphere between my married friends was not to be borne by me. When I went to pay my bill Mme Dessain sent a maid to take the money and with the message that she was occupied.

But Raymond came running after me as my luggage went into the taxi. His face was fairly frantic. It struck me that he would have been rather handsome without his beard.

"Lucy," he said. "Lucy."

"I'm sorry, Raymond. But I have to go."

He was really inarticulate and I thought it quite civil of him to feel for me and my embarrassment at being on the scene of a messed-up marriage.

"Lucy."

"My apologies to Sylvia," I said. "She'll understand."

That was the last I saw of Raymond, watching my taxi depart, as he did.

Everything but the physical memory of the lovely château went far away to the back of my mind in the general nuisance of changing my holiday plans. The next week I returned to London and took up my life. Mme Dessain and the telling of her cards slept latent for year after year, but with each detail regularly arranged in case it should ever be needed, as is the way with memory.

Some time over the following year I heard that Sylvia and Raymond had finally separated; I was told that Sylvia was married again, to a social worker much younger than herself, and that after the divorce Raymond had given up his good job and gone to live abroad. Abroad is a big place and the rumours were equally too large and amorphous for me to take any account of, so busy with my own life as I was. When occasionally I thought of that holiday I shared with them I thought of the beautiful château, but a cloud came over my thoughts when I remembered how uncomfortable I felt as the third party. I didn't know till much later that they stayed on at the château for another week.

Not long ago I came across M. Dessain. I didn't recognize him at first. I was aware only of a little wizened man walking out of the Black Forest at Baden-Baden. I should say that it isn't unusual for anything whatsoever to walk out of the Black Forest, so I took no particular notice. Moreover he was dressed in beige, and I might say that every visitor to Baden-Baden wears beige, both men and women. Their clothes and their shoes are beige and their faces are beige; in which respect they are quite lovable.

But I noticed him again that day seated alone at a lunch table in the dining room of my hotel. Even then, I failed to see anything familiar about him; I only noticed that he looked at me once or twice, briefly, but in a decidedly curious way.

That evening I was sitting in the public room of the hotel playing with my cards. I was alone, waiting for a friend to join me there the next day. I shuffled my cards and dealt them out in my own style which seems so haphazard; I don't ever tell my own fortune, but I can't keep away from the cards. I shuffle and deal and see what comes up, and in the meantime my ideas take form as if the cards were a sort of sacrament, "an outward and visible sign of an inward and spiritual grace," as the traditional definition goes.

Up to me at my table came the wizened guest, him of the Black Forest. He sat down on the edge of a sofa, watching me. I felt he was sad, and I was about to ask him if he would like me to tell his fortune.

"Mlle Lucy," he said.

Then I recognized him, the once chubby little husband of Mme Dessain, and I saw how the years had withered him. In all its formal detail of ten years ago or more, I remembered the features of the room in the château where I told Mme Dessain's fortune while she, intense and distressed, perceived in her clairvoyance all that I was about. I remembered the two chess players sitting quietly apart, the tall shapes of Sylvia and Raymond moving away impatiently from the scene, the worn floral fabric on the chairs. I wondered if Mme Dessain's lover had materialized, and I recalled vaguely some of my light-hearted predictions which hadn't fooled Mme Dessain one bit. "You are hoping for a visit from a tall, bearded Englishman, interested in the garden." And my own sincere prediction, "You will have a family letter."

I looked at M. Dessain and said, "What a long time ago. Are you on holiday?"

"I am here for my health."

"How is Mme Dessain?" I said.

"She does very well. As you predicted, the letter came next day."

"Oh, dear. I hope it was a good letter."

"Yes. It came from her cousin Claude. It announced his engagement. I was delighted, because Claude was my wife's lover."

"Oh," I said. "Well, that must have solved a problem for you, M. Dessain."

"It was a good thing for Claude," he said. "And a good thing for you, Mlle Lucy."

"For me?"

"My wife changed your destiny," said the sad and withered man. He repeated, "Your destiny, Mlle Lucy. She saw that you were destined to marry your friend Raymond, and she intervened."

"Marry Raymond? I never thought of such a thing. There was nothing at all between us. He was on bad terms with his wife but that had nothing to do with me."

"Nevertheless, my wife foresaw the outcome. You would have married Raymond, but after your departure, before the week was out she had him for her new lover. He is still at the château. She forestalled your destiny."

"Not my destiny, then," I said, "only my destination." And seeing that he looked so sad and so beige, I asked, "Would you like me to tell your fortune, M. Dessain?"

He didn't answer the question. He only said, "Raymond is very good in the garden and in the grounds."

THE FATHERS' DAUGHTERS

She left the old man in his deck-chair on the front, having first adjusted the umbrella awning with her own hand, and, with her own hand, put his panama hat at a comfortable angle. The beach attendant had been sulky, but she didn't see why one should lay out tips only for adjusting an umbrella and a panama hat. Since the introduction of the new franc it was impossible to tip less than a franc. There seemed to be a conspiracy all along the coast to hide the lesser coins from the visitors, and one could only find franc pieces in one's purse, and one had to be careful not to embarrass Father, and one . . .

She hurried along the Rue Paradis, keeping in the hot shade, among all the old, old smells of Nice, not only garlic wafting from the cafês, and of the hot invisible air itself, but the smells from her memory, from thirty-five summers at Nice in apartments of long ago, Father's summer salon, Father's friends' children, Father's friends, writers, young artists dating back five years at Nice, six, nine years; and then, before the war, twenty years ago – when we were at Nice, do you remember, Father? Do you remember the pension on the Boulevard Victor Hugo when we were rather poor? Do you remember the

Americans at the Negresco in 1937 – how changed, how demure they are now! Do you remember, Father, how in the old days we disliked the thick carpets – at least, you disliked them, and what you dislike, I dislike, isn't it so, Father?

Yes, Dora, we don't care for luxury. Comfort, yes, but luxury, no.

I doubt if we can afford to stay at an hotel on the front this year, Father.

What's that? What's that you say?

I said I doubt if we ought to stay on the front this year, Father; the Promenade des Anglais is becoming very trippery. Remember you disliked the thick carpets . . .

Yes, yes, of course.

Of course, and so we'll go, I suggest, to a little place I've found on the Boulevard Gambetta, and if we don't like that there's a very good place on the Boulevard Victor Hugo. Within our means, Father, modest and . . .

What's that you say?

I said it wasn't a vulgar place, Father.

Ah. No.

And so I'll just drop them a note and book a couple of bedrooms. They may be small, but the food . . .

Facing the sea, Dora.

They are all very vulgar places facing the sea, Father. Very distracting. No peace at all. Times have changed, you know.

Ah. Well, I leave it to you, dear. Tell them I desire a large room, suitable for entertaining. Spare no expense, Dora.

Oh, of course not, Father.

And I hope to God we've won the lottery, she thought,

as she hurried up the little street to the lottery kiosk. Someone's got to win it out of the whole of France. The dark-skinned blonde at the lottery kiosk took an interest in Dora, who came so regularly each morning rather than buy a newspaper to see the results. She leaned over the ticket, holding her card of numbers, comparing it with Dora's ticket, with an expression of earnest sympathy.

"No luck," Dora said.

"Try again tomorrow," said the woman. "One never knows. Life is a lottery . . ."

Dora smiled as one who must either smile or weep. On her way back to the sea-front she thought, tomorrow I will buy five hundred francs' worth. Then she thought, no, no, I'd better not, I may run short of francs and have to take Father home before time. Dora, the food here is inferior. – I know, Father, but it's the same everywhere in France now, times have changed. – I think we should move to another hotel, Dora. – The others are all very expensive, Father. – What's that? What's that you say? – There are no other rooms available, Father, because of the tourists, these days.

The brown legs of lovely young men and girls passed her as she approached the sea. I ought to appreciate every minute of this, she thought, it may be the last time. This thoroughly blue sea, these brown limbs, these white teeth and innocent inane tongues, these palm trees – all this is what we are paying for.

"Everything all right, Father?"

"Where have you been, dear?"

"Only for a walk round the back streets to smell the savours."

"Dora, you are a chip off the old block. What did you see?"

"Brown limbs, white teeth, men in shirt-sleeves behind café windows, playing cards with green bottles in front of them."

"Good – you see everything with my eyes, Dora."

"Heat, smell, brown legs – it's what we are paying for, Father."

"Dora, you are becoming vulgar, if you don't mind my saying so. The eye of the true artist doesn't see life in the way of goods paid for. The world is ours. It is our birthright. We take it without payment."

"I'm not an artist like you, Father. Let me move the umbrella – you mustn't get too much sun."

"Times have changed," he said, glancing along the pebble beach, "the young men today have no interest in life."

She knew what her father meant. All along the beach, the young men playing with the air, girls, the sun; they were coming in from the sea, shaking the water from their heads; they were walking over the pebbles, then splashing into the water; they were taking an interest in their environment with every pore of their skin, as Father would have said in younger days when he was writing his books. What he meant, now, when he said, "the young men today have no interest in life", was that his young disciples, his admirers, had all gone, they were grown old and preoccupied, and had not been replaced. The last young man to seek out Father had been a bloodless-looking youth – not that one judged by appearances – who had called about seven years ago at their house in Essex. Father had made the most of him, giving up many of his mornings to sitting in the library talking about books with the young man, about life and the old days. But this, the last of Father's disciples, had left after two weeks with a promise to send them the article he was going to write about Father and his works. Indeed he had sent a letter: "Dear Henry Castlemaine, – Words cannot express my admiration . . ." After that they had heard no more. Dora was not really sorry. He was a poor specimen compared with the men who, in earlier days, used to visit Father. Dora in her late teens could have married one of three or four vigorous members of the Henry Castlemaine set, but she had not done so because of her widowed father and his needs as a public figure; and now she sometimes felt it would have served Father better if she had married, because of Father – one could have contributed from a husband's income, perhaps, to his declining years.

Dora said, "We must be going back to the hotel for lunch."

"Let us lunch somewhere else. The food there is . . ."

She helped her father from the deck-chair and, turning to the sea, took a grateful breath of the warm blue breeze. A young man, coming up from the sea, shook his head blindly and splashed her with water; then noticing what he had done he said – turning and catching her by the arm – "Oh, I'm so sorry." He spoke in English, was an Englishman, and she knew already how unmistakably she was an Englishwoman. "All right," she said, with a quick little laugh. The father was fumbling with his stick, the incident had passed, was immediately forgotten by Dora as she took his arm and propelled him across the wide hot boulevard where the white-suited policemen held up the impetuous traffic. "How would you like to be arrested by one of those, Dora?" He gave his deep short laugh and looked down at her. "I'd love it, Father." Perhaps he wouldn't insist on lunching elsewhere. If only they could reach the hotel, it would be all right; Father would be too exhausted to insist. But already he was saying, "Let's find somewhere for lunch."

"Well, we've paid for it at the hotel, Father."

"Don't be vulgar, my love."

In the following March, when Dora met Ben Donadieu for the first time, she had the feeling she had seen him somewhere before, she knew not where. Later, she told him of this, but he could not recall having seen her. But this sense of having seen him somewhere remained with Dora all her life. She came to believe she had met him in a former existence. In fact, it was on the beach at Nice that she had seen him, when he came up among the pebbles from the sea, and shook his hair, wetting her, and took her arm, apologizing.

"Don't be vulgar, my love. The hotel food is appalling. Not French at all."

"It's the same all over France, Father, these days."

"There used to be a restaurant – what was its name? – in one of those little streets behind the Casino. Let's go there. All the writers go there."

"Not any more, Father."

"Well, so much the better. Let's go there in any case. What's the name of the place? – Anyway, come on, I could go there blindfold. All the writers used to go . . ."

She laughed, because, after all, he was sweet. As she walked with him towards the Casino she did not say – Not any more, Father, do the writers go there. The writers don't come to Nice, not those of moderate means. But there's one writer here this year, Father, called Kenneth Hope, whom you haven't heard about. He uses our beach, and I've seen him once – a shy, thin, middle-aged man. But he won't speak to anyone. He writes wonderfully, Father. I've read his novels, they open windows in the mind that have been bricked-up for a hundred years. I have read *The Inventors*, which made great fame and fortune for him. It is about the inventors of patent gadgets, what lives they lead, how their minds apply themselves to invention and to love, and you would think, while you were reading *The Inventors*, that the place they live in was dominated by inventors. He has that magic, Father – he can make you believe anything. Dora did not say this, for her father had done great work too, and deserved a revival. His name was revered, his books were not greatly spoken of, they were not read. He would not understand the fame of Kenneth Hope. Father's novels were about the individual consciences of men and women, no one could do the individual conscience like Father. "Here we are, Father – this is the place, isn't it?"

"No, Dora, it's further along."

"Oh, but that's the Tumbril; it's wildly expensive."

"Really, darling!"

She decided to plead the heat, and to order only a slice of melon for lunch with a glass of her father's wine. Both tall and slim, they entered the restaurant. Her hair was drawn back, the bones of her face were good, her eyes were small and fixed ready for humour, for she had decided to be a spinster and do it properly; she looked forty-six and she did not look forty-six; her skin was dry; her mouth was thin, and was growing thinner with the worry about money. The father looked eighty years old, as he was. Thirty years ago people used to turn round and say, as he passed. "That's Henry Castlemaine."

Ben lay on his stomach on his mattress on the beach enclosure. Carmelita Hope lay on her mattress, next to him. They were eating rolls and cheese and drinking white wine which the beach attendant had brought to them from the café. Carmelita's tan was like a perfect garment, drawn skin-tight over her body. Since leaving school she had been in numerous jobs behind the scenes of film and television studios. Now she was out of a job again. She thought of marrying Ben, he was so entirely different from all the other men of her acquaintance, he was joyful and he was serious. He was also good-looking: he was half-French, brought up in England. And an interesting age, thirty-one. He was a schoolteacher, but Father could probably get him a job in advertising or publishing. Father could do a lot of things for them both if only he would exert himself. Perhaps if she got married he would exert himself.

"Did you see your father at all yesterday, Carmelita?"

"No; as a matter of fact he's driven up the coast. I think he's gone to stay at some villa on the Italian border."

"I should like to see more of him," said Ben. "And have a talk with him. I've never really had a chance to have a talk with him."

"He's awfully shy," said Carmelita, "with my friends."

Sometimes she felt a stab of dissatisfaction when Ben talked about her father. Ben had read all his books through and through – that seemed rather obsessive to Carmelita, reading books a second time and a third, as if one's memory was defective. It seemed to her that Ben loved her only because she was Kenneth Hope's daughter, and then, again, it seemed to her that this couldn't be so, for Ben wasn't attracted by money and success. Carmelita knew lots of daughters of famous men, and they were beset by suitors who were keen on their fathers' money and success. But it was the books that Ben liked about her father.

"He never interferes with me," she said. "He's rather good that way."

"I would like to have a long talk with him," Ben said.

"What about? – He doesn't like talking about his work."

"No, but a man like that. I would like to know his mind."

"What about my mind?"

"You've got a lovely mind. Full of pleasant laziness. No guile." He drew his forefinger from her knee to her ankle. She was wearing a pink bikini. She was very pretty and had hoped to become a starlet before her eighteenth birthday. Now she was close to twenty-one and was thinking of marrying Ben instead, and was relieved that she no longer wanted to be an actress. He had lasted longer than any other boyfriend. She had often found a boy exciting at first but usually went off him quite soon. Ben was an intellectual, and intellectuals, say what you like, seemed to last longer than anyone else. There was more in them to find out about. One was always discovering new things – she supposed it was Father's blood in her that drew her towards the cultivated type, like Ben.

He was staying at a tiny hotel in a back street near the old quay. The entrance was dark, but the room itself was right at the top of the house, with a little balcony. Carmelita was staying with friends at a villa. She spent a lot of time in Ben's room, and sometimes slept there. It was turning out to be a remarkably happy summer.

"You won't see much of Father," she said, "if we get married. He works and sees nobody. When he doesn't write he goes away. Perhaps he'll get married again and –"

"That's all right," he said, "I don't want to marry your father."

Dora Castlemaine had several diplomas for elocution which she had never put to use. She got a part-time job, after the Christmas holidays that year, in Basil Street Grammar School in London, and her job was to try to reform the more pronounced Cockney accents of the more promising boys into a near-standard English. Her father was amazed.

"Money, money, you are always talking about money. Let us run up debts. One is nobody without debts."

"One's credit is limited, Father. Don't be an old goose."

"Have you consulted Waite?" Waite was the publisher's young man who looked after the Castlemaine royalties, diminishing year by year.

"We've drawn more than our due for the present."

"Well, it's a bore, you going out to teach."

"It may be a bore for you," she said at last, "but it isn't for me."

"Dora, do you really mean you want to go to this job in London?"

"Yes, I want to. I'm looking forward to it."

He didn't believe her. But he said, "I suppose I'm a bit of a burden on you, Dora, these days. Perhaps I ought to go off and die."

"Like Oates at the South Pole," Dora commented.

He looked at her and she looked at him. They were shrewd in their love for each other.

She was the only woman teacher in the school, with hardly the status of a teacher. She had her own corner of the common room and, anxious to reassure the men that she had no intention of intruding upon them, would, during free periods, spread out on the table one of the weekly journals and study it intently, only looking up to say good morning or good afternoon to the masters who came in with piles of exercise books under their arms. Dora had no exercise books to correct, she was something apart, a reformer of vowel sounds. One of the masters, and then another, made conversation with her during morning break, when she passed round the sugar for the coffee. Some were in their early thirties. The ginger-moustached science master was not long graduated from Cambridge. Nobody said to her, as intelligent young men had done as late as fifteen years ago, "Are you any relation, Miss Castlemaine, to Henry Castlemaine the writer?"

Ben walked with Carmelita under the trees of Lincoln's Inn Fields in the spring of the year, after school, and watched the children at their games. They were a beautiful couple. Carmelita was doing secretarial work in the City. Her father was in Morocco, having first taken them out to dinner to celebrate their engagement.

Ben said, "There's a woman at the school, teaching elocution."

"Oh?" said Carmelita. She was jumpy, because since her father's departure for Morocco Ben had given a new turn to their relationship. He would not let her stay overnight in his flat in Bayswater, not even at the weekends. He said it would be nice, perhaps, to practise restraint until they were married in the summer, and that would give them something to look forward to. "And I'm interested to see," said Ben, "what we mean to each other without sex."

This made her understand how greatly she had become obsessed with him. She thought perhaps he was practising a form of cruelty to intensify her obsession. In fact, he did want to see what they meant to each other without sex.

She called at his flat unexpectedly and found him reading, with piles of other books set out on the table as if waiting to be read.

She accused him: You only want to get rid of me so that you can read your books.

"The fourth form is reading Trollope," he explained, pointing to a novel of Trollope's among the pile.

"But you aren't studying Trollope just now."

He had been reading a life of James Joyce. He banged it down and said, "I've been reading all my life, and you won't stop me, Carmelita."

She sat down. "I don't want to stop you," she said.

"I know," he said.

"We aren't getting on at all well without sex," she said, and on that occasion stayed the night.

He was writing an essay on her father. She wished that her father had taken more interest in it. Father had taken them out to dinner with his party face, smiling and boyish. Carmelita had seen him otherwise – in his acute dejection, when he seemed hardly able to endure the light of day.

"What's the matter, Father?"

"There's a comedy of errors going on inside me, Carmelita." He sat at his desk most of the day while he was in these moods, doing nothing. Then, during the night, he would perhaps start writing, and sleep all the next morning, and gradually in the following days the weight would pass.

"There's a man on the phone wants you, Father – an interview."

"Tell him I'm in the Middle East."

"What did you think of Ben, Father?"

"A terribly nice man, Carmelita. You've made the right choice, I think."

"An intellectual – I do like them best, you know."

"I'd say he was the student type. Always will be."

"He wants to write an essay about you, Father. He's absolutely mad about your books."

"Yes."

"I mean, couldn't you help him, Father? Couldn't you talk to him about your work, you know?"

"Oh, God, Carmelita. It would be easier to write the bloody essay myself."

"All right, all right. I was only asking."

"I don't want any disciples, Carmelita. They give me the creeps."

"Yes, yes, all right. I know you're an artist, Father, there's no need to show off your temperament. I only wanted you to help Ben. I only . . ."

I only, she thought as she walked in Lincoln's Inn Fields with Ben, wanted him to help me. I should have said, "I want you to talk more to Ben, to help me." And Father would have said, "How do you mean?" And I would have said, "I don't know, quite." And he would have said, "Well, if you don't know what you mean, how the hell do I?"

Ben was saying, "There's a woman at the school, teaching elocution."

"Oh?" said Carmelita jumpily.

"A Miss Castlemaine. She's been there four months, and I only found out today that she's the daughter of Henry Castlemaine."

"But he's dead!" said Carmelita.

"Well, I thought so too. But apparently he isn't dead, he's very much alive in a house in Essex."

"How old is Miss Castlemaine?" said Carmelita.

"Middle-aged. Middle forties. Perhaps late forties. She's a nice woman, a classic English spinster. She teaches the boys to say 'How now brown cow.' You could imagine her doing wood-engravings in the Cotswolds. I only found out today –"

"You might manage to get invited to meet him, with any luck," Carmelita said.

"Yes, she said I must come and see him, perhaps for a weekend. Miss Castlemaine is going to arrange it. She was awfully friendly when she found I was a Castlemaine admirer. A lot of people must think he's dead. Of course, his work belongs to a past world, but it's wonderful. Do you know *The Pebbled Shore*? – that's an early one."

"No, but I've read *Sin of Substance*, I think. It –"

"You mean *The Sinner and the Substance*. Oh, it has fine things in it. Castlemaine's due for a revival."

Carmelita felt a sharp stab of anger with her father, and then a kind of despair which was not as yet entirely familiar to her, although already she wondered if this was how Father felt in his great depressions when he sat all day, staring and enduring, and all night miraculously wrote the ache out of his system in prose of harsh merriment.

Helplessly, she said, "Castlemaine's novels aren't as good as Father's, are they?"

"Oh, there's no comparison. Castlemaine is quite different. You can't say one type is *better* than another – goodness me!" He was looking academically towards the chimney stacks of Lincoln's Inn. This was the look in which she loved him most. After all, she thought, the Castlemaines might make everything easier for both of us.

"Father, it's really absurd. A difference of sixteen years … People will say –"

"Don't be vulgar, Dora dear. What does it matter what people say? Mere age makes no difference when there's a true affinity, a marriage of true minds."

"Ben and I have a lot in common."

"I know it," he said, and sat a little higher in his chair.

"I shall be able to give up my job, Father, and spend my time here with you again. I never really wanted that job. And you are so much better in health now …"

"I know."

"And Ben will be here in the evenings and the weekends. You get on well with Ben, don't you?"

"A remarkably fine man, Dora. He'll go far. He's perceptive."

"He's keen to revive your work."

"I know. He should give up that job, as I told him, and devote himself entirely to literary studies. A born essayist."

"Oh, Father, he'll have to keep his job for the meantime, anyhow. We'll need the money. It will help us all; we –"

"What's that? What's that you say?"

"I said he finds work in the grammar school stimulating, Father."

"Do you love the man?"

"It's a little difficult to say, at my age, Father."

"To me, you both seem children. Do you love him?"

"I feel," she said, "that I have known him much longer than I have. Sometimes I think I've known him all my life. I'm sure we have met before, perhaps even in a former existence. That's the decisive factor. There's something of *destiny* about my marrying Ben; do you know what I mean?"

"Yes, I think I do."

"He was engaged, last year for a short time, to marry quite a young girl," she said. "The daughter of a novelist called Kenneth Hope. Have you heard of him, Father?"

"Vaguely," he said. "Ben," he said, "is a born disciple."

She looked at him and he looked at her, shrewd in their love for each other.

OPEN TO THE PUBLIC

This story, written in 1989, is a sequel to "The Fathers' Daughters", 1959

Warily she moves from room to room, lingering over the mortal furniture which resembles in style, but has long since replaced, the lost originals. This is the house of the young Jean-Jacques Rousseau, Les Charmettes, on the outskirts of Chambéry in the Savoie district of France, where from 1736 to 1742 he vitally resided with clever Mme de Warens, his mature friend, thirteen years his senior, to whom he was official lover and whom he called "Maman". It was their summer residence.

It is early spring. There had been few visitors, the guardian has told her when she bought her ticket and a brochure, downstairs at the entrance. As in most of these out-of-the-way preserved houses of the famous, the good guardian was willing to unfold the history of the place down there in his lodge beside a stove, and not at all anxious about letting a well-behaved and quiet-looking visitor roam free among the chilly rooms, downstairs and up.

It is upstairs that she finds a fellow-visitor. She is not

sure why she is surprised but possibly this is because she hasn't heard him moving about until she comes upon him staring into the little alcove where Jean-Jacques Rousseau's bed, or a replica of his bed, is fitted.

The man is tall and thin, somewhere about thirty, casually dressed in a black short coat and greenish-brown trousers. When he turns to look at her she sees his jersey is black with a rim of his white shirt showing at the neck, so that one might take him for a clergyman, but for the trousers. He has a long face, fairish hair, greyish eyes. His casual outfit is slightly outdated although in fact quite smart and expensive. And she has seen him before. He looks away and then he looks again in her direction. Why?

Because he has seen her before.

She continues her tour of the rooms, noticing details as is her way. Close details. The wallpaper in Mme de Warens's room is original eighteenth century, it is said, with small hand-painted flowers. This is the grandest room in the house. Two great windows look out on to the cold garden of early spring and beyond that, the valley and the mountains. Down there in the garden the enamoured young man Rousseau waited each morning, looking up for the shutters to open and "it was day *chez maman* –"

She goes downstairs again, having another look at all there is to see. She sees the other visitor at the porter's vestibule, his back turned towards her. He is buying postcards. She leaves the museum and goes her way. Outside the gates a small cream-coloured Peugeot is parked.

* * *

You must have heard of Ben Donadieu, the biographer and son-in-law of Henry Castlemaine the novelist. He had married Dora Castlemaine in 1960, passionate about her ageing father's once-famous novels which were already falling into a phase of obscurity. About Dora herself he was not at all passionate and for this she was rather thankful. Sixteen years older than Ben, she was then forty-six, spinsterish. Her true object of love was her once-famous father. She married Ben, then about thirty, mainly because he had a job as a schoolmaster, a means of livelihood to assist her father's dwindling income and to enable her to give up her job and devote herself to her father.

Henry Castlemaine loved his daughter dearly, and himself a little more. He accepted the basis of the marriage as he had in the long past accepted the adulation of his readers and the discipleship of young critics. Ben moved into the Castlemaine house and in the evenings and school holidays set about sorting the Castlemaine papers, and taking voluminous notes on his conversations with the ageing novelist. Castlemaine was now eighty-five.

It was about three years later, after the biography was published, that the Castlemaine revival set in. The Castlemaine novels were reprinted, they were filmed and televised. When Henry Castlemaine died he was once again at the height of his fame.

He left his house to his daughter, Dora. All his papers, all his literary estate, everything. Ben, however, had the royalties from his biography of Henry Castlemaine. They were fairly substantial.

In those last years of Castlemaine's life, their financial position had improved, largely through the initial efforts of

Ben to revive his father-in-law's fame. They were able to employ a cook and a maid, leaving Dora free to be a real companion to her father and take him for drives in their new Volkswagen.

Nobody was surprised when, after Castlemaine's death, the marriage broke up. It's only real basis had been the couple's devotion to Dora's father. Ben, now still a young and sprightly thirty-five and Dora fifty-one, oldish for her age, had nothing in common except their memories of the old man. He had been authoritative and tiresome, but Dora hadn't minded. Ben had felt the personal weight of his famous father-in-law. He had put up with it, for the sake of the admired works, and his own efforts to promote them, day by day, in his study, docketing the archives, on the telephone to television and film producers.

In the early days of his marriage he had tried to make love to Dora, and succeeded fairly often out of sheer enthusiasm for her father. Dora herself couldn't keep it up. She was obsessed by her father, and Ben was no substitute. Now Ben was left with the proceeds of his biography. His work was done. Dora was immensely rich.

Henry Castlemaine was buried. A crowded memorial service, reporters, television; and the next week it was over. Henry Castlemaine lived on in his posthumous fame, but Dora and Ben were no longer a couple.

It was at this point that very little was publicly known. It was understood that Dora refused to leave the house of her childhood and her father's life. Ben took a flat in London and grumbled to his friends that Dora was stingy. She gave him an allowance. The proceeds from his biography could not last forever.

He wrote a lot of Castlemaine essays, and was said to be thinking of some other subject, something fresh to write about.

Within a few months Dora suggested a divorce:

Dear Ben,

I intend to see my lawyer, Bassett. He will no doubt be in touch with you. I know Father would have wished us to stay together and to love each other as he wished from the start. It was Father's wish that I should never want for anything, indeed he hated to talk about the financial details of life in those old days when his books had started to fade out, and we met. I know that Father would have wished me to show my appreciation, and express his acknowledgment, of the part you played in our life, (even although I am of course convinced that the revival of Father's great reputation would have been inevitable in any case). That is why I have instructed Bassett to offer you a monthly allowance which you are free to accept or reject according to your conscience. The divorce should go through as quietly and smoothly as possible. Father would have wished that at least. Above all, Father, I think, would have wished for complete discretion on the fact that our union was a marriage in name only, even although the situation could be amply testified to by the domestics (who are of course always aware of everything, as Father always said.) So I could have obtained a divorce quite easily on other grounds than mutual consent thus saving the allowance I am offering you in amicable settlement. I trust you have benefited by your stay with us under our roof for these years past.

Father would wish me to enjoy the fruits of his

labours, and soon I shall be taking a trip abroad, especially to those haunts so beloved of Father.

Yours, in good faith,
Dora Castlemaine

It was that "in good faith", more than her formal signature, that chilled Ben's bones. He recalled a phrase from one of Henry Castlemaine's books: "Beware the wickedness of the righteous."

What is there to see in the austere and awesome birthplace of Joan of Arc at Domrémy-la-Pucelle in the Vosges? It is full of grey-walled emptiness, and there is no doubt, someone has been here and has gone. It stands just off the road, in the shade of a large tree. Near by is a bridge over the Meuse where a man hovers, looking down at the water. A small cream-coloured Peugeot is parked close by, waiting for him, with the driver's door open. He has got in once and got out again. He has looked round at the woman who has been watching him while he tours the simple birthplace, now open to the public. The woman watches him as he drives away, too fast, away and away, so that the guardian at the ticket entrance comes out to join her on the road, staring after him.

Ben and Dora were never divorced. He showed her letter round their friends. It had been the couple's boast that they had few friends, but, as always when "a few friends" come to be counted up, they amounted to a surprising number. Most of them were indignant.

"That's a shabby way to treat you, Ben. First, you build up a fortune for her, and now she . . ."

"Ben, you must see a lawyer. You are entitled to . . ."

"What a cold, what a very frigid letter. But between you and me, she was always in love with her father. It was incestuous."

"I won't go to a lawyer," Ben said. "I'll go to see Dora."

He went to see her, unannounced. The door was opened by a tall, fat youth who beamed with delight when Ben gave his name and demanded his wife.

"Dora's in the kitchen."

The father's smell had gone from the house. Ben glanced through the dining-room door on the way to the kitchen. There was new wallpaper, a new carpet. Dora was there in the kitchen, unhappy of face, beating up an omelette. The kitchen table was laid for a meal, which meal no one could guess, whether lunch or breakfast. It was four-fifteen in the afternoon. Anyway, Dora was unhappy. She clung to her unhappiness, Ben saw clearly. It was all she had.

The flaccid youth scraped a chair across the kitchen floor towards Ben. "Make yourself at home," he said.

Ben turned to leave.

"Stay, don't go," said Dora. "We should sit down and discuss the situation like three civilized people."

"I've had enough of three civilized people," Ben said. "There was your father and you, so very civilized; and I was civilized enough to let myself be used and then thrown out when I was no more use."

The flabby youth said, "As I understand it you were never a husband to Dora. She let herself be used as a means to your relationship with her father."

"Who is he?" Ben demanded, indicating the young man.

Dora brought an omelette to the table and set it before her friend. "Eat it while it's hot. Don't wait for me." She started breaking eggs into the bowl. The youth commenced to eat.

"Isn't there a drink in the house?" said Ben. "This is sordid." He got up and went into the living-room where the drinks were set out, as always, on a tray. When he got back with his whisky and soda, the young man's place was empty, part of his omelette still on his plate. Ben then saw through the kitchen window the ends of the young man's trousers and his shoes disappearing up the half-flight of steps which led to the garden and a door to the lane behind. Dora, with her omelette-turner still in her hand went to shut the kitchen door which had been left open.

"You can have this omelette," said Dora. "I'll make another for myself."

"I couldn't eat it, thanks, at this hour. What happened to your friend?"

"I suppose he was embarrassed when he saw you," said Dora.

"About what?"

"About his coming to live here and opening the house to the public. I owe it to Father. First I'll have a trip abroad and then, believe me, I'll arrange for a companion, an assistant, somebody, to help me turn the house into a museum. Father's rooms, his manuscripts."

"Well, that was my idea," Ben said. "That's what we were always planning to do when Henry was dead."

"You aren't the only Castlemaine enthusiast," Dora said. "I'm not too old to marry again and I could open the house to the public, only certain rooms, the important ones. I've had the house repainted and the floors mended. I could do it with a new partner."

"Why on earth should you want to marry again?"

"The usual reasons," Dora said. "Love, sex, companionship. The Castlemaine idea wasn't enough, after all. You can't go to bed with an idea."

"You used to," he said, "when Henry was alive."

"Well, I don't now."

"Do you mind if I look over the house before I go?" Ben said.

Dora studied her watch. She sighed. She put the dishes in the sink.

"I'll come with you," she said. "What exactly do you want?"

"To see for myself what it's like now."

They went from room to room. The chairs were newly upholstered, the walls and woodwork freshly painted. In Henry Castlemaine's study his papers were piled on the floor on a plastic sheet, his desk had been replaced by a trestle-table on which more papers and manuscripts were piled. "I'm working on the papers," said Dora. "It'll take time. A lot of his books have been re-bound and some are still at the binders."

Ben looked at the shelves. The books that Henry had used most, his shabby poetry, his worn reference books, were now done up in glittering gold and half-calf bindings.

"You'll never get through those papers yourself," Ben said. "It's an enormous job. The letters alone –"

"I'll have them in showcases," Dora said, her voice monotonous and weary. "I can get help, lots of help."

"Look," said Ben. "I know you can get help. But it's a professional job. You need scholars, people with taste."

"All right, I'll get scholars, people with taste."

"Do you intend to marry that young man, what was his name?"

"I could marry him. I haven't decided," she said.

"Do you mean he's a manuscript expert?"

"Oh, no," she said. "I wouldn't let a fellow like that touch Father's papers. But he'd be very good at the entrance-hall, giving out tickets, when I open the house to the public. Can't you see him in that role?"

"Yes, I can," said Ben.

"The divorce should go through –"

"Look, Dora, I must tell you that I'm going to make a claim. I'm entitled to a share of what I've built up for you over the last seven years."

"I expected you would. The lawyer expected it. We'll make a settlement."

"Castlemaine was nowhere when I married you."

"I said we'll make a settlement."

"It's a sad end to our ambitions," Ben said. "We were always going to open the house to the public, Henry knew that. Now you'll make a mess of it, are making a mess of it. You'll never get through those archives."

"Are you proposing to come back here and work on the papers?" she said.

"I might consider it. For Henry's sake."

"But for my sake?"

"For Henry's sake. You didn't marry me for my sake. It was always Father, Father."

"Yes," she said, "and now Father's dead. We have no more in common."

"We still have our ambition for the Castlemaine museum in common, our dreams."

"It's time for you to go. I want some sleep," Dora said, her eyes fixed on her watch.

As she closed the study door there was the sound behind them in the study of a bundle of papers slithering to the floor, blown by the draught. Then, another thump of paper urged on by the displacement of the first lot. Dora took no notice.

The visitors, it seems to the young girl-student who is taking her turn at the entrance-desk, appear to be nervously aware of each other, although they have arrived separately. There is something old-fashioned about them both. It is not exactly the cut and style of their clothes that gives them this impression; it is not exactly anything; it is something inexact. They are both English or perhaps American: the girl's ear is not attuned to the difference, especially as they have each said so few words when buying their ticket. "How long has the museum been open?" and "Is that really Freud's hat?" Freud's hat, a bourgeois light-brown felt hat, is hanging on the coat-stand with Freud's walking stick. The girl follows the visitors. The man is tall, good-looking, around thirty. The woman, prim with her hair combed back into a bun is older. They look studious, as do most people who come to visit the house of Sigmund Freud at 19 Berggasse, Vienna. But the fact that they look at each other from time to time anxiously, then anxiously look away, makes the young guardian of the shrine feel increasingly nervous. There are precious objects lying about: a collection of primitive artefacts on the studio table, manuscripts and letters in the glass-topped show-tables. Could the visitors be accomplices in a projected robbery?

"That is the Couch," says the girl-student. "Yes, the original Couch." The couch is large, floppy and soft. One could go to sleep forever in it, sinking deeper and deeper.

"And this is the waiting-room."

"Ah, the waiting-room," says the young man.

"Is it haunted?" says the woman, touching one of the red plush chairs lined up against the wall, themselves waiting for something.

"Hunted?" says the puzzled girl.

"No, haunted. Ghosts."

"No," says the young woman, looking behind her in sharp surprise, for the man has left abruptly, and is already outside the door of the flat. When she turns back to the woman she is amazed to find nobody there.

At the family home of Louis Pasteur the bacteriologist at Arbois, in the rainy Jura, she is there and so is he. "This was the dining table. This is the board where he carved. What rain! – will it never stop? You would like to see the laboratory, Madame, Monsieur, this way." It is taken for granted they are a couple. The laboratory is scrubbed but somehow dusty, and a few old books are lying about realistically: ". . . his researches into organisms and fermentations."

"Few people," says the young man, in lucid but foreign French, "realize that pasteurized milk comes from Pasteur."

"True," says the guide.

The couple leave together. Outside in the rain she says, "It's time for you to stop following me."

"I'm not following you," he says, "I'm following our ambition. It's for you to go back where you came from. It was you who broke away."

"There is no contract," she says. "No pledge. It was you who provoked the rift. We never had a marriage that you could call a marriage. As I've told you, I have always intended to open Father's house to the public after Father's death."

"You'll never do it," he says. "Not without me. I'm part of the ambition. I have to go on."

"You're the ghost of an ambition," she says.

"So are you, the ghost of a dream and a plan."

He gets into his car and drives off leaving her in the wet, old street.

Dora opened the door of her father's study and closed it again. It was two years since he died. Her new young man was the third in the series and, like his two predecessors, his enthusiasm for helping to put the papers in order and setting up the house as a museum, had waned or perhaps was never there. But unlike the others he has had a good effect on Dora. This young man was in the wholesale fashion business; his attempts to smarten up Dora's appearance had been successful. In her fifties Dora looked healthy for the first time in her life. His devotion to her, or rather, his quite eccentric passion, always did wonders for her morale, as she herself put it.

"Apart from being Henry Castlemaine's daughter,

what is there in me for you?" she once asked the new young man.

"You're fascinating by yourself."

It was, in a way, all she wanted to hear or know from him. The very next day she had telephoned to Ben. A woman's voice answered the phone, a silly voice. "Who's speaking?" – "His wife." – "Oh, wife." – "Yes, wife." (Voice off: "Ben, it's for you. She says she's your wife.") – A pause and Ben is on the phone. "Yes, Dora, what do you want?" – "Lionel and I have to make a decision about Father's papers. I think you could be helpful." – "Who's Lionel?" – "My friend." – "I thought he was Tim." – "No, Tim was last year. Anyway . . ." – "I'll come round one day." – "Better make it soon." – "Some time in the next couple of weeks, I can't manage sooner."

She is appalled to see him at the Brontë's house of doom and dread, at Haworth in Yorkshire.

"This is where they walked up and down at night, after dinner, here in this dining-room, planning the future –"

Outside, in the graveyard among the tombstones, there by Emily Brontë's grave, she turns and says,

"Stop following me."

A small group of American visitors are watching them. They see a neurotic-looking woman in her mid-forties apparently trying to shake off a bewildered man in his late twenties or early thirties, both slightly outmoded in their appearance.

"People are looking at us," he says.

"It is my one hope," she says, "that we should open the house for Father. I've been round so many houses. They are all so bleak. Museums have no heart."

"Stop haunting them," he says. "That's what I've come to tell you."

"Then you'll be free, is that it?"

"Don't tell me," he says, "that you're free, wandering around in this timelessness, as you do."

They walk away, he to his car and she to nowhere. The American group are already standing before the solemn Brontë graves, reading the inscriptions.

It is at Lamb House, Rye, in East Sussex that the ghosts of their ambition finally reach a decision.

"Would you like to sign the book?" says the curator. "This is where James received his visitors; yes, it is rather small, quite poky; yes, indeed with his bulk he must have found it quite cramped. But upstairs –"

Out in the garden beside the graves of Henry James's dogs Ben says,

"I don't know how you could bear to open your old home to the public. It's so charming as it is."

"If it wasn't for Father I would feel the same," Dora says. "But Father's ambition was always for his fame to be perpetuated, for ever and ever, it seems, elongated, on and on into the future."

"The future has arrived," he says, "and you've done nothing about it but sit around drinking with your young men, thinking of your father."

"And what have you been doing?"

"Sitting around drinking with my girls, thinking of your father."

"To hell with Father," she says.

Dora opened the door.

"Lionel was desolate," she said. "I was a bit sad myself, for he was the best of the lot. But he knew he had to go."

"You've got a new haircut," he said.

"Have you come for Father, his papers?"

"No, I've come for you."

She led the way upstairs in the new freedom of her trousers, and opened the door to the hopeless study, with its piles of archives going back to 1890 or worse.

"I suppose we should give them to a university," she said.

"We would never be free," he said. "Those ghosts, those ghosts, would never let us go. Letters from students, letters from scholars. It would be the same old industry."

They lit a bonfire in the garden that night. It took them many hours to burn all the Castlemaine papers. But they sat around drinking in the back wash-house, watching the flames curl round the papers and going out every now and again to feed the fire with a new armful, until they were all consumed.

THE DRAGON

I was standing talking at a cocktail party when I was saddened to see that everybody formed a forest. I felt defeated. The Dragon had taken over.

No sooner did I feel this, than I decided it was only a temporary defeat, for that is what I am like. I didn't see then how I could possibly do it, but certainly, I decided, I was going to stop the Dragon. The party was people again. I picked up the conversation at the point where a man in the group was talking. He was good-looking, about sixty. "My address book," he was saying, "is becoming like a necropolis, so many people dying every month, this friend, that friend. You have to draw a line through their names. It's very sad." "I always use pencil," said a lady, a little younger, "then when people pass on I can rub them out."

We were in a shady part of the garden. It was six o'clock on a hot evening in the north of Italy. It was my garden, my party. The Dragon came oozing through the foliage. She was holding her drink, a Pimm's No. 1, and was followed by a tall, strikingly handsome truck-driver whom she had brought along to the party on the spur of the moment. To her dismay, discernible only to myself, he was a genial, easy-mannered young man, rather amused to be taking half-an-hour off the job with his truck parked outside the gate. I knew very well that when she had picked him up at the bar across the street she had hoped he would be an embarrassment, a nuisance.

Oh, the Dragon! Dragon was what it was her job to be. She had been highly and pressingly recommended by one of my clients, the widow of a well-known dramatist. It didn't occur to me, then, that the vertiginous blurb that was written to me about the girl was in fact so excessive as to be suspicious. Perhaps I did feel uneasy about the eulogies that came over the telephone, and the letters which the widow wrote to me from Gstaad about the Dragon and her virtues as such. Perhaps I did. But, as often when I want to believe something enough because I am in need of help, I didn't listen to the small inner voice which said, Something is wrong, or which said, Be careful. I was optimistic and enthusiastic.

I was first and foremost a needlewoman. I have been called a *couturier*, a dressmaker, a designer. But it was my fascination with the needle and thread that earned me my reputation. I could have gone into big business, I could have merged with any of the world's famous houses of *haute couture*. But I would have none of that. I preferred to keep my own exclusive and small clientele. It wasn't everybody I would sew for.

When I left school at the beginning of the sixties there were two things I could do well. One was write a good letter in fine calligraphy, and the other was sew, by hand, with every stitch perfect. I worked as a seamstress, in the alterations department of a London store. This taught me a lot, but it didn't satisfy me. At home, I started making my own clothes.

I had learned at my evening classes how to make an individual working dummy for each client. I was very careful about this, and I practised on my grandmother with whom I lived. You cut a length of buckram into a body-shape and sew your lady into it over the minimum of underwear. I did this with my grandmother, basting the buckram on her body with only an exact inch to spare. She thought she would never get out of it again. Then, I slit it up the front with my scissors, sewed it up again the exact one-inch seam. When I had perfected the sewing on the buckram with even, small, back-stitching I filled the shape with fine-teased raw wool. There was my grandmother's perfect shape to set on my stand. Some dressmakers use synthetic fabrics, if they still employ this process, but I wouldn't touch them.

I made my grandmother a dress she was proud of to the day she died. It was velvet lined with silk, every inside-seam edged with narrow lace, both dress and lining. Nobody could see how beautifully it was finished inside. I have always stitched lace to my inside seams. Even if nobody ever saw the reverse side, my clients were the sort of women who are satisfied with the knowledge that they are beautifully dressed in garments made by hand and edged inside with very narrow lace, even when a silk lining hides the whip-stitched lace-edged seams. Hem-stitch, back-stitch, cross-stitch, slip-stitch, buttonhole-stitch – I can do them to perfection. No sewing machine has ever stood in my workshop. You might say it was my obsession to turn out a hand-made dress. My clients would say, "Do you mean that you even do the long seams by hand?" "Everything by hand," I replied. It's been the secret of my success. You would be surprised at the demand for dresses and blouses and skirts and underwear all made by hand – I've accomplished entire *trousseaux* for clients who were prepared to give me time and pay the price.

A long time has passed since I made my grandmother's dress, and since I set up on my own. My reputation as a superb seamstress was growing all the time, so that I no longer made clothes from paper patterns but employed my own men as cutters and designers. For cutting and designing you can't beat a man; and the clients prefer them, too. The cutters and designers have come and gone over the years. I never married any of them although I came near to doing so very often. Something within me told me not to make a permanent life with any of the cutters and designers. Fashions change so much from season to season, year to year. Cutters and designers often get stuck in a certain period, and never move on; their best work is over. Needleworkers, on the other hand, never go out of date, and I was always a needlewoman with a difference. There is a big difference between the seams that are right for velvet and those for chiffon, and I have devised ways of sewing a lace dress where you wouldn't know there was any seam at all. Lately I got my needles from Frankfurt, and my threads from London. My speciality was in the textiles that I obtained from all over the world.

So I had come to Como for silk, and was already fairly comfortably placed with my exclusive clientele. Like my textiles, they came from all parts of the world, even the wives of ambassadors from Eastern Europe. I saw a lovely house for sale on the shores of Lake Como and decided to settle there, and make a new workshop.

Now I was so well known for my hand-made dresses that

I had to have some sort of protection. It takes a long time to make one hand-made evening dress or wedding-gown, so I couldn't possibly answer the telephone to all the millionairesses and their secretaries, who wanted me to work for them. Ordinary maids and *au pair* helpers were very weak, and easily bribed. They would let people in or call me to the phone just when I was stitching a circular piece or a corner – very much precision-work. My temperament wouldn't stand it. At the same time, I had learned over the years that the more you discourage your prospective clients the more they want your work, and the higher the price they are prepared to pay.

I decided to take on a Dragon, whose job it was to keep new clients at a distance, to tell them that they must write for an appointment; and she was to be very firm about this. Her other job was to look after the files of all my clients of the past, so that my business could go forward in good order, with that personal touch of remembering small items when the client finally succeeded in making an appointment. At this time I had a brilliant cutter called Daniele; he couldn't design originals, but that is a small matter; Daniele could copy and adapt. I would advise him a little – which materials to cut on the bias and which to cut, for instance, with the patterns not matching at the seams, to make an intriguing change. I usually did the fittings and pinnings myself, because I have that very exact eye. Daniele was well-paid. He was inclined to be arrogant; he felt the traditional *couture* business, where the designers employ the cutters and seamstresses, was the true thing, and that my method was the wrong way round. But I soon let him know how to mind his business, and the pay kept him quiet.

I started to interview Dragons. A sewing assistant, I explained, was out of the question for me. All the more did I need protection, and time, long stretches of time all to myself. Every stitch had to be perfect, I explained, small and perfect. Even the basting and tacking stitches, which later had to be drawn out, had to be done by me, or I could not sleep at night. Sometimes, to make an elaborate dress, I needed two clear months, working on that one dress alone. With embroidery, I needed three or four months. All this I explained to the candidates for the job. There were eight. I brought them out from England to be interviewed on the spot where the job was offered. A frightened bunch, with one exception. The others were glad to get away after the interview and profit by their trip to Italy to go and see the sights and have a good time. The eighth looked more suspicious than afraid while I explained what the job was to be. She frowned a lot. Emily Butler. Tall, skinny, with her top teeth protruding, and a lot of red hair. She understood a little Italian and spoke French, as indeed had the other girls whom I'd brought out to be interviewed, otherwise I wouldn't have brought them. But Emily: I thought she would make a good Dragon. She was to keep everybody away from me except an approved short list of clients, or people highly recommended by the clients. Even then, I was never to be called to the telephone. The client must either write or leave a number for me to call back at my leisure. Emily had brought an additional good reference from an opera singer she had worked for; she seemed to understand what was wanted. I remembered having heard somewhere that women with protruding teeth are very attractive to men, but I didn't see that this was a factor that mattered, anyway. In fact, what happened had nothing to do with Emily's teeth.

The Dragon was a marvel that spring and early summer. I worked without a break, seven days a week, sometimes twelve hours a day, frequently in a summer-house in the garden except during the very hot hours of the day when I kept to my air-conditioned workroom. I must tell you about the garden and about the house.

The house was set well back from the road on a high cliff looking over the lake. It had been built at the turn of the century with many features of *art-nouveau*, such as stained-glass windows, curly banisters, and fruity decorations above the doors. From the outside, the villa seemed to have more colonnades, arches, terraces, bow-windows and turrets than its size really warranted; this means, for instance, that there were two turrets, and none would have been enough. The garden was large, really out of proportion to the house; but this suited me very well. I liked to sit and sew in the garden, especially under a mighty cedar tree that had become my banner; you could see it from the opposite shore of the lake, you could look down on it from the cliff-road; wherever you were, or from wherever you approached in those parts you couldn't miss the cedar tree. It soared above the statues in the garden. There, on the garden seat I would do my button-holing in tranquillity – for I would never sew a zip fastener into a dress – looping the thread as I made each stitch; and if it was a blouse to be embroidered I used to sit coolly and do my satin-stitch or split-stitch.

In the garden were white stone statues of the period. They represented the Four Seasons and Four Arts (Painting,

Sculpture, Music and Literature). The Seasons were female figures and the Arts, male, but all garbed so that it made very little difference. The Painter held a palette in one hand and a paint-brush in the other; the Sculptor worked on a stone lion; the Musician held a flute in his left hand, with his arm stretched out, and with the other, corrected a music score that was cleverly set up in stone in front of him; the Writer reclined, making notes in a book. The Seasons were garlanded according to the time of year they represented; their hair flowed; Winter was adorned with holly and icicles; Spring with flowers of the field; Summer with roses and cherries; Autumn had a necklace of grapes, and leaned on a sheaf of corn. The garden was very striking. Some of my clients would exclaim over it, with delight; others would just stare and, with a strange silence, say nothing at all. As for the statues, they struck me as odd sometimes when I turned suddenly and looked back at them. They looked exactly the same as before; that is, they seemed to have recomposed their features. What had been their expression behind my back?

The Dragon erupted in her spare time with Daniele the cutter, and they made love after lunch in the room off the cool back kitchen where the Dragon slept. Her red hair was growing longer and she kept it flying loose. She said it was Pre-Raphaelite, to go with the house.

In August came extraordinary rains, leaving the air between downfalls soporific and bewildered. The Dragon said to me, "Why do you work so hard? What is it all for?" Nobody had ever before asked me a question like that. It seemed sacrilegious. I began to notice that my clients arrived late for their fittings. When you live out of town, you must expect certain delays. But, in fact they didn't come so very late to the house; rather, they were kept gossiping with the Dragon in her office, no matter that I was kept waiting in my workroom. Later, she wouldn't tell me what my clients had to say to her or she to them. I noticed that, with me, curiously enough, people started to speak in a low careful voice after they had first talked to the Dragon. When the Dragon took a boat out on the lake with Daniele, her red hair blew over her face; mostly, she came back drenched from the rain. Now, one day, I observed that she was breathing fire.

"Emily," I said, "I think you're not very well."

"Can you wonder?" she said; and the smoke rose from her nostrils, flaming like her hair. "Can you wonder? Always no, no, no on the telephone. Always, keep away, nobody come here, Madam is busy, have you an appointment? It wears you down," she said, "always playing the negative role." Her nose was perfectly cool by now as if there had been no smoke, no flame flaring.

I agreed to let her invite the local people for an evening party. She brought a group from the smart hotel across the lake whom she had somehow got friendly with. She brought a number of Spaniards who were touring the lake, to make Daniele happy, and Daniele's sister from Milan also arrived. I noticed that three of my most exclusive clients were among the women who came to that party. And there was the handsome truck-driver. The Dragon had called in a caterer of the first importance and ordered refreshments of the last rarity. She was efficient.

The Dragon had taken over, and I knew it when the forest formed around me. She came through the people, the trees, towards me, blowing fire. Then I saw that the statues, the Four Seasons, the Four Artists, were wearing materials from my workroom. They were pinned and draped as if the statues were my working manikins, and my guests marvelled at them. One of the statues, the Winter one, was actually wearing an evening dress that I was in the process of sewing. I looked round for Daniele. He was entertaining the boat-officer from the little lake port by blowing smoke through two cigarettes stuck one in each of his nostrils. The Dragon was drinking her Pimm's, green-eyed, watching me. I went up to the good-looking truck-driver who was standing around not knowing what to do with himself, and I said, "Where are you going with your truck?" He was going to Düsseldorf with a load, and back again across Europe. His name was Simon K. Clegg, the "K" standing for Kurt. For a few moments we discussed the adventures of heavy transport in the Common Market. Finally, I said, "Let's go."

I left the party and climbed into the truck beside him and off we went. Suddenly I remembered my raincoat and my passport, the two indispensable vade-mecums of travel, but Simon Kurt said, for a raincoat and a passport leave it to him. The Dragon ran up the road after us a little way, snorting and breathing green fire from her mouth – perhaps it had a copper sulphate or copper chloride basis; I have heard that you can get a green flame from skilfully blowing green Chartreuse on to a lighted candle. She was followed by Daniele. However, off we went, waving, leaving the Dragon and Daniele and the party and all my household to sort out the mess and the anxiety, and the stitching and matching, forever.

Forever? Before we reached the city of Como, nearly

twenty-five miles from my house, my conversation with Simon K. Clegg had turned on the meaning of forever. We parked the truck and went for a walk into town to a bar where we ordered coffee and ice-creams. Simon said he definitely felt that he didn't understand "forever", and doubted if there was any such thing as always and always, if that's what it meant. I told him that so far as I knew to date, forever was slip-stitch, split-stitch, cross-stitch, back-stitch; and also buttonhole and running-stitches.

"You've got me guessing," said Simon. "It's above my head, all that. Don't you want a lift, then? Get away from the party and all?"

I explained that the Dragon was in my home, questioning the value of all the materials and the sewing, the buckram, the soft, soft silk; and the run-and-fell seams, the fine lace edging. Buttonholes. Satin-stitch. I told him about her liaison with Daniele the cutter.

"Her what?"

"Her love affair."

"They should go away on holiday," was Simon's point of view.

"There's too much work to do."

"Well, if she's the lady in charge, it's up to her what she does in business hours. The garment industry's flourishing."

"I am the lady in charge," I said.

He was taken aback, as if he had been deceived.

"I thought," he said, "that you were some sort of employee."

Really, he was a nice-looking truck-driver. He pushed away his glass of ice-cream as if he had something newly on his mind.

He said, "My sister works in a textile and garment factory in Lyons. Good pay, short hours. She's a seamer."

"A seamstress," I said.

"She calls it seamer."

"I sew my seams by hand," I said.

"By hand? How do you do that?"

"With a needle and thread."

"What does that involve?" he said, in a way that forced me to realize he had never seen a needle and thread.

I explained the technique of how you use the fingers of your right hand to replace the needle and shuttle of the sewing machine, while holding the material with your left hand. He listened carefully. He was almost deferential. "It must save you a lot of electricity," he observed.

"But surely," I said, "you've seen someone sewing on a button?"

"I don't have any clothes with buttons. Not in my line."

But he was thinking of something else.

"Would you mind lying low in the cabin of the truck while I pass the customs and immigration?" he said. "It's quite comfortable and they won't look in there. They just look at my papers. I've delivered half my load and I've got to take the rest across the St Gotthard to a hotel at Brunnen in Switzerland. Then on to Düsseldorf. Health crackers from Lyons."

But I, too, was thinking of something else, and I didn't answer immediately.

"I thought you were an employee," he said. "If I'd known you were the employer I'd have thought up something better."

It saddened me to hear the anxiety in his voice. I said,

"I'm afraid I'm in charge of my business." I was thinking of the orders mounting up for next winter. I had a lady from Boston who was coming specially next Tuesday across the Atlantic, across the Alps, to order her dresses from my range of winter fabrics which included a length of wool so soft you would think it was muslin, coloured pale shrimp, and I had that deep blue silk-velvet, not quite midnight blue, but something like midnight with a glisten of royal blue which I would line with identical coloured silk, for an evening occasion, with the quarter-centimetre wide lace hand-sewn on all the seams. I had another client from Milan for my grey wool-chiffon with the almost indiscernible orange stripe, to be made up as a three-piece garment flowing like a wintry cloud; I had the design ready for the cutter and I had matched all the threads.

I was going on to think of other lengths and bales and clients when Simon penetrated my thoughts and ideas with his voice. "Look, you're breathing fire. You must have some sort of electricity," he said; and he stood up and took the check off the table. He looked shaken. "I can see that you could be a Dragon in your way."

I slipped out of the bar while he was paying the bill at the counter. I waited till after dark and hired a car to take me back to my villa. Everyone had gone home. The statues in the garden stood again unclothed. Emily Butler was in the living-room talking to Daniele. I had been sorry to part with the nice-looking truck-driver. He seemed to have a certain liking for me, a sympathy with my nature and my looks which I know are very much those of the serious unadorned seamstress. Some people like that sort of personality. But when I thought of how, as Simon had observed, I was really the

Dragon in the case I couldn't have gone over the border with him. Perhaps forever. Neither my temperament nor my temperature would stand it.

I stood, now, at the living-room door and looked at Emily and Daniele. Emily gasped; Daniele sprang to his feet, his eyes terrified.

"She's breathing fire," said Emily, and escaped through the French windows. Daniele followed her quickly, knocking over a chair as he went. He looked once over his shoulder, and then he was away after Emily.

I went to the kitchen and made some hot milk. I waited there while the sound of their creeping back, and the bumps of hasty packing went on in Daniele's room upstairs and Emily's at the back of the house.

Finally, they bundled themselves into the hall and out of the house, into Daniele's car, and away, without even waiting for their wages.

My business flourishes and I manage it without a Dragon. Without a cutter too, for I've found I have a talent for cutting. I've also invented a new stitch, the dragon-stitch. It looks lovely on the uneven hems of those dresses people like, which suggest the nineteen-thirties – for the evening but not too much. The essence of the dragon-stitch is that you see all the stitches; they are large, in a bright-coloured thick thread to contrast with the colour of the dress; one line and two forks, one line and two forks, in, out and away, all along the dipping and rising hemline, as if for always and always.

THE LEAF-SWEEPER

Behind the town hall there is a wooded parkland which, towards the end of November, begins to draw a thin blue cloud right into itself; and as a rule the park floats in this haze until mid-February. I pass every day, and see Johnnie Geddes in the heart of this mist, sweeping up the leaves. Now and again he stops, and jerking his long head erect, looks indignantly at the pile of leaves, as if it ought not to be there; then he sweeps on. This business of leaf-sweeping he learnt during the years he spent in the asylum; it was the job they always gave him to do; and when he was discharged the town council gave him the leaves to sweep. But the indignant movement of the head comes naturally to him, for this has been one of his habits since he was the most promising and buoyant and vociferous graduate of his year. He looks much older than he is, for it is not quite twenty years ago that Johnnie founded the Society for the Abolition of Christmas.

Johnnie was living with his aunt then. I was at school, and in the Christmas holidays Miss Geddes gave me her nephew's pamphlet, *How to Grow Rich at Christmas*. It sounded very likely, but it turned out that you grow rich at Christmas by doing away with Christmas, and so pondered Johnnie's pamphlet no further.

But it was only his first attempt. He had, within the next three years, founded his society of Abolitionists. His new book, *Abolish Christmas or We Die*, was in great demand at the public library, and my turn for it came at last. Johnnie was really convincing, this time, and most people were completely won over until after they had closed the book. I got an old copy for sixpence the other day, and despite the lapse of time it still proves conclusively that Christmas is a national crime. Johnnie demonstrates that every human-unit in the kingdom faces inevitable starvation within a period inversely proportional to that in which one in every six industrial-productivity units, if you see what he means, stops producing toys to fill the stockings of the educational-intake units. He cites appalling statistics to show that 1.024 per cent of the time squandered each Christmas in reckless shopping and thoughtless churchgoing brings the nation closer to its doom by five years. A few readers protested, but Johnnie was able to demolish their muddled arguments, and meanwhile the Society for the Abolition of Christmas increased. But Johnnie was troubled. Not only did Christmas rage throughout the kingdom as usual that year, but he had private information that many of the Society's members had broken the Oath of Abstention.

He decided, then, to strike at the very roots of Christmas. Johnnie gave up his job on the Drainage Supply Board; he gave up all his prospects, and, financed by a few supporters, retreated for two years to study the roots of Christmas. Then, all jubilant, Johnnie produced his next and last book, in which he established, either that Christmas was an invention of the Early Fathers to propitiate the pagans, or it was invented by the pagans to placate the Early Fathers, I forget which. Against the advice of his friends, Johnnie entitled it *Christmas and Christianity*. It sold eighteen copies. Johnnie never really recovered from this; and it happened, about that time, that the girl he was engaged to, an ardent Abolitionist, sent him a pullover she had knitted, for Christmas; he sent it back, enclosing a copy of the Society's rules, and she sent back the ring. But in any case, during Johnnie's absence, the Society had been undermined by a moderate faction. These moderates finally became more moderate, and the whole thing broke up.

Soon after this, I left the district, and it was some years before I saw Johnnie again. One Sunday afternoon in summer, I was idling among the crowds who were gathered to hear the speakers at Hyde Park. One little crowd surrounded a man who bore a banner marked "Crusade against Christmas"; his voice was frightening; it carried an unusually long way. This was Johnnie. A man in the crowd told me Johnnie was there every Sunday, very violent about Christmas, and that he would soon be taken up for insulting language. As I saw in the papers, he was soon taken up for insulting language. And a few months later I heard that poor Johnnie was in a mental home, because he had Christmas on the brain and couldn't stop shouting about it.

After that I forgot all about him until three years ago, in December, I went to live near the town where Johnnie had spent his youth. On the afternoon of Christmas Eve I was walking with a friend, noticing what had changed in my absence, and what hadn't. We passed a long, large house, once famous for its armoury, and I saw that the iron gates were wide open.

"They used to be kept shut," I said.

"That's an asylum now," said my friend; "they let the mild cases work in the grounds, and leave the gates open to give them a feeling of freedom."

"But," said my friend, "they lock everything inside. Door after door. The lift as well; they keep it locked."

While my friend was chattering, I stood in the gateway and looked in. Just beyond the gate was a great bare elm-tree. There I saw a man in brown corduroys, sweeping up the leaves. Poor soul, he was shouting about Christmas.

"That's Johnnie Geddes," I said. "Has he been here all these years?"

"Yes," said my friend as we walked on. "I believe he gets worse at this time of year."

"Does his aunt see him?"

"Yes. And she sees nobody else."

We were, in fact, approaching the house where Miss Geddes lived. I suggested we call on her. I had known her well.

"No fear," said my friend.

I decided to go in, all the same, and my friend walked on to the town.

Miss Geddes had changed, more than the landscape. She had been a solemn, calm woman, and now she moved about quickly, and gave short agitated smiles. She took me to her sitting-room, and as she opened the door she called to someone inside,

"Johnnie, see who's come to see us!"

A man, dressed in a dark suit, was standing on a chair, fixing holly behind a picture. He jumped down.

"Happy Christmas," he said. "A Happy and a Merry

Christmas indeed. I do hope," he said, "you're going to stay for tea, as we've got a delightful Christmas cake, and at this season of goodwill I would be cheered indeed if you could see how charmingly it's decorated; it has 'Happy Christmas' in red icing, and then there's a robin and –"

"Johnnie," said Miss Geddes, "you're forgetting the carols."

"The carols," he said. He lifted a gramophone record from a pile and put it on. It was "The Holly and the Ivy".

"It's 'The Holly and the Ivy'," said Miss Geddes. "Can't we have something else? We had that all morning."

"It is sublime," he said, beaming from his chair, and holding up his hand for silence.

While Miss Geddes went to fetch the tea, and he sat absorbed in his carol, I watched him. He was so like Johnnie, that if I hadn't seen poor Johnnie a few moments before, sweeping up the asylum leaves, I would have thought he really was Johnnie. Miss Geddes returned with the tray, and while he rose to put on another record, he said something that startled me.

"I saw you in the crowd that Sunday when I was speaking at Hyde Park."

"What a memory you have!" said Miss Geddes.

"It must be ten years ago," he said.

"My nephew has altered his opinion of Christmas," she explained. "He always comes home for Christmas now, and don't we have a jolly time, Johnnie?"

"Rather!" he said. "Oh, let me cut the cake."

He was very excited about the cake. With a flourish he dug a large knife into the side. The knife slipped, and I saw it run deep into his finger. Miss Geddes did not move. He wrenched his cut finger away, and went on slicing the cake.

"Isn't it bleeding?" I said.

He held up his hand. I could see the deep cut, but there was no blood.

Deliberately, and perhaps desperately, I turned to Miss Geddes.

"That house up the road," I said, "I see it's a mental home now. I passed it this afternoon."

"Johnnie," said Miss Geddes, as one who knows the game is up, "go and fetch the mince pies."

He went, whistling a carol.

"You passed the asylum," said Miss Geddes wearily.

"Yes," I said.

"And you saw Johnnie sweeping up the leaves."

"Yes."

We could still hear the whistling of the carol.

"Who is *he*?" I said.

"That's Johnnie's ghost," she said. "He comes home every Christmas. But," she said, "I don't like him. I can't bear him any longer, and I'm going away tomorrow. I don't want Johnnie's ghost, I want Johnnie in flesh and blood."

I shuddered, thinking of the cut finger that could not bleed. And I left, before Johnnie's ghost returned with the mince pies.

Next day, as I had arranged to join a family who lived in the town, I started walking over about noon. Because of the light mist, I didn't see at first who it was approaching. It was a man, waving his arm to me. It turned out to be Johnnie's ghost.

"Happy Christmas. What do you think," said Johnnie's ghost, "my aunt has gone to London. Fancy, on Christmas Day, and I thought she was at church, and here I am without anyone to spend a jolly Christmas with, and, of course, I forgive her, as it's the season of goodwill, but I'm glad to see you, because now I can come with you, wherever it is you're going, and we can all have a Happy . . ."

"Go away," I said, and walked on.

It sounds hard. But perhaps you don't know how repulsive and loathsome is the ghost of a living man. The ghosts of the dead may be all right, but the ghost of mad Johnnie gave me the creeps.

"Clear off," I said.

He continued walking beside me. "As it's the time of goodwill, I make allowances for your tone," he said. "But I'm coming."

We had reached the asylum gates, and there, in the grounds, I saw Johnnie sweeping the leaves. I suppose it was his way of going on strike, working on Christmas Day. He was making a noise about Christmas.

On a sudden impulse I said to Johnnie's ghost, "You want company?"

"Certainly," he replied. "It's the season of . . ."

"Then you shall have it," I said.

I stood in the gateway. "Oh, Johnnie," I called.

He looked up.

"I've brought your ghost to see you, Johnnie."

"Well, well," said Johnnie, advancing to meet his ghost. "Just imagine it!"

"Happy Christmas," said Johnnie's ghost.

"Oh, really?" said Johnnie.

I left them to it. And when I looked back, wondering if they would come to blows, I saw that Johnnie's ghost was sweeping the leaves as well. They seemed to be arguing at the same time. But it was still misty, and really, I can't say whether, when I looked a second time, there were two men or one man sweeping the leaves.

Johnnie began to improve in the New Year. At least, he stopped shouting about Christmas, and then he never mentioned it at all; in a few months, when he had almost stopped saying anything, they discharged him.

The town council gave him the leaves of the park to sweep. He seldom speaks, and recognizes nobody. I see him every day at the late end of the year, working within the mist. Sometimes, if there is a sudden gust, he jerks his head up to watch a few leaves falling behind him, as if amazed that they are undeniably there, although, by rights, the falling of leaves should be stopped.

HARPER AND WILTON

In the afternoons there was seldom anybody about except for the young cross-eyed gardener. He was so cross-eyed that if you stood talking to him with a friend it was impossible to know which of you he was addressing. And when alone, it was almost as if he was conversing with the nearest tree if not with myself. I meant to summon courage to ask him if there was no corrective treatment, or special eye-glasses, he could have, but I never got round to it. The house was not mine. I was merely house-sitting for a month for my friends, the Lowthers. It was an arrangement which suited me well. I had a book to finish and this house in the depth of Hampshire was ideal for my purpose. In the morning Harriet, the part-time daily came and tidied up. She cooked my meals for the day then left me to myself about midday.

I worked hard, and I slept well. Nothing disturbed me during the night. It was about two in the afternoon that I felt uneasy. An oddness in the house. This went on for some weeks. The spring weather was capricious.

But it was not when the wind whistled round the house and moaned in the eaves that the house felt weird. The weather and sound effects in fact normalized the old edifice. It was on clear sunny days, spring rain sprinkling and spraying the windows, that something was decidedly odd. Under the need to work I determinedly shook off the feeling, often sitting in the garden or else the garden room to apply myself to my work. I began to notice that Joe the gardener often stood under the great cedar tree on the lawn looking up apparently at a window of one of the two guest bedrooms to the left above the front door. They were divided by a drainpipe which I felt rather spoilt the aspect of the house. It was impossible to say which of the windows he was paying attention to because of his squint.

"Is anything the matter, Joe?" I asked him after a few days of watching his performance.

He said "No" and continued staring. Joe was after all, not my concern, not my employee. The house was well protected by burglar alarms. I had my work to do and decided to ignore Joe; I continued to shake off the feeling of chilling weirdness that I felt every afternoon.

The fourth week of my stay I heard voices, the voices of young women. I opened the door of the garden room and called out "Joe, who's there?" But Joe had disappeared. I decided this listening to "voices" and puzzling about Joe was a waste of time. I really had a great compulsion and economic need to finish my book. I was getting on well with it and refused to be waylaid from the job I had come to accomplish.

But no sooner had I settled down at my desk than I heard the voices again, outside the house, quite near. I wasn't expecting any visitors, so went to look out of the window. The house was attached to a stretch of woodland from where the voices came. Then two women came in sight. I was not at first surprised that they were dressed in Edwardian-type long skirts and shawls, with their long hair knotted up severely. They might well have bought their outfits at London's Miss Selfridge, in Beauchamp Place or in Manhattan's Village. Nothing in the way of garments is surprising in these days of merry freedom.

I thought I recognized them, but couldn't tell where I had seen them before. Certainly I had a sense of having seen them both together, young and gaunt, one tall, one less so.

As they approached the house I saw Joe lurking on the edge of the woods behind them. He seemed interested.

The front-door bell was ringing, now. I was not at all sure I should answer it. There was no reason to expect visitors and I had been assured by the Lowthers of my complete solitude. But I opened the garden room window, smitten with nerves, and called out,

"Who is it you want? I'm afraid the Lowthers are away. I'm only a temporary tenant."

"We want you," said the woman who seemed to be the younger of the two.

I was still almost sure I had seen them before. They gave me the creeps. The older woman pressed the bell again. "Let us in."

"Who are you?" I said.

"Harper and Wilton," said the younger one. "Don't panic. We are merely outraged."

Harper and Wilton – where had I heard their names before?

"Do I know you?" I said.

"Do you know us?" said one of the women, the taller. "You made us. My name is Marion Harper known as Harper and my friend is Marion Wilton known as Wilton. We fight for the Vote for Women."

Oh God, I remembered then that years ago, many, many years ago, some time in the 1950s, I wrote a story about two Edwardian suffragettes. What could I recall of that story? It was never published. Was it finished? I didn't find the two characters, Harper and Wilton, very sympathetic but I had certainly had some fun with them.

"What do you want from me?" I inquired from the window. I had no intention of letting them into the house.

"You cast the story away," said little Wilton. "We've been looking for you for some time. Now you've got to give us substance otherwise we'll haunt you."

For my part Harper and Wilton were lying at the back of a drawer in which I used to put unfinished stories and poems when, long ago, I started writing fiction and verse.

I packed up my belongings, packed them in the car, and drove off, watched at a distance by Harper, Wilton and Joe. At home I searched for the missing manuscript and eventually found it, curled at the edges. I read it through:

> One day there appeared at the window a youth of about twenty. Unfortunately, he had a squint.
>
> There was another boarding-house opposite. Here, on the second floor, lived Miss Wilton and Miss Harper, members of the suffragette movement. Their parents, who lived in the country, gave them money to keep away.
>
> Three weeks later, when Miss Wilton could stand it no longer, she went along the landing to Miss Harper's room. "Harper," she said, "I can stand it no longer."

"Why Wilton," said Harper, "don't be discouraged. We had three hundred and four new recruits last month. Remember the words of Pankhurst –"

"Harper," said Wilton severely, "I refer to a personal matter."

"Really?" said Harper, losing interest and starting to roll a pair of stays very tight and neat. "Well, I haven't time to discuss anything personal. I'm busy with my Reports."

"I'll be brief," said Wilton. "Every afternoon there's a young man at the window across the road –"

"I *thought* as much," said Harper.

"Don't think I've been spying," her friend protested. "But I can't avoid seeing what I see. He has been making signs."

"I have observed it," Harper said. "I advise you to live elsewhere if you can't resist temptation. I cannot do more for you Wilton. There are larger issues, important things."

"Indeed. You consider it important to encourage the advances of a strange man. I hardly think the Committee will take that view," stated Wilton.

"Ah!" said Harper. "Ah!"

"Ah!" said Wilton. "Yes, I intend to report this to the Bayswater Committee."

"You're too late," Harper said, "with your wily scheme. I have already reported the matter. You may read a copy of my statement."

Wilton moved over to the gas light with the paper, and read:

"With regret, I have to report that Miss M. Wilton of our Ranks, has lately behaved in a manner prejudicial to our Cause. She has openly encouraged a male person, presumably a student, to make overtures from a window opposite her residence. I fear we will soon have to call upon Miss Wilton to resign from the Movement."

Wilton handed back the report. "It's a clever plan of yours," she said scornfully, "to cover your traces by implicating me in your unworthy undertakings. But I will prove my innocence. You will be exposed."

"Remember," she added, "the Secretary already has doubts regarding your feminist zeal. The fact that you wear those stays to give you a figure, is alone an indication that –"

"Kindly depart," Harper said.

"Moreover, I disagree that he is a student," said Wilton.

Next day, the youth opposite appeared to believe he was getting somewhere with one of the girls. At her unmistakable bidding he crossed the road, and looked up expectantly at Wilton's window. She observed that the idiot seemed to be watching Harper's window. He needn't worry; Harper was out. Wilton dropped an envelope. It contained a note, unsigned, executed on Harper's typewriting-machine. It also contained a key.

It was the front-door key, and the note explained how to get to her room, at ten that night. Only, of course, it was Harper's room she directed him to, this Wilton.

She heard Harper come in. Wilton composed herself

to wait for justice at ten o'clock. She would fetch the landlady. A man in Harper's room. A noisy scene. The Committee would be informed.

As the hour advanced, the youth was forced to consider an alternative method of keeping the assignment, because, due to excitement, he had lost the key. Courageous, though unimaginative, he started climbing the drainpipe which ran between Wilton's window and Harper's. Wilton watched this lamp-lit performance, appalled. Harper, too, observed it; and before he had got two feet, the water from Harper's wash-jug descended. Wilton worked quickly. Her jug was empty, so she threw out the jug. Harper swooped downstairs to the door. Wilton followed.

The young man was very wet, very stunned.

"Don't move," said Harper. "I shall hand you over."

"Harper," said Wilton, "I'm arresting him. He had an appointment with you. It's shameful. You are exposed at last."

The landlady was suddenly in the doorway. "Constable!" she called. A policeman at the top of the street turned and ambled towards them.

Harper was, in spite of her stays, the more emancipated of the two; she looked at Wilton. "This is my man," she said. "You get the hell out of it."

"What's going on?" said the policeman.

"Language!" said the landlady. "These suffragettes!"

"Suffragettes, eh?" said the policeman.

"Constable," said Wilton, a-flutter, "this man was attempting to climb up this lady. This drainpipe was encouraging him."

"It's her fault," the young man gasped, glaring at Wilton. Owing to the squint, the policeman was unable to decide which girl was meant. Not that it mattered.

"Oh, suffragettes!" said the policeman.

"Yes, I was attacked," sighed the youth.

The constable took all the particulars. He took Harper and Wilton by the sleeves. "This way," he said, "and come quiet. Disturbing the Peace. Suffragettes."

"I hope they get a month," said the landlady.

"Three months more likely," said the policeman. "You all right now, sir!"

"More or less," replied the young man cheerfully. "Good night, Constable. Good night, sweet ladies."

They only got a month. But you see, sweet ladies, what they all had to suffer to get us the vote.

I raced back to the country with this manuscript in my handbag. It had been one of many and many that I had always intended to revise when I had a spare day or two. Those spare days had never come. But looking at the story I didn't see what was missing. Harper and Wilton had adequately fulfilled their destiny for that little space of history at the turn of the twentieth century that their story occupied.

Harper and Wilton were waiting for me on the doorstep of my country retreat.

"How about it?" This was Wilton.

I noticed that Joe the gardener was observing us from the mysterious wooded part of the garden which I had greatly taken to. I love mysterious gardens. I felt that Joe should come and join us. I was dangling the door keys in my hand.

On no account would I let any of them cross the threshold. I was carried away by the fact of Joe's intensely squinting eyes as he approached. Again I wondered why he wore no corrective glasses. How could I have envisaged and foreseen this boy with the great squint all those years ago when I had written this episodic little story of Harper and Wilton?

Joe was obviously fascinated by the two girls in their unconventional clothes. But here again it was difficult to see which one he was observing at any one time.

"He has given us no peace," said Wilton. "He follows us everywhere. Don't you know that is a crime? In the world of today, more than ever."

"Sexual molestation," said Harper.

"Oh, what has he done?" I said.

"Followed us everywhere. He is molesting us. It was he who should have gone to prison, not us."

I saw my chance. I sat down on the doorstep and re-wrote the ending of the story in the light of current correctness. The girls, Harper and Wilton, were vindicated and it was the squint-eyed student who was taken off by the police. I showed it to Harper and Wilton.

Not only that, since they were tepid in their satisfaction, I let myself into the house while the group remained uneasily in the garden. I called the police and said that our garden boy was troubling two young women by his unwanted attention. Rather languidly, they agreed to come along and see what it was all about.

They took Joe away. Harper and Wilton disappeared, evidently satisfied. Joe came back shortly, having been merely cautioned, and got on with his weeding of the garden.

THE EXECUTOR

When my uncle died all the literary manuscripts went to a university foundation, except one. The correspondence went too, and the whole of his library. They came (a white-haired man and a young girl) and surveyed his study. Everything, they said, would be desirable and it would make a good price if I let the whole room go – his chair, his desk, the carpet, even his ashtrays. I agreed to this. I left everything in the drawers of the desk just as it was when my uncle died, including the bottle of Librium and a rusty razor blade.

My uncle died this way: he was sitting on the bank of the river, playing a fish. As the afternoon faded a man passed by, and then a young couple who made pottery passed him. As they said later, he was sitting peacefully awaiting the catch and of course they didn't disturb him. As night fell the colonel and his wife passed by; they were on their way home from their daily walk. They knew it was too late for my uncle to be simply sitting there, so they went to look. He had been dead, the doctor pronounced, from two to two and a half hours. The fish was still struggling with the bait. It was a mild heart attack. Everything my uncle did was mild, so different from everything he wrote. Yet perhaps not so different. He was supposed to be "far out", so one didn't know what went on out there. Besides, he had not long returned from a trip to London. They say, still waters run deep.

But far out was how he saw himself. He once said that if you could imagine modern literature as a painting, perhaps by Brueghel the Elder, the people and the action were in the foreground, full of colour, eating, stealing, copulating, laughing, courting each other, excreting, and stabbing each other, selling things, climbing trees. Then in the distance, at the far end of a vast plain, there he would be, a speck on the horizon, always receding and always there, and always a necessary and mysterious component of the picture; always there and never to be taken away, essential to the picture – a speck in the distance, which if you were to blow up the detail would simply be a vague figure, plodding on the other way.

I am no fool, and he knew it. He didn't know it at first, but he had seven months in which to learn that fact. I gave up my job in Edinburgh in the government office, a job with a pension, to come here to the lonely house among the Pentland Hills to live with him and take care of things. I think he imagined I was going to be another Elaine when he suggested the arrangement. He had no idea how much better I was for him than Elaine. Elaine was his mistress, that is the stark truth. "My common-law wife," he called her, explaining that in Scotland, by tradition, the woman you are living with is your wife. As if I didn't know all that nineteenth-century folklore; and it's long died out. Nowadays you have to do more than say "I marry you, I marry you, I marry you," to make a woman your wife. Of course, my uncle was a genius and a character. I allowed for that. Anyway, Elaine died and I came here a month later. Within a month I had cleared up the best part of the disorder. He called me a Scottish puritan girl, and at forty-one it was nice to be a girl and I wasn't against the Scottish puritanical attribution either since I am proud to be a Scot; I feel nationalistic about it. He always had that smile of his when he said it, so I don't know how he meant it. They say he had that smile of his when he was found dead, fishing.

"I appoint my niece Susan Kyle to be my sole literary executor." I don't wonder he decided on this course after I had been with him for three months. Probably for the first time in his life all his papers were in order. I went into Edinburgh and bought box-files and cover-files and I filed away all that mountain of papers, each under its separate heading. And I knew what was what. You didn't catch me filing away a letter from Angus Wilson or Saul Bellow in the same place as an ordinary "W" or "B", a Miss Mary Whitelaw or a Mrs Jonathan Brown. I knew the value of these letters, they went into a famous-persons file, bulging and of value. So that in a short time my uncle said, "There's little for me to do now, Susan, but die." Which I thought was melodramatic, and said so. But I could see he was forced to admire my good sense. He said, "You remind me of my mother, who prepared her shroud all ready for her funeral." His mother was my grandmother Janet Kyle. Why shouldn't she have sat and sewn her shroud? People in those days had very little to do, and here I was running the house and looking after my uncle's papers with only the help of Mrs Donaldson three mornings a week, where my grandmother had four pairs of hands for indoor help and three out. The rest of the family never went near the house after my grandmother died, for Elaine was always there with my uncle.

The property was distributed among the family, but I was the sole literary executor. And it was up to me to do what I liked with his literary remains. It was a good thing I had everything inventoried and filed, ready for sale. They came and took the total archive as they called it away, all the correspondence and manuscripts except one. That one I kept for myself. It was the novel he was writing when he died, an unfinished manuscript. I thought, Why not? Maybe I will finish it myself and publish it. I am no fool, and my uncle must have known how the book was going to end. I never read any of his correspondence, mind you; I was too busy those months filing it all in order. I did think, however, that I would read this manuscript and perhaps put an ending to it. There were already ten chapters. My uncle had told me there was only another chapter to go. So I said nothing to the Foundation about that one unfinished manuscript; I was only too glad when they had come and gone, and the papers were out of the house. I got the painters in to clean the study. Mrs Donaldson said she had never seen the house looking so like a house should be.

Under my uncle's will I inherited the house, and I planned eventually to rent rooms to tourists in the summer, bed and breakfast. In the meantime I set about reading the unfinished manuscript, for it was only April, and I'm not a one to let the grass grow under my feet. I had learnt to decipher that old-fashioned handwriting of his which looked good on the page but was not too clear. My uncle had a treasure in me those last months of his life, although he said I was like a book without an index – all information, and no way of getting at it. I asked him to tell me what information he ever got out of Elaine, who never passed an exam in her life.

This last work of my uncle's was an unusual story for him, set in the seventeenth century here among the Pentland Hills. He had told me only that he was writing something strong and cruel, and that this was easier to accomplish in a historical novel. It was about the slow identification and final trapping of a witch, and I could see as I read it that he hadn't been joking when he said it was strong and cruel; he had often said things to frighten and alarm me, I don't know why. By chapter ten the trial of the witch in Edinburgh was only halfway through. Her fate depended entirely on chapter eleven, and on the negotiations that were being conducted behind the scenes by the opposing factions of intrigue. My uncle had left a pile of notes he had accumulated towards this novel, and I retained these along with the manuscript. But there was no sign in the notes as to how my uncle had decided to resolve the fate of the witch – whose name was Edith but that is by the way. I put the notebooks and papers away, for there were many other things to be done following the death of my famous uncle. The novel itself was written by hand in twelve notebooks. In the twelfth only the first two pages had been filled, the rest of the pages were blank; I am sure of this. The two filled pages came to the end of chapter ten. At the top of the next page was written "Chapter Eleven". I looked through the rest of the notebook to make sure my uncle had not made some note there on how he intended to continue; all blank, I am sure of it. I put the twelve notebooks, together with the sheaf of loose notes, in a drawer of the solid-mahogany dining-room sideboard.

A few weeks later I brought the notebooks out again,

intending to consider how I might proceed with the completion of the book and so enhance its value. I read again through chapter ten; then, when I turned to the page where "Chapter Eleven" was written, there in my uncle's handwriting was the following:

> *Well, Susan, how do you feel about finishing my novel? Aren't you a greedy little snoot, holding back my unfinished work, when you know the Foundation paid for the lot? What about your puritanical principles? Elaine and I are waiting to see how you manage to write Chapter Eleven. Elaine asks me to add it's lovely to see you scouring and cleaning those neglected corners of the house. But don't you know, Jaimie is having you on. Where does he go after lunch?*
>
> *– Your affect Uncle*

I could hardly believe my eyes. The first shock I got was the bit about Jaimie, and then came the second shock, that the words were there at all. It was twelve-thirty at night and Jaimie had gone home. Jaimie Donaldson is the son of Mrs Donaldson, and it isn't his fault he's out of work. We have had experiences together, but nobody is to know that, least of all Mrs Donaldson who introduced him into the household merely to clean the windows and stoke the boiler. But the words? Where did they come from?

It is a lonely house, here in a fold of the Pentlands, surrounded by woods, five miles to the nearest cottage, six to Mrs Donaldson's, and the buses stop at ten p.m. I felt a great fear there in the dining-room, with the twelve notebooks on the table, and the pile of papers, a great cold, and a panic. I ran to the hall and lifted the telephone but didn't know how to explain myself or whom to phone. My story would sound like that of a woman gone crazy. Mrs Donaldson? The police? I couldn't think what to say to them at that hour of night. "I have found some words that weren't there before in my uncle's manuscript, and in his own hand." It was unthinkable. Then I thought perhaps someone had played me a trick. Oh no, I knew that this couldn't be. Only Mrs Donaldson had been in the dining-room, and only to dust, with me to help her. Jaimie had no chance to go there, not at all. I never used the dining-room now and had meals in the kitchen. But in fact I knew it wasn't them, it was Uncle. I wished with all my heart that I was a strong woman, as I had always felt I was, strong and sensible. I stood in the hall by the telephone, shaking. "O God, everlasting and almighty," I prayed, "make me strong, and guide and lead me as to how Mrs Thatcher would conduct herself in circumstances of this nature."

I didn't sleep all night. I sat in the big kitchen stoking up the fire. Only once I moved, to go back into the dining-room and make sure that those words were there. Beyond a doubt they were, and in my uncle's handwriting – that handwriting it would take an expert forger to copy. I put the manuscript back in the drawer; I locked the dining-room door and took the key. My uncle's study, now absolutely empty, was above the kitchen. If he was haunting the house, I heard no sound from there or from anywhere else. It was a fearful night, waiting there by the fire.

Mrs Donaldson arrived in the morning, complaining that Jaimie was getting lazy; he wouldn't rise. Too many late nights.

"Where does he go after lunch?" I said.

"Oh, he goes for a round of golf after his dinner," she said. "He's always ready for a round of golf no matter what else there is to do. Golf is the curse of Scotland."

I had a good idea who Jaimie was meeting on the golf course, and I could almost have been grateful to Uncle for pointing out to me in that sly way of his that Jaimie wandered in the hours after the midday meal which we called lunch and they called their dinner. By five o'clock in the afternoon Jaimie would come here to the house to fetch up the coal, bank the fire, and so forth. But all afternoon he would be on the links with that girl who works at the manse, Greta, younger sister of Elaine, the one who moved in here openly, ruining my uncle's morals, leaving the house to rot. I always suspected that family. After Elaine died it came out he had even introduced her to all his friends; I could tell from the letters of condolence, how they said things like "He never got over the loss of Elaine" and "He couldn't live without her". And sometimes he called me Elaine by mistake. I was furious. Once, for example, I said, "Uncle, stop pacing about down here. Go up to your study and do your scribbling; I'll bring you a cup of cocoa." He said, with that glaze-eyed look he always had when he was interrupted in his thoughts, "What's come over you, Elaine?" I said, "I'm not Elaine, thank you very much." "Oh, of course," he said, "you are not Elaine, you are most certainly not her." If the public that read his books by the tens of thousands could have seen behind the scenes, I often wondered what they would have thought. I told him so many a time, but he smiled in that sly way, that smile he still had on his face when they found him fishing and stone dead.

After Mrs Donaldson left the house, at noon, I went

up to my bedroom, half dropping from lack of sleep. Mrs Donaldson hadn't noticed anything; you could be falling down dead – they never look at you. I slept till four. It was still light. I got up and locked the doors, front and back. I pulled the curtains shut, and when Jaimie rang the bell at five o'clock I didn't open, I just let him ring. Eventually he went away. I expect he had plenty to wonder about. But I wasn't going to make him welcome before the fire and get him his supper, and take off my clothes there in the back room on the divan with him, in front of the television, while Uncle and Elaine were looking on, even though it is only Nature. No, I turned on the television for myself. You would never believe, it was a programme on the Scottish BBC about Uncle. I switched to TV One, and got a quiz show. And I felt hungry, for I'd eaten nothing since the night before.

But I couldn't face any supper until I had assured myself about that manuscript. I was fairly certain by now that it was a dream. "Maybe I've been overworking," I thought to myself. I had the key of the dining-room in my pocket and I took it and opened the door; I closed the curtains, and I went to the drawer and took out the notebook.

Not only were the words that I had read last night there, new words were added, a whole paragraph:

> *Look up the Acts of the Apostles, Chapter 5, verses 1 to 10. See what happened to Ananias and Sapphira his wife. You're not getting on very fast with your scribbling, are you, Susan? Elaine and I were under the impression you were going to write Chapter Eleven. Why don't you*

take a cup of cocoa and get on with it? First read Acts, V, 1–10.

– Your affec Uncle

Well, I shoved the book in the drawer and looked round the dining-room. I looked under the table and behind the curtains. It didn't look as if anything had been touched. I got out of the room and locked the door, I don't know how. I went to fetch my Bible, praying, "O God omnipotent and all-seeing, direct and instruct me as to the way out of this situation, astonishing as it must appear to Thee." I looked up the passage:

> But a certain man named Ananias, with Sapphira his wife, sold a possession.
>
> And kept back part of the price, his wife also being privy to it, and brought a certain part and laid it at the apostles' feet.
>
> But Peter said, Ananias, why hath Satan filled thine heart to lie to the Holy Ghost, and to keep back part of the land?

I didn't read any more because I knew how it went on. Ananias and Sapphira, his wife, were both struck dead for holding back the portion of the sale for themselves. This was Uncle getting at me for holding back his manuscript from the Foundation. That's an impudence, I thought, to make such a comparison from the Bible, when he was an open and avowed sinner himself.

I thought it all over for a while. Then I went into the dining-room and got out that last notebook. Something else had been written since I had put it away, not half an hour before:

> *Why don't you get on with Chapter Eleven? We're waiting for it.*

I tore out the page, put the book away and locked the door. I took the page to the fire and put it on to burn. Then I went to bed.

This went on for a month. My uncle always started the page afresh with "Chapter Eleven", followed by a new message. He even went so far as to put in that I had kept back bits of the housekeeping money, although, he wrote, I was well paid enough. That's a matter of opinion, and who did the economising, anyway? Always, after reading Uncle's disrespectful comments, I burned the page, and we were getting near the end of the notebook. He would say things to show he followed me round the house, and even knew my dreams. When I went into Edinburgh for some shopping he knew exactly where I had been and what I'd bought. He and Elaine listened in to my conversations on the telephone if I rang up an old friend. I didn't let anyone in the house except Mrs Donaldson. No more Jaimie. He even knew if I took a dose of salts and how long I had sat in the bathroom, the awful old man.

Mrs Donaldson one morning said she was leaving. She said to me, "Why don't you see a doctor?" I said, "Why?" But she wouldn't speak.

One day soon afterwards a man rang me up from the Foundation. They didn't want to bother me, they said, but they were rather puzzled. They had found in Uncle's letters many references to a novel. *The Witch of the Pentlands*, which he had been writing just before his death; and they had found among the papers a final chapter to this novel, which he had evidently written on loose pages on a train, for a letter of his, kindly provided by one of his many correspondents, proved this. Only they had no idea where the rest of the manuscript could be. In the end the witch Edith is condemned to be burned, but dies of her own will power before the execution, he said, but there must be ten more chapters leading up to it. This was Uncle's most metaphysical work, and based on a true history, the man said, and he must stress that it was very important.

I said that I would have a look. I rang back that afternoon and said I had found the whole book in a drawer in the dining-room.

So the man came to get it. On the phone he sounded very suspicious, in case there were more manuscripts. "Are you sure that's everything? You know, the Foundation's price included the whole archive. No, don't trust it to the mail, I'll be there tomorrow at two."

Just before he arrived I took a good drink, whisky and soda, as, indeed, I had been taking from sheer need all the past month. I had brought out the notebooks. On the blank page was written:

Goodbye, Susan. It's lovely being a speck in the distance.
Your affec Uncle

ANOTHER PAIR OF HANDS

I am the only son of parents old enough to be grandparents. This has advantages and disadvantages, for although I was out of touch with the intervening generation, my mother's friends when I was born being forty and upwards and my father's contemporaries mostly over sixty, I inherited a longer sense of living history than most people do. It was quite natural for my elders to talk about the life of the early part of the century to which they belonged, and I grew up knowing instinctively how things were done in those days and how they thought.

My mother died aged ninety-six, just after my fiftieth birthday. She had survived my father by nearly thirty years. She was active almost to the last, the only difficulty being her failing eyesight; her movements had slowed down a bit. But really she was, as everyone said, wonderful for her age. She died quickly of a stroke. To the last she was still wondering why I hadn't found the right woman to marry. Maybe she's wondering even yet. She belonged to the wondering generation.

My mother, originally mistress of a great house with countless servants, had moved down with the times like everyone else, each move to a smaller house and fewer servants being somewhat of a trauma to her. She called every new house poky, every domestic arrangement makeshift. It was not till well after the First World War that she got used to only four indoor servants including a manservant and three outdoor. Somewhere about the end of the fifties she was reduced to a compact Georgian house in Sussex with twelve bedrooms surrounded by woodland. It became more and more enormous for one person as time went on. Her means were sufficient but she couldn't get the staff she needed. A few rooms were closed off entirely. Some years before she died she was doing very well with a gardener to keep going a token piece of lawn and some kitchen-garden patches, and, indoors, her cook-housekeeper, Miss Spigot, and Winnie the maid. By the end of her life, two years ago, she was left with only Winnie.

After Miss Spigot's death Winnie struggled on, in deep chaos, burning the food and quite unable to shop and clean. My mother wouldn't lift a finger beyond picking flowers; she sat calmly with her eternal sewing, which she called "my work", giving orders. Up to then I had been accustomed to go down to spend Sunday and Monday with a few friends to cheer Ma up, and she had always looked forward to these visits. She had outlived her sisters and her friends, and she enjoyed company. My own work, a regular theatre column, prevented me from spending much more time with her. I don't notice dust but I do notice bad food; I must say Miss Spigot, who was already in her late seventies, had cooked very well. Our rooms had always been ready and bright when we arrived during Miss Spigot's lifetime. But suddenly all that ended. Winnie was frantic. I could see that my mother would have to move again. I begged her to let me get her a small flat in

London. She was very old but by no means infirm, especially of purpose. "Winnie can manage alone. I shall have a Word with her," said Ma, and went on with her needlepoint or whatever. I could have killed her, but Ma wasn't the sort of person you could easily be nasty to.

I decided to stop bringing my friends to my mother's. My own visits were hell. There was a terrible smell everywhere of burnt food, unaired rooms and sheer neglect. My mother's tastes in food were simple and I dare say so were Winnie's, but as for me I like my square meals. The dining-room floor was littered with old bits of toast and egg-shells. The table hadn't been cleared for weeks, the place-mats were greasy. I did my best to help clear up on my miserable Sundays and Mondays. Personally, I'm quite used to shifting for myself in London; in fact, having been brought up with servants, I hate them. Your life's never your own. In London I always managed with a morning woman.

But I wasn't up to coping with a vast house like Ma's. Nothing would disturb Ma's resolve to put up with it or Winnie's exasperating loyalty; she took my mother's part. It went on for a month. I spent all my spare time in employment agencies and on various other means to get someone to replace Miss Spigot, but nothing came of my efforts or those of my friends; nothing. "I am going to have a Word with Winnie," said Ma.

On the fifth Sunday I drove down to Sussex late intending to cut short the horror of it all. Amazingly, there was no horror. Winnie had become a super-efficient cook-housekeeper all in the course of a week. As I passed the dining-room I could see the table was laid ready, sparkling with silver and glass, and the table-linen was up to Ma's best standard. The drawing-room was fresh and the windows looked like glass once more.

Ma was knitting. It was almost time to go in to dinner.

"Have you found someone to help?" I said.

"No," said Ma.

"Well, how has Winnie managed all this on her own?"

"I had a Word with her," said my mother.

Winnie served an excellent dinner on the whole; perhaps it wasn't quite up to the late cook's quality but certainly ambitious enough to include a rather flat soufflé.

"It's her first soufflé," said Ma, when Winnie went to get the meat course. "If she doesn't improve I'll have a Word."

But now something had happened to Winnie. She was perfectly happy, indeed almost blissful. She went around whispering to herself in a decidedly odd way. She served the vegetables with great care, but whispering, whispering, all the time.

"What did you say, Winnie?" I said.

"The soufflé was flat," said Winnie.

"Turn on the BBC news," said my mother.

For the whole of Monday Winnie went round chattering to herself. Breakfast was, however, set out on the table with nothing forgotten. The house was already in good order before half-past eight, the fire new and crackling. And Winnie conversed with herself, merrily, and quite a lot. I supposed that finding herself alone in the kitchen was now showing. However, my mother seemed to have solved her domestic problem which had fast been developing into mine. I didn't give time to worrying lest Winnie was turning a little funny.

* * *

I went back cheerfully to my own bachelor life and regaled my friends with the news of the change that had come over Winnie and of how well she was coping. They were quite eager to come and join me in Sussex again, assuring me they would make their own beds, help with the shopping and generally refrain from giving Winnie a hard time. I thought I'd better wait a few weeks before making up a party as of old. These visitors to my mother's house were either unmarried and younger colleagues of mine who, like myself, had to work on Saturdays for their newspapers, or middle-aged widows who had nothing to tie them to any day of the week. All were very keen to come, but I waited.

Winnie was even more efficient the next week. I came to the conclusion that it was Winnie who had been the guiding spirit in the kitchen all along; she was a good cook. Ma took no notice of her whatsoever, as was always her way, preferring not to praise or blame, just to give orders. Winnie was an unguessable age between fifty-five and seventy, her face was big with a lot of folds, her body thin and angular, her hair chocolate-rinsed. My mother who long ago had been used to picking and choosing maids "of good appearance" had taken some time to resign herself to uncomely Winnie, and, having done so, she was not now inclined to waste consideration on any further divergence from the norm that Winnie might display.

Winnie in fact could now be heard in the kitchen kicking up a dreadful racket. One evening the noise filled the house for about ten minutes. My bed was turned down neatly. The stair carpets were spotless as of old, and the furniture and banisters shone. Winnie conducted a further brief altercation in the kitchen and then was quiet till tea when my mother went to bed and so did she. I had a comfortable night. In the morning Winnie started fighting with herself again, or so it seemed. On investigation, I found her smiling while she argued. My mother's breakfast tray was all prepared and Winnie was about to carry it up to Ma's room. "What's the matter, Winnie?" I said.

"Oh, the butter was forgot to be put on the tray. Too old for the job."

"Would you like to leave, Winnie?" I said, somewhat desperately, but feeling that this was Winnie's way of saying just that.

"How could I leave your mother?" said Winnie, marching off with the tray.

Well, my mother, aged ninety-six, died suddenly during the following week. Winnie phoned me quite calmly from Sussex and I went down right away. There was a little quiet funeral. The house was to be sold. Winnie was still having occasional outbreaks against herself, such as "*The Times* didn't get cancelled at the newsagent like I said," and she muttered a bit as she went around. However, I spent a last, comfortable night in the house and after breakfast prepared to settle Winnie's pay and pension. I believed she would be glad of a rest. She had relations in Yorkshire and I thought she would probably want to return to them.

"I'm not leaving the family," said Winnie.

She didn't mean her family, she meant me.

"Well, Winnie, the house will be sold. There's no family left, is there?"

"I'm coming with you," Winnie said. "I've no doubt it's a pigsty but I can live in the basement."

My pigsty, my paradise. It was a small narrow house in a Hampstead lane, which I had acquired over twelve years ago. I never got round to putting it straight. It was so much my life to be out late at night at the theatre, then usually some sort of supper after the theatre with friends; in the morning doing my notes for the theatre column, shuffling about in my dressing-gown; then after a quick lunch I would work in my study, or maybe go out to a cinema or an art show, or if not attend to something bureaucratic; or I would play some music on the piano. I worked hardest Fridays and Saturdays, for my last show was Friday and the column had to be in on Saturday at three in the afternoon. And since, until Ma died, I would go down to Sussex for Sunday and Monday with my friends, there was no time to put things straight. Sometimes there were people staying at my house and they would try to help. But it was better when they didn't, for after one of those friendly tidy-ups I couldn't find anything. Never, on any occasion, did I allow anyone into my little study upstairs. A sullen and lady-like domestic help called Ida came mincing in three mornings a week for a couple of hours, painful all round; that is, to herself, to me and to my cat Francis. Ida took the clean dishes out of the dishwasher and stacked them away; she changed the towels and bedsheets and left them at the laundry. She swept the kitchen floor, making short work of Francis with her broom, and sometimes she dusted the sitting-room and vacuumed the carpet. Francis cowered in the basement three mornings a week till she had gone.

It was not altogether the undesirability of Ida that persuaded me to take on Winnie. At first, I was decidedly dissuaded. The family fortunes had just managed to eke themselves out over my mother's lifetime. I am comfortably off, I have a job, but I'm by no means wealthy. Like most of my friends I wasn't in a position to take on a full-time housekeeper. And for another thing, I had no room. There was the damp basement full of rotting boxes which contained a great many other rotting objects that I always intended to do something about. These included some boxes of my mother's that had somehow landed at my house during one of her moves, and never been forwarded; once I had looked inside one of them; it had held two ostrich feather fans falling apart with moth, some carved wood chessmen the worse for the damp, some soggy books and some wine. On that occasion I threw back the contents into the box, less the wine which was still enjoyable. But I never again opened one of those boxes. The basement contained two rooms, a little dank bathroom and a frightful kitchen. It had plainly been inhabited before I acquired the house.

"I can't put you in the basement, Winnie," I said, instead of saying outright "I can't afford a cook-housekeeper, Winnie."

"What's wrong with the basement?"

"It's damp."

"I don't need much money," said Winnie. "Your mother underpaid me, anyway. Old-fashioned ideas. You need me to cook for you. I can go into the attic and make it over for a room."

How she knew about the attic I don't know. I had once thought of making it into a one-room apartment and renting it, but it was just above the two bedrooms of the house, one of which was my study, and I hadn't liked the thought of people moving about over my head. So the attic was empty. The other rooms in my house apart from my bedroom and my study were on the ground floor, a sitting-room and a dining-room with a divan where I put up occasional friends. The only place for Winnie was the attic, warm and empty. What made me waver in my resolve not to take on Winnie was that remark of hers, "You need me to cook for you." That was indeed a temptation. I visualized the effortless and good little supper parties I could give after the theatre. The nice lunches I would have, always so well-planned, well-served; and Winnie was a very economical shopper.

"Save you a fortune in restaurants," decided Winnie; for it really was all decided. "And with the sale of your mother's house, you'll be in clover."

I didn't go into the fact that death duties were taking care of my late mother's property, she having stubbornly arranged her affairs so badly. But it was true that restaurant-eating in London was becoming more and more difficult as the food and service were ever more inferior. I just said, "Well, Winnie, you'll have to settle yourself in the attic as best you can. I'll help you up with your things but beyond that, I'm a busy man."

"I haven't many things," Winnie said.

When she saw my house she said, "The Slough of Despond, if you remember your Bunyan." Nevertheless she settled into the attic. I paid off Ida and from then on was in Winnie's hands.

It was true my life was transformed. It was amazing what Winnie could do. Except for the study which I locked up every time I left the house and where Winnie could not penetrate, she penetrated everywhere. A new kitchen stove was her only extravagance. I paid no attention to Winnie's comings and goings but it was truly remarkable how she managed to clean out the house from the basement to the attic so well that I saw through the sitting-room windows as it seemed for the first time, and my bed was actually made every day. Winnie achieved all this in a very short time. Within a week I began to have friends to meals, delicious, interesting, just right.

"How lucky you are!" was what I heard from one friend after another. There were few who would not willingly have taken Winnie away from me if they'd had the chance. My mother's silver and crystal sparkled on the table. Winnie was quite up to serving at a late hour. And her meals were always marvellous. "Oh what elegance! How does she manage it?"

"Who is she arguing with, there in the kitchen?"

"Herself."

For one could hear Winnie, after she had cleared away and served us coffee, muttering to herself meanwhile, in the sitting-room, still fighting her lonely battles in the kitchen.

I am a man of the theatre, and this oddity of Winnie's certainly appealed to my sense of theatre. Nor were my friends unappreciative of the carry-on. They thought it was delightful. As soon as she had left the room they called her a joy and they called her a treasure. One of my younger friends, an actress who had formerly liked to visit my mother in the country, had the quick eye to notice, what I hadn't noticed, that a couple of my chairs had been newly upholstered in genuine petit-point.

"You've had your mother's petit-point finished," she said.

"I remember she was working on it all last summer. The last time I saw her just before she died she was sitting out on the terrace working at this."

"How do you know it's Ma's work?" I said.

"I recognize the pattern, look, that's the Venetian design, she had it done specially, look at that red."

"Well she must have finished it."

"Oh, that's impossible. It's very slow work. For your mother, impossible."

"Well, Winnie must have finished it."

"Winnie? How could she have managed it with all the other things she had to do?"

"One never knows what Winnie's up to."

I was suspicious. But, looking back on it, I think that the truth is I didn't want to know how Winnie did it. It was like admitting you didn't believe in Santa Claus: all those lovely surprises might stop.

Winnie's success with my friends wasn't lost on her. She, too, developed a sense of her theatrical side, muttering ever the more as she served the vegetables or the coffee; and one evening when I had a few guests, for no apparent reason she entered the room with one of my mother's mothy great ostrich feather fans in her hand and gave a performance of a pre-war debutante being presented at court, sweeping the fan before her and curtseying low, with the feathers flying all over the carpet. She solemnly left the room, backwards, treating us to another low genuflection before she left. Nobody spoke till she had gone, but Winnie's dottiness occupied the conversation merrily for the rest of the evening; secretly, I was a little embarrassed. Another time I was having a quiet game of chess with a friend when Winnie came in unnecessarily to tidy the fire. She had cleaned up those old chess pieces from Ma's trunk, they were positively a work of restoration. As she passed us she cast an eye at the board and said, "Undemocratic." I suppose she was referring to the kings and castles. But where Winnie was getting beyond a joke was on those days when, after lunch, I sat in my study trying to compose my theatre column.

Winnie at that time of day was usually up in her room in the attic wildly remonstrating with herself. I could get no peace. Finally and reluctantly I had it out with her.

"Winnie," I said, very tactfully, "you're beginning to talk to yourself, you know. There's nothing to worry about, many people do it, in fact there are great geniuses who go about talking to themselves. It's only that I can't get on with my work when I hear these arguments going on over my head."

"Well, I'm much provoked," Winnie said.

"I've no doubt of that. And I think you really do too much for me. Will you agree to see a doctor?"

"In an institution?" Winnie wanted to know.

"Oh, Winnie, of course not. Only privately. Maybe you need some medicine. Otherwise, I'm afraid we'll have to part. But I do urge you –"

I urged her into going to a young psychiatrist I'd heard of, in private practice. I have no idea what account she gave of herself and her condition but I've no doubt he got some illogical story out of her. She didn't appear to think there was anything wrong with her, and neither, apparently, did he. She refused to go into hospital under observation and he sent her away after a few visits with some medicine. I made enquiries of the doctor but he wouldn't say much. "She has a few hallucinations, nothing to worry about. She should get over it. Of course I can't diagnose in depth without her cooperation in a clinic." I settled his exorbitant bill. Winnie carried on in much the same way as before for about a week. She told me she was taking the medicine.

Then she did get quieter. Within two weeks she had stopped her racketing and shouting. I was able to get on with my work.

But slowly the house degenerated. It was like old times, only worse, because, although I began to eat out, Winnie burnt the food she prepared for herself. There was a super-chaos, a smell of burning and old rubbish all over the house. She bustled about brightly enough, but simply couldn't manage.

"Perhaps you need a holiday, Winnie."

"I stopped taking them pills," she said. "Rose didn't like them. They had an effect."

"Rose?"

"Rose Spigot."

I remembered Miss Spigot, the cook who died. I remembered Miss Spigot with her specially careful enunciation, her prim and well-trained ways, and how she was said to have travelled with a duke's family all over the Orient. "Are you talking about some relation of our late cook?" I said.

"I'm talking about our late cook herself," said Winnie. "She's gone away. When I started to take the pills they put her off her stroke."

"By no means," I said wildly, "take anything whatsoever that doesn't suit you, Winnie."

"It's not me, it's Rose. She was a very provoking woman,

acting the lady with your mother's needlework and objecting to me showing off in front of company. But she was a good cook-housekeeper, she's a good manager, and I can't cope alone with all the mess. She was another pair of hands."

"Definitely, you should stop the pills," I said. "Wouldn't you like me to have another word with the doctor?"

"Certainly not," said Winnie. "There was nothing wrong with the doctor."

I had to go away for a week to a theatre festival in the north. I was glad to go, notwithstanding my crumpled shirts and unwashed socks crammed into my bag. I felt I could face the problem of Winnie better after a break.

When I got back, as I put my key in the door, I knew something had happened by the fact that my old brass nameplate was twinkling and by the sound of Winnie's voice from the back of the house raised in argument.

Only Winnie was in the kitchen when I put my head round the door. "Rose is back," said Winnie.

I could see what she meant. The house was clean and shining; my supper that night was excellent.

But it was all too much for my no doubt weak character. I thought it over for a bit and finally persuaded Winnie to retire. She went back to Yorkshire, accompanied by Miss Spigot or not I don't know. My house is the pigsty of old. My friends are awfully good to me and I dine out a lot. The stuff that used to moulder in the basement is now rotting in the attic. Nobody combs Francis the cat, but he doesn't mind. When I'm on my own I can always sit down among the dust and the litter, and play the piano.

THE GIRL I LEFT BEHIND ME

It was just gone quarter past six when I left the office.

"Teedle-um-tum-tum" – there was the tune again, going round my head. Mr Letter had been whistling it all throughout the day between his noisy telephone calls and his dreamy sessions. Sometimes he whistled "Softly, Softly, Turn the Key", but usually it was "The Girl I Left Behind Me" rendered at a brisk hornpipe tempo.

I stood in the bus queue, tired out, and wondering how long I would endure Mark Letter (Screws & Nails) Ltd. Of course, after my long illness, it was experience. But Mr Letter and his tune, and his sudden moods of bounce, and his sudden lapses into lassitude, his sandy hair and little bad teeth, roused my resentment, especially when his tune barrelled round my head long after I had left the office; it was like taking Mr Letter home.

No one at the bus stop took any notice of me. Well, of course, why should they? I was not acquainted with anyone there, but that evening I felt particularly anonymous among the homegoers. Everyone looked right through me and even, it seemed, walked through me. Late autumn always sets my fancy towards sad ideas. The starlings were crowding in to roost on all the high cornices of the great office buildings. And I located, among the misty unease of my feelings, a very strong conviction that I had left something important behind me or some job incompleted at the office. Perhaps I had left the safe unlocked, or perhaps it was something quite trivial which nagged at me. I had half a mind to turn back, tired as I was, and reassure myself. But my bus came along and I piled in with the rest.

As usual, I did not get a seat. I clung to the handrail and allowed myself to be lurched back and forth against the other passengers. I stood on a man's foot, and said, "Oh, sorry." But he looked away without response, which depressed me. And more and more, I felt that I had left something of tremendous import at the office. "Teedle-um-tum-tum" – the tune was a background to my worry all the way home. I went over in my mind the day's business, for I thought, now, perhaps it was a letter which I should have written and posted on my way home.

That morning I had arrived at the office to find Mark Letter vigorously at work. By fits, he would occasionally turn up at eight in the morning, tear at the post and, by the time I arrived, he would have dispatched perhaps half a dozen needless telegrams; and before I could get my coat off, would deliver a whole day's instructions to me, rapidly fluttering his freckled hands in time with his chattering mouth. This habit used to jar me, and I found only one thing amusing about it; that was when he would say, as he gave instructions for dealing with each item, "Mark letter urgent." I thought that rather funny coming from Mark Letter, and I often thought of him, as he was in those moods, as Mark Letter Urgent.

As I swayed in the bus I recalled that morning's excess of energy on the part of Mark Letter Urgent. He had been more urgent than usual, so that I still felt put out by the urgency. I felt terribly old for my twenty-two years as I raked round my mind for some clue as to what I had left unfinished. Something had been left amiss; the further the bus carried me from the office, the more certain I became of it. Not that I took my job to heart very greatly, but Mr Letter's moods of bustle were infectious, and when they occurred I felt fussy for the rest of the day; and although I consoled myself that I would feel better when I got home, the worry would not leave me.

By noon, Mr Letter had calmed down a little, and for an hour before I went to lunch he strode round the office with his hands in his pockets, whistling between his seedy brown teeth that sailors' song "The Girl I Left Behind Me". I lurched with the bus as it chugged out the rhythm, "Teedle-um-tum-tum. Teedle-um . . ." Returning from lunch I had found silence, and wondered if Mr Letter was out, until I heard suddenly, from his tiny private office, his tune again, a low swift hum, trailing out towards the end. Then I knew that he had fallen into one of his afternoon daydreams.

I would sometimes come upon him in his little box of an office when these trances afflicted him. I would find him sitting in his swivel chair behind his desk. Usually he had taken off his coat and slung it across the back of his chair. His right elbow would be propped on the desk, supporting his chin, while from his left hand would dangle his tie. He would gaze at this tie; it was his main object of contemplation. That afternoon I had found him tie-gazing when I went into his room for some papers. He was gazing at it with parted lips so that I could see his small, separated discoloured teeth, no larger than a child's first teeth. Through them he whistled his tune. Yesterday, it had been "Softly, Softly, Turn the Key", but today it was the other.

I got off the bus at my usual stop, with my fare still in my hand. I almost threw the coins away, absentmindedly thinking they were the ticket, and when I noticed them I thought how nearly no one at all I was, since even the conductor had, in his rush, passed me by.

Mark Letter had remained in his dream for two and a half hours. What was it I had left unfinished? I could not for the life of me recall what he had said when at last he emerged from his office-box. Perhaps it was then I had made tea. Mr Letter always liked a cup when he was neither in his frenzy nor in his abstraction, but ordinary and talkative. He would speak of his hobby, fretwork. I do not think Mr Letter had any home life. At forty-six he was still unmarried, living alone in a house at Roehampton. As I walked up the lane to my lodgings I recollected that Mr Letter had come in for his tea with his tie still dangling from his hand, his throat white under the open-neck shirt, and his "Teedle-um-tum-tum" in his teeth.

At last I was home and my Yale in the lock. Softly, I said to myself, softly turn the key, and thank God I'm home. My landlady passed through the hall from kitchen to dining-room with a salt and pepper cruet in her crinkly hands. She had some new lodgers. "My guests", she always called them. The new guests took precedence over the old with my land-lady. I felt desolate. I simply could not climb the stairs to my room to wash, and then descend to take brown soup with the new guests while my landlady fussed over them, ignoring me. I sat for a moment in the chair in the hall to collect my strength. A year's illness drains one, however young. Suddenly the repulsion of the brown soup and the anxiety about the office made me decide. I would not go upstairs to my room. I must return to the office to see what it was that I had overlooked.

"Teedle-um-tum-tum" – I told myself that I was giving way to neurosis. Many times I had laughed at my sister who, after she had gone to bed at night, would send her husband downstairs to make sure all the gas taps were turned off, all the doors locked, back and front. Very well, I was as silly as my sister, but I understood her obsession, and simply opened the door and slipped out of the house, tired as I was, making my weary way back to the bus stop, back to the office.

"Why should I do this for Mark Letter?" I demanded of myself. But really, I was not returning for his sake, it was for my own. I was doing this to get rid of the feeling of incompletion, and that song in my brain swimming round like a damned goldfish.

I wondered, as the bus took me back along the familiar route, what I would say if Mark Letter should still be at the office. He often worked late, or at least, stayed there late, doing I don't know what, for his screw and nail business did not call for long hours. It seemed to me he had an affection for those dingy premises. I was rather apprehensive lest I should find Mr Letter at the office, standing, just as I had last seen him, swinging his tie in his hand, beside my desk. I resolved that if I should find him there, I should say straight out that I had left something behind me.

A clock struck quarter past seven as I got off the bus. I realized that again I had not paid my fare. I looked at the money in my hand for a stupid second. Then I felt reckless. "Teedle-um-tum-tum" – I caught myself humming the tune as I walked quickly up the sad side street to our office. My heart knocked at my throat, for I was eager. Softly, softly, I said to myself as I turned the key of the outside door. Quickly, quickly, I ran up the stairs. Only outside the office door I halted, and while I found its key on my bunch it occurred to me how strangely my sister would think I was behaving.

I opened the door and my sadness left me at once. With a great joy I recognized what it was I had left behind me, my body lying strangled on the floor. I ran towards my body and embraced it like a lover.

MISS PINKERTON'S APOCALYPSE

One evening, a damp one in February, something flew in at the window. Miss Laura Pinkerton, who was doing something innocent to the fire, heard a faint throbbing noise overhead. On looking up, "George! come here! come quickly!"

George Lake came in at once, though sullenly because of their quarrel, eating a sandwich from the kitchen. He looked up at the noise then sat down immediately.

From this point onward their story comes in two versions, his and hers. But they agree as to the main facts; they agree that it was a small round flattish object, and that it flew.

"It's a flying object of some sort," whispered George eventually.

"It's a saucer," said Miss Pinkerton, keen and loud, "an antique piece. You can tell by the shape."

"It can't be an antique, that's absolutely certain," George said.

He ought to have been more tactful, and would have been, but for the stress of the moment. Of course it set Miss Pinkerton off, she being in the right.

"I know my facts," she stated as usual, "I should hope

I know my facts. I've been in antique china for twenty-three years in the autumn," which was true, and George knew it.

The little saucer was cavorting round the lamp.

"It seems to be attracted by the light," George remarked, as one might distinguish a moth.

Promptly, it made as if to dive dangerously at George's head. He ducked, and Miss Pinkerton backed against the wall. As the dish tilted on its side, skimming George's shoulder, Miss Pinkerton could see inside it.

"The thing might be radioactive. It might be dangerous." George was breathless. The saucer had climbed, was circling high above his head, and now made for him again, but missed.

"It is not radioactive," said Miss Pinkerton, "it is Spode."

"Don't be so damn silly," George replied, under the stress of the occasion.

"All right, very well," said Miss Pinkerton, "it is not Spode. I suppose you are the expert, George, I suppose you know best. I was only judging by the pattern. After the best part of a lifetime in china –"

"It must be a forgery," George said unfortunately. For, unfortunately, something familiar and abrasive in Miss Pinkerton's speech began to grind within him. Also, he was afraid of the saucer.

It had taken a stately turn, following the picture rail in a steady career round the room.

"Forgery, ha!" said Miss Pinkerton. She was out of the room like a shot, and in again carrying a pair of steps.

"I will examine the mark," said she, pointing intensely at the saucer. "Where are my glasses?"

Obligingly, the saucer settled in a corner; it hung like a

spider a few inches from the ceiling. Miss Pinkerton adjusted the steps. With her glasses on she was almost her sunny self again, she was ceremonious and expert.

"Don't touch it, don't go near it!" George pushed her aside and grabbed the steps, knocking over a blue glass bowl, a Dresden figure, a vase of flowers and a decanter of sherry; like a bull in a china shop, as Miss Pinkerton exclaimed. But she was determined, and struggled to reclaim the steps.

"Laura!" he said desperately. "I believe it is Spode. I take your word."

The saucer then flew out of the window.

They acted quickly. They telephoned to the local paper. A reporter would come right away. Meanwhile, Miss Pinkerton telephoned to her two scientific friends – at least, one was interested in psychic research and the other was an electrician. But she got no reply from either. George had leaned out of the window, scanning the rooftops and the night sky. He had leaned out of the back windows, had tried all the lights and the wireless. These things were as usual.

The news man arrived, accompanied by a photographer.

"There's nothing to photograph," said Miss Pinkerton excitably. "It went away."

"We could take a few shots of the actual spot," the man explained.

Miss Pinkerton looked anxiously at the result of George and the steps.

"The place is a wreck."

Sherry from the decanter was still dripping from the sideboard.

"I'd better clear the place up. George, help me!" She

fluttered nervously, and started to pack the fire with small coals.

"No, leave everything as it is," the reporter advised her. "Did the apparition make this mess?"

George and Miss Pinkerton spoke together.

"Well, indirectly," said George.

"It wasn't an apparition," said Miss Pinkerton.

The reporter settled on the nearest chair, poising his pencil and asking, "Do you mind if I take notes?"

"Would you mind sitting over here?" said Miss Pinkerton. "I don't use the Queen Annes, normally. They are very frail pieces."

The reporter rose as if stung, then perched on a table which Miss Pinkerton looked at uneasily.

"You see, I'm in antiques," she rattled on, for the affair was beginning to tell on her, as George told himself. In fact he sized up that she was done for; his irritation abated, his confidence came flooding back.

"Now, Laura, sit down and take it easy." Solicitously he pushed her into an easy chair.

"She's overwrought," he informed the pressmen in an audible undertone.

"You say this object actually flew in this window?" suggested the reporter.

"That is correct," said George.

The cameraman trained his apparatus on the window.

"And you were both here at the time?"

"No," Miss Pinkerton said. "Mr Lake was in the kitchen and I called out, of course. But he didn't see inside the bowl, only the outside, underneath where the manufacturer's mark is. I saw the pattern so I got the steps to make sure. That's how Mr Lake knocked my things over. I saw inside."

"I am going to say something," said George.

The men looked hopefully towards him. After a pause, George continued, "Let us begin at the beginning."

"Right," said the reporter, breezing up.

"It was like this," George said. "I came straight in when Miss Pinkerton screamed, and there was a white convex disc, you realize, floating around up there."

The reporter contemplated the spot indicated by George.

"It was making a hell of a racket like a cat purring," George told him.

"Any idea what it really was?" the reporter inquired.

George took his time to answer. "Well, yes," he said, "and no."

"Spode ware," said Miss Pinkerton.

George continued, "I'm not up in these things. I'm extremely sceptical as a rule. This was a new experience to me."

"That's just it," said Miss Pinkerton. "Personally, I've been in china for twenty-three years. I recognized the thing immediately."

The reporter scribbled and inquired, "These flying discs appear frequently in China?"

"It was a saucer. I've never seen one flying before," Miss Pinkerton explained.

"I am going to ask a question," George said.

Miss Pinkerton continued, "Mr Lake is an art framer. He handles old canvases but next to no antiques."

"I am going to ask. Are you telling the story or am I?" George said.

"Perhaps Mr Lake's account first and then the lady's," the reporter ventured.

Miss Pinkerton subsided crossly while he turned to George.

"Was the object attached to anything? No wires or anything? I mean, someone couldn't have been having a joke or something?"

George gave a decent moment to the possibility.

"No," he then said. "It struck me, in fact, that there was some sort of Mind behind it, operating from outer space. It tried to attack me, in fact."

"Really, how was that?"

"Mr Lake was not attacked," Miss Pinkerton stated. "There was no danger at all. I saw the expression on the pilot's face. He was having a game with Mr Lake, grinning all over his face."

"Pilot?" said George. "What are you talking about – pilot!"

Miss Pinkerton sighed. "A tiny man half the size of my finger," she declared. "He sat on a tiny stool. He held the little tiny steering-wheel with one hand and waved with the other. Because, there was something like a sewing-machine fixed near the rim, and he worked the tiny treadle with his foot. Mr Lake was not attacked."

"Don't be so damn silly," said George.

"You don't mean this?" the reporter asked her with scrutiny.

"Of course I do."

"I would like to know something," George demanded.

"You only saw the underside of the saucer, George."

"You said nothing about any pilot at the time," said George. "I saw no pilot."

"Mr Lake got a fright when the saucer came at him. If he hadn't been dodging he would have seen for himself."

"You mentioned no pilot," said George. "Be reasonable."

"I had no chance," said she. She appealed to the cameraman. "You see, I know what I'm talking about. Mr Lake thought he knew better, however. Mr Lake said, 'It's a forgery.' If there's one thing I do know, it's china."

"It would be most unlikely," said George to the reporter. "A steering-wheel and a treadle machine these days, can you credit it?"

"The man would have fallen out," the cameraman reflected.

"I must say," said the reporter, "that I favour Mr Lake's long-range theory. The lady may have been subject to some hallucination, after the shock of the saucer."

"Quite," said George. He whispered something to the photographer. "Women!" Miss Pinkerton heard him breathe.

The reporter heard him also. He gave a friendly laugh. "Shall we continue with Mr Lake's account, and then see what we can make of both stories?"

But Miss Pinkerton had come to a rapid decision. She began to display a mood hitherto unknown to George. Leaning back, she gave way to a weak and artless giggling. Her hand fluttered prettily as she spoke between gurgles of mirth. "Oh, what a mess! What an evening! We aren't accustomed to drink, you see, and now oh dear, oh dear!"

"Are you all right, Laura?" George inquired severely.

"Yes, yes, yes," said Miss Pinkerton, drowsy and amiable.

"We really oughtn't to have done this, George. Bringing these gentlemen out. But I can't keep it up, George. Oh dear, it's been fun though."

She was away into her giggles again. George looked bewildered. Then he looked suspicious.

"It's definitely the effect of this extraordinary phenomenon," George said firmly to the press.

"It was my fault, all my fault," spluttered Miss Pinkerton.

The reporter looked at his watch. "I can quite definitely say you saw a flying object?" he asked. "And that you were both put out by it?"

"Put down that it was a small, round, flattish object. We both agree to that," George said.

A spurt of delight arose from Miss Pinkerton again.

"Women, you know! It always comes down to women in the finish," she told them. "We had a couple of drinks."

"Mr Lake had rather more than I did," she added triumphantly.

"I assure you," said George to the reporter.

"We might be fined for bringing the press along, George. It might be an offence," she put in.

"I assure you," George insisted to the photographer, "that we had a flying saucer less than an hour ago in this room."

Miss Pinkerton giggled.

The reporter looked round the room with new eyes; and with the air of one to whom to understand all is to forgive all, he folded his notebook. The cameraman stared at the pool of sherry, the overturned flowers, the broken glass and china. He packed up his camera, and they went away.

George gave out the tale to his regular customers. He

gave both versions, appealing to their reason to choose. Further up the road at her corner shop, Miss Pinkerton smiled tolerantly when questioned. "Flying saucer? George is very artistic," she would say, "and allowances must be made for imaginative folk." Sometimes she added that the evening had been a memorable one, "Quite a party!"

It caused a certain amount of tittering in the neighbourhood. George felt this; but otherwise, the affair made no difference between them. Personally, I believe the story, with a preference for Miss Pinkerton's original version. She is a neighbour of mine. I have reason to believe this version because, not long afterwards, I too received a flying visitation from a saucer. The little pilot, in my case, was shy and inquisitive. He pedalled with all his might. My saucer was Royal Worcester, fake or not I can't say.

THE PEARLY SHADOW

"I'll track him down," said Mr Neviss. "I'll be relentless."

Dr Felicity Grayland offered him a caramel of which there was a bowl on her table (for the children?).

"Thanks. I'll do away with him," said Mr Neviss, "as soon as I get my hands on him."

"Yes, Mr Neviss," said Felicity, who was a resident psychiatrist at the nursing home. "We'll *both* do away with him, in fact. That's what we're here for. I see you're down as Mr O. Neviss. What does 'O' stand for?"

"I can't think of anyone I dislike more," Mr Neviss said. "I'll break his –"

"Mr Neviss," said Felicity. "Relax. Just relax."

"O stands for Olaf. It isn't easy to relax," said the patient, "with him standing there." He pointed to a spot behind her chair.

Felicity leaned back. "Please describe this pearly shadow, Olaf," she said. "Simply tell me what you see, with the details. Call me Felicity – please do."

"Well," he said, "you can see for yourself. He's standing behind you."

"What is he doing?" Felicity inquired.

"Just standing," said Mr Neviss. "He's always just standing, except when I try to get hold of him, and then –"

"Try," said Felicity, "to relax. What exactly do you mean by a *pearly* shadow?"

"For goodness' sake, woman," said the patient, "look round and see for yourself."

Indulgently, with a small smile, she looked round, and looked back very quickly at her patient. "That's the way – keep relaxed," she said, helping herself to a sweet. "Now, tell me, when did this pearly shadow business first start?"

Felicity gave Olaf an hour. Then she showed him out to the nurse, who conveyed him to an attendant, to take him to his ward. Felicity lingered outside her consulting-room. She hesitated, then entered abruptly. Yes, the pearly shadow was still there.

She gave the matter a moment's thought before deciding to see the Chief about herself. Overwork, clearly. As she reached for the house phone, the nurse entered with the appointment book. "Only one more patient today, doctor," said the nurse pleasantly.

"Oh," Felicity said, "I thought Neviss was the last." She looked at the book. "P. Shadow," she repeated. "He must be a new patient; have we got his previous record?"

"It's on your desk," said the nurse. "Will I show him in?"

"I'm here already," said the pearly shadow.

The nurse jumped. "Oh, Mr Shadow," she said, "you should have waited in the waiting-room, you know."

"Sit down, Mr Shadow," said Felicity, as the nurse withdrew. She opened a drawer and took out a packet of cigarettes. "Cigarette?"

"Thank you," said the patient hoarsely, while Felicity glanced at his record.

"I shouldn't really offer you cigarettes," she smiled. "I see you've had lung trouble. *And* anaemia."

"I'm very bloodless," said the pearly shadow, "and my voice has almost gone.

"But," said the pearly shadow, as Felicity tried to distinguish his features, "I've come here about my nerves, you know. There's something on my mind."

This put Felicity finally at her ease. She applied herself calmly to the problem before her. The luminous vagueness of the patient's face became irrelevant. "I see you're down as P. Shadow. What does 'P' stand for?"

"Pearly. You can call me Pearly."

"Just relax," said Felicity. "Pearly, relax."

"It isn't easy to relax," said the pearly shadow, "when every hand is against you.

"Everyone is against me. You," he continued, "are against me. You want to do away with me. You intend to exterminate me."

"Relax, Mr Shadow," said Felicity, who did not really believe in first-name relationships with patients. "Now, tell me, what gives you this idea?"

"You told Neviss you'd both get rid of me. That's what you're here for, I heard," said the pearly shadow. "You're giving him sedatives, aren't you? You're going to work me out of his system, aren't you?"

Felicity kept her eye fixed on what looked like a pearl tie-pin at the level of his chest. "I can't discuss another patient's treatment with you," she explained. "That would be unethical. One patient has nothing to do with another."

"They gave him a drug last night," the pearly shadow said, "and I nearly died of it. If you give him anything stronger I shall probably fade away.

"You're trying to murder me," the patient insisted. "You and all the rest of them. I know."

Felicity gave him an hour. Then she opened the door and let him out. She carefully wrote her report on P. Shadow, and took it to the nurse. It was her habit to exchange a friendly few words with the nurse, after the last patient had left. Felicity leaned in the doorway. "Another day over, nurse," she remarked. "It's been rather a bore. In fact," she went on, "we don't get any interesting cases these days. All quite cut to the pattern, these days. Take those last two, for instance. Neviss – illusions of being haunted; perfectly simple. Shadow – straightforward illusions of persecution. Now, if you'd been here last year, we had some really complicated . . . Nurse! What's wrong with you?"

"He walked right through me," said the nurse, heaving, "and he came out at the other side."

"You've been overworking, Nurse," Felicity said. "Take a sweet, a cigarette . . . Here's some water. Now relax . . . just relax. He could not have walked right through you, but I think I know what you mean. He is a very insubstantial type." Felicity regarded the prosperous shape of the nurse. "Did you feel any sensation when he appeared to walk through you?"

"Well, he's luminous, isn't he? Where's he gone?"

"Home, I imagine. He's an out-patient. If you're feeling better, Nurse, I'm afraid I have to close the office. It's been a heavy day."

* * *

Felicity was still firmly decided to consult the Chief about herself and her confused delusion, but it was too late. Everyone had gone home.

Dr Felicity Grayland, as she left her office, regretted that she had not been able to remember the name of the nurse, and so make her chatty interlude more personal. She rarely remembered the names of the people around her or of the people she met. Without referring to the cards, she did not remember many of her patients. She drove home, trying hard, for some reason, to think of her last patient's name. She had no success, and when she put the car away she deliberately gave up.

Her supper of mixed green salad, Roquefort cheese and fruit, with brown bread and butter, was laid out on the dining-room table. Felicity set about it with relish, reading the morning's newspaper. She could never read the papers until the evening. Now she also remembered that she had decided to see the Chief about herself.

About herself? Herself? Why? There must be some mistake. She went into the sitting-room and turned on the television, tuning in to a quiz show, her favourite programme. The subject was the Armada. What age exactly was Philip of Spain when he embarked upon this enterprise? The girl student with black glossy hair and round-eyed glasses, who was already winning thousands of pounds, opened her mouth confidently to answer. But just at that moment the television turned itself off although the lights were still on. "I hate quiz programmes," said a thin voice. "They get too much money."

Felicity looked round and saw that patient of hers. The name?

"How did you get in here?" she said.

"Through the door."

The front door was locked, but she supposed he meant that he always proceeded like a ghost through walls and doors.

"If you want to consult me professionally," Felicity said, "you'll have to see me at my office in the clinic. This is my home, Mr—?"

"P. Shadow," he said. "First name, Pearly. I prefer not to attend that clinic. I frighten the nurses."

Felicity was used to strange patients, but she was thoroughly annoyed that her privacy had been violated. Quite sensibly, she didn't see the point of arguing with Shadow. Instead, she decided to ring a colleague to see if he would come round and help her to chuck out the unwanted patient. She phoned a number while P. Shadow made himself comfortable in an armchair with the newspaper.

There was no reply to the number Felicity rang. She paused a moment and started looking up another number in her address book.

She came to the name she was looking for: Margaret Arkans, a gynaecologist married to James Arkans, another gynaecologist. When she thought of them, sun-bronzed, young, with white teeth flashing as they laughed, she felt a fool.

The shadow sat on. He had put aside her paper and from what she could make out of his features, he looked more anxious than before.

"Mr Shadow, what's troubling you?" she said.

"I gather you're looking for medical friends," said the pearly shadow. "They might advise you to take a sleeping pill or something."

"Undoubtedly," said Felicity, beginning to see some way out of the situation. "I'll take a sleeping pill anyway."

"It might kill me if you did that."

"Relax. Just relax. I'll only take a light one. But I do feel the need of something to make me sleep, quite honestly."

In the bathroom Felicity took a white tablet from her medicine cupboard. She cleaned her teeth. Then she looked round the door of the sitting-room. Already, the pearly shadow had gone. To be quite sure, she searched the rest of the house before going to bed. Yes, the pill had worked. She slept well.

"Nurse, relax. Just relax."

"He's in the waiting-room," said the nurse. It was nine-thirty the next morning, the time when the psychiatrist's office opened.

"Any other patients?" said Felicity.

"Three more. But they don't seem to notice him."

Felicity could quite believe this. Most psychiatric patients look weird, especially while waiting for consultation.

"He might walk through me again," wailed the nurse loudly. "It makes me feel awful."

"Hush," said the doctor. "Someone might hear you."

The office door was open. Someone had heard her. Dr Margaret Arkans put her head round the door. "Anything wrong?"

"Nurse Simmons isn't very well," said Felicity in a voice which suggested she had decided everything – on a course of action, everything, from now on.

"I've had a terrible experience," Nurse Simmons said. "Last night; and now it's going to happen again this morning."

Margaret and Felicity were extremely solicitous. Felicity

herself gave the nurse an injection to make her relax, and took her to the staff rest-room to lie down.

"Overwork." The two doctors looked at each other and shook their heads knowingly. They were both long since convinced that everyone in their department was overworked, including themselves.

On her way back to her office Felicity looked in on the waiting-room. The pearly shadow was not there.

Felicity recommended that Nurse Simmons should have a month's rest, with a course of sedatives. Nurse Simmons lived with a large family who were extremely alarmed when she felt a "presence" in the room every time she forgot to take her pills. She screamed a great deal. "She still has her delusions," said her sister on the phone.

One night Pearly Shadow visited Felicity again.

"Are you hoping to kill me with all these sedatives you're giving her?"

"Yes," said Felicity.

"She might take an overdose."

"Almost certainly she will," Felicity said.

"But that would kill me."

"I know," she said. "If you don't leave us alone you'll be finished soon."

"But I'm your patient."

"You won't feel a thing," said the doctor. "Not a thing."

The pearly shadow looked terribly frightened.

"Your only hope," said Felicity, as she switched the television from station to station, "is to leave us alone and go elsewhere for treatment."

Nurse Simmons improved. Neither she nor Dr Felicity

Grayland saw Pearly Shadow again, but a few years later they heard of a psychiatrist in the north who had died of an overdose of barbiturates which had curiously made his skin translucent and pearly.

GOING UP AND COMING DOWN

How many couples have met in an elevator (lift, *ascenseur*, *ascensore* or whatever you call it throughout the world)? How many marriages have resulted?

In their elevator there is usually an attendant, sometimes not.

She goes up and down every weekday. At the 1.05 crush and the 2.35 return she generally finds him in the crowded box; looking up at the floor number display, looking down at the floor. Sometimes they are alone. He, she discovers, comes down from the twenty-first.

His office? On the board downstairs six offices are listed on the twenty-first floor: a law firm, a real estate office, an ophthalmologist, a Swiss chemicals association, a Palestine Potassium (believe it or not) agency, a rheumatologist. Which of these offices could he belong to? She doesn't look at him direct, but always, at a glance, tests the ramifying possibilities inherent in all six concerns.

He is polite. He stands well back when the crowd presses. They are like coins in a purse.

One day she catches his eye and looks away.

He notices her briefcase while she has her eyes on the

floor numbers. Going down. Out she pours with the chattering human throng, turns left (the lobby has two entrances) and is gone. On the board down there are listed four offices on Floor 16, her floor. Two law firms, a literary agency and an office named W. H. Gilbert without further designation. Does she work for Mr Gilbert, he wonders. Is Gilbert a private detective? W. H. Gilbert may well be something furtive.

Day by day she keeps her eyes on his briefcase of pale brown leather and wonders what he does. The lift stops at Floor 9, and in sidles the grey-haired stoutish man with the extremely cheerful smile. On we go; down, down. She wonders about the young man's daily life, where does he live, where and what does he eat, has he ever read the Bible? She knows nothing, absolutely nothing except one thing, which is this: he tries to catch a glimpse of her when she is looking elsewhere or leaving the elevator.

On the ground floor – seconds, and he's gone. It is like looking out of the window of a train, he flashes by so quickly. She thinks he might be poorly paid up there on the twenty-first, possibly in the real estate office or with the expert on rheumatism. He must be barely twenty-five. He might be working towards a better job, but at the moment with very little left in his pocket after paying out for his rent, food, clothes and insect spray.

Her long fair hair falls over her shoulders, outside her dark green coat. Perhaps she spends her days sending out membership renewal forms for Mr Gilbert's arcane activity: "Yes, I want to confirm my steadfast support for the Cosmic Paranormal Apostolic Movement by renewing my subscription", followed by different rates to be filled in for the categories: Individual Member, Couple, and Senior Citizen/Unwaged/Student.

Suppose there is a power failure?

She looks at his briefcase, his tie. Everything begins in a dream. In a daydream she has even envisaged an inevitable meeting in a room in some place where only two could be, far from intrusions, such as in a barn, taking shelter from a storm, snowed up. Surely there is some film to that effect.

He does not have the married look. That look, impossible to define apart from a wedding ring, absent in his case, is far from his look. All the same, he could be married, peeling potatoes for two at the weekend. What sign of the zodiac is his? Has there been an orchard somewhere in his past life as there has in hers? What TV channels does he watch?

Her hair hangs over her shoulders. He wonders if she dyes it blonde; her pubic hairs are possibly dark. Is she one of those girls who doesn't eat, so that you pay an enormous restaurant bill for food she has only picked at?

One night the attendant is missing. They are alone. Homicidal? – Could it possibly be? He would only have to take off his tie if his hands alone weren't enough. But his hands could strangle her. When they get out at the ground floor he says, "Good night," and is lost in the crowd.

Here in the enclosed space is almost like bundling. He considers how, in remote parts, when it was impossible for a courting man to get home at night, the elders would bundle a couple; they would bundle them together in their clothes. The pair breathed over each other but were mutually inaccessible, in an impotent rehearsal of the intimacy to come. Perhaps, he flounders in his mind, she goes to church and is better than me. This idea of her being morally better hangs about him all night, and he brings it to the elevator next morning.

She is not there. Surely she has flu, alone in her one-room apartment. Her one room with a big bed and a window overlooking the river? Or is Mr Gilbert there with her?

When she appears next day in the elevator he is tempted to follow her home that night. But then she might know; feel, guess, his presence behind her. Certainly she would. She might well think him a weirdy, a criminal. She might turn and catch sight of him, crossing the park:

> Like one, that on a lonesome road
> Doth walk in fear and dread,
> And having once turned round walks on,
> And turns no more his head;
> Because he knows, a frightful fiend
> Doth close behind him tread.

Does she go to a gym class? She must have caught me looking just now. He knows she does not wear a wedding ring or an engagement ring. But that does not mean very much.

She looks at his briefcase, his tie, the floor, the floor number. Could he be a diamond merchant with a fold of tissue paper, containing five one-carat diamonds, nestling in his inner pocket? One of the names on the board could be a cover.

Other, familiar people join them on every floor. A woman with a white smile that no dentist could warm edges towards him while he edges away.

*   *   *

One day at the lunch hour he looks at her and smiles. She is there, too, in the evening with only four other people plus the attendant for the elevator. He takes the plunge. Would she be free for dinner one night? Thursday? Friday?

They have made a date. They eat in a Polish restaurant where the clients are served by waitresses with long hair even blonder and probably more natural than Doreen's.

How long does it take for floating myths and suppositions to form themselves into the separate still digits of reality? Sometimes it is as quick or as slow, according to luck, as fixing the television screen when it has gone haywire. Those stripes and cloudscapes are suddenly furniture and people.

He is employed by one of the law firms up there on the twenty-first, his speciality is marine insurance claims. Doreen, as she is called, remarks that it must be a great responsibility. He realizes she is intelligent even before Doreen Bridges (her full name) tells him she works for W. H. Gilbert, ("Bill"), an independent literary agent, and that she has recently discovered an absolutely brilliant new author called Dak Jan whose forthcoming first novel she has great hopes for. Michael Pivet lives in a bachelor apartment; she shares rooms with another girl in another part of the city.

And the curious thing is, that all the notions and possibilities that have gone through their minds for the past five weeks or more are totally forgotten by both of them. In the fullness of the plain real facts their speculations disappear into immaterial nothingness, never once to be remembered in the course of their future life together.

YOU SHOULD HAVE SEEN THE MESS

I am now more than glad that I did not pass into the grammar school five years ago, although it was a disappointment at the time. I was always good at English, but not so good at the other subjects!!

I am glad that I went to the Secondary Modern School, because it was only constructed the year before. Therefore, it was much more hygienic than the Grammar School. The Secondary Modern was light and airy, and the walls were painted with a bright, washable, gloss. One day, I was sent over to the Grammar School, with a note for one of the teachers, and you should have seen the mess! The corridors were dusty, and I saw dust on the window ledges, which were chipped. I saw into one of the classrooms. It was very untidy in there.

I am also glad that I did not go to the Grammar School, because of what it does to one's habits. This may appear to be a strange remark, at first sight. It is a good thing to have an education behind you, and I do not believe in ignorance, but I have had certain experiences, with educated people, since going out into the world.

I am seventeen years of age, and left school two years ago last month. I had my A certificate for typing, so got my first job, as a junior, in a solicitor's office. Mum was pleased at this, and Dad said it was a first-class start, as it was an old-established firm. I must say that when I went for the interview I was surprised at the windows, and the stairs up to the offices were also far from clean. There was a little waiting-room, where some of the elements were missing from the gas fire, and the carpet on the floor was worn. However, Mr Heygate's office, into which I was shown for the interview, was better. The furniture was old, but it was polished, and there was a good carpet, I will say that. The glass of the book-case was very clean.

I was to start on the Monday, so along I went. They took me to the general office, where there were two senior shorthand typists, and a clerk, Mr Gresham, who was far from smart in appearance. You should have seen the mess!! There was no floor covering whatsoever, and so dusty everywhere. There were shelves all round the room, with old box files on them. The box files were falling to pieces, and all the old papers inside them were crumpled. The worst shock of all was the tea-cups. It was my duty to make tea, mornings and afternoons. Miss Bewlay showed me where everything was kept. It was kept in an old orange box, and the cups were all cracked. There were not enough saucers to go round, etc. I will not go into the facilities, but they were also far from hygienic. After three days, I told Mum, and she was upset, most of all about the cracked cups. We never keep a cracked cup, but throw it out, because those cracks can harbour germs. So Mum gave me my own cup to take to the office.

Then at the end of the week, when I got my salary, Mr Heygate said, "Well, Lorna, what are you going to do with your first pay?" I did not like him saying this, and I nearly passed a comment, but I said, "I don't know." He said, "What do you do in the evenings, Lorna? Do you watch telly?" I did take this as an insult, because we call it TV, and his remark made me out to be uneducated. I just stood, and did not answer, and he looked surprised. Next day, Saturday, I told Mum and Dad about the facilities, and we decided I should not go back to that job. Also, the desks in the general office were rickety. Dad was indignant, because Mr Heygate's concern was flourishing, and he had letters after his name.

Everyone admires our flat, because Mum keeps it spotless, and Dad keeps doing things to it. He has done it up all over, and got permission from the Council to re-modernize the kitchen. I well recall the Health Visitor remarking to Mum, "You could eat off your floor, Mrs Merrifield." It is true that you could eat your lunch off Mum's floors, and any hour of the day or night you will find every corner spick and span.

Next, I was sent by the agency to a publisher's for an interview, because of being good at English. One look was enough!! My next interview was a success, and I am still at Low's Chemical Co. It is a modern block, with a quarter of an hour rest period, morning and afternoon. Mr Marwood is very smart in appearance. He is well spoken, although he has not got a university education behind him. There is special lighting over the desks, and the typewriters are the latest models.

So I am happy at Low's. But I have met other people, of an educated type, in the past year, and it has opened my eyes. It so happened that I had to go to the doctor's house, to fetch a prescription for my young brother, Trevor, when the epidemic was on. I rang the bell, and Mrs Darby came to the door. She was small, with fair hair, but too long, and a green maternity dress. But she was very nice to me. I had to wait in their living-room, and you should have seen the state it was in! There were broken toys on the carpet, and the ashtrays were full up. There were contemporary pictures on the walls, but the furniture was not contemporary, but old-fashioned, with covers which were past standing up to another wash, I should say. To cut a long story short, Dr Darby and Mrs Darby have always been very kind to me, and they meant everything for the best. Dr Darby is also short and fair, and they have three children, a girl and a boy, and now a baby boy.

When I went that day for the prescription, Dr Darby said to me, "You look pale, Lorna. It's the London atmosphere. Come on a picnic with us, in the car, on Saturday." After that I went with the Darbys more and more. I liked them, but I did not like the mess, and it was a surprise. But I also kept in with them for the opportunity of meeting people, and Mum and Dad were pleased that I had made nice friends. So I did not say anything about the cracked lino, and the paintwork all chipped. The children's clothes were very shabby for a doctor, and she changed them out of their school clothes when they came home from school, into those worn-out garments. Mum always kept us spotless to go out to play, and I do not like to say it, but those Darby children frequently looked like the Leary family, which the Council evicted from our block, as they were far from houseproud.

One day, when I was there, Mavis (as I called Mrs Darby by then) put her head out of the window, and shouted to the boy, "John, stop peeing over the cabbages at once. Pee on the lawn." I did not know which way to look. Mum would never say a word like that from the window, and I know for a fact that Trevor would never pass water outside, not even bathing in the sea.

I went there usually at the weekends, but sometimes on weekdays, after supper. They had an idea to make a match for me with a chemist's assistant, whom they had taken up too. He was an orphan, and I do not say there was anything wrong with that. But he was not accustomed to those little extras that I was. He was a good-looking boy, I will say that. So I went once to a dance, and twice to films with him. To look at, he was quite clean in appearance. But there was only hot water at the weekend at his place, and he said that a bath once a week was sufficient. Jim (as I called Dr Darby by then) said it was sufficient also, and surprised me. He did not have much money, and I do not hold that against him. But there was no hurry for me, and I could wait for a man in a better position, so that I would not miss those little extras. So he started going out with a girl from the coffee bar, and did not come to the Darbys very much then.

There were plenty of boys at the office, but I will say this for the Darbys, they had lots of friends coming and going, and they had interesting conversation, although sometimes it gave me a surprise, and I did not know where to look. And sometimes they had people who were very down and out, although there is no need to be. But most of the guests were different, so it made a comparison with the boys at the office, who were not so educated in their conversation.

Now it was near the time for Mavis to have her baby, and I was to come in at the weekend, to keep an eye on the children, while the help had her day off. Mavis did not go away to have her baby, but would have it at home, in their double bed, as they did not have twin beds, although he was a doctor. A girl I knew, in our block, was engaged, but was let down, and even she had her baby in the labour ward. I was sure the bedroom was not hygienic for having a baby, but I did not mention it.

One day, after the baby boy came along, they took me in the car to the country, to see Jim's mother. The baby was put in a carry-cot at the back of the car. He began to cry, and without a word of a lie, Jim said to him over his shoulder, "Oh shut your gob, you little bastard." I did not know what to do, and Mavis was smoking a cigarette. Dad would not dream of saying such a thing to Trevor or I. When we arrived at Jim's mother's place, Jim said, "It's a fourteenth-century cottage, Lorna." I could well believe it. It was very cracked and old, and it made one wonder how Jim could let his old mother live in this tumble-down cottage, as he was so good to everyone else. So Mavis knocked at the door, and the old lady came. There was not much anyone could do to the inside. Mavis said, "Isn't it charming, Lorna?" If that was a joke, it was going too far. I said to the old Mrs Darby, "Are you going to be re-housed?" but she did not understand this, and I explained how you have to apply to the Council, and keep at them. But it was funny that the Council had not done something already, when they go round condemning. Then old Mrs Darby said, "My dear, I shall be re-housed in the Grave." I did not know where to look.

There was a carpet hanging on the wall, which I think was there to hide a damp spot. She had a good TV set, I will say that. But some of the walls were bare brick, and the facilities were outside, through the garden. The furniture was far from new.

One Saturday afternoon, as I happened to go to the Darbys, they were just going off to a film and they took me too. It was the Curzon, and afterwards we went to a flat in Curzon Street. It was a very clean block, I will say that, and there were good carpets at the entrance. The couple there had contemporary furniture, and they also spoke about music. It was a nice place, but there was no Welfare Centre to the flats, where people could go for social intercourse, advice and guidance. But they were well-spoken, and I met Willy Morley, who was an artist. Willy sat beside me, and we had a drink. He was young, dark, with a dark shirt, so one could not see right away if he was clean. Soon after this, Jim said to me, "Willy wants to paint you, Lorna. But you'd better ask your Mum." Mum said it was all right if he was a friend of the Darbys.

I can honestly say that Willy's place was the most unhygienic place I have seen in my life. He said I had an unusual type of beauty, which he must capture. This was when we came back to his place from the restaurant. The light was very dim, but I could see the bed had not been made, and the sheets were far from clean. He said he must paint me, but I told Mavis I did not like to go back there. "Don't you like Willy?" she asked. I could not deny that I liked Willy, in a way. There was something about him, I will say that. Mavis said, "I hope he hasn't been making a pass at you, Lorna." I said he had not done so, which was almost true, because he did not attempt to go to the full extent. It was always unhygienic when I went to Willy's place, and I told him so once, but he said, "Lorna, you are a joy." He had a nice way, and he took me out in his car, which was a good one, but dirty inside, like his place. Jim said one day, "He has pots of money, Lorna," and Mavis said, "You might make a man of him, as he is keen on you." They always said Willy came from a good family.

But I saw that one could not do anything with him. He would not change his shirt very often, or get clothes, but he went round like a tramp, lending people money, as I have seen with my own eyes. His place was in a terrible mess, with the empty bottles, and laundry in the corner. He gave me several gifts over the period, which I took as he would have only given them away, but he never tried to go to the full extent. He never painted my portrait, as he was painting fruit on a table all that time, and they said his pictures were marvellous, and thought Willy and I were getting married.

One night, when I went home, I was upset as usual, after Willy's place. Mum and Dad had gone to bed, and I looked round our kitchen which is done in primrose and white. Then I went into the living-room, where Dad has done one wall in a patterned paper, deep rose and white, and the other walls pale rose, with white woodwork. The suite is new, and Mum keeps everything beautiful. So it came to me, all of a sudden, what a fool I was, going with Willy. I agree to equality, but as to me marrying Willy, as I said to Mavis, when I recall his place, and the good carpet gone greasy, not to mention the paint oozing out of the tubes, I think it would break my heart to sink so low.

QUEST FOR LAVISHES GHAST

Lavishes ghast! – this phrase haunted me for years. When I first came to London I worked for a man who was always losing his papers. Hours I would spend, looking for those bits of paper, until suddenly he would say, "Lavishes ghast." After a while I got used to this man. Northerner though I was, and with only the short "a" of lavishes and the long "a" of ghast to work on, I came to understand that lavishes ghast stood for "I have it at last." And in spite of his habit of talking hand-over-fist and disdaining consonants, it became possible for me to decode an irrelevant statement like "Clot on the brain" into the relevant "Lost it again!"

I have kept coming across people like him. As a rule I have managed to fill in the missing letters and guess the whole. As a rule; but lavishes ghast remains an exception. In the same way that the yellowhammer chirps continually, "A little piece of bread and no cheese," and the cuckoo croaks nothing but "cuckoo," so, I swear, does everyone at the usual crowded party say "lavishes ghast" all the time.

At the beginning of my quest I was quite unnerved by it. The phrase meant something different each time, but plainly it stemmed from a general, perhaps mystical meaning. Lavishes was so substantial and ghast so evanescent; all the anxious ingredients of Pavlov's nasty practical jokes were there in essence. Were people talking of radishes vast? Did they hang from the mast? Once I met a soldier in the train who was trying to dodge the military police. "They'll ask me to lavishes ghast and I *lavishes* ghast, can't be done," he explained through his teeth. With due cunning I inquired, "Why not?" The question goaded him to articulate speech. "How," he demanded, "can I hand 'em me pass if I haven't a pass?" And a girl I knew told me, "I lavishes ghast to marry him." Ungenerously, I took this to mean she hadn't been asked, but it turned out she hadn't the heart. I recall, too, a visit to the country . . . a rabbit in the grass . . . "Yes, he does look happy at his task," I said to my host, who had seemed to point at a ploughman as he spoke.

There was also the earlier and more deranging occasion when I stayed overnight with a friend's mother. At breakfast she was reading a letter from her son. She put down the letter, and, gazing wistfully at a bowl of flowers, murmured, "Lavishes ghast, don't you think?" Well, of course I thought Anthony was fast. I could have told her a lot about Anthony, but after all, she was the mother, so I said, "Oh, not really!" She paused, and, keeping her eye still on the flowers, repeated firmly, "Well, my dear, I think they *are* ravishing flaahers."

I entered the obsessional phase. L. G. became meaningful, threatening. I began to suspect that it was a person. I didn't want to meet Mrs Ghast, for at the time I decided it must be a woman, a widow, formerly married to a Mr Ghast who was seen only once with his wife, on a desolate cliff top in the Orkneys or Land's End, before he disappeared. Mrs Ghast would be very lavish at first. She would be ever so hospitable, to start with. At times I speculated whether Ghast might be a thing, a powerful magnetic mineral to which I alone was allergic. But pondering the question at the dead of night, I felt sure again it was a person.

The situation had reached Gothic proportions. I decided to pursue the monster, hunt it down before it hunted me, and thus I came to do so. I took to frequenting the sort of place which is not my sort of place at all: cosy tea shops in Hampstead, Kensington, and even Ealing, with names like Araminta's Kettle or The Ginger Jug. Here, in these Jugs and Kettles, lavishes ghast flourishes most. And it rages most between the afternoon hours of four and five-thirty. My plan was simple: all I had to do was sit and listen, take notes of everything I heard by way of lavishes, do it into English and, when my collection reached a decent size, extract the common factors of sense. In this way I would locate lavishes ghast, its origin, nature, nationality of parents and present address.

The first afternoon, this seemed easy. I fixed on a mother and daughter having tea. "They're very lavish here," said the mother, beaming on the cakes as the daughter replied, "But the tea's ghastly." I took this to be a good omen. But within a few days sinister complications like "lavishes ghast lavishes" began to set in. A creature comprising Alex's car, aspects of art, anarchist bard, amorous chars, hand on my heart, Battersea Park, masses of stars, passion aha! remained beyond my comprehension.

My last tea shop was ominously called The African Palm by virtue of a large tough fern in the window. I chose a table next to a young couple who were conversing audibly.

"What was the lavishes ghast on lavishes ghast like?" rattled the girl.

"No, thanks," said the youth, "I'll have a bun."

The girl looked cross. He had obviously misunderstood her, had this likable young man. She repeated her question. Practice had given me a flair for rapid decoding: "What was the Charity Dance on Saturday last like?"

"Ghast!" he replied. "Lavishes!"

"I only went to please my mother," he added obligingly, from which I deduced that the dance had been ghastly and shattering. I now craned eagerly. The girl gave utterance again . . . She meant, surely, "Harriet's mannerly ma's having a bath at last." No doubt Harriet's ma lived in a boarding-house where there was so little hot water, and she so mannerly, that she had always sacrificed her bath to the other residents.

But the young man was apparently a little deaf. The girl had to repeat her piece of information over and over. The arrogant heart of the guard carried him far too far . . . Tragic that happy young Mark fancies his chance at art . . . If the tea shop had been an opium den the nightmare quality of the afternoon could not have been improved upon. "Lavishes lavishes ghast lavishes ghast ghast," the girl insisted. I really believed I had it then: "Sad that a man like Papa had to depart fast." This was obviously connected with the charity dance. An emerald bracelet had been missed. Papa, who was present, was also, later, missed. I could see Papa, small and round, skipping on to the plane – no, the Golden Arrow at Victoria Station. Papa, feeling for the bulge in his breast pocket, dressed so businesslike, but emanating such a sublime . . . Ma was prostrate. His firm were already going into the accounts. Sad that a man like Papa . . .

But who was Lavishes Ghast? Could it be that Papa . . .

At that moment someone entered the shop. The girl at the table looked up. Pamela!" she called out. "Hallo, Pamela," said the young man, "we were just talking about you." Well, it had all been about Pamela and, for all I knew, her angular charms. As it happened I knew this Pamela. She came and spoke to me, then introduced me to her friends, and we stuck together for the evening.

We went to a pub and then to another. Then we went to a pub that served those watery meals comprising something with two vegetables, and decided we were hungry enough to take it. Two men sat at the table nearest ours. As the larger man ordered a rum with his supper, I noticed his voice above the hubbub from the bar, oiled and purring, like a cat of Rolls Royce make. He wore a broad ring studded with onyx, and although his clothes were dark, he looked profuse, his face, fruitlike above the white leaves of his collar, glowing with higher and richer thoughts. He said nothing to his companion who, poor thing, seemed distressed; this man, nervous and haggard, made repeated movements with his throat, as though swallowing down some dreadful sorrow.

The landlord approached the pair. "How's business?" he said with a more-than-hearty laugh. The large man seemed delighted by the question. "Lavishes ghast!" he proclaimed with a deep ripple of wheel-borne laughter. His friend closed his eyelids and softly ordered a beer.

The waitress came along with our plates splashing over each other. She set them down and said, jerking her head to indicate the two men, "Did you hear that? I don't call that a joke. Very bad taste." She explained that the men worked in the funeral parlour around the corner, and that it was the landlord's indelicate habit to inquire how business was, and the big fellow's habit to reply, "Absolutely marvellous."

Suddenly I saw the whole thing quite clearly and the weight lifted for ever: this was Mr Lavishes and that was the unfortunate Mr Ghast. My friends were smiling at the landlord's joke, and I, secure in my private enlightenment, smiled too, and continued to work out the simple details. The partners had begun as Lavishes, Ghast & Co., now known generally as Lavishes Ghast, Undertakers. Mr Lavishes preferred to deal with the bereaved relatives, leaving Mr Ghast to see to the actual body.

Lavishes Ghast. I like to think of Mr Lavishes and Mr Ghast performing, each in his own way, their selfless functions, so necessary to all. I feel it is rather touching, and only right, that when we gather together at parties we should pass those hours, as we do, in fervent acclamation of the Lavishes Ghast combine. In their way they are as much the backbone of the country as is the Housewife or the Coldstream Guard. And it is a memory to be cherished, that evening at the pub, when they settled to their late-snatched supper, in a silence of mutual understanding, interrupted only when shrunken Mr Ghast looked up from his plate, and having brokenly uttered the national phrase to which he had contributed his name, swallowed a mouthful of cabbage, alas.

THE YOUNG MAN WHO DISCOVERED THE SECRET OF LIFE

The main fact was, he was haunted by a ghost about five feet high when unfurled and standing upright. For the ghost unfurled itself from the top drawer of a piece of furniture that stood in the young man's bed-sitting room every night, or failing that, every morning. The young man was a plasterer's apprentice, or so he claimed.

But I have been told on good authority that this is absolutely absurd. There is no such thing: plasterers do not have apprentices. Ben, as the young man was called, was very concerned when I wrote to point this out. He decidedly preferred to change his status to that of "bricklayer's" or, better still, "kerblayer's apprentice", even though this meant putting himself in an unemployed category while doing a bit of plastering on the side to make a weekly wage of sorts.

I myself had only heard of Ben through correspondence, for he had written to me a most unusual letter, care of my publisher. In it, the then "plasterer's apprentice" told about the visitations of the ghost. Normally, I would have torn up the letter; I only replied to him because one of his statements contained the challenging one that through his ghost Ben had discovered, or was by way of discovering “the secret of life”. In my reply I was cautious about the “apparition”, as I called his ghost, but I more definitely pointed out that “the secret of life” was most likely to mean the secret of his own personal life, not life in general. The lives of people hold many secrets, I emphasized. There was possibly no one “secret” applying to us all. So, anyway, I wished him luck, and mailed off the letter. Goodbye.

But no, it wasn’t goodbye, as I might have foreseen. It was true that I didn’t write to him for some time, but he continued to write letters to me in some inexplicable need that he felt to express his odd experiences, real or imagined as the case might be.

According to Ben’s letters to me, his greatest problem with the ghost was now blackmail and jealousy, for the ghost was truly jealous of Ben’s girlfriend.

“I can haunt whoever and wherever I wish,” the ghost told Ben. “It is easy for me to inform the whole of your acquaintance that you are only a plasterer looking for a steady job, and as for being a kerblayer or even a bricklayer, that is far from the truth.”

“Please yourself who you haunt,” said Ben. “I am totally indifferent. The fact remains that I am a kerblayer at heart, whatever the nature of the temporary job as plasterer, etc., etc., that I am economically forced to accept from time to time.”

“And what is ‘etc., etc.’?” said the ghost nastily. “Do you mind explaining?”

“Curl up and return to your drawer,” Ben bade him. “And mind you don’t crush my pyjamas.”

"Your pyjamas," said the ghost, "have no place in the top drawer where I come from. They are not pure silk; they are Marks & Spencer's."

Ben was secretly very anxious lest it should be known he was not a kerblayer after all. But he was a brave fellow. "Get back to your place or else," he said.

The ghost curled up again, murmuring, "At least you admit that I have a right to be here. As it happens I know what is going to win the three-thirty tomorrow. It is Bartender's Best."

True enough that horse won the race and Ben was furious with himself for failing to take the tip, for he liked to play the horses when he had some money.

"Any more tips?" he asked the ghost that night.

"I thought you would ask that question," said the ghost. "But as you know, your girlfriend doesn't like betting. If you give her up I'll tell no one your secret and I'll give you good racing tips."

"Do you know what?" said Ben. "You are getting on my nerves. You are the result of stale air, neither more nor less. Stale air becomes radioactive. It becomes luminous. If I open the window you will gradually disappear."

"Not me," said the ghost. "Not me, I won't."

"I can't think of any more mindless occupation than to be a ghost in that post-mortem way you have in coming and going. So very unnecessary. I could have you psychoanalysed away."

Enter the story Genevieve, young and fair, a designer of scarecrows, Ben's girlfriend: Ben was convinced that her occupational status, the only type of status that apparently he knew, was beneath his, particularly now that he had become "Profession: kerblayer's apprentice". The passion with which the ghost despised Genevieve could only be matched by Ben's genuine and desperate love for her. In the meantime the ghost continued to unfurl its five feet and to give Ben advice like "psychoanalyse your crazy pavements."

"The ghost is a terrible snob," Ben wrote. "He makes me feel great and terrible –"

In fact, Ben changed his patronizing attitude towards the girl only after Genevieve borrowed his sun-hat, his jeans and one of his shirts to make up one of her scarecrows. She painted a turnip in the likeness of Ben's face. When she had set up this scarecrow in a field everyone knew that it was modelled on Ben. Everyone smiled. The terrible snob ghost came to report this to Ben, adding that a cow's milk had already been turned by the scarecrow.

On the previous day Ben had won twenty-four pounds on a horse, quite on his own hunch. So he skipped his usual visit to the job centre and took a bus out of town to the field where Genevieve's handiwork was flapping. Two cars had drawn up by the side of the road, and the occupants were admiring the work of art, as one of them called it. "It's the image of a young builder's mate who once worked on my property," she said.

So instead of taking the effigy amiss Ben was full of admiration for Genevieve. He rang her up and made her fix a date for their marriage, never mind that he was at present out of work.

The ghost unfurled himself again that night, but when he heard of Ben's proposal to Genevieve, he returned to the top drawer from whence he came, curled up and disappeared. "This quenching of the ghost," Ben wrote, "is to me the secret of life." He said "quenching" for he felt the ghost had been thirsty for his soul, and had in fact drunk his fill.

Ben never again won on the horses, although he became a master-bricklayer, a prosperous man, specializing in crazy-paving.

DAISY OVEREND

It is hardly ever that I think of her, but sometimes, if I happen to pass Clarges Street or Albemarle Street on a sunny afternoon, she comes to mind. Or if, in a little crowd waiting to cross the road, I hear behind me two women meet, and the one exclaim:

"Darling!" (or "Bobbie!" or "Goo!") and the other answer: "Goo!" (or "Billie!" or "Bobbie!" or "Darling!") – if I hear these words, spoken in a certain trill which betokens the period 1920–29, I know that I have by chance entered the world of Daisy Overend, Bruton Street, WI.

Ideally, these Bobbies and Darlings are sheathed in short frocks, the hems of which dangle about their knees like seaweed, the waistlines of which encircle their hips, loose and effortless, following the droop of shoulder and mouth. Ideally, the whole is upheld by a pair of shiny silk stockings of a bright hue known as, but not resembling, a peach.

But in reality it is only by the voice you can tell them. The voice harks back to days bright and young and unredeemable whence the involuntary echoes arise – *Billie! . . . Goo! . . . heavenly! . . . divine!* like the motto and crest which adorn the letter paper of a family whose silver is pawned and forgotten.

Daisy Overend, small, imperious, smart, was to my mind the flower and consummation of her kind, and this is not to discount the male of the species *Daisy Overend*, with his wee face, blue eyes, bad teeth and nerves. But if you have met Mrs Overend, you have as good as met him too, he is so unlike her, and yet so much her kind.

I met her, myself, in the prodigious and lovely summer of 1947. Very charming she was. A tubular skirt clung to her hips, a tiny cap to her hair, and her hair clung, bronzed and shingled, to her head, like the cup of a toy egg of which her face was the other half. Her face was a mere lobe. Her eyes were considered to be expressive and they expressed avarice in various forms; the pupils were round and watchful. Mrs Overend engaged me for three weeks to help her with some committee work. As you will see, we parted in three days.

I found that literature and politics took up most of Daisy's days and many of her nights. She wrote a regular column in a small political paper and she belonged to all the literary societies. Thus, it was the literature of politics and the politics of literature which occupied Daisy, and thus she bamboozled many politicians who thought she was a writer, and writers who believed her to be a political theorist. But these activities failed to satisfy, that is to say, intoxicate her.

Now, she did not drink. I saw her sipping barley water while her guests drank her gin. But Daisy had danced the Charleston in her youth with a royal prince, and of this she assured me several times, speaking with swift greed while an alcoholic look came over her.

"Those times were divine," she boozily concluded, "they

were ripping." And I realized she was quite drunk with the idea. Normally as precise as a bird, she reached out blunderingly for the cigarettes, knocking the whole lot over. Literature and politics failed to affect her in this way, though she sat on many committees. Therefore she had taken – it is her expression – two lovers: one an expert, as she put it, on politics, and the other a poet.

The political expert, Lotti, was a fair Central European, an exiled man. The skin of his upper lip was drawn taut across his top jaw; this gave Lotti the appearance, together with his high cheekbones, of having had his face lifted. But it was not so; it was a natural defect which made his smile look like a baring of the teeth. He was perhaps the best of the lot that I met at Daisy Overend's.

Lotti could name each member of every Western Cabinet which had sat since the Treaty of Versailles. Daisy found this invaluable for her monthly column. Never did Lotti speak of these men but with contempt. He was a member of three shadow cabinets.

On the Sunday which, as it turned out, was my last day with Daisy, she laid aside her library book and said to Lotti:

"I'm bored with Cronin."

Lotti, to whom all statesmen were as the ash he was just then flicking to the floor, looked at her all amazed.

"Daisy, mei gurl, you crazy?" he said.

"A Cronin!" he said, handing me an armful of air to convey the full extent of his derision. "She is bored with a Cronin."

At that moment, Daisy's vexed misunderstood expression

reminded me that her other lover, the poet Tom Pfeffer, had brought the same look to her face two days before. When, rushing into the flat as was her wont, she said, gasping, to Tom, "Things have been happening in the House." – Tom, who was reading the *Notebooks of Malte Laurids Brigge*, looked up. "Nothing's been happening in the house," he assured her.

Tom Pfeffer is dead now. Mrs Overend told me the story of how she rescued him from lunacy, and I think Tom believed this. It is true she had prevented his being taken to a mental home for treatment.

The time came when Tom wanted, on an autumn morning, a ticket to Burton-on-Trent to visit a friend, and he wanted this more than he wanted a room in Mrs Overend's flat and regular meals. In his own interests she refused, obliterating the last traces of insurrection by giving Lotti six pound notes, clean from the bank, in front of Tom.

How jealous Tom Pfeffer was of Lotti, how indifferent was Lotti to him! But on this last day that I spent with Mrs Overend, the poet was fairly calm, although there were signs of the awful neurotic dance of his facial muscles which were later to distort him utterly before he died insane.

Daisy was preparing for a party, the reason for my presence on a Sunday, and for the arrival at five o'clock of her secretary Miss Rilke, a displaced European, got cheap. When anyone said to Daisy "Is she related to the poet Rilke?" Daisy replied, "Oh, I should *think* so," indignant almost, that it should be doubted.

"Be an angel," said Daisy to Miss Rilke when she arrived, "run down to the cafe and get me two packets of twenty. Is it still raining? How priceless the weather is. Take my awning."

"Awning?"

"*Umbrella, umbrella, umbrella,*" said Daisy, jabbing her finger at it fractiously.

Like ping-pong, Miss Rilke's glance met Lotti's, and Lotti's hers. She took the umbrella and went.

"What are you looking at?" Daisy said quickly to Lotti.

"Nothing," said Tom Pfeffer, thinking he was being addressed and looking up from his book.

"Not you," said Daisy.

"Do you mean me?" I said.

"No," she said, and kept her peace.

Miss Rilke returned to say that the shop would give Mrs Overend no more credit.

"This is the end," said Daisy as she shook out the money from her purse. "Tell them I'm livid."

"Yes," said Miss Rilke, looking at Lotti.

"What are you looking at?" Daisy demanded of her.

"Looking at?"

"Have you got the right money?" Daisy said.

"Yes."

"Well, go."

"I think," said Daisy when she had gone, "she's a bit dotty owing to her awful experiences."

Nobody replied.

"Don't you think so?" she said to Lotti.

"Could be," said Lotti.

Tom looked up suddenly. "She's bats," he hastened to say, "the silly bitch is bats."

As soon as Miss Rilke returned Daisy started becking and calling in preparation for her party. Her papers, which lay on every plane surface in the room, were moved into her bedroom in several piles.

The drawing-room was furnished in a style which in many ways anticipated the members' room at the Institute of Contemporary Arts. Mrs Overend had recently got rid of her black-and-orange striped divans, cushions and sofas. In their place were curiously cut slabs, polygons, and three-legged manifestations of Daisy Overend's personality, done in El Greco's colours. As Daisy kept on saying, no two pieces were alike, and each was a contemporary version of a traditional design.

In her attempt to create a Contemporary interior she was, I felt, successful, and I was quite dazzled by its period charm. "A rare old Contemporary piece," some curio dealer, not yet born, might one day aver of Daisy's citrine settle or her blue glass-topped telephone table, adding in the same breath and pointing elsewhere, "A genuine brass-bracket gas-jet, nineteenth century . . ." But I was dreaming, and Daisy was working, shifting things, blowing the powdery dust off things. She trotted and tripped amid the pretty jigsaw puzzle of her furniture, making a clean sweep of letters, bills, pamphlets, and all that suggested a past or a future, with one exception. This was the photograph of Daisy Overend, haughty and beplumed in presentation dress, queening it over the Contemporary prospect of the light-grey grand piano.

Sometimes, while placing glasses and plates now here, now there, Daisy stopped short to take in the effect; and at this sign we all of us did the same. I realized then how silently and well did Daisy induce people to humour her. I discovered that the place was charged on a high voltage with the constant menace of a scene.

"I've put the papers on your bed," said Miss Rilke from the bedroom.

"Is *she* saying something?" said Daisy, as if it were the last straw.

"Yes," said Miss Rilke in a loud voice.

"They are not to go on my bed," replied Daisy, having heard her in the first place.

"She's off her head, my dear," said the poet to his mistress, "putting your papers on your bed."

"Go and see what she's doing," said Daisy to me.

I went, and there found Miss Rilke moving the papers off the bed on to the floor. I was impressed by the pinkness of Daisy's bedroom. Where on earth did she get her taste in pink? Now this was not in the Contemporary style, nor was it in the manner of Daisy's heyday, the 1920s. The kidney-shaped dressing-table was tricked out with tulle, unhappy spoiled stuff which cold cream had long ago stained, cigarettes burned, and various jagged objects ripped. In among the folds the original colour had survived here and there, and this fervid pink reminded me of a colour I had seen before, a pink much loved and worn by the women of the Malay colony at Cape Town.

No, this was not a bedroom of the twenties; it belonged, surely, to the first ten years of the century: an Edwardian bedroom. But then, even then, it was hardly the sort of room Daisy would have inherited, since neither her mother nor her grandmother had kicked her height at the Gaiety. No, it was

Daisy's own inarticulate exacting instinct which had bestowed on this room its frilly bed, its frilly curtains, the silken and sorry roses on its mantelpiece, and its all-but-perished powder-puffs. And all in pink, and all in pink. I did not solve the mystery of Daisy's taste in bedrooms, not then nor at any time. For, whenever I provide a category of time and place for her, the evidence is in default. A plant of the twenties, she is also the perpetrator of that vintage bedroom. A lingering limb of the old leisured class, she is also the author of that pink room.

I devoted the rest of the evening to the destruction of Daisy's party, I regret to say, and the subversion of her purpose in giving it.

Her purpose was the usual thing. She had joined a new international guild, and wanted to sit on the committee. Several Members of Parliament, a director of a mineral-water factory, a Brigadier-General who was also an Earl, a retired Admiral, some wives, a few women journalists, were expected. In addition, she had asked some of her older friends, those who were summoned to all her parties and whom she called her "basics"; they were the walkers-on or the chorus of Daisy's social drama. There was also a Mr Jamieson, who was not invited but who played an unseen part as the chairman of the committee. He did not want Mrs Overend to sit on his committee. We were therefore assembled, though few guessed it, to inaugurate a campaign to remove from office this Mr Jamieson, whose colleagues and acquaintances presently began to arrive.

Parted from the drawing-room by folding doors was an ante-room leading out of the flat. I was put in charge of this room where a buffet had been laid. Here Daisy had repaired, when dressing for the party, to change her stockings. It was her habit to dress in every room in the house, anxiously moving from place to place. Miss Rilke had been sent on a tour of the premises to collect the discarded clothes, the comb, the lipstick from the various stations of Daisy's journey; but the secretary had overlooked, on a table in the centre of this ante-room, a pair of black satin garters a quarter of a century old, each bearing a very large grimy pink disintegrating rosette.

Just before the first guests began to arrive, Daisy Overend saw her garters lying there.

"Put those away," she commanded Miss Rilke.

The Admiral came first. I opened the door, while with swift and practised skill Daisy and Lotti began a lively conversation, in the midst of which the Admiral was intended to come upon them. Behind the Admiral came a Member of Parliament. They had never been to the house before, not being among Daisy's "basics".

"Do come in," said Miss Rilke, holding open the folding doors.

"This way," said Tom Pfeffer from the drawing-room.

The two guests stared at the table. Daisy's garters were still there. The Admiral, I could see, was puzzled. Not knowing Daisy very well, he thought, no doubt, she was eccentric. He tried to smile. The political man took rather longer to decide on an attitude. He must have concluded that the garters were not Daisy's, for next I saw him looking curiously at me.

"They are not mine," I rapidly said, "those garters."

"Whose are they?" said the Admiral, drawing near.

"They are Mrs Overend's garters," I said, "she changed her stockings in here."

Now the garters had never really been serviceable; even now, with the help of safety pins, they did not so much keep Daisy's stockings, as her spirits up, for she liked them. They were historic in the sense that they had at first, I suppose, looked merely naughty. In about five years they had entered their most interesting, their old-fashioned, their lewd period. A little while, and the rosettes had begun to fray: the decadence. And now, with the impurity of those to whom all things pertaining to themselves are pure, Daisy did not see them as junk, but as part of herself, as she had cause to tell me later.

The Admiral walked warily into the drawing-room, but the Member of Parliament lingered to examine a picture on the wall, one eye on the garters. I was, I must say, tempted to hide them somewhere out of sight. More people were arriving, and the garters were causing them to think. If only for this reason, it was perhaps inhospitable to leave them so prominently on the table.

I resisted the temptation. Miss Rilke had suddenly become very excited. She flew to open the door to each guest, and, copying my tone, exclaimed:

"Please to excuse the garters. They are the garters of Mrs Overend. She changed her stockings in here."

Daisy, Daisy Overend! I hope you have forgotten me. The party got out of hand. Lotti was not long in leaving the relatively sedative drawing-room in favour of the little room where Daisy's old basics were foregathered. These erstwhile adherents to the Young Idea, arriving in twos and threes, were filled with a great joy on hearing Miss Rilke's speech:

"Please to excuse those garters which you see. They are the garters of Mrs Overend . . ."

But there was none more delighted than Lotti.

It was some minutes before the commotion was heard by Daisy in the drawing-room, where she was soliciting the badwill of a journalist against Mr Jamieson. Meanwhile, the ante-room party joined hands, clinked glasses and danced round Lotti who held the garters aloft with a pair of sugar tongs. Tom Pfeffer so far forgot himself as to curl up with mirth on a sofa.

I remember Daisy as she stood between the folding doors in her black party dress, like an infolded undernourished tulip. Behind her clustered her new friends, slightly offended, though prepared to join in the spirit of the thing, whatever it should be. Before her pranced the old, led by Lotti in a primitive mountain jig. The sugar tongs with the garters in their jaws Lotti held high in one hand, and with the other he plucked the knee of his trouser-leg as if it were a skirt.

"*Ai*, *Ai*, *Ai*," chanted Lotti, "Daisy's dirty old garters, *Ai!*"

"*Ai*, *Ai*, *Ai*," responded the chorus, while Miss Rilke looked lovingly on, holding in one hand Lotti's drink, in the other her own.

I remember Daisy as she stood there, not altogether without charm, beside herself. While laughter rebounded like plunging breakers from her mouth, she guided her eyes towards myself and trained on me the missiles of her fury. For a full three minutes Daisy's mouth continued to laugh.

I am seldom in the West End of London. But sometimes I have to hurry across the Piccadilly end of Albemarle Street where the buses crash past like giant orgulous parakeets, more thunderous and more hectic than the Household Cavalry. The shops are on my left and the Green Park lies on my right under the broad countenance of drowsy summer. It is then that, in my mind's eye, Daisy Overend gads again, diminutive, charming, vicious, and tarted up to the nines.

By district messenger she sent me a note early on the morning after the party. I was to come no more. Herewith a cheque. The garters were part of herself and I would understand how she felt.

The cheque was a dud. I did not pursue the matter, and in fact I have forgotten the real name of Daisy Overend. I have forgotten her name but I shall remember it at the Bar of Judgement.

THE HOUSE OF THE FAMOUS POET

In the summer of 1944, when it was nothing for trains from the provinces to be five or six hours late, I travelled to London on the night train from Edinburgh, which, at York, was already three hours late. There were ten people in the compartment, only two of whom I remember well, and for good reason.

I have the impression, looking back on it, of a row of people opposite me, dozing untidily with heads askew, and, as it often seems when we look at sleeping strangers, their features had assumed extra emphasis and individuality, sometimes disturbing to watch. It was as if they had rendered up their daytime talent for obliterating the outward traces of themselves in exchange for mental obliteration. In this way they resembled a twelfth-century fresco; there was a look of medieval unself-consciousness about these people, all except one.

This was a private soldier who was awake to a greater degree than most people are when they are not sleeping. He was smoking cigarettes one after the other with long, calm puffs. I thought he looked excessively evil – an atavistic type. His forehead must have been less than two inches high above dark, thick eyebrows, which met. His jaw was not large, but it was apelike; so was his small nose and so were his deep, close-set eyes. I thought there must have been some consanguinity in the parents. He was quite a throwback.

As it turned out, he was extremely gentle and kind. When I ran out of cigarettes, he fished about in his haversack and produced a packet for me and one for a girl sitting next to me. We both tried, with a flutter of small change, to pay him. Nothing would please him at all but that we should accept his cigarettes, whereupon he returned to his silent, reflective smoking.

I felt a sort of pity for him then, rather as we feel towards animals we know to be harmless, such as monkeys. But I realized that, like the pity we expend on monkeys merely because they are not human beings, this pity was not needed.

Receiving the cigarettes gave the girl and myself common ground, and we conversed quietly for the rest of the journey. She told me she had a job in London as a domestic helper and nursemaid. She looked as if she had come from a country district – her very blond hair, red face and large bones gave the impression of power, as if she was used to carrying heavy things, perhaps great scuttles of coal, or two children at a time. But what made me curious about her was her voice, which was cultivated, melodious and restrained.

Towards the end of the journey, when the people were beginning to jerk themselves straight and the rushing to and fro in the corridor had started, this girl, Elise, asked me to come with her to the house where she worked. The master, who was something in a university, was away with his wife and family.

I agreed to this, because at that time I was in the way

of thinking that the discovery of an educated servant girl was valuable and something to be gone deeper into. It had the element of experience – perhaps, even of truth – and I believed, in those days, that truth is stranger than fiction. Besides, I wanted to spend that Sunday in London. I was due back next day at my job in a branch of the civil service, which had been evacuated to the country and for a reason that is another story, I didn't want to return too soon. I had some telephoning to do. I wanted to wash and change. I wanted to know more about the girl. So I thanked Elise and accepted her invitation.

I regretted it as soon as we got out of the train at King's Cross, some minutes after ten. Standing up tall on the platform, Elise looked unbearably tired, as if not only the last night's journey but every fragment of her unknown life was suddenly heaping up on top of her. The power I had noticed in the train was no longer there. As she called, in her beautiful voice, for a porter, I saw that on the side of her head that had been away from me in the train, her hair was parted in a dark streak, which, by contrast with the yellow, looked navy blue. I had thought, when I first saw her, that possibly her hair was bleached, but now, seeing it so badly done, seeing this navy blue parting pointing like an arrow to the weighted weariness of her face, I, too, got the sensation of great tiredness. And it was not only the strain of the journey that I felt, but the foreknowledge of boredom that comes upon us unaccountably at the beginning of a quest, and that checks, perhaps mercifully, our curiosity.

And, as it happened, there really wasn't much to learn about Elise. The explanation of her that I had been prompted to seek, I got in the taxi between King's Cross and the house at Swiss Cottage. She came of a good family, who thought her a pity, and she them. Having no training for anything else, she had taken a domestic job on leaving home. She was engaged to an Australian soldier billeted also at Swiss Cottage.

Perhaps it was the anticipation of a day's boredom, maybe it was the effect of no sleep or the fact that the V-1 sirens were sounding, but I felt some sourness when I saw the house. The garden was growing all over the place. Elise opened the front door, and we entered a darkish room almost wholly taken up with a long, plain wooden work-table. On this were a half-empty marmalade jar, a pile of papers, and a dried-up ink bottle. There was a steel-canopied bed, known as a Morrison shelter, in one corner and some photographs on the mantelpiece, one of a schoolboy wearing glasses. Everything was tainted with Elise's weariness and my own distaste. But Elise didn't seem to be aware of the exhaustion so plainly revealed on her face. She did not even bother to take her coat off, and as it was too tight for her I wondered how she could move about so quickly with this restriction added to the weight of her tiredness. But, with her coat still buttoned tight Elise phoned her boyfriend and made breakfast, while I washed in a dim, blue, cracked bathroom upstairs.

When I found that she had opened my hold-all without asking me and had taken out my rations, I was a little pleased. It seemed a friendly action, with some measure of reality about it, and I felt better. But I was still irritated by the house. I felt there was no justification for the positive lack of consequence which was lying about here and there. I asked no questions about the owner who was something in a university, for fear of getting the answer I expected – that he was away visiting his grandchildren, at some family gathering in the home counties. The owners of the house had no reality for me, and I looked upon the place as belonging to, and permeated with, Elise.

I went with her to a nearby public house, where she met her boyfriend and one or two other Australian soldiers. They had with them a thin Cockney girl with bad teeth. Elise was very happy, and insisted in her lovely voice that they should all come along to a party at the house that evening. In a fine aristocratic tone, she demanded that each should bring a bottle of beer.

During the afternoon Elise said she was going to have a bath, and she showed me a room where I could use the telephone and sleep if I wanted. This was a large, light room with several windows, much more orderly than the rest of the house, and lined with books. There was only one unusual thing about it: beside one of the windows was a bed, but this bed was only a fairly thick mattress made up neatly on the floor. It was obviously a bed on the floor with some purpose, and again I was angered to think of the futile crankiness of the elderly professor who had thought of it.

I did my telephoning, and decided to rest. But first I wanted to find something to read. The books puzzled me. None of them seemed to be automatically part of a scholar's library. An inscription in one book was signed by the author, a well-known novelist. I found another inscribed copy, and this had the name of the recipient. On a sudden idea, I went to the desk, where while I had been telephoning I had noticed a pile of unopened letters. For the first time, I looked at the name of the owner of the house.

I ran to the bathroom and shouted through the door to Elise, "Is this the house of the famous poet?"

"Yes," she called. "I *told* you."

She had told me nothing of the kind. I felt I had no right at all to be there, for it wasn't, now, the house of Elise acting by proxy for some unknown couple. It was the house of a famous modern poet. The thought that at any moment he and his family might walk in and find me there terrified me. I insisted that Elise should open the bathroom door and tell me to my face that there was no possible chance of their returning for many days to come.

Then I began to think about the house itself, which Elise was no longer accountable for. Its new definition, as the house of a poet whose work I knew well, many of whose poems I knew by heart, gave it altogether a new appearance.

To confirm this, I went outside and stood exactly where I had been when I first saw the garden from the door of the taxi. I wanted to get my first impression for a second time.

And this time I saw an absolute purpose in the overgrown garden, which, since then, I have come to believe existed in the eye of the beholder. But, at the time, the room we had first entered, and which had riled me, now began to give back a meaning, and whatever was, was right. The caked-up bottle of ink, which Elise had put on the mantelpiece, I replaced on the table to make sure. I saw a photograph I hadn't noticed before, and I recognized the famous poet.

It was the same with the upstairs room where Elise had put me, and I handled the books again, not so much with the sense that they belonged to the famous poet but with some curiosity about how they had been made. The sort of question that occurred to me was where the paper had come from and from what sort of vegetation was manufactured the black print, and these things have not troubled me since.

The Australians and the Cockney girl came around about seven. I had planned to catch an eight-thirty train to the country, but when I telephoned to confirm the time I found there were no Sunday trains running. Elise, in her friendly and exhausted way, begged me to stay without attempting to be too serious about it. The sirens were starting up again. I asked Elise once more to repeat that the poet and his family could by no means return that night. But I asked this question more abstractedly than before, as I was thinking of the sirens and of the exact proportions of the noise they made. I wondered, as well, what sinister genius of the Home Office could have invented so ominous a wail, and why. And I was thinking of the word "siren". The sound then became comical, for I imagined some maniac sea nymph from centuries past belching into the year 1944. Actually, the sirens frightened me.

Most of all, I wondered about Elise's party. Everyone roamed about the place as if it were nobody's house in particular, with Elise the best-behaved of the lot. The Cockney girl sat on the long table and gave of her best to the skies every time a bomb exploded. I had the feeling that the house had been requisitioned for an evening by the military. It was so hugely and everywhere occupied that it became not the house I had first entered, nor the house of the famous poet, but a third house – the one I had vaguely prefigured when I stood, bored, on the platform at King's Cross station. I saw a great amount of tiredness among these people, and heard, from the loud noise they made, that they were all lacking sleep. When the beer was finished and they were gone, some to their billets, some to pubs, and the Cockney girl to her Underground shelter where she had slept for weeks past, I asked Elise, "Don't you feel tired?"

"No," she said with agonizing weariness, "I never feel tired."

I fell asleep myself, as soon as I had got into the bed on the floor in the upstairs room, and overslept until Elise woke me at eight. I had wanted to get up early to catch a nine o'clock train, so I hadn't much time to speak to her. I did notice, though, that she had lost some of her tired look.

I was pushing my things into my hold-all while Elise went up the street to catch a taxi when I heard someone coming upstairs. I thought it was Elise come back, and I looked out of the open door. I saw a man in uniform carrying an enormous parcel in both hands. He looked down as he climbed, and had a cigarette in his mouth.

"Do you want Elise?" I called, thinking it was one of her friends.

He looked up, and I recognized the soldier, the throwback, who had given us cigarettes in the train.

"Well, anyone will do," he said. "The thing is, I've got to get back to camp and I'm stuck for the fare – eight and six."

I told him I could manage it, and was finding the money when he said, putting his parcel on the floor, "I don't want to borrow it. I wouldn't think of borrowing it. I've got something for sale."

"What's that?" I said.

"A funeral," said the soldier. "I've got it here."

This alarmed me, and I went to the window. No hearse, no coffin stood below. I saw only the avenue of trees.

The soldier smiled. "It's an abstract funeral," he explained, opening the parcel.

He took it out and I examined it carefully, greatly comforted. It was very much the sort of thing I had wanted – rather more purple in parts than I would have liked, for I was not in favour of this colour of mourning. Still, I thought I could tone it down a bit.

Delighted with the bargain, I handed over the eight shillings and sixpence. There was a great deal of this abstract funeral. Hastily, I packed some of it into the hold-all. Some I stuffed in my pockets, and there was still some left over. Elise had returned with a cab and I hadn't much time. So I ran for it, out of the door and out of the gate of the house of the famous poet, with the rest of my funeral trailing behind me.

You will complain that I am withholding evidence. Indeed, you may wonder if there is any evidence at all. "An abstract funeral," you will say, "is neither here nor there. It is only a notion. You cannot pack a notion into your bag. You cannot see the colour of a notion."

You will insinuate that what I have just told you is pure fiction.

Hear me to the end.

I caught the train. Imagine my surprise when I found, sitting opposite me, my friend the soldier, of whose existence you are so sceptical.

"As a matter of interest," I said, "how would you describe all this funeral you sold me?"

"Describe it?" he said. "Nobody describes an abstract funeral. You just conceive it."

"There is much in what you say," I replied. "Still, describe it I must, because it is not every day one comes by an abstract funeral."

"I am glad you appreciate that," said the soldier.

"And after the war," I continued, "when I am no longer a civil servant, I hope, in a few deftly turned phrases, to write of my experiences at the house of the famous poet, which has culminated like this. But of course," I added, "I will need to say what it looks like."

The soldier did not reply.

"If it were an okapi or a sea-cow," I said, "I would have to say what it looked like. No one would believe me otherwise."

"Do you want your money back?" asked the soldier. "Because if so, you can't have it. I spent it on my ticket."

"Don't misunderstand me," I hastened to say. "The funeral is a delightful abstraction. Only, I wish to put it down in writing."

I felt a great pity for the soldier on seeing his worried look. The ape-like head seemed the saddest thing in the world.

"I make them by hand," he said, "these abstract funerals."

A siren sounded somewhere, far away.

"Elise bought one of them last month. She hadn't any complaints. I change at the next stop," he said, getting down his kit from the rack. "And what's more," he said, "your famous poet bought one."

"Oh, did he?" I said.

"Yes," he said. "No complaints. It was just what he wanted – the idea of a funeral."

The train pulled up. The soldier leaped down and waved. As the train started again, I unpacked my abstract funeral and looked at it for a few moments.

"To hell with the idea," I said. "It's a real funeral I want."

"All in good time," said a voice from the corridor.

"*You* again," I said. It was the soldier.

"No," he said, "I got off at the last station. I'm only a notion of myself."

"Look here," I said, "would you be offended if I throw all this away?"

"Of course not," said the soldier. "You can't offend a notion."

"I want a real funeral," I explained. "One of my own."

"That's right," said the soldier.

"And then I'll be able to write about it and go into all the details," I said.

"Your own funeral?" he said. "You want to write it up?"

"Yes," I said.

"But," said he, "you're only human. Nobody reports on their own funeral. It's got to be abstract."

"You see my predicament?" I said.

"I see it," he replied. "I get off at this stop."

This notion of a soldier alighted. Once more the train put on speed. Out of the window I chucked all my eight and sixpence worth of abstract funeral. I watched it fluttering over the fields and around the tops of camouflaged factories with the sun glittering richly upon it, until it was out of sight.

In the summer of 1944 a great many people were harshly and suddenly killed. The papers reported, in due course, those whose names were known to the public. One of these, the famous poet, had returned unexpectedly to his home at Swiss Cottage a few moments before it was hit direct by a flying bomb. Fortunately, he had left his wife and children in the country.

When I got to the place where my job was, I had some time to spare before going on duty. I decided to ring Elise and thank her properly, as I had left in such a hurry. But the lines were out of order, and the operator could not find words enough to express her annoyance with me. Behind this overworked, quarrelsome voice from the exchange I heard the high, long hoot which means that the telephone at the other end is not functioning, and the sound made me infinitely depressed and weary; it was more intolerable to me than the sirens, and I replaced the receiver; and, in fact, Elise had already perished under the house of the famous poet.

The blue cracked bathroom, the bed on the floor, the caked ink bottle, the neglected garden, and the neat rows of books – I try to gather them together in my mind whenever I am enraged by the thought that Elise and the poet were killed outright. The angels of the Resurrection will invoke the dead man and the dead woman, but who will care to restore the fallen house of the famous poet if not myself? Who else will tell its story?

When I reflect how Elise and the poet were taken in – how they calmly allowed a well-meaning soldier to sell them the notion of a funeral, I remind myself that one day I will accept, and so will you, an abstract funeral, and make no complaints.

THE PLAYHOUSE CALLED REMARKABLE

I was telling my friend Moon Biglow the other day that I was going to Hampstead to see some literary people.

"Oh, littery people," said Moon – because that's how he talks.

"Oh, Hampstead!" said Moon.

"Yes," I said, "I'm going to read a story to illustrate the Uprise of my Downfall."

Moon turned a little jerky. It's strange how you think you know people, and then they do something odd, and you have to start on virgin ground again.

"What's the matter, Moon?" I asked him. We were sitting in a milk-bar drinking coffee, or whatever it really was.

"Have another coffee," I suggested.

"*The Uprise*," said Moon, "*of your Downfall*? Did you say . . . ?"

"Oh," I said hastily, "it's got nothing to do with the Fall of Man, you know. This is just a way of expressing my venture into that bourne from which no traveller returns, I mean . . ."

"Then you know the secret!" Moon exclaimed.

"Secret?" I said. "There's no secret about it. It comes to me naturally.

"A mere gift," I added modestly.

I was thinking of some means of extracting myself from Moon's company. I didn't like the look of him in the least, desperately afraid of me for some reason.

Suddenly Moon's will seemed to slump. I said I must go.

"Don't go until you've told me how you came to *know*." Moon was quite mild now, quite blank.

"Know *what?*" I said impatiently. "What *have* you been drinking?"

"Either tea or coffee," Moon replied, gazing into his cup, for he was extremely truthful. One thing about Moon, he is always very fond of the truth.

"The uprise of your downfall," said Moon. "I must say when you came out with it just now, I was fit to bust, but I'll get over it in a day or two. Only tell me how . . ."

"That phrase," I said, "refers to my downward progress up to the dizzy heights, as they concern the art of letters."

"I *know*," said Moon. "I mean," he added, having conceived a new thought, "I *think* I know."

I said, "What are you talking about and why are you talking in italics?"

"*You* say first," said Moon suspiciously, "what *you're* talking about."

"Nothing doing," I said mysteriously – because I'd begun to get interested in the thing in Moon's mind.

"Well," said Moon, "it's the Moon, isn't it?"

"Yes," I said, because I never have scruples about artistic lies.

Moon breathed a long draught of invisible nourishment from the air, then sighed it out again.

"Anything else?" Moon inquired.

"Hampstead," I ventured, remembering that this word had started him off.

"Ah," said Moon. "Well, now, I'll tell you the *true* story, because whoever told you the secret has ten to one told you the wrong thing. You'll get the truth from me."

Before I tell you Moon Biglow's story, I must tell you something about him. He's the sort of friend whose family and background you know nothing about. I always felt he came from Ireland or Chicago or somewhere like that – because of the name, rather strange, of Moon Biglow. Moon must be about forty, and he describes himself as a freelance, which I suppose means journalism once a month. The strange thing is, I can't remember where I first met Moon. It was probably at a party. I must have known him for ten years. I would often see him in Kensington High Street in the late morning, short and fair and dressed in brown. His face is small, but his features are big, a pleasant face. I doubt if I shall see it again for some time, for Moon has left London now.

Well, to get back to the story that Moon Biglow told me when I was downcast about my downfall rising up.

"I used to live at Hampstead," said Moon. "That was just after the Flood."

"Did they have a flood?" I said. "When would that be?"

"The *Flood*," said Moon. "I mean Noah's Flood – the big one. You just listen to me. I'm telling no lies.

"I lived at Hampstead just after the Flood. Of course, it was very different then, but there was a pleasant little society of people – long before the palaeolithic savages appeared, of course. The son of Noah called Ham begat this particular crowd – hence the name Hampstead. There were six of us," said Moon, "six to begin with – later seven. Of course, we were total strangers to the place, but everyone made us welcome."

"Where had you come from?" I asked.

"The Moon," said Moon. "You know that very well. Don't interrupt me with insincere questions. We came of our own free will on the Downfall of our Uprise, and we settled at Hampstead; seeing it was the most civilized place on the globe in the post-Flood years. It was almost like the Moon – of course, the Moon has changed since then, but I remember the Moon in her prime. She was a beauty to live on. Still, we left her and came to settle in Hampstead.

"The nice thing about the people," said Moon, "was their discretion. They never inquired why we came, they simply accepted us.

"After the first eighteen months, when the ice was broken, we told them why we had come to the earth. We got the Mayor of Hampstead and his wife to call a meeting at the Town Hall. That was where Keats's house is now. I wrote out my speech and learnt it by heart. Of course, I was more eloquent in those days than I am now. I still remember every word.

"'Friends, brothers and sisters,' I said, 'The Six Brothers of the Moon give you greeting, and beg the privilege, nay the honour, of addressing your inmost hearts. There will, brothers and sisters, sisters and brothers, – there will come a time when these words will no longer reverberate new and thrilling to the ear. And why? Will your progeny, generation upon generation, remain unmoved by a brotherly appeal to the heart of man? No. Why then, will they shun and mock at such a speech as I deliver to you this evening? – For upon my prophetic honour, they will do so. They will call it, my friends, empty rhetoric. They will term it by the names of blah, drip, ham, and bloody awful.

"'That things should not be otherwise than thus, my brothers and my sisters, is in the nature of this earth, your home. I need not dwell on the cycles of birth, growth, decay and death, which you sum up in your profound philosophy, "Nothing lasts long." It is the same, my dear children, with all expressions of life, and if I may say so without offence to that tenderness, that ineffable refinement of spirit which I perceive within you, your language is in a shocking condition. As for your art, it does not exist.

"'Sisters, we are come from the Moon to teach you the language of poetry. Brothers, we are here on what you might term an art mission.'"

At this point Moon Biglow stopped talking and took a large bite from a Chelsea bun. As you can imagine, I was somewhat puzzled by his story. If you had met Moon Biglow, you would never doubt the sincerity of the man. There was something very honest, also, about the way he was eating the bun; it seemed as undebatable as the story he was telling. Of course, I wanted to question him, but decided this might put him off. As a provisional measure, I worked it out that either he was mad or that he was not mad.

"What happened next?" I said.

"Well," said Moon, "I finished my speech, shook hands

with the gentlemen, kissed all the ladies, and went home to bed."

I could see that somehow I had hurt Moon's feelings.

"*Do* tell me what transpired," I said urgently.

"I am *not* mad," said Moon; then he continued his story.

"To tell you the truth," said Moon, "the whole race of Hampstead was dying out from the sheer lack of something to do in its spare time. They had only one recreation. In the evenings they would get together at the local Welfare Centre. All they did was to sit on the floor and chant. The chant went like this: Tum tum *ya*, tum tum *ya* – the same thing over and over again. Nothing else. Just tum tum *ya* the whole evening until they were tired. And it was the same every night. Naturally, at this rate, the race was beginning to die out.

"Well, we put it to them that what we had to offer was a very good thing. We proposed to set up a playhouse at Hampstead, and give nightly performances for a small fee. We proposed to bring them the Changing Drama of the Moon. I told them," said Moon. "'Once you have seen and heard the Changing Drama of the Moon,' I said, 'you will never more be content, my friends, with your own national classic, the Unchanging Tum tum *ya*. It is not,' I added, 'that we of the Moon do not hold the classical tradition in the greatest possible reverence. But you will have observed amongst yourselves that the time-honoured tum tum *ya* no longer possesses the power to keep you interested in life. Many of your youth have died from the disease of boredom. No babies have been born for the past two years.

"'Friends,' I concluded, 'the tum tum *ya* is not enough.'

"We had only one opponent – young Johnnie Heath, assistant editor of the *Tum Tum Times*. Johnnie set up the slogan: 'Hampstead for the sons of Ham,' and pasted up bills all over the town with headlines like 'Down with the Moon,' and 'Protect Our Women from the Arty Crafties.' But no one took any notice of Johnnie Heath – there was terrific excitement over the new scheme. We took over the Welfare Centre and got it reconstructed into a large theatre. First we called it the Moon Playhouse, but Johnnie Heath started agitating about this name, so to keep him quiet we changed it simply to the Playhouse.

"The opening night was a tremendous triumph. I must tell you something about the Changing Drama of the Moon.

"The artists of the Moon had only one principal theme, and this was the story on which our show was based. It happens to be a true story. On top of a high mountain on the Moon there was at that time a singing voice. It did not sing in words, only pure notes. There had always been much speculation on the Moon as to whether this was a man's voice or a woman's voice; it was very difficult to tell. From time to time an expedition set out to the singing mountain to try to locate the singer. The approach to the singing mountain was pitted with deep concealed craters. No one had ever returned from an expedition. But there was once a young girl, an acrobat and singer by profession, who taught herself to mimic the voice. She decided to fit its music to words, and set off for the mountain, intending to find out what inspired the singer. If she knew the source of the melody, she would know what words to fit in.

"By her acrobatic skill, this Moon girl managed to reach

the mountain, swinging from rock to tree to rock. All the people in that territory of the Moon could hear her singing to cheer herself up as she climbed the mountain, because it was night. She sang a song about her journey, the warm, strange-smelling forests and the lakes of phosphorus. As she approached the top, the song combined with the voice of the singing mountain like a duet. She reached the summit at dawn. Suddenly the Moon girl was silent. Only the mountain notes could be heard. The people waited anxiously all that day for some sign from the Moon girl, but no sound came. Towards evening they gave her up as lost. She had been murdered, they concluded, by the jealous voice of the mountain.

"But just as the sun had set, they heard a cry from the mountain-top. The Moon girl began to sing again, her voice beating against the mountain melody in a kind of desperate dialogue. It made a strange harmony. The Moon girl sang a narrative song which told how she was imprisoned by the voice of the mountain. The voice, she sang, had no body attached to it, but it surrounded her and held her fast on the mountain peak in a whirling spiral of sound. She could not move to left or right, neither forward nor backward, but was compelled to spin round and round with the voice of the mountain spirit. Our Moon girl is still there. She pirouettes on the mountain peak every night, imprisoned in the spinning voice, and singing a continual song of defiance, in harmony with the mountain spirit. Every day at sunrise she stops singing, and her whirling body comes to a standstill. On clear days the Moon people can make out her small figure standing motionless on the mountain peak while the voice of the mountain mocks her with its high wordless music.

Eventually the Moon girl told us in her song how it is that she can't make any sound or movement during the day. Every morning there is a certain ray of the sun which stabs her through the throat more sharply than a fine steel blade. She is pinioned against the sky throughout the day, unable to cry or move until the terrible blade of the sun withdraws itself from her throat at nightfall. The Moon girl's song tells us that this hard ray of the sun is what inspires the musical mountain. And the Moon girl sings of other things too. She tells us in her nightly song all she has seen on the landscape of the moon. It was the Moon girl who told us in her song to bring her drama to the earth."

Moon Biglow was beginning to look dreary. He was obviously much taken up with this Moon girl, and seemed likely to discourse upon the wonder of the lady all morning.

"What about your Playhouse?" I said, "– at Hampstead, you know."

"Yes," said Moon. "I was just coming down to earth.

"Well," he continued, "we put on the Changing Drama of the Moon, based on this history of the Moon girl – that's the active part of it, the drama. The Changing part comes in the words and music; because, you see, the Moon girl sings a different song every night. She saves up everything she sees by day, and hurls it in her song against the walls of the voice which imprisons her.

"And so we followed her story; we showed her journey to the mountain – dancing and singing. We reproduced her changing dialogue with the mountain, reproaching the invisible voice with everything under the sun – we put the glittering blue salt-banks on the shores of the Moon lakes into human language; we satirized the incoming tides of the earth, and the landmarks of Hampstead Heath from season to season; we even put our enemy Johnnie Heath to music, to try and placate him, praising his intelligence. But he didn't care for it much. Our decor was magnificent. Since we took it from the shapes and colours of the Moon, no one had seen anything like it.

"No one, in fact, had seen anything like our Playhouse show before. It was a tremendous success. We had to extend the premises, for the Playhouse had become a sort of communal centre.

"'A remarkable performance,' everyone said. 'Quite remarkable.'

"In fact the Playhouse came to be known as the Remarkable. People would arrange to meet each other at the Remarkable, and we six Moon Brothers were known as the Young Remarkables. A new spirit had entered the people of Hampstead. Not only were they wildly in love with the Moon girl whose history and whose changing song we depicted nightly, but they were more in love with each other. The youth of the community stopped dying young; the maternity wards opened again; the Remarkable was packed to the doors each evening.

"For my part, I was in love with Dolores, the daughter of the Mayor of Hampstead. We had not brought any girls from the moon, as the earth doesn't agree with the Moonish female. So we got Dolores to play the part of the Moon girl, which she did in a most lifelike manner. Of course, we were all six very fond of Dolores, but eventually she became attached to me.

"This was about five years after we opened the

Remarkable. Then Dolores' father, the Mayor, died, and we were all very irritated when Johnnie Heath took his place. The *Tum Tum Times* was, of course, no longer functioning, but Johnnie had worked himself up on some of the new civic welfare plans occasioned by the revitalized life of the community. He was becoming very influential.

"We had planned to branch off into a new field and set up a sort of academy of art. Perhaps it was just as well we never got the chance, but our reasons were quite *reasonable*. Although the Remarkable show continued to flourish, we somehow couldn't induce the people to practise any form of our art themselves. No Hampstead poets, no painters, no musicians. The general feeling was that art was a Moon affair; and only the Young Remarkables could really handle it. When we pointed out how well Dolores expressed the Moon girl, they replied that she was a bit of a born Moon girl herself. Perhaps they were right. We never got very far with our academic project, and some months after Johnnie Heath became the Mayor, we began to have difficulties with the Playhouse called Remarkable. Johnnie had somehow introduced an acid note into the life of Hampstead. (It was a descendant of Johnnie's, by the way, who founded the London School of Economics.)

"He started a campaign of inquiry against us. We had to fill in forms about our origin. We had to fill in an enormous questionnaire for our licence to run the Playhouse.

"On the grounds that we were not born on earth, and because there was no evidence of life on the Moon, Johnnie tried to prove that we did not exist at all. He sent us an official note objecting to our description of the Playhouse. He could not accept the phrase 'known as the Remarkable', he wrote, and begged to point out that whereas 'Playhouse' was a noun, 'Remarkable' was an adjective. The two could not be reconciled as signifying one and the same object.

"As the year wore on, so did Johnnie's nuisance-campaign. His tone became more and more peremptory. He tightened up on the vigilance of the police, and we were frequently fined for small infringements.

"Johnnie defeated us, in fact. We gave our last performance one evening in February. It was seven years since our first performance. The people were very upset, but Johnnie had so worked on them that they were afraid to express their grief.

"We had decided to take Dolores back to the Moon with us, in the usual way, you know."

"What way?" I asked, eagerly.

"Don't interrupt," said Moon. "And anyhow you know the way to the Moon. You go on the Uprise of your Downfall, you told me yourself!"

"Listen," I said desperately, "I know nothing about how to get to the Moon. There's a lot of talk about spaceships, but what have they got to do with the Uprise . . . ?"

"Quite," said Moon. "Quite."

I had better say straight away that so far as getting to the Moon is concerned, that was all the information I extracted from Moon Biglow. It has something to do with uprising and downfalling, we may be sure. But the end of his story is still to be told.

"On what I thought was my last night on earth," Moon continued, "I took a walk over Hampstead Heath. We had closed the doors of the Remarkable for the last time and were all prepared for the last Uprise of our Downfall. Dolores was to come with us. We were both sorry and glad to go. We felt sad about leaving Hampstead, but the place and people had changed under Johnnie's influence, and also largely under our own in the last seven years.

"I brooded on these things and was turning back to our quarters where I was to meet Dolores, when suddenly I heard a curious sound on my right.

"As I walked towards the place, I became aware that a number of people were gathered together hidden from my sight behind a large boulder. Presently I could hear more clearly what the noise was: these people were chanting together the old refrain. Tum tum *ya*, tum tum *ya*. Silently, I peered round the boulder, and stopped short, sick and terrified and appalled by what I saw.

"Before I describe what I saw, I must tell you that Johnnie Heath had recently revived the *Tum Tum Times*. One of its columns was regularly devoted to a plea for a return to what was described variously as 'the native purity of our customs', or 'the purity of our native customs', or else 'the customs of our native purity'. I had not thought very much about this, for Johnnie's ideas were always rather cranky. But one day I had chanced to read in this column a reference to an organization which was recommended as offering 'an outlet through a classical mode of expressions of our most pure and primitive passions'. On reading this, I shuddered, then thought no more about it.

"I remembered this some time after the incident on Hampstead Heath.

"Now," said Moon Biglow, "I will tell you what I saw there.

"A group of young men and women, well known to me, and many of whom had been close friends, were seated cross-legged in a circle round a stone slab. By the light of the Moon I saw them led by Johnnie Heath clapping their hands to the rhythm of tum tum *ya*, tum tum *ya*. On the slab inside the circle lay the dead body of Dolores, with a knife stuck in her throat. The blood was congealed on her neck, where it had flowed and ceased to flow.

"Then I saw, watching from behind them, two of my Moon Brothers. They moved round silently to where I was standing. Hand in hand we fled home.

"My five Moon Brothers left the earth secretly during the night. I could not, myself, face the Moon without Dolores. I felt it necessary to remain on earth and die here where she died.

"Of course, I cleared out of Hampstead.

"But the strange thing is, that our mission wasn't a failure, after all. The revival of the tum tum *ya* cult did not last. It still crops up from time to time here and there, for these things spread. But the absence of the Changing Drama of the Moon began to be felt. The sense of loss led to a tremendous movement of the human spirit. The race of the artist appeared on the earth, everywhere attempting to express the lost Moon drama. Long after the people who had frequented the old Remarkable Playhouse were dead and forgotten the legend survived; and long after the legend was forgotten, the sense of loss survived.

"So it happens," said Moon Biglow, "that whenever the

tum tum *ya* movement gets afoot, and the monotony and horror start taking hold of people, the artists rise up and proclaim the virtue of the remarkable things that are missing from the earth.

"And so," said Moon Biglow, "you owe your literature, your symphonies, your old masters and your new masters, to the Six Moon Brothers and Dolores. It was a good thing we had to go. We could never have induced you to shift for yourselves by any other means.

"You and your littery friends," said Moon Biglow, "ought to know the true position, which is what I've told you. And if ever you produce a decent poem or a story, it won't be on account of anything you've got in this world but of something remarkable which you haven't got. There is always a call for the Remarkable from time to time, simply because we closed the doors of the Playhouse called Remarkable, and because the Young Remarkables have gone off home, and because there is nothing left Remarkable beneath the visiting Moon."

CHIMES

Tonight is the anniversary of one of my most puzzling murders. It was the autumn of 1954, when life was sleepier than it is now. Saturday, the second of October, to be exact.

For a detective, I haven't a particularly good memory as a rule. But you will see presently why I remember this particular date. It was nearly an unsolved murder. Old Matthews was a farmer of the village of Mellow in the West Country. He was found dead on the morning of the third of October in an outhouse of his own farm, lying at the foot of the ladder leading to the hayloft. He was eighty-two.

At the inquest the local doctor gave evidence that Matthews's death was due to a fractured skull. It was assumed he had been up in the hayloft during the night and had fallen down the ladder. The verdict was death by misadventure.

You will wonder what old Matthews was doing in the hayloft during the night.

He slept in the hayloft. It is true he owned the farm. And there was a large farmhouse where his wife lived. You must understand that Matthews was rather peculiar. So was his wife. They didn't get on together and he preferred to sleep in the outhouse. Situations like that are not unusual in the deep country.

The inquest was soon over and Matthews was buried on the sixth of October. A fortnight after the funeral the police received an anonymous letter accusing Harold Matthews, the son, of having murdered his father. It was not generally known at the time, but in fact Harold was not old Matthews's legitimate son.

The police frequently receive anonymous letters and so they took no great notice of this one. They tried to trace the author, whom they suspected to be some village woman, but they were unsuccessful. Before long, however, rumours were going about the village to the effect that Harold had murdered his father. The police questioned Harold. He was unhelpful, but that wasn't his fault, for he was rather simple.

Within three months the rumours had increased, and a reporter from a national newspaper was said to have visited the area. The police had to act. They disinterred Matthews's body. The Home Office pathologist found that the fracture on his skull had been caused by a blow. It was now certain that Matthews had been murdered during the night of the second–third of October.

Poor Harold tried to explain to the police that he could not have killed his father, since old Matthews was *not* his father. That's how the police came to know about his illegitimacy. But in any case, they didn't waste time trying to get sense out of Harold, for the man had a perfect alibi.

During the night of the murder he had been watching the others playing cards in the kitchen, and then had gone to bed in a room which he shared with one of the farm hands.

It was at this point in the investigations that we from London were called in. First we were presented with a number of established facts. On the afternoon of the second of October Matthews had gone to a farm two miles from Mellow to help with a difficult calving. He left this place just after nine that night and was seen to cross some fields, slowly because of his age. This would bring him to the main road at about 10.20. The doctor was passing in his car and stopped, apparently to give Matthews a lift. Matthews entered the car, where he sat talking to the doctor. A courting couple who passed them at 10.30 said they seemed to be arguing rather violently. No one observed the car drive off.

You will wonder how the witnesses remembered these encounters three months after the event. Well, mainly because it *was* the night old Matthews was killed. People said, when they heard the news of Matthews's death, "Why, I saw him that very night!" and so on. It's surprising the things people remember and what they forget, especially in this case, as you'll see.

Everyone at the farmhouse was equally clear about what had happened that night, with the exception of Harold who wasn't clear about much. They had been playing cards in the kitchen – some farm labourers who lived at the house, and Mrs Matthews – with Harold looking on. At midnight they heard a car drive up the farm lane and stop outside the outhouse. They assumed that old Matthews had got a lift home. They heard him, as they supposed, enter the outhouse, the door of which had a noisy hinge. A few seconds later the car drove off.

This was at midnight. They all swore they heard the

church clock strike twelve when the car arrived. By our reckoning, it was not old Matthews whom they heard entering the outhouse, but the murderer dumping the body. A murderer with a car. Now Matthews had been seen arguing with the doctor at 10.30, only a few minutes' drive from the farm. Yet these noises were not heard till twelve.

We questioned the doctor, of course. His name was Fell. He lived in another village – Otling, three miles from Mellow along the main road. His story was that he had sat chatting to Matthews – a patient of his – for over half an hour in the car. They had had a little argument about politics. He had then driven Matthews to his farm, arriving there at eleven o'clock. After that he had proceeded home where he arrived at ten past eleven.

There he found an urgent message to visit a sick patient, and set off immediately. He attended to his patient – a childbirth case – and was home again just as the church clock struck midnight.

Dr Fell's manner was extremely helpful. He actually wrote out a statement for us, giving all his movements that night and citing his witnesses. We checked up on everything and could find no flaw in his alibi. There was no doubt he had visited his patient at twenty past eleven, for the child was registered as having been born at ten minutes to twelve. His housekeeper's niece, who had just returned home from a dance, as well as his wife, gave evidence of his return home as the clock struck midnight. He couldn't have been both at Mellow and at Otling as the church clock struck midnight.

And I was assured that the church clock always kept perfect time.

And you will say, were the farm people lying? Did they really hear those noises at the outhouse at midnight?

Do you know, it was a strange thing – we are all of us experienced in detecting lies – but we couldn't break down one of those witnesses, either at Otling or at Mellow, in the slightest detail. We had no evidence against Dr Fell. It was quite a puzzle. Three months after the event, you know, there isn't much physical evidence to go by – fingerprints and so on.

But we suspected Dr Fell. Our investigations had brought another important fact to light. Old Matthews had been receiving monthly payments from Dr Fell for thirty-odd years.

Of course, we thought of blackmail. We questioned Mrs Matthews about this. She denied knowledge of the money, but eventually told us that Dr Fell was Harold's real father. It looked very much to us that the monthly payments were made to keep old Matthews quiet. A country doctor can't afford to lose his reputation.

And we found that a few months before the murder these payments had increased. The increase coincided exactly with Dr Fell's marriage to a much younger woman. If our theory was correct Matthews had seized the opportunity of the marriage to increase his demands, for in those days – perhaps even now – a doctor would not wish his bride to know of an illegitimate son in the neighbourhood. Here, then, was a clear motive for murder. But Dr Fell had his alibi. We could not prove it.

I questioned him again. His eyes fixed themselves on me. I was almost hypnotized. I must say I felt very uneasy in his presence. But of course in our profession we are trained to discount most of our personal feelings when dealing with a suspect. Still, the old rhyme went round my head as I drove away from his house:

I do not like thee, Dr Fell.
The reason why I cannot tell.
But this one thing I know full well:
I do not like thee, Dr Fell.

Shortly after this a member of the local police made a discovery which earned him promotion. He was looking through the statement which Dr Fell had written out for us when he noticed a peculiarity in the writing which coincided with that of the anonymous letter they had received accusing Harold of the crime. The letter had been written in a disguised hand, but still the experts confirmed the suspicions of that clever policeman. Now, at least, we had something concrete to tax Dr Fell with – and a concrete charge is always a help in a murder case.

He was, of course, upset at our discovery. Eventually he admitted writing it, said he had genuinely suspected Harold but could not bring himself to say so at the inquest. We suggested to him that the letter was written as a defence against blackmail on the part of Harold. The doctor denied it.

However, I went off to interview Harold, hoping to discover what he knew about Dr Fell. With simple people it is best to be direct. I said, "Harold, why did you try to get money out of Dr Fell?"

He said, "Eh?"

I said, "You think he killed the old man, don't you?"

He said, "That's right, sir, I do."

But, like ourselves, poor Harold had no evidence to produce against the doctor. There were probabilities, but simply no answer to the fact that he had been seen at Otling at the very time the car had been heard at Mellow.

I can't tell you how disappointed I was after that interview with Harold. There was no further point in our men hanging on at Mellow. We were to return to London next morning, our criminal in sight but not brought to justice.

I was so disappointed that I said, half to myself and half to Harold, "If only we could shake his alibi for that particular midnight!" Harold didn't seem to take this in. I went my way.

But in a moment Harold was running after me. "You'll never get him, sir," he said.

I said, "No, that's just what I mean."

He said, "You see, sir, there was two midnights, like, that night. That's why you'll never get him. You can't get a man between two midnights."

"Two midnights?" I said.

"Right you are, sir," Harold said. "It was end of summer time, wasn't it? And they put the clocks back. Old Fell done it between the two midnights, and you'll never get him."

"Harold," I said. "You're a genius."

"You'll never get him," he said.

I went to see the verger who recalled, yes, come to think of it, the church clock wasn't put back till a couple of days after the official date. The town clerk, on the other hand, was proud to declare that he had arranged for the town hall's clock to be put back on the afternoon of the previous day, 1 October. "You don't catch us napping!" said the Clerk.

"Won't we?" I said.

It didn't take us long to put our point of view over to Dr Fell. He confessed to the murder. It had taken place in a field. He had hit old Matthews over the head with a wooden leg. He had the wooden leg in his car, for earlier that week he'd been getting it mended for an old pensioner in the village. In some ways Dr Fell was quite a kindly man. Well, having killed old Matthews he dumped his body in the outhouse at eleven o'clock by Winter Time, twelve by British Summer Time and the church clock. These were the days of capital punishment, but his sentence was commuted to life imprisonment. The law doesn't like blackmail.

LADIES AND GENTLEMEN

Author's note: The following is based on a true incident, perhaps made more macabre by the fact that the man in question was afraid of being seen with a girl by his mother, not his wife. In the true version the man was not caught, only observed as he crept round the public lavatory in a way that struck the author as being quite hilarious.

Past the Cathedral, past the "Fighting Cocks" which will not be open till later, past the ice-cream stand, past the mill-race, past the lake which was once a monastic fishpond, they come. The year is 1950. June Flinders is her name, Bill Dobson his. The ancient site of Verulamium is the place. Arm in arm they advance towards us.

Miss Flinders was still a student at a university in the north of England. Mr Dobson was a teacher of domestic science at a technical college in the Midlands. They had met at a holiday course. There was a Mrs Dobson but she was far from their thoughts.

They dallied awhile by the mill-race, leaning over the bridge. A cow came down and stepped daintily into the water farther up where the river was calm. Silent and patient as a tree standing in its own shadow, she stood and accepted the cool water about her feet. Where the stream broke up noisily at the mill-race a few barefoot boys were playing. Neither June nor Bill were fond of children, but they felt pleasantly inclined towards these boys. Because they were two together, illicitly, and in secret, a sentiment of indulgence entered their hearts and caused them to buy five cones at the kiosk, and distribute them among the children.

The boys took the ice-creams and deserted the mill-stream right away as if they felt this unforeseen treat might be snatched away.

"Don't go, boys," said Bill. But that finished it. They recognized the teacher in him, and were gone.

"It must be funny," said June, "suddenly inheriting a fortune."

He was glad she had opened the subject. There was something he wanted to tell her.

"I couldn't believe it," he said, "at first."

"I'm sure," said June.

"I showed Maisie the letter. Maisie couldn't believe it," he said; "at first."

A look of sad reflection overcame June's face. Maisie was Bill's wife and June felt sad and reflective whenever she was mentioned. Moreover, this expression was one to which June was adapted by nature. She wore her light hair parted in the middle and drawn back in a bun, and she had rather a long white nose, think of this, and you will understand how the dolorous look fitted in with the whole.

She pursued the subject, however.

"It will make it easier when we break the news," said June.

"Yes," he replied eagerly, "that's the important thing about the money. Maisie won't be dependent upon me, now or later.

"As a matter of fact, June," he said, "I have left her the lot in my will. I'm sure you will agree, that's the best thing in the circumstances. But, of course, we shall have enough to live on, June. Only, I thought it only right, June, to leave her the lot in my will. It will make it easier when we break the news."

"The lot?" said June.

"Yes," said Bill. "It will make it easier for us, you see."

"It's a great deal of money," said June.

"The tax would come off it, the death duties," he said pacifically. "But we've got our life ahead of us, and who knows who will die first?

"Don't let's talk about it," he added.

"Let's live and make the most of it," he added further.

Bill was forty-two. To June who was eighteen, he did not seem to have his life ahead of him. But then, she was in love with Bill; surely that was all that mattered. His ways were almost exactly like the ways of the Professor of Botany, with this exception, that Bill had run away with her and the Professor of Botany had not and never would.

It worried June that Bill had not made a clean break with his wife. Indeed, Maisie knew nothing about her husband's romance, and fancied he was gone to give a series of lectures.

"I wish you had made a clean break with Maisie," said June, "I always hate deception in cases like this."

"Why," said Bill, "have you done it before?"

"Oh no," June said swiftly, "I just meant that I always hate deception."

June had not done it before. This worried her. They had left their luggage in the hotel bedroom. Bill had signed "Wm and Mrs Dobson" in the book. Suppose he ceased to want to live with her always? Suppose he only wanted her for one thing. If he only wanted her for that, it would explain why he had not told Maisie. It would be too late afterwards. What a muddle.

"I always hate deception," June repeated.

"I thought we should see how we get on together before doing anything final," Bill was careless enough to say.

"You said it was all over between you in any case," said June.

"It is," said Bill. "It is."

"Bill," she said, "will you do something for me?"

"Of course," he said.

"Just for tonight," she said, "I'd rather we didn't – I'd prefer not to – I mean let's not –"

June sought round in her mind for the correct phrase. She was anxious to convey her meaning without seeming either coarse or prim. With relief she lit on the words she wanted.

"I would rather we were not intimate tonight," she said.

Bill looked put out. There were some very surprising elements in June.

"Don't you want to stop at the hotel?" he said.

"Oh yes," said June impatiently, "but I'd rather we waited. Don't you see. It's a very important and big thing for me.

"Tomorrow night, though," she added, with a searching look at Bill.

"That's all right," said Bill who was still a bit bewildered.

"If you don't want to come across with it – I mean," he said, "if you would rather wait my dear, then naturally I will respect your wishes.

"I hope," he said, warming to the idea, "I hope that I am man enough for that. And I love you very dearly, June."

June felt relieved. She would have liked to go on about the final break with Maisie, but she thought it wiser to wait.

"Let's go and see the old Roman wall," she suggested.

She had thought it wiser to wait before mentioning Maisie again. However, she was only eighteen and very excited.

"I'm only eighteen and very excited, what with it all," she told herself.

In a few seconds she was back on the subject of Maisie.

"Have you made a settlement on Maisie?" she inquired. "Because I hope you will make her a small income. Have you done that?"

"Yes," said Bill.

"Sufficient for her needs?" said June. "They can't be much, there are no children involved."

"Yes," said Bill.

June was longing to ask "How much?" She was thinking of the best way to frame this question when Bill spoke again.

"I must remember to send a fiver to my old cousin Leonard. He lives near this place, in fact. At Bricket Wood."

"Who is he?" said June. "Oh, I hope we shan't meet him."

"Don't worry," Bill laughed. "He wouldn't recognize me. He's been simple all his life. He lives all alone, poor chap. I daresay he gets a disability pension now," Bill mused on. "Still, I must get Maisie to send him a fiver, now I can afford it."

"Why Maisie?" said June. "Can't you do it yourself?"

"I don't know his address," said Bill. "Maisie knows it. She has kept up with him. Out of charity, you know.

"Maisie has got her better side," Bill said, stopping in the pathway to stress his point. "I'll say that for her, darling."

"Oh, everyone's got their good side," said June, looking at him anxiously. "But she sounds a terror otherwise."

"Yes," said Bill. "I'm afraid she is a terror all right. But I'm going to buy my freedom now, at last."

"Come on," he said, "let's go and look at the Roman wall."

He took a few paces forward and stopped. "Stop," he said.

About fifty yards ahead, on the left side of the path facing the lake, was a bench. It was placed on a small raised bank under a hawthorn. A man and a woman were seated on the bench. Owing to the bending sprays of hawthorn, it was impossible to see their faces properly.

"That looks like Maisie," he said.

"I'm not sure," he said. "Don't move, dear. Let's wait a moment."

"Oh, no!" she said. "Oh, Bill!" she said. "I'm going back to the town."

"Don't be silly," he said, "I'm not at all certain it is Maisie. It just looks a bit like her. I can't quite see the face. But I'm certain she never comes here."

"Maybe she has come to see your old cousin," said June. "Oh, let me get back, quick."

"That's possible," said Bill. "It might be old Leonard with her there. But I'm sure she would have told me she was coming."

"I'm going," said June.

"No. Wait here. Don't panic," said Bill. "I'll find out."

"It might all get into the papers," said June, "my name and all."

"It won't get into the papers," said Bill.

Alas, it got into the papers.

In their present predicament, Bill kept his head.

"Wait here," he repeated. "I'll skirt round that wooden hut and get a look at their faces. I'll soon see if the woman is Maisie or not."

I daresay that even if you once knew the place you would not remember the wooden hut. It was a modest building situated on the lake side of the path, about halfway between the mill-race and the bench where the couple were seated. It was a building less crude than it looked. Perhaps it was built to look rustic, with its rough overlaid planks. It was lined with brick. All round this simple structure was a narrow space fenced off with wavy wire. You might enter this enclosure at either end, according as you were a Gentleman or a Lady in large print. These were the days before a skirted or trousered figure indicated your rightful door. The two ends of the public lavatory were separated by a shaky fence.

It is doubtful if Bill noticed this. In any case, he went in at the right end, and passing the wooden door marked Gentlemen, began to skirt round the building with his eyes fixed on the bench.

He could not make out their faces. Keeping close to the wooden walls he passed under the Gentlemen's windows. Still he could not see the couple on the bench. The hawthorn tree was still in the way. If, at first, he had observed what the building was, he had by now forgotten it. He was intent on seeing the occupants of that bench.

It took him three movements to climb over the wire fence separating the two ends of the enclosure. A second, and he was under the windows of the Ladies.

Nearer, nearer, he crept. Yes – it is Maisie! But, is it? No. She has no hat on. Maisie always wears a hat. It is not Maisie. But look – she is holding her hat! Yes, and isn't that Leonard there beside her, with his mouth wide open?

To make quite certain, Bill started to heave himself up on to the sagging wire. He gripped the ledge of one of the Ladies' windows; he placed his hand on the ledge of another Ladies' window. Thus poised, he turned and got a clear view of the bench. It was Maisie! It occurred to him how like June she looked; older, of course. Yes, and that was Leonard sitting all slack and silly beside her.

Thus poised, he surveyed them, calculating his retreat with June. They had better leave the town. No one would see them. Thus poised, he signalled to June; and thus it was that they caught him.

Advance warning of the ensuing disturbance came with a fanfare of outraged shrieks from inside the building. There was a splash followed by a child's loud yell.

"Hold him!" said a thin wiry woman, rushing out of the Ladies. "The dirty Peeping Tom, the swine!"

She got hold of Bill's feet, and with the aid of two passing girls who laid down their bicycles for the purpose, floored him.

June turned and started to run for it.

"Wait here, you!" shouted the wiry woman. "Stop her, someone. She's a witness, an accomplice."

A middle-aged couple caught at June, who did not resist.

"I know nothing about it," she said.

"I saw nothing," she said.

"Didn't you?" said the thin woman. "Well I did."

"So did I," said one of the girls. "He was peeping into the Ladies. Broad daylight, too."

"Low," said the middle-aged man. "I call it low. You hold him down while I get a policeman."

Three more women had emerged from the Ladies a-tremble with the fuss. One woman held a little girl under her arm, and with her other arm she wielded her handbag, landing it on Bill's upturned face.

"Let me get up," cried Bill, "I can explain."

"Yes, you sneaky peeper," said the mother of the wailing child, "You'll explain all right. You wait till my husband hears of this."

"Ask my friend there," gasped Bill, pointing to June.

"Your friend!" said a pretty young redhead who had been inside the Ladies. "If she's your friend, she's for it too. Part of the game, she is, I'll bet."

"With a face like hers," added Redhead inconsequently.

"I didn't see anything," said June helplessly.

Bill managed to lean up on his elbows. The thin woman was sitting firmly on his legs. His feet were being secured by the child's mother.

As Bill saw the policeman approach, so also did he see Maisie arise from the bench. Curious about the little crowd which had gathered, Maisie ambled in her familiar casual way, over to where he was lying. Behind her shuffled Leonard, shaking his head a little.

Suddenly, Maisie jammed on the brakes, her nonchalant stride ceased. "Bill!" she said.

"This," she informed the crowd haughtily, "is my husband. Is he ill? Make way for me if you please."

"Oh, is he?" said the wiry woman, "Well, he's been up to his tricks, the back-door squinter."

June made one more attempt to retreat.

"You stop right there," said the redhead.

The policeman arrived. "Stand up," he said to Bill.

It was a very distressing case. The mother of the small girl was the chief witness for the Prosecution.

"I was out for a walk with my daughter," she said in the witness box, "and she wanted to go. I was holding her out when suddenly I saw the face of the accused at the window.

"I am afraid," she added, "that the shock was too much for me. I let go of Betty and poor little thing, she went right in."

"Was the child hurt?" inquired the magistrate.

"Well, there's nothing to actually see," said the mother. "But it can't be good for a child, a thing like that."

If it had been left to the other witnesses, the Prosecution might perhaps have lost the case.

Redhead let them down by saying she had only gone in to tidy up when she saw Bill at the window.

No one would say what they were really doing when they saw Bill at the window. As you know, the year was 1950. Not that it made much difference; peeping is peeping, no matter what you see. Still, they were glad of the mother of Betty to make a clear case of it.

The magistrate spoke severely to Maisie, being under the impression that she was June. This was not surprising, because with her fair hair parted in the middle and pulled back into a bun, Maisie looked remarkably like her rival, as do so many women whose men cannot really escape from them, but seek the same person in other arms.

When the magistrate was put right as to the mistaken identity, he spoke severely to June.

"You come to this place with another woman's husband and condone his offence," he said. "You even attempt to impersonate," he added, "this good, this honest woman."

Bill was fined ten pounds with an option of three weeks.

June emigrated to Australia to forget. Maisie went to the hairdresser without telling a soul, and had her hairstyle changed in favour of something different. Bill went to his lawyer without telling a soul and had his will changed in favour of his simple cousin Leonard.

COME ALONG, MARJORIE

Not many days had passed since my arrival at Watling Abbey when I realized that most of us were recovering from nerves. The Abbey, a twelfth-century foundation, lies in Worcestershire on the site of an ancient Temple of Mithras. It had recently been acquired and restored by its original religious Order at that time, just after the war, when I went to stay there and found after a few days that most of us were nervous cases.

By "most of us" I mean the lay visitors who resided in the pilgrims' quarters on two sides of the Annexe. We were all known as pilgrims. Apart from us, there was a group of permanent lay residents known as the Cloisters, because they lived in rooms above the cloisters.

Neurotics are awfully quick to notice other people's mentalities, everyone goes into an exaggerated category. I placed four categories at the Abbey. First ourselves, the visiting neurotic pilgrims. Second the Cloisters, they were cranks on the whole. Third the monks; they seemed not to have nerves, but non-individualized, non-neurotic, so I thought then, they billowed about in their white habits under the gold of that October, or swung out from the cloisters in processions on Feast Days. Into the fourth category I placed Miss Marjorie Pettigrew.

Indeed, she did seem sane. I got the instant impression that she alone among the lay people, both pilgrims and Cloisters, understood the purpose of the place. I did get that impression.

Three of us had arrived at Watling together. It was dark when I got off the train, but under the only gas bracket on the platform I saw the two women standing. They looked about them in that silly manner of women unused to arriving at strange railway stations. They heard me asking the ticket man the way to the Abbey and chummed up with me immediately. As we walked along with our suitcases I made note that there was little in common between them and me except Catholicism, and then only in the mystical sense, for their religious apprehensions were different from mine. "Different from" is the form my neurosis takes. I do like the differentiation of things, but it is apt to lead to nerve-racking pursuits. On the other hand, life led on the different-from level is always an adventure.

Those were quite nice women. One was Squackle-wackle, so I called her to myself, for she spoke like that, squackle-wackle, squackle-wackle – it was her neurosis – all about her job as a nurse in a London hospital. She had never managed to pass an exam but was content, squackle-wackle, to remain a subordinate, though thirty-three in December. All this in the first four minutes. The other woman would be nearer forty. She was quieter, but not much. As we approached the Abbey gates she said, "My name's Jennifer, what's yours?"

"Gloria Deplores-you," I answered. It is true my Christian name is Gloria.

"Gloria what?"

"It's a French name," I said, inventing in my mind the spelling "des Pleuresyeux" in case I should be pressed for it.

"We'll call you Gloria," she said. I had stopped in the Abbey gateway, wondering if I should turn back after all. "Come along, Gloria," she said.

It was not till some days later that I found that Jennifer's neurosis took the form of "same as". We are all the same, she would assert, infuriating me because I knew that God had made everyone unique. "We are all the same" was her way of saying we were all equal in the sight of God. Still, the inaccuracy irritated me. And still, like Squackle-wackle, she was quite an interesting person. It was only in my more vibrant moments that I deplored them.

Oh, the trifles, the people, that get on your nerves when you have a neurosis!

Don't I remember the little ginger man with the bottle-green cloak? He was one of the Cloisters, having been resident at Watling for over three years. He was compiling a work called *The Monkish Booke of Brewes*. Once every fortnight he would be absent at the British Museum and I suppose other record houses, from where he would return with a great pad of notes on the methods and subtleties of brewing practised in ancient monasteries, don't I remember? And he, too, was a kindly sort in between his frightful fumes against the management of Watling Abbey. When anything went wrong he blamed the monks, unlike the Irish who blamed the Devil. This sometimes caused friction between the ginger man and the Irish, for which the monks blamed the Devil.

There were ladies from Cork and thereabouts, ladies from

Tyrone and Londonderry, all having come for a rest or a Retreat, and most bearing those neurotic stigmata of South or North accordingly. There were times when bitter bits of meaning would whistle across the space between North and South when they were gathered together outside of their common worship. Though all were Catholics, "Temperament tells," I told myself frequently. I did so often tell myself remarks like that to still my own nerves.

I joined Squackle-wackle and Jennifer each morning to recite the Fifteen Mysteries. After that we went to the town for coffee. Because I rested in the afternoons Jennifer guessed I was recovering from nerves. She asked me outright, "Is it nerves?" I said "Yes," outright.

Squackle-wackle had also been sent away with nervous exhaustion, she made no secret of it, indeed no.

Jennifer was delighted. "I've got the same trouble. Fancy, all three of us. That makes us *all the same*."

"It makes us," I said, "more different from each other than other people are."

"But, all the same," she said, "we're all *the same*."

But there was Miss Marjorie Pettigrew. Miss Pettigrew's appearance and bearing attracted me with a kind of consolation. I learned that she had been at Watling for about six months and from various hints and abrupt silences I gathered that she was either feared or disliked. I put this down to the fact that she wasn't a neurotic. Usually, neurotics take against people whose nerves they can't jar upon. So I argued to myself; and that I myself rather approved of Miss Pettigrew was a sign that I was a different sort of neurotic from the others.

Miss Pettigrew was very tall and stick-like, with very high shoulders and a square face. She seemed to have a lot of bones. Her eyes were dark, her hair black; it was coiled in the earphone style but she was not otherwise unfashionable.

I thought at first she must be in Retreat, for she never spoke at mealtimes, though she always smiled faintly when passing anything at table. She never joined the rest of the community except for meals and prayers. She was often in the chapel praying. I envied her resistance, for though I too wanted solitude I often hadn't the courage to refuse to join the company, and so make myself unpopular like Miss Pettigrew. I hoped she would speak to me when she came out of her Retreat.

One day in that first week a grand-looking north-countrywoman said to me at table, nodding over to where Miss Pettigrew sat in her silence,

"There's nothing wrong with *her* at all."

"Wrong with her?"

"It's pretence, she's clever, that's it."

By clever she meant cunning, I realized that much.

"How do you mean, pretence?" I said.

"Her silence. She won't speak to anyone."

"But she's in Retreat, isn't she?"

"Not her," said this smart woman. "She's been living here for over six months and for the past four she hasn't opened her mouth. It isn't mental trouble, it is not."

"Has she taken some religious vow, perhaps?"

"Not her; she's clever. She won't open her mouth. They brought a doctor, but she wouldn't open her mouth to him."

"I'm glad she's quiet, anyhow," I said. "Her room's next door to mine and I like quietness."

Not all the pilgrims regarded Miss Pettigrew as "clever". She was thought to be genuinely touched in the head. And it was strange how she was disapproved of by the Cloisters, for they were kind – only too intrusively kind – towards obvious nervous sufferers like me. Their disapproval of Miss Pettigrew was almost an admission that they believed nothing was wrong with her. If she had gone untidy, made grotesque faces, given jerks and starts and twitches, if she had in some way lost their respect I do not think she would have lost their approval.

I began to notice her more closely in the hope of finding out more about her mental aberration; such things are like a magnet to neurotics. I would meet her crossing the courtyard, or come upon her kneeling in the lonely Lady Chapel. Always she inclined her coiled head towards me, ceremonious as an Abbess greeting a nun. Passing her in a corridor I felt the need to stand aside and make way for her confident quiet progress. I could not believe she was insane.

I could not believe she was practising some crude triumphant cunning, enduring from day to day, with her silence and prayers. It was said she had money. Perhaps she was very mystical. I wondered how long she would be able to remain hermited so within herself. The monks were in a difficult position. It was against their nature to turn her out; maybe it was against their Rule; certainly it would cause a bad impression in the neighbourhood which was not at all Abbey-minded. One after another the monks had approached her, tactful monks, sympathetic, firm and curious ones.

"Well, Miss Pettigrew, I hope you've benefited from your stay at the Abbey? I suppose you have plans for the winter?"

No answer, only a mild gesture of acknowledgement.

No answer, likewise, to another monk, "Now, Miss Pettigrew, dear child, you simply can't go on like this. It isn't that we don't want to keep you. Glory be to God, we'd never turn you out of doors, nor any soul. But we need the room, d'you see, for another pilgrim."

And again, "Now tell us what's the trouble, open your heart, poor Miss Pettigrew. This isn't the Catholic way at all. You've got to communicate with your fellows."

"Is it a religious vow you've taken all on your own? That's very unwise, it's . . ."

"See, Miss Pettigrew, we've found you a lodging in the town . . ."

Not a word. She was seen to go weekly to Confession, so evidently she was capable of speech. But she would not talk, even to do her small bits of shopping. Every week or so she would write on a piece of paper, "Please get me a Snowdrop Shampoo, is. 6d. encl." or some such errand, handing it to the laundry-girl who was much attached to her, and who showed me these slips of paper as proudly as if they were the relics of a saint.

"Gloria, are you coming for a walk?"

No, I wasn't going for a trudge. It was my third week. Squackle-wackle was becoming most uninteresting.

I sat by my window and thought how happy I would be if I wasn't waiting uncertainly for a telephone call. I still have in mind the blue and green and gold of that October afternoon which was spoiled for me at the time. The small ginger man with his dark green cloak slipping off his shoulders crossed the grass in the courtyard below. Two lay brothers in blue workmen's overalls were manipulating a tractor away in the distance. From the Lady Chapel came the chant of the monks at their office. There is nothing like plainsong to eternalize a memory, it puts a seal on whatever is happening at the time. I thought it a pity that my appreciation of this fact should be vitiated by an overwhelming need for the telephone call.

I had hoped, in fact, that the ginger man had crossed the courtyard to summon me to the telephone, but he disappeared beneath my window and his footsteps faded out somewhere round the back. Everything's perfect, I told myself, and I can't enjoy it. Brown, white and purple, I distinguished the pigeons on the grass.

Everyone else seemed to be out of doors. My room was on the attic floor, under the dusty beams of the roof. All along this top floor the rooms were separated by thin partitions which allowed transit to every sound. Even silent Miss Pettigrew, my immediate neighbour, could not lie breathing on her still bed without my knowing it. That afternoon she too was out, probably over in the chapel.

The telephone call was to be from Jonathan, my very best friend. I had returned from my coffee session in the town that morning to find a letter from him which had been delayed in the post. "I'll ring you at 11.30," he had written, referring to that very day. It was then past twelve. At eleven-thirty I had been drinking coffee with unutterable Squackle-wackle and Jennifer.

"Has there been a call for me?" I inquired.

"Not that I know," said the secretary vaguely. "I've been

away from the phone all morning, of course, so there may have been, I don't know."

Not that there was anything important to discuss with Jonathan; the idea was only to have a chat. But at that moment I felt imperatively dependent on his voice over the telephone. I stopped everyone, monks and brothers and pilgrims. "Did you take a telephone message for me? I should have received a very urgent call. It should have come at eleven-thirty."

"Sorry, I've been out," or "Sorry, I haven't been near the phone."

"Doesn't anyone attend to your telephone?" I demanded.

"Hardly ever, dear. We're too busy."

"I've missed an important telephone call, a vital –"

"Can't you telephone to your friend from here?"

"No," I said. "It's impossible, it's too bad."

Jonathan did not have a telephone in his studio. I wondered whether I should send him a wire and even drafted one, "Sorry love your letter arrived too late was out please ring at once love Gloria." I tore this up on the grounds that I couldn't afford the expense. And something about the torment of the affair attracted me, it was better than boredom. I decided that Jonathan would surely ring again during the afternoon. I prepared, even, to sit in the little office by the telephone with my sense of suspense and vigilance, all afternoon. But, "I'll be here till five o'clock," said the secretary; "of course, of course, I'll send for you if the call comes."

And so there I was by the window waiting for the summons. At three o'clock I washed and made up my face and changed my frock as if this were a propitiation to whatever stood between Jonathan's telephone call and me. I decided to stroll round the green-gold courtyard where I could not fail to miss any messenger. Once round, and still no one came. Only Miss Pettigrew emerged from the cloisters, crossing the courtyard towards me.

I was so bemused by my need to talk to Jonathan that I thought, as she approached, "Perhaps they've sent her to call me." Immediately I remembered, that was absurd, for she carried no messages ever. But she continued so directly towards me that I thought again; "She's going to speak." She had her dark eyes on my face.

I made as if to pass her, not wishing to upset her by inviting approach. But she stopped me. "Excuse me," she said, "I have a message for you."

I was so relieved that I forgot to be surprised by her speaking.

"Am I wanted on the telephone?" I said, half-ready to run across to the office.

"No, I have a message for you," she said.

"What's the message?"

"The Lord is risen," she said.

It was not until I had got over my disappointment that I felt the shock of her having spoken, and recalled an odd focus of her eyes that I had not seen before. "After all," I thought, "she has a religious mania. She *is* different from the neurotics, but not because she is sane."

"Gloria!" – this was the girl from the repository poking her head round the door. She beckoned to me, and, still disturbed, I idled over to her.

"I say, did I see Miss Pettigrew actually speaking to you, or was I dreaming?"

"You were dreaming." If I had said otherwise the news would have bristled round the monastery. It would have seemed a betrayal to reveal this first crack in Miss Pettigrew's control. The pilgrims would have pitied her more if they had known of it, they would have respected her less. I could not bear to think of their heads shaking sorrowfully over Miss Pettigrew's vital "The Lord is risen."

"But surely," this girl pursued, "she stopped beside you just now".

"You've got Miss Pettigrew on the brain," I said. "Leave her alone, poor soul."

"Poor soul!" said the girl. "I don't know about poor soul. There's nothing wrong with that one. She's got foolish medieval ideas, that's all."

"There's nothing to be done with her," I said.

And yet it was not long before something had to be done with Miss Pettigrew. From the Sunday of the fourth week of my stay she went off food. It was not till supper-time on the Monday that her absence was noticed from the refectory.

"Anyone seen Miss Pettigrew?"

"No, she hasn't been down here for two days."

"Does she eat in the town, perhaps?"

"No, she hasn't left the Abbey."

A deputation with a tray of food was sent to her room. There was no answer. The door was bolted from the inside. But I heard her moving calmly as ever in her room that evening.

Next morning she came in to breakfast after Mass, looking distant and grey, but still very neat. She took up a glass of milk, lifted the crust end of the bread from the board and carried them shakily off to her room. When she did not appear for lunch the cook tried her room again, without success. The door was bolted, there was no answer.

I saw Miss Pettigrew again at Mass next morning, kneeling a little in front of me, resting her head upon her missal as if she could not bear the weight of head on neck. When at last she left the chapel she walked extremely slowly but without halting in her measure. Squackle-wackle ran to help her down the steps. Miss Pettigrew stopped and looked at her, inclining her head in recognition, but clearly rejecting her help.

The doctor was waiting in her room. I heard later that he asked her many questions, used many persuasives, but she simply stared right through him. The Abbot and several of the monks visited her, but by then she had bolted the door again, and though they tempted her with soups and beef broth. Miss Pettigrew would not open.

News went round that her relatives had been sent for. The news went round that she had no relatives to send for. It was said she had been certified insane and was to be taken away.

She did not rise next morning at her usual seven o'clock. It was not till after twelve that I heard her first movement, and the protracted sounds of her slow rising and dressing. A tiny clatter – that would be her shoe falling out of her weak hands; I knew she was bending down, trying again. My pulse was pattering so rapidly that I had to take more of my sedative than usual, as I listened to this slow deliberated performance. Heavy rhythmic rain had started to ping on the roof.

"Neurotics never go mad," my friends had always told me. Now I realized the distinction between neurosis and madness, and in my agitation I half-envied the woman beyond my bedroom wall, the sheer cool sanity of her behaviour within the limits of her impracticable mania. Only the very mad, I thought, can come out with the information "The Lord is risen", in the same factual way as one might say, "You are wanted on the telephone", regardless of the time and place.

A knock at my door. I opened it, still shaking with my nerves. It was Jennifer. She whispered, with an eye on the partition dividing me from Miss Pettigrew,

"Come along, Gloria. They say you are to come away for half an hour. The nurses are coming to fetch *her*."

"What nurses?"

"From the asylum. And there will be men with a stretcher. We haven't to distress ourselves, they say."

I could see that Jennifer was agog. She was more transparent than I was. I could see she was longing to stay and overhear, watch out of the windows, see what would happen. I was overcome with disgust and indignation. Why should Jennifer want to satisfy her curiosity? She believed everyone was "the same", she didn't acknowledge the difference of things, what right had she to possess curiosity? My case was different.

"I shall stay here," I said in a normal voice, signifying that I wasn't going to participate in any whispering. Jennifer disappeared, annoyed.

Insanity was my great sort of enemy at that time. And here, clothed in the innocence and dignity of Miss Pettigrew, was my next-door enemy being removed by ambulance. I would not miss it. Afterwards I learned that Jennifer too was lurking around when the ambulance arrived. So were most of the neurotics.

The ambulance came round the back. My window looked only on the front but my ears were windows. I heard a woman's voice, then in reply the voice of one of our priests. Heavy footsteps and something bumping on the stairs and strange men's voices ascending.

"What's her name, did you say?"

"Marjorie Pettigrew."

The hauling and bumping up the stairs continued.

"Ain't no key. Bolt from the inside."

Whenever they paused I could hear Miss Pettigrew's tiny movements. She was continuing to do what she was doing.

They knocked at the door. I pulled like mad at the rosary which I was telling for Miss Pettigrew. A man's voice said, kindly but terribly loud,

"Open up the door, dear. Else we shall have to force it, dear."

She opened the door.

"That's a good girl," said the man. "What was the name again?"

The other man replied, "Marjorie Pettigrew."

"Well, come on, Marjorie dear. You just follow me and you won't go wrong. Come along, Marjorie."

I knew she must have been following, though I could not hear her footsteps. I heard the heavy men's boots descending the stairs, and their unnecessary equipment bumping behind them.

"That's right, Marjorie. That's a good girl."

Down below the nurse said something, and I heard no more till the ambulance drove off.

"Oh, I saw her!" This was the laundry-girl who had been fond of Miss Pettigrew. "She must have been combing her hair," she said, "when they came for her. It was all loose and long, not at all like Miss Pettigrew. She was always just so. And that going out in the rain, I hope she doesn't catch cold. But they'll be good to her."

Everyone was saying, "They will be kind to her." "They will look after her." "They might cure her."

I never saw them so friendly with each other.

After supper someone said, "I had a respect for Miss Pettigrew."

"So did I," said another.

"Yes, so did I."

"They will be very kind. Those men – they sounded all right."

"They meant well enough."

Suddenly the ginger man came out with that one thing which stood at the core of this circuitous talk.

"Did you hear them," he said, "calling her Marjorie?"

"My God, yes!"

"Yes, it made me feel funny."

"Same here. Fancy calling her Marjorie."

After that the incident was little discussed. But the community was sobered and united for a brief time, contemplating with fear and pity the calling of Miss Pettigrew Marjorie.

THE TWINS

When Jennie was at school with me, she was one of those well-behaved and intelligent girls who were, and maybe still are, popular with everyone in Scottish schools. The popularity of boys and girls in English schools, so far as I gather, goes by other, less easily definable qualities, and also by their prowess at games. However, it was not so with us, and although Jennie was not much use at hockey, she was good and quiet and clever, and we all liked her. She was rather nice-looking too, plump, dark-haired, clean, neat.

She married a Londoner, Simon Reeves. I heard from her occasionally. She was living in Essex, and once or twice, when she came to London, we met. But it was some years before I could pay my long-promised visit to them, and by the time I got round to it, her twins, Marjie and Jeff, were five years old.

They were noticeably beautiful children; dark, like Jennie, with a charming way of holding their heads. Jennie was, as she always had been, a sensible girl. She made nothing of their beauty, on which everyone felt compelled to remark. "As long as they behave themselves –" said Jennie; and I thought what a pretty girl she was herself, and how little notice she took of her looks, and how much care she took with other people. I noticed that Jennie assumed that everyone else was inwardly as quiet, as peacefully inclined, as little prone to be perturbed, as herself. I found this very restful and was grateful to Jennie for it. Her husband resembled her in this; but otherwise, Simon was more positive. He was brisk, full of activity, as indeed was Jennie; the difference between them was that Jennie never appeared to be bustling, even at her busiest hours, while Simon always seemed to live in the act of doing something. They were a fine match. I supposed he had gained from Jennie, during their six years of marriage, a little of her sweet and self-denying nature for he was really considerate. Simon would stop mowing the lawn at once, if he caught sight of the old man next door asleep in a deck-chair, although his need to do something about the lawn was apparently intense. For Jennie's part, she had learned from Simon how to speak to men without embarrassment. This was something she had been unable to do at the age of eighteen. Jennie got from Simon an insight into the mentalities of a fair variety of people, because his friends were curiously mixed, socially and intellectually. And in a way, Simon bore within himself an integrated combination of all those people he brought to the house; he represented them, almost, and kept his balance at the same time. So that Jennie derived from Simon a knowledge of the world, without actually weathering the world. A happy couple. And then, of course, there were the twins.

I arrived on a Saturday afternoon, to spend a week. The lovely twins were put to bed at six, and I did not see them much on the Sunday, as a neighbouring couple took them off for a day's picnicking with their own children. I spent most of Monday chatting with Jennie about old times and new times, while little Marjie and Jeff played in the garden. They were lively, full of noise and everything that goes with healthy children. And they were advanced for their years; both could read and write, taught by Jennie. She was sending them to school in September. They pronounced their words very clearly, and I was amused to notice some of Jennie's Scottish phraseology coming out in their English intonation.

Well, they went off to bed at six sharp that day: Simon came home shortly afterwards, and we dined in a pleasant humdrum peace.

It wasn't until the Tuesday morning that I really got on close speaking terms with the twins. Jennie took the car to the village to fetch some groceries, and for an hour I played with them in the garden. Again, I was struck by their loveliness and intelligence, especially of the little girl. She was the sort of child who noticed everything. The boy was quicker with words, however; his vocabulary was exceptionally large.

Jennie returned, and after tea, I went indoors to write letters. I heard Jennie telling the children "Go and play yourselves down the other end of the garden and don't make too much noise, mind." She went to do something in the kitchen. After a while, there was a ring at the back door. The children scampered in from the garden, while Jennie answered the ring.

"Baker," said the man.

"Oh, yes," said Jennie: "wait, I'll get my purse."

I went on writing my letter, only half-hearing the sound of Jennie's small change as she, presumably, paid the baker's man.

In a moment, Marjie was by my side.

"Hallo," I said.

Marjie did not answer.

"Hallo, Marjie," I said. "Have you come to keep me company?"

"Listen," said little Marjie in a whisper, looking over her shoulder. "Listen."

"Yes," I said.

She looked over her shoulder again, as if afraid her mother might come in.

"Will you give me half-a-crown?" whispered Marjie, holding out her hand.

"Well," I said, "what do you want it for?"

"I want it," said Marjie, looking furtively behind her again.

"Would your mummy want you to have it?" I said.

"Give me half-a-crown," said Marjie.

"I'd rather not," I said. "But I'll tell you what, I'll buy you a –"

But Marjie had fled, out of the door, into the kitchen. "She'd rather not," I heard her say to someone.

Presently, Jennie came in, looking upset.

"Oh," she said, "I hope you didn't feel hurt. I only wanted to pay the baker, and I hadn't enough change. He hadn't any either; so just on the spur of the moment I sent Marjie for a loan of half-a-crown till tonight. But I shouldn't have done it. I *never* borrow anything as a rule."

"Well, of course!" I said. "Of course I'll lend you half-a-crown. I've got plenty of change. I didn't understand and I got the message all wrong; I thought she wanted it for herself and that you wouldn't like that."

Jennie looked doubtful. I funked explaining the whole of Marjie's act. It isn't easy to give evidence against a child of five.

"Oh, they never ask for money," said Jennie. "I would never allow them to ask anyone for anything. They never do *that*."

"I'm sure they don't," I said, floundering a bit.

Jennie was much too kind to point out that this was what I had just been suggesting. She was altogether too nice to let the incident make any difference during my stay. That night, Simon came home just after six. He had bought two elaborate spinning-tops for the twins. These tops had to be wound up, and they sang a tinny little tune while they spun.

"You'll ruin those children," said Jennie.

Simon enjoyed himself that evening, playing with the tops.

"You'll break them before the children even see them," said Jennie.

Simon put them away. But when one of his friends, a pilot from a nearby aerodrome, looked in later in the evening, Simon brought out the tops again; and the two men played delightedly with them, occasionally peering into the works and discussing what made the tops go; while Jennie and I made scornful comments.

Little Marjie and Jeff were highly pleased with the tops next morning, but by the afternoon they had tired of them and gone on to something more in the romping line. After dinner Simon produced a couple of small gadgets. They were the things that go inside musical cigarette-boxes, he explained, and he thought they would fit into the spinning-tops, so that the children could have a change of tune.

"When they get fed up with 'Pop Goes the Weasel'," he said, "they can have 'In and Out the Windows'."

He got out one of the tops to take it apart and fit in the new tune. But when he had put the pieces together again, the top wouldn't sing at all. Jennie tried to help, but we couldn't get "In and Out the Windows". So Simon patiently unpieced the top, put the gadgets aside, and said they would do for something else.

"That's Jeff's top," said Jennie, in her precise way, looking at the pieces on the carpet. "Jeff's is the red one, Marjie has the blue."

Once more, Simon started piecing the toy together, with the old tune inside it, while Jennie and I went to make some tea.

"I'll bet it won't work now," said Jennie with a giggle.

When we returned, Simon was reading and the top was gone.

"Did you fix it?" said Jennie.

"Yes," he said absently. "I've put it away."

It rained the next morning and the twins were indoors.

"Why not play with your tops?" Jennie said.

"Your Daddy took one of them to pieces last night," Jennie informed them, "and put all the pieces back again."

Jennie had the stoic in her nature and did not believe in shielding her children from possible disappointment.

"He was hoping," she added, "to fit new tunes inside it. But it wouldn't work with the new tune . . . But he's going to try again."

They took this quite hopefully, and I didn't see much of them for some hours although, when the rain stopped and I went outside, I saw the small boy spinning his bright-red top on the hard concrete of the garage floor. About noon little Jeff came running into the kitchen where Jennie was baking. He was howling hard, his small face distorted with grief. He held in both arms the spare parts of his top.

"My top!" he sobbed. "My top!"

"Goodness," said Jennie, "what did you do to it? Don't cry, poor wee pet."

"I found it," he said. "I found my top all in pieces under that box behind Daddy's car.

"My top," he wept. "Daddy's broken my top." Marjie came in and looked on unmoved, hugging her blue top.

"But you were playing with the top this morning!" I said. "Isn't yours the red one? You were spinning it."

"I was playing with the blue one," he wept. "And then I found my own top all broken. Daddy broke it."

Jennie sat them up to their dinner, and Jeff presently stopped crying.

Jennie was cheerful about it, although she said to me afterwards, "I think Simon might have told me he couldn't put it together again. But isn't it just like a man? They're that proud of themselves, men."

As I have said, it isn't easy to give evidence against a child of five. And especially to its mother.

Jennie tactfully put the pieces of the top back in the box behind the garage. They were still there, rusty and untouched, in a pile of other rusty things, seven years later, for I saw them. Jennie got skipping ropes for the twins that day and when they had gone to bed, she removed Marjie's top from the toy-cupboard. "It'll only make wee Jeff cry to see it," she said to me. "We'll just forget about the tops."

"And I don't want Simon to find out that I found *him* out," she giggled.

I don't think tops were ever mentioned again in the household. If they were, I am sure Jennie would change the subject. An affectionate couple; it was impossible not to feel kindly towards them; not so, towards the children.

I was abroad for some years after that, and heard sometimes from Jennie at first; later, we seldom wrote, and then not at all. I had been back in London for about a year when I met Jennie in Baker Street. She was excited about her children, now aged twelve, who had both won scholarships and were going off to boarding schools in the autumn.

"Come and see them while they've got their holidays," she said. "We often talk about you, Simon and I." It was good to hear Jennie's kind voice again.

I went to stay for a few days in August. I felt sure the twins must have grown out of their peculiarities, and I was right. Jennie brought them to meet me at the station. They had grown rather quiet; both still extremely good-looking. These children possessed an unusual composure for their years. They were well-mannered as Jennie had been at their age, but without Jennie's shyness.

Simon was pruning something in the garden when we got to the house.

"Why, you haven't changed a bit," he said. "A bit thinner maybe. Nice to see you so flourishing."

Jennie went to make tea. In these surroundings she seemed to have endured no change; and she had made no change in her ways in the seven years since my last visit.

The twins started chatting about their school life, and

Simon asked me questions I could not answer about the size of the population of the places I had lived in abroad. When Jennie returned, Simon leapt off to wash.

"I'm sorry Simon said that," said Jennie to me when he had gone. "I don't think he should have said it, but you know how tactless men are."

"Said what?" I asked.

"About you looking thin and ill," said Jennie.

"Oh, I didn't take it *that* way!" I said.

"Didn't you?" said Jennie with an understanding smile. "That was sweet of you."

"Thin and haggard indeed!" said Jennie as she poured out the tea, and the twins discreetly passed the sandwiches.

That night I sat up late talking to the couple. Jennie retained the former habit of making a tea-session at nine o'clock and I accompanied her to the kitchen. While she was talking, she packed a few biscuits neatly into a small green box.

"There's the kettle boiling," said Jennie, going out with the box in her hand. "You know where the teapot is. I won't be a minute."

She returned in a few seconds, and we carried off our tray.

It was past one before we parted for the night. Jennie had taken care to make me comfortable. She had put fresh flowers on the dressing-table, and there, beside my bed, was the little box of biscuits she had thoughtfully provided. I munched one while I looked out of the window at the calm country sky, ruminating upon Jennie's perennial merits. I have always regarded the lack of neurosis in people with awe. I am too much with brightly intelligent, highly erratic friends. In this Jennie, I decided, reposed a mystery which I and my like could not fathom.

Jennie had driven off next day to fetch the twins from a swimming-pool near by, when Simon came home from his office.

"I'm glad Jennie's out," he said, "for I wanted a chance to talk to you.

"I hope you won't mind," he said, "but Jennie's got a horror of mice."

"Mice?" I said.

"Yes," said Simon, "so don't eat biscuits in your room if you wouldn't mind. Jennie was rather upset when she saw the crumbs but of course she'd have a fit if she knew I'd told you. She'd die rather than tell you. But there it is, and I know you'll understand."

"But Jennie put the biscuits in my room herself," I explained. "She packed them in a box and took them up last night."

Simon looked worried. "We've had mice before," he said, "and she can't bear the thought of them upstairs."

"Jennie put the biscuits there," I insisted, feeling all in the wrong.

"And," I said, "I saw Jennie pack the box. I'll ask her about it."

"*Please*," said Simon, "please don't do that. She would be so hurt to think I'd spoken about it. Please," he said, "go on eating biscuits in your room; I shouldn't have mentioned it."

Of course I promised not to eat any more of the things. And Simon, with a knowing smile, said he would give me larger helpings at dinner, so that I wouldn't go hungry.

The biscuit-box had gone when I went to my room. Jennie was busy all next day preparing for a cocktail party they were giving that night. The twins devotedly gave up their day to the cutting of sandwiches and the making of curious patterns with small pieces of anchovy on diminutive squares of toast.

Jennie wanted some provisions from the village, and I offered to fetch them. I took the car, and noticed it was almost out of petrol; I got some on the way. When I returned, these good children were eating their supper standing up in the kitchen, and without a word of protest, cleared off to bed before the guests arrived.

When Simon came home I met him in the hall. He was uneasy about the gin; he thought there might not be enough. He decided to go straight to the local and get more.

"And," he said, "I've just remembered. The car's almost out of petrol. I promised to drive the Rawlings home after the party. I nearly forgot. I'll get some petrol too."

"Oh, I got some today," I said.

There were ten guests, four married couples and two unattached girls. Jennie and I did the handing round of snacks and Simon did the drinks. His speciality was a cocktail he had just discovered, called Loopamp. This Loopamp required him to make frequent excursions to the kitchen for replenishments of prune-juice and ice. Simon persuaded himself that Loopamp was in great demand among the guests. We all drank it obligingly. As he took his shakers to the kitchen for the fourth time, he called out to one of the unattached girls who was standing by the door, "Mollie, bring that lemon jug too, will you?"

Mollie followed him with the lemon jug.

"Very good scholarships," Jennie was saying to an elderly man. "Jeff came fourth among the boys, and Marjie took eleventh place in the girls. There were only fourteen scholarships, so she was lucky. If it hadn't been for the geography she'd have been near the top. Her English teacher told me."

"Really!" said the man.

"Yes," said Jennie. "Mollie Thomas; you know Mollie Thomas. That's Marjie's English mistress. She's here tonight. Where's Mollie?" said Jennie, looking round.

"She's in the kitchen," I said.

"Making Loopamp, I expect," said Jennie. "What a name, Loopamp!"

Simon and Jennie looked rather jaded the next morning. I put it down to the Loopamp. They had very little to say, and when Simon had left for London, I asked Jennie how she was feeling.

"Not too good," she said. "Not too good. I am really sorry, my dear, about the petrol. I wish you had asked me for the money. Now, here it is, and don't say another word. Simon's so touchy."

"Touchy?"

"Well," said Jennie; "you know what men are like. I wish you had come to me about it. You know how scrupulous I am about debts. And so is Simon. He just didn't know you had got the petrol, and, of course, he couldn't understand why you felt hurt."

I sent myself a wire that morning, summoning myself back to London. There wasn't a train before the 6.30, but I caught this. Simon arrived home as I was getting into the taxi, and he joined Jennie and the children on the doorstep to wave goodbye.

"Mind you come again soon," said Jennie.

As I waved back, I noticed that the twins, who were waving to me, were not looking at me, but at their parents. There was an expression on their faces which I have only seen once before. That was at the Royal Academy, when I saw a famous portrait painter standing bemused, giving a remarkable and long look at the work of his own hands. So, with wonder, pride and bewilderment, did the twins gaze upon Jennie and Simon.

I wrote and thanked them, avoiding any reference to future meetings. By return I had a letter from Simon. "I am sorry," he wrote, "that you got the impression that Mollie and I were behaving improperly in the kitchen on the night of our party. Jennie was very upset. She does not, of course, doubt my fidelity, but she is distressed that you could suggest such a thing. It was very embarrassing for Jennie to hear it in front of all her friends, and I hope, for Jennie's sake, you will not mention to her that I have written you about it. Jennie would rather die than hurt your feelings. Yours ever, Simon Reeves."

"A SAD TALE'S BEST FOR WINTER"

There was a man lived by a graveyard. His name was Selwyn Macgregor, the nicest boy who ever committed the sin of whisky.

"Selwyn, what a place to live."

"Have a tot for the road, dear."

"Oh, Selwyn!"

"I get my letter tomorrow. Tomorrow I get the letter."

"Now, Selwyn Macgregor!"

"It always arrives the first of the month. The first it always comes."

"Macgregor, you're a case. Make it a small one."

"For the road, mind."

"Mac, I'm on my way. What a place to live, what a graveyard and the mucky old church with the barbed wire round it, who'd ever want to trespass within yon?"

"Cheerio, cheers!"

"Here's to you, Mr Macgregor. I would have to be a sore old tramp to shelter in yon for the night. The barbed wire I cannot understand, I can not."

"The money comes on the first."

"I'm away, Selwyn, the night's begun to rise."

So it continued for thirteen years, with Selwyn increasing in age from twenty-five to thirty-eight. At twenty-five he was invalided out of the army, at thirty-eight was still living in the shack in the garden of the fallen manse. There by the graveyard he was still getting his letter from Edinburgh every month on the 1st, when he would cash the cheque.

"Good evening, Mr Macgregor."

"Just a tot, the both of you, come on now."

"Mr Macgregor, we beg to inquire, will you play the piano at the concert?"

"Aw, but that's to be the middle of the month."

"Mac, you will play us a piece."

"Mid-month I'll be in contemplation."

"No more for me – well, a small . . . that's enough, Mr M."

"Cheerio!"

"We'll put you down for a tune then, Selwyn."

"Aw no, I said."

"Mr Selwyn, you'll go melancholy mad. What a place to dwell by!"

"Here's luck t'you both."

Always, about the middle of the month, Selwyn's money ran dry. Then he would go thirsty; he wouldn't open the door to anyone even if they had a plate of dinner in their hands. He lived on what he could get, turnips and sometimes the loaves and dinners which they left on the doorstep. The 25th of the month he opened his doors again, borrowed a bit till the 1st, received visitors, brought out the bottle.

But in those ten silent days between the middle of the

month and the 25th Selwyn Macgregor would sit by his window and contemplate the graves of the dead.

Selwyn's aunt lived in a tenement flat in the Warrender district of Edinburgh. Those flats were once occupied by people of good substance and still here and there contain a whole lot of wealth behind the lack of show.

"The district's going down," Selwyn's aunt was saying for twenty years. But let anyone come and tell her, "This quarter's going down":

"Not in my consideration, it isn't," she would say.

It was Selwyn's Aunt Macgregor who, in view of the fact that his mother had been Welsh, sent him his monthly cheque, for it wasn't Selwyn's fault that his mother had been Welsh and mad or at least bone lazy. What's bred in the bone comes out.

There wouldn't be much point in going into many details about Aunt Macgregor, what she looked like in her navy blue and how her eyes, nose and mouth were disposed among the broken veins of her fine severe old face, because her features went, as Selwyn said, under the earth where corruption is, and her navy blue went to the nurse.

Well, she died. Some months before, you must know, she visited Selwyn up there in that shack by the graveyard. She wore her brown, for she was careful with the navy. So up she went on the excursion to Selwyn Macgregor. He wasn't contemplating just then, so the doors were open.

"Auntie Macgregor! A little drop, Auntie, oh come on, a bit of a drop. That's the girl."

"Selwyn," she said, "you're the worse."

"Worse than what?" Although Selwyn knew she meant for the drink.

"Worse than what? Worse than who? Than who-oo-ooo?" Selwyn kept on chanting, and she started to laugh. She had a soft spot really for Selwyn.

Well, she died and left him a packet. Selwyn travelled to the funeral, a bitter cold day. Bitter cold, and naturally he had his flask in his pocket. For you must know Selwyn entertained a lively faith in the Resurrection; work it out, there was no dishonour meant to Aunt Macgregor by Selwyn's taking precautions against the cold at the graveside though he tottered and there was talk.

"Dust to dust . . ."

"That's never Miss Macgregor's nephew! Surely yon's never!"

"That's the chief mourner, her brother's boy. What's he up to for the Lord's sake?"

Selwyn lifted a handful of earth. But then, then, he stood looking at it with his smile. There was the coffin waiting and all the people waiting. So when the minister nodded as if to say, "All right, toss it on the coffin," Selwyn flung the earth over his left shoulder out of force of habit, as he did at home with the salt. After that he beamed round at the mourners as much as to say, "Here's health!" or "Cheerio!" or some similar saying.

"Poor Miss Macgregor. The only relative, poor soul."

Shortly afterwards Selwyn received a letter about his aunt's will from one of the trustees. It was rather complicated, and so Selwyn wrote, "Come and see me after the 25th." And he busied himself with contemplation until that date. On the 26th the trustee arrived at Selwyn's door with his healthy face and dark overcoat. Selwyn thought, what a nice wee trustee, here's hoping he's brought some ready.

"Make yourself at home," said Selwyn, getting out another glass.

"Ta," said the man.

"Here's hoping," Selwyn said.

And eventually this trustee said to Selwyn, "You know the provision in Miss Macgregor's will?"

"I did notice something," Selwyn declared, "in that letter you sent me but I was busy at the time."

So the man read out the will, and when he came to the bit ". . . to my nephew Selwyn Macgregor . . ." he stopped and looked at Selwyn, ". . . providing," he continued, "he looks after his health."

"My auntie all over," Selwyn said and filled up the glasses. "A very fine woman, Mr –?"

"Brown," said the man. "My partner Mr Harper is the other trustee. You'll get on fine with him. When will you be moving from here?"

"Aw when I'm dead," said Selwyn.

"Now, Mr Macgregor, this is not a healthy spot. The will says –"

"To hell with the will," said Selwyn, and patted Mr Brown on the shoulder, so that Mr Brown couldn't help warming to him, what with the whisky-tingle inside him, and the pleasant Welsh lilt of the "l's" when Selwyn had said, "To hell with the will."

"My work keeps me here," Selwyn added.

"What is your work, Mr Macgregor?"

"The contemplation of corruption."

"Now, Mr Macgregor, that is not a healthy occupation. I don't wish to be difficult but my partner Mr Harper takes his duty as a trustee very much to heart. Miss Macgregor was an old client of ours and she always worried about your health."

"Bung ho, press on!" said Selwyn.

"Same to you, Mr Mac. Here's to you, sir."

"You can tell Harper," Selwyn pointed out, "that you found me in good health and busy working."

"You look a bit thin, Mr Macgregor. This doesn't look a healthy spot to me."

Selwyn played him a tune and sang him a song. "O mother, mother," he sang, "make my bed. O make it soft and narrow . . ."

"Very nice," said the trustee when he'd finished. "That was rare."

"I'm a musician," said Selwyn. "You needn't mention my other work to Harper."

"Here, you're trying to corrupt me, that'll never do. Didn't you say corruption was your line?"

"No, no. I do contemplation of corruption," Selwyn explained. "A very different thing, very high. Drink up."

"Here's wishing you all you wish yourself," said Mr Brown. "You don't corrupt me, mind!"

"It's either I corrupt you or you corrupt me," Selwyn stated, and he went on to explain himself, and they argued the point while the time became timeless and they got muddled over the word corrupt, calling it cupped.

"Who's cupping who?" said Mr Brown. "Who's cups?"

Eventually Selwyn couldn't laugh for coughing, and again, he couldn't cough for laughing. When he recovered he passed the bottle and went deep into the question of cups being a corrupt form of corrupt.

He sang out, "Ha, ha, ha. Hee, hee, hee. I'll cup you or you'll cup me."

"Here's a short life and a merry one!" said Mr Brown.

Well, it was Selwyn corrupted the trustee. His monthly cheque, bigger than before, continued to come in. All through the winter he carried on his routine, doors open for company on the 25th, and on the 15th doors shut, and Selwyn at his window contemplating the dead graves.

He died the following spring. There had been an X-ray two years back, when Selwyn had said, "Aw to hell with my chest, I've work to do. Here's a health!"

Mr Brown said to his partner, "He never told me of his chest. If I'd known of it I would have seen him into a warm house and a new suit. I would have seen him with a housekeeper and I would have seen him into medical hands."

"These musicians," said Mr Harper. "Too dedicated. One must admire them, though."

"Oh, must one? Oh, must one?" said Mr Brown irritably, for he couldn't himself think highly of Selwyn who had been so shabby as to actually die when he had more or less agreed only to contemplate.

"A sad tale," said Mr Harper dreamily. "Macgregor was a hero in his way."

"Oh, was he? Oh, was he?" At that moment Mr Brown despised his stupid partner almost more than he resented the dead man. Though lately, chancing to be in those parts where Selwyn had lived, even Mr Brown couldn't help the thought, "Oh, Selwyn Macgregor, what a manner you had!" And when he saw that they had levelled out the old graveyard to make a playground for the children, he contemplated Selwyn's corruption for a long time.

CHRISTMAS FUGUE

As a growing schoolgirl Cynthia had been a nature-lover; in those days she had thought of herself in those terms. She would love to go for solitary walks beside a river, feel the rain on her face, lean over old walls, gazing into dark pools. She was dreamy, wrote nature-poetry. It was part of a Home Counties culture of the 1970s, and she had left all but the memories behind her when she left England to join her cousin Moira, a girl slightly older than herself, in Sydney, where Moira ran a random boutique of youthful clothes, handbags, hand-made slippers, ceramics, cushions, decorated writing paper, and many other art-like objects. Moira married a successful lawyer and moved to Adelaide. Beautiful Sydney suddenly became empty for Cynthia. She had a boyfriend. He, too, suddenly became empty. At twenty-four she wanted a new life. She had never really known the old life.

So many friends had invited her to spend Christmas Day with them that she couldn't remember how many. Kind faces, smiling, "You'll be lonely without Moira . . . What are your plans for Christmas?" Georgie (her so-called boyfriend): "Look, you must come to us. We'd love you to come to us for Christmas. My kid brother and sister . . ."

Cynthia felt terribly empty, "Actually, I'm going back to England." "So soon? Before Christmas?"

She packed her things, gave away all the stuff she didn't want. She had a one-way air ticket, Sydney–London, precisely on Christmas Day. She would spend Christmas Day on the plane. She thought all the time of all the beauty and blossoming lifestyle she was leaving behind her, the sea, the beaches, the shops, the mountains, but now it was like leaning over an old wall, dreaming. England was her destination, and really her destiny. She had never had a full adult life in England. Georgie saw her off on the plane. He was going for a new life, too, to the blue hills and wonderful colours of Brisbane, where his only uncle needed him on his Queensland sheep farm. For someone else, Cynthia thought, he won't be empty. Far from it. But he is empty for me.

She would not be alone in England. Her parents, divorced, were in their early fifties. Her brother, still unmarried, was a City accountant. An aunt had died recently; Cynthia was the executor of her will. She would not be alone in England, or in any way wondering what to do.

The plane was practically empty.

"Nobody flies on Christmas Day," said the hostess who served the preliminary drinks. "At least, very few. The rush is always before Christmas, and then there's always a full flight after Boxing Day till New Year when things begin to normalize." She was talking to a young man who had remarked on the number of empty seats. "I'm spending Christmas on the plane because I'd nowhere else to go. I thought it might be amusing."

"It will be amusing," said the pretty hostess. "We'll make it fun."

The young man looked pleased. He was a few seats in front of Cynthia. He looked around, saw Cynthia and smiled. In the course of the next hour he made it known to this small world in the air that he was a teacher returning from an exchange programme.

The plane had left Sydney at after three in the afternoon of Christmas Day. There remained over nine hours to Bangkok, their refuelling stop.

Luxuriously occupying two vacant front seats of the compartment was a middle-aged couple fully intent on their reading: he, a copy of *Time*; she, a tattered paperback of Agatha Christie's: *The Mysterious Affair at Styles*.

A thin, tall man with glasses passed the couple on the way to the lavatories. On his emergence he stopped, pointed at the paperback and said, "Agatha Christie! You're reading Agatha Christie. She's a serial killer. On your dark side you yourself are a serial killer." The man beamed triumphantly and made his way to a seat behind the couple.

A steward appeared and was called by the couple, both together. "Who's that man?" – "Did you hear what he said? He said I am a serial killer."

"Excuse me, sir, is there something wrong?" the steward demanded of the man with glasses.

"Just making an observation," the man replied.

The steward disappeared into the front of the plane, and reappeared with a uniformed officer, a co-pilot, who had in his hand a sheet of paper, evidently a list of passengers. He glanced at the seat number of the bespectacled offender, then at him: "Professor Sygmund Schatt?" "Sygmund spelt with a y," precised the professor. "Nothing wrong. I was merely making a professional observation."

"Keep them to yourself in future."

"I will not be silenced," said Sygmund Schatt. "Plot and scheme against me as you may."

The co-pilot went to the couple, bent towards them, and whispered something reassuring.

"You see!" said Schatt.

The pilot walked up the aisle towards Cynthia. He sat down beside her.

"A complete nut. They do cause anxiety on planes. But maybe he's harmless. He'd better be. Are you feeling lonely?"

Cynthia looked at the officer. He was good-looking, fairly young, young enough. "Just a bit," she said.

"First class is empty," said the officer. "Like to come there?"

"I don't want to –"

"Come with me," he said. "What's your name?"

"Cynthia. What's yours?"

"Tom. I'm one of the pilots. There are three of us today so far. Another's coming on at Bangkok."

"That makes me feel safe."

It fell about that at Bangkok, when everyone else had got off the plane to stretch their legs for an hour and a half; the passengers had gone to walk around the departments of the Duty Free shop, buy presents "from Bangkok" of a useless nature such as dolls and silk ties, to drink coffee and other beverages with biscuits and pastries; Tom and Cynthia stayed on. They made love in a beautifully appointed cabin with real curtains in the windows – unrealistic yellow flowers on a white background. Then they talked about each other, and made love again.

"Christmas Day," he said. "I'll never forget this one."

"Nor me," she said.

They had half an hour before the crew and passengers would rejoin them. One of the tankers which had refuelled the plane could be seen moving off.

Cynthia luxuriated in the washroom with its toilet waters and tooth-brushes. She made herself fresh and pretty, combed her well-cut casque of dark hair. When she got back to the cabin he was returning from somewhere, looking young, smiling. He gave her a box. "Christmas present."

It contained a set of plaster Christmas crib figures, "made in China". A kneeling Virgin and St Joseph, the baby Jesus and a shoemaker with his bench, a woodcutter, an unidentifiable monk, two shepherds and two angels.

Cynthia arranged them on the table in front of her.

"Do you believe in it?" she said.

"Well, I believe in Christmas."

"Yes, I, too. It means a new life. I don't see any mother and father really kneeling beside the baby's cot worshipping it, do you?"

"No, that part's symbolic."

"These are simply lovely," she said touching her presents. "Made of real stuff, not plastic."

"Let's celebrate," he said. He disappeared and returned with a bottle of champagne.

"How expensive . . ."

"Don't worry. It flows on First."

"Will you be going on duty?"

"No," he said. "I clock in tomorrow."

They made love again, high up in the air.

After that, Cynthia walked back to her former compartment. Professor Sygmund Schatt was having an argument with a hostess about his food which had apparently been pre-ordered, and now, in some way, did not come up to scratch. Cynthia sat in her old seat and, taking a postcard from the pocket in front of her, wrote to her cousin Moira. "Having a lovely time at 35,000 feet. I have started a new life. Love XX Cynthia." She then felt this former seat was part of the old life, and went back again to first.

In the night Tom came and sat beside her.

"You didn't eat much," he said.

"How did you know?"

"I noticed."

"I didn't feel up to the Christmas dinner," she said.

"Would you like something now?"

"A turkey sandwich. Let me go and ask the hostess."

"Leave it to me."

Tom told her he was now in the final stages of a divorce. His wife had no doubt had a hard time of it, his job taking him away so much. But she could have studied something. She wouldn't learn, hated to learn.

And he was lonely. He asked her to marry him, and she wasn't in the least surprised. But she said, "Oh, Tom, you don't know me."

"I think I do."

"We don't know each other."

"Well, I think we should do."

She said she would think about it. She said she would cancel her plans and come to spend some time in his flat in London at Camden Town.

"I'll have my time off within three days – by the end of the week," he said.

"God, is he all right, is he reliable?" she said to herself. "Am I safe with him? Who is he?" But she was really carried away.

Around four in the morning she woke and found him beside her. He said, "It's Boxing Day now. You're a lovely girl."

She had always imagined she was, but had always, so far, fallen timid when with men. She had experienced two brief love affairs in Australia, neither memorable. All alone in the first-class compartment with Tom, high in the air – this was reality, something to be remembered, the start of a new life.

"I'll give you the key of the flat," he said. "Go straight there. Nobody will disturb you. I've been sharing it with my young brother. But he's away for about six weeks I should say. In fact he's doing time. He got mixed up in a football row and he's in for grievous bodily harm and affray. Only, the bodily harm wasn't so grievous. He was just in the wrong place at the wrong time. Anyway, the flat's free for at least six weeks."

At the airport, despite the early hour of ten past five in the morning, there was quite a crowd to meet the plane. Having retrieved her lugguage, Cynthia pushed her trolley towards the exit. She had no expectation whatsoever that anyone would be there to meet her.

Instead, there was her father and his wife, Elaine; there was her mother with her husband Bill; crowding behind them at the barrier were her brother and his girlfriend, her cousin Moira's cousin by marriage, and a few other men and women whom she did not identify, accompanied, too, by some children of about ten to fourteen. In fact her whole family, known and unknown, had turned out to meet Cynthia. How had they known the hour of her arrival? She had promised, only, to ring them when she got to England. "Your cousin Moira," said her father, "told us your flight. We wanted you home, you know that."

She went first to her mother's house. It was now Boxing Day but they had saved Christmas Day for her arrival. All the Christmas rituals were fully observed. The tree and the presents – dozens of presents for Cynthia. Her brother and his girl with some other cousins came over for Christmas dinner.

When they came to open the presents, Cynthia brought out from her lugguage a number of packages she had brought from Australia for the occasion. Among them, labelled for her brother, was a plaster Nativity set, made in China.

"What a nice one," said her brother. "One of the best I've ever seen, and not plastic."

"I got it in Moira's boutique," Cynthia said. "She has very special things."

She talked a lot about Australia, its marvels. Then, at tea-time, they got down to her aunt's will, of which Cynthia was an executor. Cynthia felt happy, in her element, as an executor to a will, for she was normally dreamy, not legally minded at all and now she felt the flattery of her aunt's confidence in her. The executorship gave her some sort of authority in the family. She was now arranging, too, to spend New Year with her father and his second clan.

Her brother had set out the Nativity figures on a table. "I don't know," she said, "why the mother and the father are kneeling beside the child; it seems so unreal." She didn't hear what the others said, if anything, in response to this observation. She only felt a strange stirring of memory. There was to be a flat in Camden Town, but she had no idea of the address.

"The plane stopped at Bangkok," she told them.

"Did you get off?"

"Yes, but you know you can't get out of the airport. There was a coffee bar and a lovely shop."

It was later that day, when she was alone, unpacking, in her room, that she rang the airline.

"No," said a girl's voice, "I don't think there are curtains with yellow flowers in the first-class cabins. I'll have to ask. Was there any particular reason . . . ?"

"There was a co-pilot called Tom. Can you give me his full name please? I have an urgent message for him."

"What flight did you say?"

Cynthia told her not only the flight but her name and original seat number in Business Class.

After a long wait, the voice spoke again, "Yes, you are one of the arrivals."

"I know that," said Cynthia.

"I can't give you information about our pilots, I'm afraid. But there was no pilot on the plane called Tom . . . Thomas, no. The stewards in Business were Bob, Andrew, Sheila and Lilian."

"No pilot called Tom? About thirty-five, tall, brown hair. I met him. He lives in Camden Town." Cynthia gripped the phone. She looked round at the reality of the room.

"The pilots are Australian; I can tell you that but no more. I'm sorry. They're our personnel."

"It was a memorable flight. Christmas Day. I'll never forget that one," said Cynthia.

"Thank you. We appreciate that," said the voice. It seemed thousands of miles away.

THE FIRST YEAR OF MY LIFE

I was born on the first day of the second month of the last year of the First World War, a Friday. Testimony abounds that during the first year of my life I never smiled. I was known as the baby whom nothing and no one could make smile. Everyone who knew me then has told me so. They tried very hard, singing and bouncing me up and down, jumping around, pulling faces. Many times I was told this later by my family and their friends; but, anyway, I knew it at the time.

You will shortly be hearing of that new school of psychology, or maybe you have heard of it already, which after long and far-adventuring research and experiment has established that all of the young of the human species are born omniscient. Babies, in their waking hours, know everything that is going on everywhere in the world; they can tune in to any conversation they choose, switch on to any scene. We have all experienced this power. It is only after the first year that it was brainwashed out of us; for it is demanded of us by our immediate environment that we grow to be of use to it in a practical way. Gradually, our know-all brain-cells are blacked out although traces remain in some individuals in the form of ESP, and in the adults of some primitive tribes.

It is not a new theory. Poets and philosophers, as usual, have been there first. But scientific proof is now ready and to hand. Perhaps the final touches are being put to the new manifesto in some cell at Harvard University. Any day now it will be given to the world, and the world will be convinced.

Let me therefore get my word in first, because I feel pretty sure, now, about the authenticity of my remembrance of things past. My autobiography, as I very well perceived at the time, started in the very worst year that the world had ever seen so far. Apart from being born bedridden and toothless, unable to raise myself on the pillow or utter anything but farmyard squawks or police-siren wails, my bladder and my bowels totally out of control, I was further depressed by the curious behaviour of the two-legged mammals around me. There were those black-dressed people, females of the species to which I appeared to belong, saying they had lost their sons. I slept a great deal. Let them go and find their sons. It was like the special pin for my nappies which my mother or some other hoverer dedicated to my care was always losing. These careless women in black lost their husbands and their brothers. Then they came to visit my mother and clucked and crowed over my cradle. I was not amused.

"Babies never really smile till they're three months old," said my mother. "They're not *supposed* to smile till they're three months old."

My brother, aged six, marched up and down with a toy rifle over his shoulder:

> The grand old Duke of York
> He had ten thousand men;

He marched them up to the top of the hill
And he marched them down again.

And when they were up, they were up.
And when they were down, they were down.
And when they were neither down nor up
They were neither up nor down.

"Just listen to him!"

"Look at him with his rifle!"

I was about ten days old when Russia stopped fighting. I tuned in to the Czar, a prisoner, with the rest of his family, since evidently the country had put him off his throne and there had been a revolution not long before I was born. Everyone was talking about it. I tuned in to the Czar. "Nothing would ever induce me to sign the treaty of Brest-Litovsk," he said to his wife. Anyway, nobody had asked him to.

At this point I was sleeping twenty hours a day to get my strength up. And from what I discerned in the other four hours of the day I knew I was going to need it. The Western Front on my frequency was sheer blood, mud, dismembered bodies, blistered crashes, hectic flashes of light in the night skies, explosions, total terror. Since it was plain I had been born into a bad moment in the history of the world, the future bothered me, unable as I was to raise my head from the pillow and as yet only twenty inches long. "I truly wish I were a fox or a bird," D. H. Lawrence was writing to somebody. Dreary old creeping Jesus. I fell asleep.

Red sheets of flame shot across the sky. It was 21st March, the fiftieth day of my life, and the German Spring Offensive had started before my morning feed. Infinite slaughter. I scowled at the scene, and made an effort to kick out. But the attempt was feeble. Furious, and impatient for some strength, I wailed for my feed. After which I stopped wailing but continued to scowl.

The grand old Duke of York
He had ten thousand men . . .

They rocked the cradle. I never heard a sillier song. Over in Berlin and Vienna the people were starving, freezing, striking, rioting and yelling in the streets. In London everyone was bustling to work and muttering that it was time the whole damn business was over.

The big people around me bared their teeth; that meant a smile, it meant they were pleased or amused. They spoke of ration cards for meat and sugar and butter.

"Where will it all end?"

I went to sleep. I woke and tuned in to Bernard Shaw who was telling someone to shut up. I switched over to Joseph Conrad who, strangely enough, was saying precisely the same thing. I still didn't think it worth a smile, although it was expected of me any day now. I got on to Turkey. Women draped in black huddled and chattered in their harems; yak-yak-yak. This was boring, so I came back to home base.

In and out came and went the women in British black. My mother's brother, dressed in his uniform, came coughing. He had been poison-gassed in the trenches. "*Tout le monde à la bataille!*" declaimed Marshal Foch the old swine. He was now Commander-in-Chief of the Allied Forces. My uncle coughed from deep within his lungs, never to recover but destined to return to the Front. His brass buttons gleamed in the firelight. I weighed twelve pounds by now; I stretched and kicked for exercise, seeing that I had a lifetime before me, coping with this crowd. I took six feeds a day and kept most of them down by the time the *Vindictive* was sunk in Ostend harbour, on which day I kicked with special vigour in my bath.

In France the conscripted soldiers leapfrogged over the dead on the advance and littered the fields with limbs and hands, or drowned in the mud. The strongest men on all fronts were dead before I was born. Now the sentries used bodies for barricades and the fighting men were unhealthy from the start. I checked my toes and fingers, knowing I was going to need them. *The Playboy of the Western World* was playing at the Court Theatre in London, but occasionally I beamed over to the House of Commons which made me drop off gently to sleep. Generally, I preferred the Western Front where one got the true state of affairs. It was essential to know the worst, blood and explosions and all, for one had to be prepared, as the boy scouts said. Virginia Woolf yawned and reached for her diary. Really, I preferred the Western Front.

In the fifth month of my life I could raise my head from my pillow and hold it up. I could grasp the objects that were held out to me. Some of these things rattled and squawked. I gnawed on them to get my teeth started. "She hasn't smiled yet?" said the dreary old aunties. My mother, on the defensive, said I was probably one of those late smilers. On my wavelength Pablo Picasso was getting married and early in that month of July the Silver Wedding of King George V and Queen Mary was celebrated in joyous pomp at St Paul's

Cathedral. They drove through the streets of London with their children. Twenty-five years of domestic happiness. A lot of fuss and ceremonial handing over of swords went on at the Guildhall where the King and Queen received a cheque for £53,000 to dispose of for charity as they thought fit. *Tout le monde à la bataille!* Income tax in England had reached six shillings in the pound. Everyone was talking about the Silver Wedding; yak-yak-yak, and ten days later the Czar and his family, now in Siberia, were invited to descend to a little room in the basement. Crack, crack, went the guns; screams and blood all over the place, and that was the end of the Romanoffs. I flexed my muscles. "A fine healthy baby," said the doctor; which gave me much satisfaction.

Tout le monde à la bataille! That included my gassed uncle. My health had improved to the point where I was able to crawl in my playpen. Bertrand Russell was still cheerily in prison for writing something seditious about pacifism. Tuning in as usual to the Front Lines it looked as if the Germans were winning all the battles yet losing the war. And so it was. The upper-income people were upset about the income tax at six shillings to the pound. But all women over thirty got the vote. "It seems a long time to wait," said one of my drab old aunts, aged twenty-two. The speeches in the House of Commons always sent me to sleep which was why I missed, at the actual time, a certain oration by Mr Asquith following the armistice on 11th November. Mr Asquith was a greatly esteemed former prime minister later to be an Earl, and had been ousted by Mr Lloyd George. I clearly heard Asquith, in private, refer to Lloyd George as "that damned Welsh goat".

The armistice was signed and I was awake for that. I

pulled myself on to my feet with the aid of the bars of my cot. My teeth were coming through very nicely in my opinion, and well worth all the trouble I was put to in bringing them forth. I weighed twenty pounds. On all the world's fighting fronts the men killed in action or dead of wounds numbered 8,538,315 and the warriors wounded and maimed were 21,219,452. With these figures in mind I sat up in my high chair and banged my spoon on the table. One of my mother's black-draped friends recited:

> I have a rendezvous with Death
> At some disputed barricade,
> When spring comes back with rustling shade
> And apple blossoms fill the air –
> I have a rendezvous with Death.

Most of the poets, they said, had been killed. The poetry made them dab their eyes with clean white handkerchiefs.

Next February on my first birthday, there was a birthday cake with one candle. Lots of children and their elders. The war had been over two months and twenty-one days. "Why doesn't she smile?" My brother was to blow out the candle. The elders were talking about the war and the political situation. Lloyd George and Asquith, Asquith and Lloyd George. I remembered recently having switched on to Mr Asquith at a private party where he had been drinking a lot. He was playing cards and when he came to cut the cards he tried to cut a large box of matches by mistake. On another occasion I had seen him putting his arm around a lady's shoulder in a Daimler motor car, and generally behaving towards her in a very friendly fashion. Strangely enough she said, "If you don't stop this nonsense immediately I'll order the chauffeur to stop and I'll get out." Mr Asquith replied, "And pray, what reason will you give?" Well anyway it was my feeding time.

The guests arrived for my birthday. It was so sad, said one of the black widows, so sad about Wilfred Owen who was killed so late in the war, and she quoted from a poem of his:

What passing-bells for these who die as cattle?
Only the monstrous anger of the guns.

The children were squealing and toddling around. One was sick and another wet the floor and stood with his legs apart gaping at the puddle. All was mopped up. I banged my spoon on the table of my high chair.

But I've a rendezvous with Death
At midnight in some flaming town;
When spring trips north again this year,
And I to my pledged word am true,
I shall not fail that rendezvous.

More parents and children arrived. One stout man who was warming his behind at the fire, said, "I always think those words of Asquith's after the armistice were so apt . . ."

They brought the cake close to my high chair for me to see, with the candle shining and flickering above the pink icing. "A pity she never smiles."

"She'll smile in time," my mother said, obviously upset.

"What Asquith told the House of Commons just after

the war," said that stout gentleman with his backside to the fire, "– so apt, what Asquith said. He said that the war has cleansed and purged the world, by God! I recall his actual words: 'All things have become new. In this great cleansing and purging it has been the privilege of our country to play her part . . .'"

That did it. I broke into a decided smile and everyone noticed it, convinced that it was provoked by the fact that my brother had blown out the candle on the cake. "She smiled!" my mother exclaimed. And everyone was clucking away about how I was smiling. For good measure I crowed like a demented raven. "My baby's smiling!" said my mother.

"It was the candle on her cake," they said.

The cake be damned. Since that time I have grown to smile quite naturally, like any other healthy and house-trained person, but when I really mean a smile, deeply felt from the core, then to all intents and purposes it comes in response to the words uttered in the House of Commons after the First World War by the distinguished, the immaculately dressed and the late Mr Asquith.

THE GENTILE JEWESSES

One day a madman came into my little grandmother's shop at Watford. I say my little grandmother but "little" refers only to her height and to the dimensions of her world by the square foot – the small shop full of varieties, her parlour behind it, and behind that the stone kitchen and the two bedrooms over her head.

"I shall murder you," said the madman, standing with legs straddled in the door frame, holding up his dark big hands as one about to pounce and strangle. His eyes stared from a face covered with tangled eyebrows and beard.

The street was empty. My grandmother was alone in the house. For some years, from frequent hearing of the story, I believed I was standing by her side at the time, but my grandmother said no, this was long before I was born. The scene is as clear as a memory to me. The madman – truly escaped from the asylum in a great park nearby – lifted his hairy hands, cupped as for strangling. Behind him was the street, empty save for sunshine.

He said, "I'm going to murder you."

She folded her hands over her white apron which lay over the black apron and looked straight at him.

"Then you'll get hung," she said.

He turned and shuffled away.

She should have said "hanged" and I remember at one telling of the story remarking so to my grandmother. She replied that "hung" had been good enough for the madman. I could not impress her with words, but I was so impressed by the tale that very often afterwards I said "hung" instead of "hanged".

I seem to see the happening so plainly in my memory it is difficult to believe I know it only by hearsay; but indeed it happened before I was born. My grandfather was a young man then, fifteen years younger than his wife and dispossessed by his family for having married her. He was gone to arrange about seedlings when the madman had appeared.

My grandmother had married him for pure love, she had chased him and hunted him down and married him, he was so beautiful and useless. She never cared at all that she had to work and keep him all his life. She was astonishingly ugly, one was compelled to look at her. In my actual memory, late in their marriage, he would bring her a rose from the garden from time to time, and put cushions under her head and feet when she reclined on the sofa in the parlour between the hours of two and three in the afternoon. He could not scrub the counter in her shop for he did not know how to do it, but he knew about dogs and birds and gardens, and had photography for a pastime.

He said to my grandmother, "Stand by the dahlias and I will take your likeness."

I wished she had known how to take his likeness because he was golden-haired even in my day, with delicate features and glittering whiskers. She had a broad pug nose, she was sallow skinned with bright black eyes staring straight at the world and her dull black hair pulled back tight into a knot. She looked like a white negress; she did not try to beautify herself except by washing her face in rain water.

She had come from Stepney. Her mother was a Gentile and her father was a Jew. She said her father was a Quack by profession and she was proud of this, because she felt all curing was done by the kindly manner of the practitioner in handing out bottles of medicine rather than by the contents. I always forced my elders to enact their stories. I said, "Show me how he did it."

Willingly she leaned forward in her chair and handed me an invisible bottle of medicine. She said, "There you are, my dear, and you won't come to grief, and don't forget to keep your bowels regular." She said, "My father's medicine was only beetroot juice but he took pains with his manners, and he took pains with the labels, and the bottles were threepence a gross. My father cured many an ache and pain, it was his gracious manner."

This, too, entered my memory and I believed I had seen the glamorous Quack Doctor who was dead before I was born. I thought of him when I saw my grandfather, with his gracious manner, administering a tiny dose of medicine out of a blue bottle to one of his small coloured birds. He opened its beak with his finger and tipped in a drop. All the little garden was full of kennels, glass and sheds containing birds and flowerpots. His photographs were not quite real to look at. One day he called me Canary and made me stand by the brick wall for my likeness. The photograph made the garden look tremendous. Perhaps he was reproducing in his photographs the grander garden of his youth from which he was expelled avengingly upon his marriage to my grandmother long before I was born.

After his death, when my grandmother came to live with us I said to her one day,

"Are you a Gentile, Grandmother, or are you a Jewess?" I was wondering how she would be buried, according to what religion, when her time came to die.

"I am a Gentile Jewess," she said.

All during the time she kept the shop of all sorts in Watford she had not liked the Jewish part of her origins to be known, because it was bad for business. She would have been amazed at any suggestion that this attitude was a weak one or a wrong one. To her, whatever course was sensible and good for business was good in the sight of the Almighty. She believed heartily in the Almighty. I never heard her refer to God by any other title except to say, God bless you. She was a member of the Mothers' Union of the Church of England. She attended all the social functions of the Methodists, Baptists and Quakers. This was bright and agreeable as well as being good for business. She never went to church on Sundays, only for special services such as on Remembrance Day. The only time she acted against her conscience was when she attended a spiritualist meeting; this was from sheer curiosity, not business. There, a bench fell over on to her foot and she limped for a month; it was a judgment of the Almighty.

I inquired closely about spiritualism. "They call up the dead from their repose," she said. "It vexes the Almighty when the dead are stirred before they are ready."

Then she told me what happened to spiritualists after a number of years had passed over their heads. "They run up the garden path, look back over their shoulders, give a shudder, and run back again. I dare say they see spirits."

I took my grandmother's hand and led her out to the garden to make her show me what spiritualists did. She ran up the path splendidly with her skirts held up in her hands, looked round with sudden bright eyes, shuddered horribly, then, with skirts held higher so that her white petticoat frills flickered round her black stockings, she ran gasping back towards me.

My grandfather came out to see the fun with his sandy eyebrows raised high among the freckles. "Stop your larks, Adelaide," he said to my grandmother.

So my grandmother did it again, with a curdling cry, "Ah-ah-ah".

Rummaging in the shop, having climbed up on two empty fizzpop crates, I found on an upper shelf some old bundles of candles wrapped in interesting-looking literature. I smoothed out the papers and read, "Votes for Women! Why do you Oppress Women?" Another lot of candles was wrapped in a larger bill on which was printed an old-fashioned but military-looking young woman waving the Union Jack and saying, "I'm off to join the Suffragettes." I asked my grandmother where the papers came from, for she never threw anything away and must have had them for another purpose before wrapping up the candles before I was born. My grandfather answered for her, so far forgetting his refinement as to say, "Mrs Spank-arse's lark".

"Mrs Pankhurst, he means. I'm surprised at you, Tom, in front of the child."

My grandfather was smiling away at his own joke. And so all in one afternoon I learned a new word, and the story of my grandmother's participation in the Women's Marches down Watford High Street, dressed in her best clothes, and I learned also my grandfather's opinions about these happenings. I saw, before my very eyes, my grandmother and her banner, marching in the sunshiny street with her friends, her white petticoat twinkling at her ankles as she walked. In a few years' time it was difficult for me to believe I had not stood and witnessed the march of the Watford Suffragettes moving up the High Street, with my grandmother swiftly in the van before I was born. I recalled how her shiny black straw hat gleamed in the sun.

Some Jews came to Watford and opened a bicycle shop not far from my grandmother's. She would have nothing to do with them. They were Polish immigrants. She called them Pollacks. When I asked what this meant she said, "Foreigners." One day the mama-foreigner came to the door of her shop as I was passing and held out a bunch of grapes. She said, "Eat." I ran, amazed, to my grandmother who said, "I told you that foreigners are funny."

Among ourselves she boasted of her Jewish blood because it had made her so clever. I knew she was so clever that it was unnecessary for her to be beautiful. She boasted that her ancestors on her father's side crossed over the Red Sea; the Almighty stretched forth his hands and parted the waves, and they crossed over from Egypt on to dry land. Miriam, the sister of Moses, banged her timbrel and led all the women across the Red Sea, singing a song to the Almighty. I thought of the Salvation Army girls who quite recently had marched up

Watford High Street in the sunshine banging their tambourines. My grandmother had called me to the shop door to watch, and when they and their noise were dwindled away she turned from the door and clapped her hands above her head, half in the spontaneous spirit of the thing, half in mimicry. She clapped her hands. "Alleluia!" cried my grandmother. "Alleluia!"

"Stop your larks, Adelaide, my dear."

Was I present at the Red Sea crossing? No, it had happened before I was born. My head was full of stories, of Greeks and Trojans, Picts and Romans, Jacobites and Redcoats, but these were definitely outside of my lifetime. It was different where my grandmother was concerned. I see her in the vanguard, leading the women in their dance of triumph, clanging the tambourine for joy and crying Alleluia with Mrs Pankhurst and Miriam the sister of Moses. The hands of the Almighty hold back the walls of the sea. My grandmother's white lace-edged petticoat flashes beneath her black skirt an inch above her boots, as it did when she demonstrated up and down the garden path what happens to spiritualists. What part of the scene I saw and what happened before I was born can be distinguished by my reason, but my reason cannot obliterate the scene or diminish it.

Great-aunts Sally and Nancy, my grandfather's sisters, had been frigidly reconciled to him at some date before I was born. I was sent to visit them every summer. They lived quietly now, spinsters of small means. They occupied themselves with altar-flowers and the vicar. I was a Gentile Jewess like my grandmother, for my father was a Jew, and these great-aunts could not make it out that I did not look like a Jew as did my grandmother. They remarked on this in my presence as if I could not understand that they were discussing my looks. I said that I did look like a Jew and desperately pointed to my small feet. "All Jews have very little feet," I claimed. They took this for fact, being inexperienced in Jews, and admitted to each other that I possessed this Jewish characteristic.

Nancy's face was long and thin and Sally's was round. There seemed to be a lot of pincushions on tiny tables. They gave me aniseed cake and tea every summer while the clock ticked loudly in time to their silence. I looked at the yellowish-green plush upholstery which caught streaks of the sunny afternoon outside, I looked until I had absorbed its colour and texture in a total trance during the great-aunts' silences. Once when I got back to my grandmother's and looked in the glass it seemed my eyes had changed from blue to yellow-green plush.

On one of these afternoons they mentioned my father's being an engineer. I said all Jews were engineers. They were fascinated by this fact which at the time I thought was possibly true with the exception of an occasional Quack. Then Sally looked up and said, "But the Langfords are not engineers."

The Langfords were not Jews either, they were Gentiles of German origin, but it came to the same thing in those parts. The Langfords were not classified as foreigners by my grandmother because they did not speak in broken English, being all of a London-born generation.

The Langford girls were the main friends of my mother's youth. There was Lottie who sang well and Flora who played the piano and Susanna who was strange. I remember a long evening in their house when Lottie and my mother sang a duet to Flora's piano playing, while Susanna loitered darkly at the door of the drawing-room with a smile I had never seen on any face before. I could not keep my eyes off Susanna, and got into trouble for staring.

When my mother and Lottie were seventeen they hired a cab one day and went to an inn, some miles away in the country, where they drank gin. They supplied the driver with gin as well, and, forgetting that the jaunt was supposed to be a secret one, returned two hours later standing up in the cab, chanting "Horrid little Watford. Dirty little Watford. We'll soon say goodbye to nasty little Watford." They did not consider themselves to be village girls and were eager to be sent away to relatives elsewhere. This was soon accomplished; Lottie went to London for a space and my mother to Edinburgh. My mother told me the story of the wild return of carriage and horses up the High Street and my grandmother confirmed it, adding that the occurrence was bad for business. I can hear the clopping of hooves, and see the girls standing wobbly in the cab dressed in their spotted muslins, although I never actually saw anything but milk-carts, motor cars and buses, and girls with short skirts in the High Street, apart from such links with antiquity as fat old Benskin of Benskins' Breweries taking his morning stroll along the bright pavement, bowing as he passed to my grandmother.

"I am a Gentile Jewess."

She was buried as a Jewess since she died in my father's house, and notices were put in the Jewish press. Simultaneously my great-aunts announced in the Watford papers that she fell asleep in Jesus.

* * *

My mother never fails to bow three times to the new moon wherever she might be at the time of first catching sight of it. I have seen her standing on a busy pavement with numerous cold rational Presbyterian eyes upon her, turning over her money, bowing regardless and chanting, "New moon, new moon, be good to me." In my memory this image is fused with her lighting of the Sabbath candles on a Friday night, chanting a Hebrew prayer which I have since been told came out in a very strange sort of Hebrew. Still, it was her tribute and solemn observance. She said that the Israelites of the Bible and herself were one and the same because of the Jewish part of her blood, and I did not doubt this thrilling fact. I thought of her as the second Gentile Jewess after my grandmother, and myself as the third.

My mother carries everywhere in her handbag a small locket containing a picture of Christ crowned with thorns. She keeps on one table a rather fine Buddha on a lotus leaf and on another a horrible replica of the Venus de Milo. One way and another all the gods are served in my mother's household although she holds only one belief and that is in the Almighty. My father, when questioned as to what he believes, will say, "I believe in the Blessed Almighty who made heaven and earth," and will say no more, returning to his racing papers which contain problems proper to innocent men. To them, it was no great shock when I turned Catholic, since with Roman Catholics too, it all boils down to the Almighty in the end.

ALICE LONG'S DACHSHUNDS

The guns clank on the stone, one after the other, echoing against the walls outside the chapel, as the men come in for Mass before the shoot. Mamie, whose age is eight years and two months, kneels in the second row from the back, on the right-hand side, near the Virgin, where a warm candle is lit. There is no other warmth. Alice Long is kneeling on a front hassock. Her two brothers from London have come in – tall men in knickerbockers and green wool stockings that stride past Mamie's eyes as she kneels in her place.

Other big men have put their guns against the wall outside the chapel door. The Catholics from the cottages have come in. Everyone except the strangers is praying for more snow and a road blockage to the town, so that poor Alice Long can decently serve roe deer, roe deer, roe deer for all the meals that the London people are going to eat. The woods are cracking alive with roe deer, but meat from the town has got to be paid for with money.

Alice Long is round-shouldered and worried; she is the only daughter of old Sir Martin, and is always addressed, to her face, as Miss Long. Her money is her own, but it goes into the keeping of the House.

Alice Long's two brothers' wives have come into the chapel now. They are the last, because they have to look after their own babies when they get up. Before Mamie's birth, all the babies in the House had nurses. The two wives were differently made from the start, before they became Alice Long's sisters-in-law, and still look so, although their tweed coats were made more alike. One is called Lady Caroline and the other, Mrs Martin Long, will be Lady Long when old Sir Martin dies and Martin Long comes into the title.

Mamie is watching Lady Caroline through her fingers. Lady Caroline is big and broad, with bobbed black hair under her black lace veil; she doesn't like Alice Long's dogs, and dogs are the only things Alice Long has for herself. Alice Long was made to be kept down by upkeep.

The big clock upstairs chimes seven. The priest comes in and the feet shuffle. Mamie cannot see the altar when everyone is standing. She stares at the candle. The service begins. Will the friends who have come from warm London catch their death of colds?

Mamie stops in the snow. The ends of the dogs' leashes are wound round her hands in their woollen gloves, three round the right hand and two round the left. She unwinds the leads to give her arms scope, and the dogs take advantage of the few extra inches of freedom, snuffling and wriggling away from Mamie until the leads pull taut. But she works them back, lifting her elbows to cup her hands to her mouth.

"Come out. I can see you."

No reply.

She repeats the words and drops her arms, aching from the weight of straining dogs.

There is a thud of snowfall from the clump of trees. The noise would have been only a little plop had there been any more sound besides that of the snuffling dogs.

She is taking Alice Long's dogs for a walk.

"She'll be glad to, Miss Long," said her mother. "Tomorrow after school. It's a half day."

This morning, her mother said, "Come straight home at two for Alice Long's dogs."

To do so, Mamie has missed her dancing lesson at the convent. She is learning the sword dance. Alice Long had got her into the convent at reduced fees, and even those reduced fees Alice Long pays herself. She likes to keep the Catholic tenants Catholic.

Mamie walks on, satisfied there are no boys behind the trees. She is afraid the boys will find her and tease the dogs, laugh at her, laugh at the little padding, waddling dogs, do them harm before they can be returned to the House.

The snow in the wood is too deep for low-made dogs. Mamie wanders around the edge of the wood, on the crunchy path, with little running steps every now and then as the dogs get the better of her.

"My dachshunds," said Alice Long lovingly.

The country people said to each other, when she was out of sight, "Alice Long has only got her dogs. And all that upkeep."

"Lady Caroline hates dogs."

"No, she only hates dachshunds. German sausages. She likes big dogs for the country."

Alice Long is sitting with her tea cup in Mamie's house,

which has five rooms plus k.p.b. – standing for kitchen, pantry, and bathroom – and is semi-detached. Next door are Alice Long's Couple. Mamie's father no longer works on the estate but is a foreman in the town at Heppleford and Styles' Linoleum.

"Lady Caroline can't bear them. They've been locked in the north wing since Friday. I have to keep a fire going . . ."

"That wing's not heated, of course."

"No. They are freezing and lonely. I keep putting logs on. I get up in the middle of the night to see to the fire."

"They'll be all right, Miss Long."

"They need a good run, that's all. I won't have time for the dogs today. But the family goes home tomorrow or Wednesday . . ."

Mamie has taken the dogs out for a run before. She is not allowed to go near the wood but must keep to the inhabited paths that pass the groups of houses on the estate and lead to the shop. Near the shop are usually the children from the village school, throwing snowballs in winter, wheeling bicycles in summer. Mamie has money for toffee and an orange drink. She wanders by the wood.

Her father has been at home for three working days. There is a strike. Alice Long sits downstairs. The father has gone to wait upstairs until she leaves. Then he opens the cupboard door where the television set is placed in a recess formed by the removal of one of the shelves. Alice Long has not seen this television set. The people next door, her Couple, took on a television many years ago, and keep it out in the living room.

Mitzi, Fritzi, Blitzi, Ritzi, and Kitzy.

"Alice Long's dogs are all she's got to herself."

The dogs go about together and sometimes all answer at once when Alice Long calls one of their names. Mamie does not know them apart. They vary slightly in size, fatness, and in the black scars on their brown coats.

The path has become a ridge of frozen earth where the field has been ploughed right up to the verge of the wood. The daylight is turning blue with cold while Mamie struggles with the leads. One gumboot digs deep in a furrow and the other stabs to keep its hold on the ridge. The dogssnuffle each other and snort steam. They strain towards the wood, and Hamilton is suddenly there – Alice Long's gamekeeper – coming out of the trees, tall and broad, with his grey moustache and deep-pink face. He looks at Mamie as if to say, "Come here." The dogs fuss round him, cutting into her gloves.

Mamie says, "I've got to go that way," pointing down towards her home across the field.

"I'll see you back at the House," he says, and stoops back into the wood, examining the undergrown branches.

Hamilton looks after old Sir Martin when he becomes beyond a woman's strength.

"I'm afraid my father is not very well any more."

"I don't know how you do it, Miss Long."

Mamie's mother says that anybody else but Alice Long would have put the old man away.

Hamilton sees to the boilers that heat the heated wing. He has too much to do to air the dogs regularly.

"Without Hamilton, I don't know what we should do. Before your husband left us, we had it easier."

Mamie has turned away from the wood. She has taken

the path to the houses, looking back all the time to see whether Hamilton is following her with his eyes, those eyes that are two poached eggs grown old, looking at her every time he sees her.

She takes the footpath on the main road. The dogs are trotting now. A car passes, and a delivery van from the grocer's shop in the town. She clutches the leads.

"Don't let one of them get run over. Alice Long would be up to ninety-nine."

She presses, at the sharp bend, into the high white bank which touches again on the wood, while a very big lorry, carrying sacks of coal, creeps fearfully around as if bewaring of the dogs.

Bump on her shoulder, then bump on her cap come the snowballs. The boys are up there on the bank. She turns and looks quickly and sees parts of children ducking out of sight with short, laughing squeals. There are two girls with the boys; she has seen their hair. One of the girls wears the dark-blue convent cap.

"Connie, come down!"

"It isn't Connie," Gwen's voice answers. Gwen should be at the dancing class. She is learning to do the sword dance with Mamie.

A snowball falls on the road and bursts open. There is no stone inside it. The dogs are yelping now, pelted with snowballs! They are up to ninety-nine, not used to this.

Mamie drags them round the corner and starts to run. The children scramble down after her and catch up. She recognizes them all. She tries to gather up some snow, but it is impossible to make and throw a ball with the leads around her gloves.

"Where are you going with those dogs?" says a boy.

"To the shop, then up to the House."

"They look dirty."

Gwen says, "Do you like those dogs?"

"Not all of them together."

"Let them run loose," says the other girl. "It's good for them."

"No."

"Come on and play."

She is scrambling up the bank, while everyone is trying to pull the dogs up by their leads or push them up by their bottoms.

"Lift them up. You'll throttle them!"

"Let go the leads. We'll take one each."

"No."

Up on the bank, Mamie says, "I'll tie them to that tree." She refuses to let the leads out of her own hands, but she permits two of the boys to make the knots secure, as they have learned to do in the Scout Cubs.

Then it is boys against girls in a snow fight, with such fast pelting and splutters from drenched faces, such loud shrieks that the dogs' coughing and whining can scarcely be heard. When it is time to go, Mamie counts the dogs. Then she starts to untie them. The knots are difficult. She calls after one of the boys to come and untie the knots, but he does not look around. Gwen returns; she stands and looks. Mamie is kneeling in the slush, trying.

"How do you untie these knots?" All the leads are mixed up in a knotted muddle.

"I don't know. What's their names?"

"Mitzi, Fritzi, Blitzi, Ritzi, and Kitzy."

"Do you know one from the other?"

"No."

Mamie bends down with her strong teeth in the leather. She has loosened the first knot. All the knots are coming loose. She gets her woollen gloves on again and starts to wind the leads around her hands. One of them springs from her graps, and the little dog scuttles away into the wood among the old wet leaves, so that it seems to slither like a snake on its belly with its cord bouncing behind it.

"Mitzi! Kitzy! Blitzi!"

The dog disappears and the four in hand are excited, anxious to be free and warmed up, too.

"Catch him, Gwen! Can you see him? Where is it? Mitzi-mitzi-mitzi! Blitzi-blitzi!"

"I've got to go home," Gwen says. "You shouldn't have stopped to play."

Gwen is Sister Monica's model pupil for punctuality, neatness, and truthfulness. Mamie has no ground to answer Gwen's reproach as the girl starts to clamber down the bank.

The wood is dark and there is no sound of the dog. Mamie squelches with the four dogs among the leaves and snow lumps. "Fritzi-fritzi-fritzi mitzi!" A bark, a yap, behind her. Again a yap-yap. She turns and finds the dog tied once more to a tree. Hamilton? She peers all around her and sees nobody.

She should be hurrying towards the drive, but she is too tired to hurry. The Lodge gates are still open, although the sky looks late. The lights are on in the Lodge, which has been let to new people from Liverpool for their weekends. They are having a long weekend this time. A young woman comes out to her car as Mamie comes in the gateway with the five dogs.

"Goodness, you're wet through!"

"I got in a snowdrift."

"Hurry home then, dear, and get changed."

Mamie cannot hurry. She is not very well any more, like old Sir Martin. She is not very real any more. The colour of the afternoon seems strange and the sky is banked with snow-drifts. She runs in little spurts only in obedience to the pull of the dogs. But she draws them as tight as she can and plods in the direction of the House. She turns to the right when she reaches the wide steps and the big front doors. Around to the right and into the yard, where Hamilton's door is. She tries to open his door. It is locked. To pull the bell would require raising her arm, and she is too tired to do so. She tries to knock. The dogs are full of noise and anxiety, are scratching the door to get inside. She looks at them and with difficulty switches those leads in her right hand to her left, winding them round her wrist, since the hand is already full. While she knocks with her free hand at the door, she realizes that she has noticed something. There are only four dogs now. She counts – one, two, three, four. She counts the leads – one, two, three, four. She looks away again and knocks. It has not happened. Nothing has happened. It is not real. She knocks again. Hamilton is coming.

"Their food's in there," Hamilton says, not looking at the dogs but opening the door that leads from his room to another, more cluttered room. He lets the dogs scuttle in to their food without counting them. He does not remove their leads but throws them on to the floor to trail behind them. Finally, he shuts the inner door on them. He sits down in his chair and looks at Mamie as if to say, "Come here."

"I've got to go home."

"You're wet through. Get dry by the fire a minute. I'll get you a lift home."

"No, I'm late."

He pats his knee. "Sit here, dearie, lass." He has a glass and a bottle by him. "I want to give you a drop. Come on. I don't want sex."

She perches on his lap. He has not counted the dogs. Alice Long will be up to ninety-nine, but it's Hamilton's fault from now. Hamilton has taken the dogs.

"Now sip."

She recognizes whisky.

"Take a good swallow."

He gives her a lemon drop to hide her breath, then gives her a kiss on her mouth while she is still sucking the sweet.

"I'm going now. I hope the dogs are all right."

"Oh, the dogs, they're all right."

He takes her hand and goes to find one of the workmen who are mending the House. Alice Long is not home yet from her meeting, and she will not miss the workman for a few minutes.

Mamie climbs into the foreman's car beside the workman. The seat is covered with white dust, but she does not brush it off the seat before sliding on to it. Her clothes will be spoiled. She feels safe beside the driver. The whisky has given her back a real afternoon.

"What's the time, please?" she asks.

"About twenty past four."

The man backs and turns. Hamilton has gone into his quarters. The car skirts the House, turning by the large new clearing where, in the summer, the tourists' coaches come.

"You can't get many up here in Northumberland. They all swarm to the old houses in the South. Here, it's out of the way . . ."

"Well, it's an experience for those who do come, Miss Long. Especially the Catholics."

The House was once turned into a hospital for the wounded English soldiers after the Battle of Flodden, which the English won.

The House was a Mass centre at the times of the Catholic Persecution. Outside the armoury, there is a chalice in a glass case dating from Elizabethan times. It has been sold to a museum, but the museum allows the family to keep it at the House during Sir Martin's lifetime. Mamie has been inside the priest hole, where the priests were hidden when the House was searched for priests; they would sometimes stay there several days. The hole is a large space behind a panel that comes out of the wall, up among the attics. You can stand in the priest hole and look up at the beams, where, in those days, food was always stored in case of emergency.

The workmen are mending the roof.

"Did you see the priest hole?" Mamie feels talkative.

"What's that?"

"A place where the priests used to hide, up in the roof. It's historic. Haven't you seen it?"

"No, but I seen plenty dry rot up there in that roof."

The gates are closed. The man gets out to open them; then he drives off again.

Is it possible that one of the dogs is lost? Mamie is confused. There must have been five. I found the lost one, tied to the tree. But then she sees herself again counting them outside Hamilton's door. One, two, three, four. Only four. No, no, no, it's not real. Hamilton has taken the dogs. It's for him to count.

The workman says, "Do you like the Beatles?"

"Oh, yes, they're great. Do you like them?"

"So-so. I'd like just one day's earnings that the Beatles get. Just one day. I could retire on it."

Sister Monica has said that there is no harm in the Beatles, and then Mamie felt indignant because it showed Sister Monica did not properly appreciate them. She ought to lump them together with things like whisky, smoking, and sex; the Beatles are quite good enough to be forbidden.

"I like dancing," Mamie says.

"Rock – 'n' – roll stuff?"

"Yes, but at school we only get folk dancing. I'm learning the sword dance. It's historic in the Border country."

All the rest of the week, she hurries home from school to see if Alice Long has been to see her mother about the missing dog.

I counted. One, two, three, four. But I had five when I left the wood. I brought five out of the wood, and up the hill. I had five at the Lodge. I must have had . . .

Alice Long will be up to ninety-nine. She will come to Mamie's house to make inquiries:

"Hamilton says she only brought four . . .

"Hamilton says he didn't count them, he just took the leads from her hand . . .

"Hamilton must have been drinking and let one of them slip out of the door . . .

"I've only just counted them. One must have been missing since Monday. When Mamie . . ."

By Friday, Alice Long has not come. Mamie's mother says, "Alice Long hasn't dropped in. I must take a pie up to the House on Monday and see what's doing."

On Sunday afternoon, Alice Long's car stops at the door. "Come in, Miss Long, come in. Have you no family down this weekend?"

Mamie's father shuts away the television, puts on his coat, says good afternoon, and goes upstairs.

Alice Long sits trembling on the sofa beside Mamie while her mother puts on the tea.

She says, "It's Hamilton."

"The same thing again?"

"No, worse. A tragedy." Alice Long shuts her lips tight and pats Mamie's hair. Her hand is shaking.

"Mamie, go out and play," says her mother.

When Alice Long has driven her car away, Mamie comes in with the ends of her skipping-rope twined around her gloves. Her father comes down, takes off his coat, and opens up the television. "Oh, don't turn it on," says her mother, in anguish.

Mamie eats some of the remnants of cake and sandwiches while she listens.

"Hanging in the priest hole – all of them. She looked for them all night. Hamilton's gone, cleared off. It's the drink. The police have got a warrant out. They were found hanged on the beams after Mass this morning. Didn't I say poor Alice Long was looking bad at Mass? I thought it must be her father again. But she'd been up all night looking for the dogs, and at Mass she still didn't know where they were. It was after Mass they found them, herself and Mrs Huddlestone. Think of the sight! Five of them hanging in a row. Poor little beasts. Hamilton disappeared yesterday. They'll get him, though, just wait."

"He's a bit of a lunatic," Mamie's father says.

"Lunatic! He's vicious. He ought to be hung himself. They were all Alice Long had. But he'll be caught!"

Her father says, "I doubt it. Not Hamilton. Even the roebuck called him Pussyfoot." He laughs at his own joke. The mother turns away her head.

Mamie says, "How many were hanging in the priest hole?"

"All of them in a row."

"How many?"

"Five. You know she had five. You took them out, didn't you?"

Mamie says, "I was only wondering if there was *room* for five in the priest hole. Did she really say there were five? It wasn't four?"

"She said all five of them. What are you talking about, no room in the priest hole? There's plenty room. He'd have killed six if she'd had six. She was so good to him."

"A shocking affair," says her father.

Mamie feels weightless as daylight. She waves her arms as if they are freed of a huge harness.

"Five of them." I counted wrong. I didn't lose one. There were five.

She skips over to fetch the shining brass pokers from the fender and places them crisscross on the linoleum to practise her sword dance. Then she starts to dance, heel-and-toe, heel-and-toe, over-and-across, one-two-three, one-two-three. Her mother stands amazed and is about to say stop it at once, this is no time to practise, children have no heart, Alice Long pays your school fees and I thought you loved animals. But her father is clapping his hands in time to her dancing – one-two-three, heel-and-toe, hand-on-hip, right-hand, left-hand, cross-and-back. Then her father starts to sing as well, loudly, tara rum-tum-tum, tara rum-tum-tum, clapping his hands while she dances the jig, and there isn't a thing anyone can do about it.

THE DARK GLASSES

Coming to the edge of the lake we paused to look at our reflections in the water. It was then I recognized her from the past, her face looking up from the lake. She had not stopped talking.

I put on my dark glasses to shield my eyes from the sun and conceal my recognition from her eyes.

"Am I boring you?" she said.

"No, not a bit, Dr Gray."

"Sure?"

It is discouraging to put on sun-glasses in the middle of someone's intimate story. But they were necessary, now that I had recognized her, and was excited, and could only honourably hear what she had to say from a point of concealment.

"Must you wear those glasses?"

"Well, yes. The glare."

"The wearing of dark glasses,' she said, "is a modern psychological phenomenon. It signifies the trend towards impersonalization, the weapon of the modern Inquisitor, it –"

"There's a lot in what you say." But I did not remove my glasses, for I had not asked for her company in the first place, and there is a limit to what one can listen to with the naked eye.

We walked round the new concrete verge of the old lake, and she continued the story of how she was led to give up general medical practice and take up psychology; and I looked at her as she spoke, through my dark glasses, and because of the softening effect these have upon things I saw her again as I had seen her looking up from the lake, and again as in my childhood.

At the end of the thirties Leesden End was an L-shaped town. Our house stood near the top of the L. At the other extreme was the market. Mr Simmonds, the oculist, had his shop on the horizontal leg, and he lived there above the shop with his mother and sister. All the other shops in the row were attached to each other, but Mr Simmonds' stood apart, like a real house, with a lane on either side.

I was sent to have my eyes tested. He took me into the darkened interior and said, "Sit down, dear." He put his arm round my shoulder. His forefinger moved up and down on my neck. I was thirteen and didn't like to be rude to him. Dorothy Simmonds, his sister, came downstairs just then; she came upon us silently and dressed in a white overall. Before she had crossed the room to switch on a dim light Mr Simmonds removed his arm from my shoulder with such a jerk that I knew for certain he had not placed it there in innocence.

I had seen Miss Simmonds once before, at a garden fête, where she stood on a platform in a big hat and blue dress, and sang "Sometimes between long shadows on the grass", while I picked up windfall apples, all of which seemed to be rotten. Now in her white overall she turned and gave me a hostile look, as if I had been seducing her brother. I felt sexually in the wrong, and started looking round the dark room with a wide-eyed air.

"Can you read?" said Mr Simmonds.

I stopped looking round. I said, "Read what?" – for I had been told I would be asked to read row after row of letters. The card which hung beneath the dim light showed pictures of trains and animals.

"Because if you can't read we have pictures for illiterates."

This was Mr Simmonds' joke. I giggled. His sister smiled and dabbed her right eye with her handkerchief. She had been to London for an operation on her right eye.

I recall reading the letters correctly down to the last few lines, which were too small. I recall Mr Simmonds squeezing my arm as I left the shop, turning his sandy freckled face in a backward glance to see for certain that his sister was not watching.

My grandmother said, "Did you see –"

"– Mr Simmonds' sister?" said my aunt.

"Yes, she was there all the time," I said, to make it definite.

My grandmother said, "They say she's going –"

"– blind in one eye," said my aunt.

"And with the mother bedridden upstairs –" my grandmother said.

"– she must be a saint," said my aunt.

Presently – it may have been within a few days or a few

weeks – my reading glasses arrived, and I wore them whenever I remembered to do so.

I broke the glasses by sitting on them during my school holidays two years later.

My grandmother said, after she had sighed, "It's time you had your eyes tested –"

"– eyes tested in any case," said my aunt when she had sighed.

I washed my hair the night before and put a wave in it. Next morning at eleven I walked down to Mr Simmonds's with one of my grandmother's long hat-pins in my blazer pocket. The shop front had been done up, with gold lettering on the glass door: Basil Simmonds, Optician, followed by a string of letters which, so far as I remember, were FBOA, AIC, and others.

"You're quite the young lady, Joan," he said, looking at my new breasts.

I smiled and put my hand in my blazer pocket.

He was smaller than he had been two years ago. I thought he must be about fifty or thirty. His face was more freckled than ever and his eyes were flat blue as from a box of paints. Miss Simmonds appeared silently in her soft slippers. "You're quite the young lady, Joan," she said from behind her green glasses, for her right eye had now gone blind and the other was said to be troubling her.

We went into the examination room. She glided past me and switched on the dim light above the letter card. I began to read out the letters while Basil Simmonds stood with folded hands. Someone came into the front shop. Miss

Simmonds slid off to see who it was and her brother tickled my neck. I read on. He drew me towards him. I put my hand into my blazer pocket. He said, "Oh!" and sprang away as the hat-pin struck through my blazer and into his thigh.

Miss Simmonds appeared in the doorway in her avenging white overall. Her brother, who had been rubbing his thigh in a puzzled way, pretended to be dusting a mark off the front of his trousers.

"What's wrong? Why did you shout?" she said.

"No, I didn't shout."

She looked at me, then returned to attend to the person in the shop, leaving the intervening door wide open. She was back again almost immediately. My examination was soon over. Mr Simmonds saw me out at the front door and gave me a pleading unhappy look. I felt like a traitor and I considered him horrible.

For the rest of the holidays I thought of him as "Basil", and by asking questions and taking more interest than usual in the conversation around me I formed an idea of his private life. "Dorothy," I speculated, "and Basil." I let my mind dwell on them until I saw a picture of the rooms above the shop. I hung round at tea-time and, in order to bring the conversation round to Dorothy and Basil, told our visitors I had been to get my eyes tested.

"The mother bedridden all these years and worth a fortune. But what good is it to her?"

"What chance is there for Miss Simmonds now, with that eye?"

"She'll get the money. He will get the bare legal minimum only."

"No, they say he's to get everything. In trust."

"I believe Mrs Simmonds has left everything to her daughter."

My grandmother said, "She should divide her fortune –"

"– equally between them," said my aunt. "Fair's fair."

I invented for myself a recurrent scene in which brother and sister emerged from their mother's room and, on the narrow landing, allowed their gaze to meet in unspoken combat over their inheritance. Basil's flat-coloured eyes did not themselves hold any expression, but by the forward thrust of his red neck he indicated his meaning; Dorothy made herself plain by means of a corkscrew twist of the head – round and up – and the glitter of her one good eye through the green glasses.

I was sent for to try on my new reading glasses. I had the hat-pin with me. I was friendly to Basil while I tested the new glasses in the front shop. He seemed to want to put a hand on my shoulder, hovered, but was afraid. Dorothy came downstairs and appeared before us just as his hand wavered. He protracted the wavering gesture into one which adjusted the stem of my glasses above my ear.

"Auntie says to try them properly," I said, "while I'm about it." This gave me an opportunity to have a look round the front premises.

"You'll only want them for your studies," Basil said.

"Oh, I sometimes need glasses even when I'm not reading," I said. I was looking through a door into a small inner office, darkened by a tree outside in the lane. The office contained a dumpy green safe, an old typewriter on a table, and a desk in the window with a ledger on it. Other ledgers were placed –

"Nonsense," Dorothy was saying. "A healthy girl like you – you hardly need glasses at all. For reading, to save your eyes, perhaps *yes*. But when you're not reading . . .".

I said, "Grandmother said to inquire after your mother."

"She's failing," she said.

I took to giving Basil a charming smile when I passed him in the street on the way to the shops. This was very frequently. And on these occasions he would be standing at his shop door awaiting my return; then I would snub him. I wondered how often he was prepared to be won and rejected within the same ten minutes.

I took walks before supper round the back lanes, ambling right round the Simmondses' house, thinking of what was going on inside. One dusky time it started to rain heavily, and I found I could reasonably take shelter under the tree which grew quite close to the grimy window of the inner office. I could just see over the ledge and make out a shape of a person sitting at the desk. Soon, I thought, the shape will have to put on the light.

After five minutes' long waiting time the shape arose and switched on the light by the door. It was Basil, suddenly looking pink-haired. As he returned to the desk he stooped and took from the safe a sheaf of papers held in the teeth of a large paper clip. I knew he was going to select one sheet of paper from the sheaf, and that this one document would be the exciting, important one. It was like reading a familiar book: one knew what was coming, but couldn't bear to miss a word. He did extract one long sheet of paper, and held it up. It was typewritten with a paragraph in handwriting at the bottom on the side visible from the window. He laid it side by side with another sheet of paper which was lying on the desk. I pressed close up to the window, intending to wave and smile if I was seen, and to call out that I was sheltering from the rain which was now coming down in thumps. But he kept his eyes on the two sheets of paper. There were other papers lying about the desk; I could not see what was on them. But I was quite convinced that he had been practising handwriting on them, and that he was in the process of forging his mother's will.

Then he took up the pen. I can still smell the rain and hear it thundering about me, and feel it dripping on my head from the bough hanging above me. He raised his eyes and looked out at the rain. It seemed his eyes rested on me, at my station between the tree and the window. I kept still and close to the tree like a hunted piece of nature, willing myself to be the colour of bark and leaves and train. Then I realized how much more clearly I could see him than he me, for it was growing dark.

He pulled a sheet of blotting paper towards him. He dipped his pen in the ink and started writing on the bottom of the sheet of paper before him, comparing it from time to time with the one he had taken out of the safe. I was not surprised, but I was thrilled, when the door behind him slowly opened. It was like seeing the film of the book. Dorothy advanced on her creeping feet, and he did not hear, but formed the words he was writing, on and on. The rain pelted down regardless. She was looking crookedly, through her green glasses with her one eye, over his shoulder at the paper.

"What are you doing?" she said.

He jumped up and pulled the blotting paper over his work. Her one eye through her green glasses glinted upon him, though I did not actually see it do so, but saw only the dark green glass focused with a squint on to his face.

"I'm making up the accounts," he said, standing with his back to the desk, concealing the papers. I saw his hand reach back and tremble among them.

I shivered in my soaking wet clothers. Dorothy looked with her eye at the window. I slid sideways to avoid her and ran all the way home.

Next morning I said. "I've tried to read with these glasses. It's all a blur. I suppose I'll *have* to take them back?"

"Didn't you notice anything wrong when you tried –"

"– tried them on in the shop?"

"No. But the shop's so dark. *Must* I take them back?"

I took them into Mr Simmonds early that afternoon.

"I tried to read with them this morning, but it's all a blur." It was true that I had smeared them with cold cream first.

Dorothy was beside us in no time. She peered one-eyed at the glasses, then at me.

"Are you constipated?" she said.

I maintained silence. But I felt she was seeing everything through her green glasses.

"Put them on," Dorothy said.

"Try them on," said Basil.

They were ganged up together. Everything was going wrong, for I had come here to see how matters stood between them after the affair of the will.

Basil gave me something to read. "It's all right now," I said, "but it was all a blur when I tried to read this morning."

"Better take a dose," Dorothy said.

I wanted to get out of the shop with my glasses as quickly

as possible, but the brother said, "I'd better test your eyes again while you're here just to make sure."

He seemed quite normal. I followed him into the dark interior. Dorothy switched on the light. They both seemed normal. The scene in the little office last night began to lose its conviction. As I read out the letters on the card in front of me I was thinking of Basil as "Mr Simmonds" and Dorothy as "Miss Simmonds", and feared their authority, and was in the wrong.

"That seems to be all right," Mr Simmonds said. "But wait a moment." He produced some coloured slides with lettering on them.

Miss Simmonds gave me what appeared to be a triumphant one-eyed leer, and as one who washes her hands of a person, started to climb the stairs. Plainly, she knew I had lost my attraction for her brother.

But before she turned the bend in the stairs she stopped and came down again. She went to a row of shelves and shifted some bottles. I read on. She interrupted:

"My eye-drops, Basil. I made them up this morning. Where are they?"

Mr Simmonds was suddenly watching her as if something inconceivable was happening.

"Wait, Dorothy. Wait till I've tested the girl's eyes."

She had lifted down a small brown bottle. "I want my eye-drops. I wish you wouldn't displace – Are these they?"

I noted her correct phrase, "Are these they?" and it seemed just over the border of correctness. Perhaps, after all, this brother and sister were strange, vicious, in the wrong.

She had raised the bottle and was reading the label with

her one good eye. "Yes, this is mine. It has my name on it," she said.

Dark Basil, dark Dorothy. There was something wrong after all. She walked upstairs with her bottle of eye-drops. The brother put his hand on my elbow and heaved me to my feet, forgetting his coloured slides.

"There's nothing wrong with your eyes. Off you go." He pushed me into the front shop. His flat eyes were wide open as he handed me my glasses. He pointed to the door. "I'm a busy man," he said.

From upstairs came a long scream. Basil jerked open the door for me, but I did not move. Then Dorothy, upstairs, screamed and screamed and screamed. Basil put his hands to his head, covering his eyes. Dorothy appeared on the bend of the stairs, screaming, doubled-up, with both hands covering her good eye.

I started screaming when I got home, and was given a sedative. By evening everyone knew that Miss Simmonds had put the wrong drops in her eyes.

"Will she go blind in that eye, too?" people said.

"The doctor says there's hope."

"There will be an inquiry."

"She was going blind in that eye in any case," they said.

"Ah, but the pain . . ."

"Whose mistake, hers or his?"

"Joan was there at the time. Joan heard the screams. We had to give her a sedative to calm –"

"– calm her down."

"But who made the mistake?"

"She usually makes up the eye-drops herself. She's got a dispenser's –"

"– dispenser's certificate, you know."

"Her name was on the bottle, Joan says."

"Who wrote the name on the bottle? That's the question. They'll find out from the handwriting. If it was Mr Simmonds he'll be disqualified."

"She always wrote the names on the bottles. She'll be put off the dispensers' roll, poor thing."

"They'll lose their licence."

"I got eye-drops from them myself only three weeks ago. If I'd have known what I know now, I'd never have –"

"The doctor says they can't find the bottle, it's got lost."

"No, the sergeant says definitely they've got the bottle. The handwriting is hers. She must have made up the drops herself, poor thing."

"Deadly nightshade, same thing."

"Stuff called atropine. Belladonna. Deadly nightshade."

"It should have been stuff called eserine. That's what she usually had, the doctor says."

"Dr *Gray* says?"

"Yes, Dr Gray."

"Dr Gray says if you switch from eserine to atropine –"

It was put down to an accident. There was a strong hope that Miss Simmonds's one eye would survive. It was she who had made up the prescription. She refused to discuss it.

I said, "The bottle may have been tampered with, have you thought of that?"

"Joan's been reading books."

The last week of my holidays old Mrs Simmonds died above the shop and left all her fortune to her daughter. At the same time I got tonsillitis and could not return to school.

I was attended by our woman doctor, the widow of the town's former doctor who had quite recently died. This was the first time I had seen Dr Gray, although I had known the other Dr Gray, her husband, whom I missed. The new Dr Gray was a sharp-faced athletic woman. She was said to be young. She came to visit me every day for a week. After consideration I decided she was normal and in the right, though dull.

Through the feverish part of my illness I saw Basil at the desk through the window and I heard Dorothy scream. While I was convalescent I went for walks, and always returned by the lane beside the Simmonds' house. There had been no bickering over the mother's will. Everyone said the eye-drop affair was a terrible accident. Miss Simmonds had retired and was said to be going rather dotty.

I saw Dr Gray leaving the Simmonds at six o'clock one evening. She must have been calling on poor Miss Simmonds. She noticed me at once as I emerged from the lane.

"Don't loiter about, Joan. It's getting chilly."

The next evening I saw a light in the office window. I stood under the tree and looked. Dr Gray sat upon the desk with her back to me, quite close. Mr Simmonds sat in his chair talking to her, tilting back his chair. A bottle of sherry stood on the table. They each had a glass half-filled with sherry. Dr Gray swung her legs, she was in the wrong, sexy, like our morning help who sat on the kitchen table swinging her legs.

But then she spoke. "It will take time," she said. "A very difficult patient, of course."

Basil nodded. Dr Gray swung her legs, and looked professional. She was in the right, she looked like our games mistress who sometimes sat on a desk swinging her legs.

Before I returned to school I saw Basil one morning at his shop door. "Reading glasses all right now?" he said.

"Oh yes, thank you."

"There's nothing wrong with your sight. Don't let your imagination run away with you."

I walked on, certain that he had known my guilty suspicions all along.

"I took up psychology during the war. Up till then I was in general practice."

I had come to the summer school to lecture on history and she on psychology. Psychiatrists are very often ready to talk to strangers about their inmost lives. This is probably because they spend so much time hearing out their patients. I did not recognize Dr Gray, except as a type, when I had attended her first lecture on "the psychic manifestations of sex". She spoke of child-poltergeists, and I was bored, and took refuge in observing the curious language of her profession. I noticed the word "arousement". "Adolescents in a state of sexual arousement," she said, "may become possessed of almost psychic insight."

After lunch, since the Eng. Lit. people had gone off to play tennis, she tacked on to me and we walked to the lake across the lawns, past the rhododendrons. This lake had once been the scene of a love-mad duchess's death.

". . . during the war. Before that I was in general practice. It's strange," she said, "how I came to take up psychology. My second husband had a breakdown and was under a psychiatrist. Of course, he's incurable, but I decided . . . It's strange, but that's how I came to take it up. It saved *my* reason. My husband is still in a home. His sister, of course, became quite incurable. *He* has his lucid moments. I did not realize it, of course, when I married, but there was what I'd now call an oedipus-transference on his part, and . . ."

How tedious I found these phrases! We had come to the lake. I stooped over it and myself looked back at myself through the dark water. I looked at Dr Gray's reflection and recognized her. I put on my dark glasses, then.

"Am I boring you?" she said.

"No, carry on."

"Must you wear those glasses? . . . it is a modern psychological phenomenon . . . the trend towards impersonalization . . . the modern Inquisitor."

For a while, she watched her own footsteps as we walked round the lake. Then she continued her story. ". . . an optician. His sister was blind – *going* blind when I first attended her. Only the one eye was affected. Then there was an accident, one of those *psychological* accidents. She was a trained dispenser, but she mixed herself the wrong eye-drops. Now it's very difficult to make a mistake like that, normally. But subconsciously she wanted to, she *wanted* to. But she wasn't normal, she was not normal."

"I'm not saying she was," I said.

"What did you say?"

"I'm sure she wasn't a normal person," I said, "if you say so."

"It can all be explained psychologically, as we've tried to show to my husband. We've told him and told him, and given him every sort of treatment – shock, insulin, everything. And after all, the stuff didn't have any effect on his sister immediately, and when she did go blind it was caused by acute glaucoma. She would probably have lost her sight in any case. Well, she went off her head completely and accused her brother of having put the wrong drug in the bottle deliberately. This is the interesting part from the psychological point of view – she said she had seen something that he didn't want her to see, something disreputable. She said he wanted to blind the eye that saw it. She said . . ."

We were walking round the lake for the second time. When we came to the spot where I had seen her face reflected I stopped and looked over the water.

"I'm boring you."

"No, no."

"I wish you would take off those glasses."

I took them off for a moment. I rather liked her for her innocence in not recognizing me, though she looked hard and said, "There's a subconscious reason why you wear them."

"Dark glasses hide dark thoughts," I said.

"Is that a saying?"

"Not that I've heard. But it is one now."

She looked at me anew. But she didn't recognize me. These fishers of the mind have no eye for outward things. Instead, she was "recognizing" my mind: I daresay I came under some category of hers.

I had my glasses on again, and was walking on.

"How did your husband react to his sister's accusations?" I said.

"He was remarkably kind."

"Kind?"

"Oh, yes, in the circumstances. Because she started up a lot of gossip in the neighbourhood. It was only a small town.

It was a long time before I could persuade him to send her to a home for the blind where she could be looked after. There was a terrible bond between them. Unconscious incest."

"Didn't you know that when you married him? I should have thought it would have been obvious."

She looked at me again. "I had not studied psychology at that time," she said.

I thought, neither had I.

We were silent for the third turn about the lake. Then she said, "Well, I was telling you how I came to study psychology and practise it. My husband had this breakdown after his sister went away. He had delusions. He kept imagining he saw eyes looking at him everywhere. He still sees them from time to time. But *eyes*, you see. That's significant. Unconsciously he felt he had blinded his sister. Because unconsciously he wanted to do so. He keeps confessing that he did so."

"And attempted to forge the will?" I said.

She stopped. "What are you saying?"

"Does he admit that he tried to forge his mother's will?"

"I haven't mentioned anything about a will."

"Oh, I thought you had."

"But, in fact, that was his sister's accusation. What made you say that? How did you know?"

"I must be psychic," I said.

She took my arm. I had become a most endearing case history.

"You must be psychic indeed," she said. "You must tell me more about yourself. Well, that's the story of my taking up my present profession. When my husband started having these delusions and making these confessions I felt I had to understand the workings of the mind. And I began to study them. It has been fruitful. It has saved my own reason."

"Did it ever occur to you that the sister's story might be true?" I said. "Especially as he admits it."

She took away her arm and said, "Yes, I considered the possibility. I must admit I considered it well."

She saw me watching her face. She looked as if she were pleading some personal excuse.

"Oh do," she said, "please take off those glasses."

"Why don't you believe his own confession?"

"I'm a psychiatrist and we seldom believe confessions." She looked at her watch as if to suggest I had started the whole conversation and was boring her.

I said, "He might have stopped seeing eyes if you'd taken him at his word."

She shouted, "What are you saying? What are you thinking of? He wanted to give a statement to the police, do you realize . . ."

"You know he's guilty," I said.

"As his wife," she said, "I know he's guilty. But as a psychiatrist I must regard him as innocent. That's why I took up the subject." She suddenly turned angry and shouted, "You damned inquisitor, I've met your type before."

I could hardly believe she was shouting, who previously had been so calm. "Oh, it's not my business," I said, and took off my glasses to show willing.

I think it was then she recognized me.

THE ORMOLU CLOCK

The Hotel Stroh stood side by side with the Guesthouse Lublonitsch, separated by a narrow path that led up the mountain, on the Austrian side, to the Yugoslavian border. Perhaps the old place had once been a great hunting tavern. These days, though, the Hotel Stroh was plainly a disappointment to its few drooping tenants. They huddled together like birds in a storm; their flesh sagged over the unscrubbed tables on the dark back veranda, which looked over Herr Stroh's untended fields. Usually, Herr Stroh sat somewhat apart, in a mist of cognac, his lower chin resting on his red neck, and his shirt open for air. Those visitors who had come not for the climbing but simply for the view sat and admired the mountain and were sloppily waited upon until the weekly bus should come and carry them away. If they had cars, they rarely stayed long – they departed, as a rule, within two hours of arrival, like a comic act. This much was entertainingly visible from the other side of the path, at the Guesthouse Lublonitsch.

I was waiting for friends to come and pick me up on their way to Venice. Frau Lublonitsch welcomed all her guests in person. When I arrived I was hardly aware of the honour, she seemed so merely a local woman – undefined and dumpy

– as she emerged from the kitchen wiping her hands on her brown apron, with her grey hair drawn back tight, her sleeves rolled up, her dingy dress, black stockings, and boots. It was only gradually that her importance was permitted to dawn upon strangers.

There was a Herr Lublonitsch, but he was of no account, even though he got all the marital courtesies. He sat punily with his drinking friends at one of the tables in front of the inn, greeting the guests as they passed in and out and receiving as much attention as he wanted from the waitresses. When he was sick Frau Lublonitsch took his meals with her own hands to a room upstairs set aside for his sickness. But she was undoubtedly the boss.

She worked the hired girls fourteen hours a day, and they did the work cheerfully. She was never heard to complain or to give an order; it was enough that she was there. Once, when a girl dropped a tray with five mugs of soup, Frau Lublonitsch went and fetched a cloth and submissively mopped up the mess herself, like any old peasant who had suffered worse than that in her time. The maids called her Frau Chef. "Frau Chef prepares special food when her husband's stomach is bad," one of them told me.

Appended to the guesthouse was a butcher's shop, and this was also a Lublonitsch possession. A grocer's shop had been placed beside it, and on an adjacent plot of ground – all Lublonitsch property – a draper's shop was nearing completion. Two of her sons worked in the butcher's establishment; a third had been placed in charge of the grocer's; and the youngest son, now ready to take his place, was destined for the draper's.

In the garden, strangely standing on a path between the flowers for decorating the guests' tables and the vegetables for eating, facing the prolific orchard and overhung by the chestnut trees that provided a roof for outdoor diners, grew one useless thing – a small, well-tended palm tree. It gave an air to the place. Small as it was, this alien plant stood as high as the distant mountain peaks when seen from the perspective of the great back porch where we dined. It quietly dominated the view.

Ordinarily, I got up at seven, but one morning I woke at half-past five and came down from my room on the second floor to the yard, to find someone to make me some coffee. Standing in the sunlight, with her back to me, was Frau Lublonitsch. She was regarding her wide kitchen garden, her fields beyond it, her outbuildings and her pigsties where two aged women were already at work. One of the sons emerged from an outbuilding carrying several strings of long sausages. Another led a bullock with a bag tied over its head to a tree and chained it there to await the slaughterers. Frau Lublonitsch did not move but continued to survey her property, her pigs, her pig-women, her chestnut trees, her beanstalks, her sausages, her sons, her tall gladioli, and – as if she had eyes in the back of her head – she seemed aware, too, of the good thriving guest-house behind her, and the butcher's shop, the draper's shop, and the grocer's.

Just as she turned to attack the day's work, I saw that she glanced at the sorry Hotel Stroh across the path. I saw her mouth turn down at the corners with the amusement of one who has a certain foreknowledge; I saw a landowner's recognition in her little black eyes.

You could tell, even before the local people told you, that Frau Lublonitsch had built up the whole thing from nothing by her own wits and industry. But she worked pitiably hard. She did all the cooking. She supervised the household, and, without moving hurriedly, she sped into the running of the establishment like the maniac drivers from Vienna who tore along the highroad in front of her place. She scoured the huge pans herself, wielding her podgy arm round and round; clearly, she trusted none of the girls to do the job properly. She was not above sweeping the floor, feeding the pigs, and serving in the butcher's shop, where she would patiently hold one after another great sausage under her customer's nose for him to smell its quality. She did not sit down, except to take her dinner in the kitchen, from her rising at dawn to her retiring at one in the morning.

Why does she do it, what for? Her sons are grown up, she's got her guesthouse, her servants, her shops, her pigs, fields, cattle –

At the café across the river, where I went in the late afternoon, they said, "Frau Lublonitsch has got far more than that. She owns all the strip of land up to the mountain. She's got three farms. She may even expand across the river and down this way to the town."

"Why does she work so hard? She dresses like a peasant," they said. "She scours the pots." Frau Lublonitsch was their favourite subject.

She did not go to church, she was above church. I had hoped to see her there, wearing different clothes and perhaps sitting with the chemist, the dentist, and their wives in the second front row behind the count and his family; or perhaps she might have taken some less noticeable place among the congregation. But Frau Lublonitsch was a church unto herself, and even resembled in shape the onion-shaped spires of the churches around her.

I climbed the lower slopes of the mountains while the experts in their boots did the thing earnestly up on the sheer crags above the clouds. When it rained, they came back and reported, "Tito is sending the bad weather." The maids were bored with the joke, but they obliged with smiles every time, and served them up along with the interminable veal.

The higher mountain reaches were beyond me except by bus. I was anxious, however, to scale the peaks of Frau Lublonitsch's nature.

One morning, when everything was glittering madly after a nervous stormy night, I came down early to look for coffee. I had heard voices in the yard some moments before, but by the time I appeared they had gone indoors. I followed the voices to the dark stone kitchen and peered in the doorway. Beyond the chattering girls, I caught sight of a further doorway, which usually remained closed. Now it was open.

Within it was a bedroom reaching far back into the house. It was imperially magnificent. It was done in red and gold. I saw a canopied bed, built high, splendidly covered with a scarlet quilt. The pillows were piled up at the head – about four of them, very white. The bedhead was deep dark wood, touched with gilt. A golden fringe hung from the canopy. In some ways this bed reminded me of the glowing bed by which van Eyck ennobled the portrait of Jan Arnolfini and his wife. All the rest of the Lublonitsch establishment was scrubbed and polished local wood, but this was a poetic bed.

The floor of the bedroom was covered with a carpet of red which was probably crimson but which, against the scarlet of the bed, looked purple. On the walls on either side of the bed hung Turkish carpets whose background was an opulently dull, more ancient red – almost black where the canopy cast its shade.

I was moved by the sight. The girl called Mitzi was watching me as I stood in the kitchen doorway. "Coffee?" she said.

"Whose room is that?"

"It's Frau Chef's room. She sleeps there."

Now another girl, tall, lanky Gertha, with her humorous face and slightly comic answer to everything, skipped over to the bedroom door and said, "We are instructed to keep the door closed," and for a moment before closing it she drew open the door quite wide for me to see some more of the room. I caught sight of a tiled stove constructed of mosaic tiles that were not a local type; they were lustrous – ochre and green – resembling the tiles on the floors of Byzantine ruins. The stove looked like a temple. I saw a black lacquered cabinet inlaid with mother-of-pearl, and just before Gertha closed the door I noticed, standing upon the cabinet, a large ornamental clock, its case enamelled rosily with miniature inset pastel paintings; each curve and twirl in the case of this clock was overlaid with that gilded-bronze alloy which is known as ormolu. The clock twinkled in the early sunlight which slanted between the window hangings.

I went into the polished dining-room, and Mitzi brought

my coffee there. From the window I could see Frau Lublonitsch in her dark dress, her black boots and wool stockings. She was plucking a chicken over a bucketful of feathers. Beyond her I could see the sulky figure of Herr Stroh standing collarless, fat and unshaven, in the open door of his hotel across the path. He seemed to be meditating upon Frau Lublonitsch.

It was that very day that the nuisance occurred. The double windows of my bedroom were directly opposite the bedroom windows of the Hotel Stroh, with no more than twenty feet between – the width of the narrow path that led up to the frontier.

It was a cold day. I sat in my room writing letters. I glanced out of the window. In the window directly opposite me stood Herr Stroh, gazing blatantly upon me. I was annoyed at his interest. I pulled down the blind and switched on the light to continue my writing. I wondered if Herr Stroh had seen me doing anything peculiar before I had noticed him, such as tapping my head with the end of my pen or scratching my nose or pulling at my chin, or one of the things one might do while writing a letter. The drawn blind and the artificial light irritated me, and suddenly I didn't see why I shouldn't write my letters by daylight without being stared at. I switched off the light and released the blind. Herr Stroh had gone. I concluded that he had taken my action as a signal of disapproval, and I settled back to write.

I looked up a few moments later, and this time Herr Stroh was seated on a chair a little way back from the window. He was facing me squarely and holding to his eyes a pair of field-glasses.

I left my room and went down to complain to Frau Lublonitsch.

"She's gone to the market," Gertha said. "She'll be back in half an hour."

So I lodged my complaint with Gertha.

"I shall tell Frau Chef," she said.

Something in her manner made me ask, "Has this ever happened before?"

"Once or twice this year," she said. "I'll speak to Frau Chef." And she added, with her music-hall grimace, "He was probably counting your eyelashes."

I returned to my room. Herr Stroh still sat in position, the field-glasses in his hands resting on his knees. As soon as I came within view, he raised the glasses to his eyes. I decided to stare him out until such time as Frau Lublonitsch should return and take the matter in hand.

For nearly an hour I sat patiently at the window. Herr Stroh rested his arms now and again, but he did not leave his seat. I could see him clearly, although I think I imagined the grin on his face as, from time to time, he raised the glasses to his eyes. There was no doubt that he could see, as if it were within an inch of his face, the fury on mine. It was too late now for one of us to give in, and I kept glancing down at the entrances to the Hotel Stroh, expecting to see Frau Lublonitsch or perhaps one of her sons or the yard hands going across to deliver a protest. But no one from our side approached the Stroh premises, from either the front or the back of the house. I continued to stare, and Herr Stroh continued to goggle through his glasses.

Then he dropped them. It was as if they had been jerked

out of his hands by an invisible nudge. He approached close to the window and gazed, but now he was gazing at a point above and slightly to the left of my room. After about two minutes, he turned and disappeared.

Just then Gertha knocked at my door. "Frau Chef has protested, and you won't have any more trouble," she said.

"Did she telephone to his house?"

"No, Frau Chef doesn't use the phone; it mixes her up."

"Who protested, then?"

"Frau Chef."

"But she hasn't been across to see him. I've been watching the house."

"No, Frau Chef doesn't visit with him. But don't worry, he knows all right that he mustn't annoy our guests."

When I looked out of the window again, I saw that the blind of Herr Stroh's room had been pulled down, and so it remained for the rest of my stay.

Meantime, I went out to post my letters in the box opposite our hotel, across the path. The sun had come out more strongly, and Herr Stroh stood in his doorway blinking up at the roof of the Guesthouse Lublon-itsch. He was engrossed, he did not notice me at all.

I didn't want to draw his attention by following the line of his gaze but I was curious as to what held him staring so trancelike up at our roof. On my way back from the postbox I saw what it was.

Like most of the roofs in that province, the Lublonitsch roof had a railed ledge running several inches above the eaves, for the purpose of preventing the snow from falling in heavy thumps during the winter. On this ledge, just below an attic window, stood the gold-and-rose ormolu clock that I had seen in Frau Lublonitsch's splendid bedroom.

I turned the corner just as Herr Stroh gave up his gazing; he went indoors, sullen and bent. Two car-loads of people who had moved into the hotel that morning were now moving out, shifting their baggage with speed and the signs of a glad departure. I knew that his house was nearly empty.

Before supper, I walked past the Hotel Stroh and down across the bridge to the café. There were no other customers in the place. The proprietor brought the harsh gin that was the local speciality over to my usual table and I sipped it while I waited for someone to come. I did not have to wait long, for two local women came in and ordered ices, as many of them did on their way home from work in the village shops. They held the long spoons in their rough, knobbly hands and talked, while the owner of the café came and sat with them to exchange the news of the day.

"Herr Stroh has been defying Frau Lublonitsch," one of the women said.

"Not again?"

"He's been offending her tourists."

"Dirty old Peeping Tom."

"He only does it to annoy Frau Lublonitsch."

"I saw the clock on the roof. I saw –"

"Stroh is finished, he –"

"Which clock?"

"What she bought from him last winter when he was hard up. All red and gold, like an altarpiece. A beautiful clock – it was his grandfather's when things were different."

"Stroh is finished. She'll have his hotel. She'll have –"

"She'll have the pants off him."

"He'll have to go. She'll get the place at her price. Then she'll build down to the bridge. Just wait and see. Next winter she'll have the Hotel Stroh. Last winter she had the clock. It's two years since she gave him the mortgage."

"It's only Stroh's place that's standing in her way. She'll pull it down."

The faces of the two women and the man nearly met across the café table, hypnotized by the central idea of their talk. The women's spoons rose to their mouths and returned to their ices while the man clasped his hands on the table in front of him. Their voices went on like a litany.

"She'll expand down to the bridge."

"Perhaps beyond the bridge."

"No, no, the bridge will be enough. She's not so young."

"Poor old Stroh!"

"Why doesn't she expand in the other direction?"

"Because there isn't so much trade in the other direction."

"The business is down here, this side of the river."

"Old Stroh is upset."

"She'll build down to the bridge. She'll pull down his place and build."

"Beyond the bridge."

"Old Stroh. His clock stuck up there for everyone to see."

"What does he expect, the lazy old pig?"

"What does he expect to see with his field-glasses?"

"The tourists."

"I wish him joy of the tourists."

They giggled, then noticed me sitting within earshot, and came out of their trance.

How delicately Frau Lublonitsch had sent her deadly message! The ormolu clock was still there on the roof ledge when I returned. It was thus she had told him that time was passing and the end of summer was near, and that his hotel, like his clock, would soon be hers. As I passed, Herr Stroh shuffled out to his front door, rather drunk. He did not see me. He was looking at the clock where it hung in the sunset, he looked up at it as did the quaking enemies of the Lord upon the head of Holofernes. I wondered if the poor man would even live another winter; certainly he had taken his last feeble stand against Frau Lublonitsch.

As for her, she would probably live till she was ninety or more. The general estimate of her age was fifty-three, fifty-four, -five, -six: a healthy woman.

Next day, the clock was gone. Enough was enough. It had gone back to that glamorous room behind the kitchen to which Frau Lublonitsch retired in the early hours of the morning to think up her high conceptions, not lying supine like a defeated creature but propped up on the white pillows, surrounded by her crimson, her scarlet, her gold-and-rosy tints, which, like a religious discipline, disturbed her spirit out of its sloth. It was from here she planted the palm tree and built the shops.

When, next morning, I saw her scouring the pots in the yard and plodding about in her boots among the vegetables, I was somewhat terrified. She could have adorned her own person in scarlet and gold, she could have lived in a turreted mansion rivalling that of the apothecary in the village. But like one averting the evil eye or like one practising a pure disinterested art, she had stuck to her brown apron and her boots. And she would, without a doubt, have her reward. She would take the Hotel Stroh. She would march on the bridge, and beyond it. The café would be hers, the swimming-pool, the cinema. All the market place would be hers before she died in the scarlet bed under the gold-fringed canopy, facing her ormolu clock, her deed-boxes, and her ineffectual bottle of medicine.

Almost as if they knew it, the three tourists remaining in the Hotel Stroh came over to inquire of Frau Lublonitsch if there were any rooms available and what her terms were. Her terms were modest, and she found room for two of them. The third left on his motorcycle that night.

Everyone likes to be on the winning side. I saw the two new arrivals from the Hotel Stroh sitting secure under the Lublonitsch chestnut tree, taking breakfast, next morning. Herr Stroh, more sober than before, stood watching the scene from his doorway. I thought, Why doesn't he spit on us, he's got nothing to lose? I saw again, in my mind's eye, the ormolu clock set high in the sunset splendour. But I had not yet got over my fury with him for spying into my room, and was moved, all in one stroke, with high contempt and deep pity, feverish triumph and chilly fear.

THE PORTOBELLO ROAD

One day in my young youth at high summer, lolling with my lovely companions upon a haystack, I found a needle. Already and privately for some years I had been guessing that I was set apart from the common run, but this of the needle attested the fact to my whole public: George, Kathleen and Skinny. I sucked my thumb, for when I had thrust my idle hand deep into the hay, the thumb was where the needle had stuck.

When everyone had recovered George said, "She put in her thumb and pulled out a plum." Then away we were into our merciless hacking-hecking laughter again.

The needle had gone fairly deep into the thumby cushion and a small red river flowed and spread from this tiny puncture. So that nothing of our joy should lag, George put in quickly,

"Mind your bloody thumb on my shirt."

Then hac-hec-hoo, we shrieked into the hot Borderland afternoon. Really I should not care to be so young of heart again. That is my thought every time I turn over my old papers and come across the photograph. Skinny, Kathleen and myself are in the photo atop the haystack. Skinny had just finished analysing the inwards of my find.

"It couldn't have been done by brains. You haven't much brains but you're a lucky wee thing."

Everyone agreed that the needle betokened extraordinary luck. As it was becoming a serious conversation, George said,

"I'll take a photo."

I wrapped my hanky round my thumb and got myself organized. George pointed up from his camera and shouted,

"Look, there's a mouse!"

Kathleen screamed and I screamed although I think we knew there was no mouse. But this gave us an extra session of squalling hee-hoo's. Finally we three composed ourselves for George's picture. We look lovely and it was a great day at the time, but I would not care for it all over again. From that day I was known as Needle.

One Saturday in recent years I was mooching down the Portobello Road, threading among the crowds of marketers on the narrow pavement when I saw a woman. She had a haggard, careworn, wealthy look, thin but for the breasts forced-up high like a pigeon's. I had not seen her for nearly five years. How changed she was! But I recognized Kathleen, my friend; her features had already begun to sink and protrude in the way that mouths and noses do in people destined always to be old for their years. When I had last seen her, nearly five years ago, Kathleen, barely thirty, had said,

"I've lost all my looks, it's in the family. All the women are handsome as girls, but we go off early, we go brown and nosey."

I stood silently among the people, watching. As you will

see, I wasn't in a position to speak to Kathleen. I saw her shoving in her avid manner from stall to stall. She was always fond of antique jewellery and of bargains. I wondered that I had not seen her before in the Portobello Road on my Saturday-morning ambles. Her long stiff-crooked fingers pounced to select a jade ring from among the jumble of brooches and pendants, onyx, moonstone and gold, set out on the stall.

"What do you think of this?" she said.

I saw then who was with her. I had been half-conscious of the huge man following several paces behind her, and now I noticed him.

"It looks all right," he said. "How much is it?"

"How much is it?" Kathleen asked the vendor.

I took a good look at this man accompanying Kathleen. It was her husband. The beard was unfamiliar, but I recognized beneath it his enormous mouth, the bright sensuous lips, the large brown eyes forever brimming with pathos.

It was not for me to speak to Kathleen, but I had a sudden inspiration which caused me to say quietly,

"Hallo, George."

The giant of a man turned round to face the direction of my face. There were so many people – but at length he saw me.

"Hallo, George," I said again.

Kathleen had started to haggle with the stall-owner, in her old way, over the price of the jade ring. George continued to stare at me, his big mouth slightly parted so that I could see a wide slit of red lips and white teeth between the fair grassy growths of beard and moustache.

"My God!" he said.

"What's the matter?" said Kathleen.

"Hallo, George!" I said again, quite loud this time, and cheerfully.

"Look!" said George. "Look who's there, over beside the fruit stall."

Kathleen looked but didn't see.

"Who is it?" she said impatiently.

"It's Needle," he said. "She said 'Hallo, George'."

"*Needle*," said Kathleen. "Who do you mean? You don't mean our old friend *Needle* who –"

"Yes. There she is. My God!"

He looked very ill, although when I had said "Hallo, George" I had spoken friendly enough.

"I don't see anyone faintly resembling poor Needle," said Kathleen looking at him. She was worried.

George pointed straight at me. "Look *there*. I tell you that is Needle."

"You're ill, George. Heavens, you must be seeing things. Come on home. Needle isn't there. You know as well as I do, Needle is dead."

I must explain that I departed this life nearly five years ago. But I did not altogether depart this world. There were those odd things still to be done which one's executors can never do properly. Papers to be looked over, even after the executors have torn them up. Lots of business except, of course, on Sundays and Holidays of Obligation, plenty to take an interest in for the time being. I take my recreation on Saturday mornings. If it is a wet Saturday I wander up and down the substantial lanes of Woolworth's as I did when I was young and visible. There is a pleasurable spread of objects on the counters which I now perceive and exploit with a certain detachment, since it suits with my condition of life. Creams, toothpastes, combs and hankies, cotton gloves, flimsy flowering scarves, writing-paper and crayons, ice-cream cones and orangeade, screwdrivers, boxes of tacks, tins of paint, of glue, of marmalade; I always liked them but far more now that I have no need of any. When Saturdays are fine I go instead to the Portobello Road where formerly I would jaunt with Kathleen in our grown-up days. The barrow-loads do not change much, of apples and rayon vests in common blues and low-taste mauve, of silver plate, trays and teapots long since changed hands from the bygone citizens to dealers, from shops to the new flats and breakable homes, and then over to the barrow-stalls and the dealers again: Georgian spoons, rings, earrings of turquoise and opal set in the butterfly pattern of true-lovers' knot, patch-boxes with miniature paintings of ladies on ivory, snuff-boxes of silver with Scotch pebbles inset.

Sometimes as occasion arises on a Saturday morning, my friend Kathleen, who is a Catholic, has a Mass said for my soul, and then I am in attendance, as it were, at the church. But most Saturdays I take my delight among the solemn crowds with their aimless purposes, their eternal life not far away, who push past the counters and stalls, who handle, buy, steal, touch, desire and ogle the merchandise. I hear the tinkling tills, I hear the jangle of loose change and tongues and children wanting to hold and have.

That is how I came to be in the Portobello Road that Saturday morning when I saw George and Kathleen. I would not have spoken had I not been inspired to it. Indeed it's one of the things I can't do now – to speak out, unless inspired. And most extraordinary, on that morning as I spoke, a degree of visibility set in. I suppose from poor George's point of view it was like seeing a ghost when he saw me standing by the fruit barrow repeating in so friendly a manner, "Hallo, George!"

We were bound for the south. When our education, what we could get of it from the north, was thought to be finished, one by one we were sent or sent for to London. John Skinner, whom we called Skinny, went to study more archaeology, George to join his uncle's tobacco farm, Kathleen to stay with her rich connections and to potter intermittently in the Mayfair hat shop which one of them owned. A little later I also went to London to see life, for it was my ambition to write about life, which first I had to see.

"We four must stick together," George said very often in that yearning way of his. He was always desperately afraid of neglect. We four looked likely to shift off in different directions and George did not trust the other three of us not to forget all about him. More and more as the time came for him to depart for his uncle's tobacco farm in Africa he said,

"We four must keep in touch."

And before he left he told each of us anxiously,

"I'll write regularly, once a month. We must keep together for the sake of the old times." He had three prints taken from the negative of that photo on the haystack, wrote on the back of them, "George took this the day that Needle found the needle" and gave us a copy each. I think we all wished he could become a bit more callous.

During my lifetime I was a drifter, nothing organized. It was difficult for my friends to follow the logic of my life. By the normal reckonings I should have come to starvation and ruin, which I never did. Of course, I did not live to write about life as I wanted to do. Possibly that is why I am inspired to do so now in these peculiar circumstances.

I taught in a private school in Kensington for almost three months, very small children. I didn't know what to do with them but I was kept fairly busy escorting incontinent little boys to the lavatory and telling the little girls to use their handkerchiefs. After that I lived a winter holiday in London on my small capital, and when that had run out I found a diamond bracelet in the cinema for which I received a reward of fifty pounds. When it was used up I got a job with a publicity man, writing speeches for absorbed industrialists, in which the dictionary of quotations came in very useful. So it went on. I got engaged to Skinny, but shortly after that I was left a small legacy, enough to keep me for six months. This somehow decided me that I didn't love Skinny so I gave him back the ring.

But it was through Skinny that I went to Africa. He was engaged with a party of researchers to investigate King Solomon's mines, that series of ancient workings ranging from the ancient port of Ophir, now called Beira, across Portuguese East Africa and Southern Rhodesia to the mighty jungle-city of Zimbabwe whose temple walls still stand by the approach to an ancient and sacred mountain, where the rubble of that civilization scatters itself over the surrounding Rhodesian waste. I accompanied the party as a sort of secretary. Skinny vouched for me, he paid my fare, he sympathized by his action with my inconsequential life although when he spoke of it he disapproved. A life like mine annoys most people; they go to their jobs every day, attend to things, give orders, pummel typewriters, and get two or three weeks off every year, and it vexes them to see someone else not bothering to do these things and yet getting away with it, not starving, being lucky as they call it. Skinny, when I had broken off our engagement, lectured me about this, but still he took me to Africa knowing I should probably leave his unit within a few months.

We were there a few weeks before we began inquiring for George, who was farming about four hundred miles away to the north. We had not told him of our plans.

"If we tell George to expect us in his part of the world he'll come rushing to pester us the first week. After all, we're going on business," Skinny had said.

Before we left Kathleen told us, "Give George my love and tell him not to send frantic cables every time I don't answer his letters right away. Tell him I'm busy in the hat shop and being presented. You would think he hadn't another friend in the world the way he carries on."

We had settled first at Fort Victoria, our nearest place of access to the Zimbabwe ruins. There we made inquiries about George. It was clear he hadn't many friends. The older settlers were the most tolerant about the half-caste woman he was living with, as we found, but they were furious about his methods of raising tobacco which we learned were most unprofessional and in some mysterious way disloyal to the whites. We could never discover how it was that George's style of tobacco farming gave the blacks opinions about themselves, but that's what the older settlers claimed. The newer immigrants thought he was unsociable and, of course, his living with that nig made visiting impossible.

I must say I was myself a bit off-put by this news about the brown woman. I was brought up in a university town to which came Indian, African and Asiatic students in a variety of tints and hues. I was brought up to avoid them for reasons connected with local reputation and God's ordinances. You cannot easily go against what you were brought up to do unless you are a rebel by nature.

Anyhow, we visited George eventually, taking advantage of the offer of transport from some people bound north in search of game. He had heard of our arrival in Rhodesia and though he was glad, almost relieved, to see us he pursued a policy of sullenness for the first hour.

"We wanted to give you a surprise, George."

"How were we to know that you'd get to hear of our arrival, George? News here must travel faster than light, George."

"We did hope to give you a surprise, George."

At last he said, "Well, I must say it's good to see you. All we need now is Kathleen. We four simply must stick together. You find when you're in a place like this, there's nothing like old friends."

He showed us his drying sheds. He showed us a paddock where he was experimenting with a horse and a zebra mare, attempting to mate them. They were frolicking happily, but not together. They passed each other in their private play time and again, but without acknowledgement and without resentment.

"It's been done before," George said. "It makes a fine

strong beast, more intelligent than a mule and sturdier than a horse. But I'm not having any success with this pair, they won't look at each other."

After a while, he said, "Come in for a drink and meet Matilda."

She was dark brown, with a subservient hollow chest and round shoulders, a gawky woman, very snappy with the house-boys. We said pleasant things as we drank on the stoep before dinner, but we found George difficult. For some reason he began to rail at me for breaking off my engagement to Skinny, saying what a dirty trick it was after all those good times in the old days. I diverted attention to Matilda. I supposed, I said, she knew this part of the country well?

"No," said she, "I been a-shellitered my life. I not put out to working. Me nothing to go from place to place is allowed like dirty girls does." In her speech she gave every syllable equal stress.

George explained, "Her father was a white magistrate in Natal. She had a sheltered upbringing, different from the other coloureds, you realize."

"Man, me no black-eyed Susan," said Matilda, "no, no."

On the whole, George treated her as a servant. She was about four months advanced in pregnancy, but he made her get up and fetch for him, many times. Soap: that was one of the things Matilda had to fetch. George made his own bath soap, showed it proudly, gave us the recipe which I did not trouble to remember; I was fond of nice soaps during my life-time and George's smelt of brilliantine and looked likely to soil one's skin.

"D'yo brahn?" Matilda asked me.

George said, "She is asking if you go brown in the sun."

"No, I go freckled."

"I got sister-in-law go freckles."

She never spoke another word to Skinny nor to me, and we never saw her again.

Some months later I said to Skinny,

"I'm fed up with being a camp follower."

He was not surprised that I was leaving his unit, but he hated my way of expressing it. He gave me a Presbyterian look.

"Don't talk like that. Are you going back to England or staying?"

"Staying, for a while."

"Well, don't wander too far off."

I was able to live on the fee I got for writing a gossip column in a local weekly, which wasn't my idea of writing about life, of course. I made friends, more than I could cope with, after I left Skinny's exclusive little band of archaeologists. I had the attractions of being newly out from England and of wanting to see life. Of the countless young men and go-ahead families who purred me along the Rhodesian roads, hundred after hundred miles, I only kept up with one family when I returned to my native land. I think that was because they were the most representative, they stood for all the rest: people in those parts are very typical of each other, as one group of standing stones in that wilderness is like the next.

I met George once more in a hotel in Bulawayo. We drank highballs and spoke of war. Skinny's party were just then deciding whether to remain in the country or return home. They had reached an exciting part of their research, and whenever I got a chance to visit Zimbabwe he would take me for a moonlight walk in the ruined temple and try to make me see phantom Phoenicians flitting ahead of us, or along the walls. I had half a mind to marry Skinny; perhaps, I thought, when his studies were finished. The impending war was in our bones: so I remarked to George as we sat drinking highballs on the hotel stoep in the hard bright sunny July winter of that year.

George was inquisitive about my relations with Skinny. He tried to pump me for about half an hour and when at last I said, "You are becoming aggressive, George," he stopped. He became quite pathetic. He said, "War or no war I'm clearing out of this."

"It's the heat does it," I said.

"I'm clearing out in any case. I've lost a fortune in tobacco. My uncle is making a fuss. It's the other bloody planters; once you get the wrong side of them you're finished in this wide land."

"What about Matilda?" I asked.

He said, "She'll be all right. She's got hundreds of relatives."

I had already heard about the baby girl. Coal black, by repute, with George's features. And another on the way, they said.

"What about the child?"

He didn't say anything to that. He ordered more highballs and when they arrived he swizzled his for a long time with a stick. "Why didn't you ask me to your twenty-first?" he said then.

"I didn't have anything special, no party, George. We had a quiet drink among ourselves, George, just Skinny and the old professors and two of the wives and me, George."

"You didn't ask me to your twenty-first," he said. "Kathleen writes to me regularly."

This wasn't true. Kathleen sent me letters fairly often in which she said, "Don't tell George I wrote to you as he will be expecting word from me and I can't be bothered actually."

"But you," said George, "don't seem to have any sense of old friendships, you and Skinny."

"Oh, George!" I said.

"Remember the times we had," George said. "We used to have times." His large brown eyes began to water.

"I'll have to be getting along," I said.

"Please don't go. Don't leave me just yet. I've something to tell you."

"Something nice?" I laid on an eager smile. All responses to George had to be overdone.

"You don't know how lucky you are," George said.

"How?" I said. Sometimes I got tired of being called lucky by everybody. There were times when, privately practising my writings about life, I knew the bitter side of my fortune. When I failed again and again to reproduce life in some satisfactory and perfect form, I was the more imprisoned, for all my carefree living, within my craving for this satisfaction. Sometimes, in my impotence and need I secreted a venom which infected all my life for days on end and which spurted out indiscriminately on Skinny or on anyone who crossed my path.

"You aren't bound by anyone," George said. "You come

and go as you please. Something always turns up for you. You're free, and you don't know your luck."

"You're a damn sight more free than I am," I said sharply. "You've got your rich uncle."

"He's losing interest in me," George said. "He's had enough."

"Oh well, you're young yet. What was it you wanted to tell me?"

"A secret," George said. "Remember we used to have those secrets."

"Oh, yes we did."

"Did you ever tell any of mine?"

"Oh no, George." In reality, I couldn't remember any particular secret out of the dozens we must have exchanged from our schooldays onwards.

"Well, this is a secret, mind. Promise not to tell."

"Promise."

"I'm married."

"Married, George! Oh, who to?"

"Matilda."

"How dreadful!" I spoke before I could think, but he agreed with me.

"Yes, it's awful, but what could I do?"

"You might have asked my advice," I said pompously.

"I'm two years older than you are. I don't ask advice from you, Needle, little beast."

"Don't ask for sympathy then."

"A nice friend you are," he said, "I must say after all these years."

"Poor George!" I said.

"There are three white men to one white woman in this country," said George. "An isolated planter doesn't see a white woman and if he sees one she doesn't see him. What could I do? I needed the woman."

I was nearly sick. One, because of my Scottish upbringing. Two, because of my horror of corny phrases like "I needed the woman", which George repeated twice again.

"And Matilda got tough," said George, "after you and Skinny came to visit us. She had some friends at the Mission, and she packed up and went to them."

"You should have let her go," I said.

"I went after her," George said. "She insisted on being married, so I married her."

"That's not a proper secret, then," I said. "The news of a mixed marriage soon gets about."

"I took care of that," George said. "Crazy as I was, I took her to the Congo and married her there. She promised to keep quiet about it."

"Well, you can't clear off and leave her now, surely," I said.

"I'm going to get out of this place. I can't stand the woman and I can't stand the country. I didn't realize what it would be like. Two years of the country and three months of my wife has been enough."

"Will you get a divorce?"

"No, Matilda's Catholic. She won't divorce."

George was fairly getting through the highballs, and I wasn't far behind him. His brown eyes floated shiny and liquid as he told me how he had written to tell his uncle of his plight, "Except, of course, I didn't say we were married, that would have been too much for him. He's a prejudiced hardened old colonial. I only said I'd had a child by a coloured woman and was expecting another, and he perfectly understood. He came at once by plane a few weeks ago. He's made a settlement on her, providing she keeps her mouth shut about her association with me."

"Will she do that?"

"Oh, yes, or she won't get the money."

"But as your wife she has a claim on you, in any case."

"If she claimed as my wife she'd get far less. Matilda knows what she's doing, greedy bitch she is. She'll keep her mouth shut."

"Only, you won't be able to marry again, will you, George?"

"Not unless she dies," he said. "And she's as strong as a trek ox."

"Well, I'm sorry, George," I said.

"Good of you to say so," he said. "But I can see by your chin that you disapprove of me. Even my old uncle understood."

"Oh, George, I quite understand. You were lonely, I suppose."

"You didn't even ask me to your twenty-first. If you and Skinny had been nicer to me, I would never have lost my head and married the woman, never."

"You didn't ask me to your wedding," I said.

"You're a catty bissom, Needle, not like what you were in the old times when you used to tell us your wee stories."

"I'll have to be getting along," I said.

"Mind you keep the secret," George said.

"Can't I tell Skinny? He would be very sorry for you, George."

"You mustn't tell anyone. Keep it a secret. Promise."

"Promise," I said. I understood that he wished to enforce some sort of bond between us with this secret, and I thought, "Oh well, I suppose he's lonely. Keeping his secret won't do any harm."

I returned to England with Skinny's party just before the war.

I did not see George again till just before my death, five years ago.

After the war Skinny returned to his studies. He had two more exams, over a period of eighteen months, and I thought I might marry him when the exams were over.

"You might do worse than Skinny," Kathleen used to say to me on our Saturday morning excursions to the antique shops and the junk stalls.

She too was getting on in years. The remainder of our families in Scotland were hinting that it was time we settled down with husbands. Kathleen was a little younger than me, but looked much older. She knew her chances were diminishing but at that time I did not think she cared very much. As for myself, the main attraction of marrying Skinny was his prospective expeditions to Mesopotamia. My desire to marry him had to be stimulated by the continual reading of books about Babylon and Assyria; perhaps Skinny felt this, because he supplied the books and even started instructing me in the art of deciphering cuneiform tablets.

Kathleen was more interested in marriage than I

thought. Like me, she had racketed around a good deal during the war; she had actually been engaged to an officer in the US navy, who was killed. Now she kept an antique shop near Lambeth, was doing very nicely, lived in a Chelsea square, but for all that she must have wanted to be married and have children. She would stop and look into all the prams which the mothers had left outside shops or area gates.

"The poet Swinburne used to do that," I told her once.

"Really? Did he want children of his own?"

"I shouldn't think so. He simply liked babies."

Before Skinny's final exam he fell ill and was sent to a sanatorium in Switzerland.

"You're fortunate after all not to be married to him," Kathleen said. "You might have caught TB."

I was fortunate, I was lucky . . . so everyone kept telling me on different occasions. Although it annoyed me to hear, I knew they were right, but in a way that was different from what they meant. It took me very small effort to make a living; book reviews, odd jobs for Kathleen, a few months with the publicity man again, still getting up speeches about literature, art and life for industrial tycoons. I was waiting to write about life and it seemed to me that the good fortune lay in this, whenever it should be. And until then I was assured of my charmed life, the necessities of existence always coming my way and I with far more leisure than anyone else. I thought of my type of luck after I became a Catholic and was being confirmed. The Bishop touches the candidate on the cheek, a symbolic reminder of the sufferings a Christian is supposed to undertake. I thought, how lucky, what a feathery symbol to stand for the hellish violence of its true meaning.

I visited Skinny twice in the two years that he was in the sanatorium. He was almost cured, and expected to be home within a few months. I told Kathleen after my last visit.

"Maybe I'll marry Skinny when he's well again."

"Make it definite, Needle, and not so much of the maybe. You don't know when you're well off," she said.

This was five years ago, in the last year of my life. Kathleen and I had become very close friends. We met several times each week, and after our Saturday morning excursions in the Portobello Road very often I would accompany Kathleen to her aunt's house in Kent for a long weekend.

One day in the June of that year I met Kathleen specially for lunch because she had phoned me to say she had news.

"Guess who came into the shop this afternoon," she said.

"Who?"

"George."

We had half imagined George was dead. We had received no letters in the past ten years. Early in the war we had heard rumours of his keeping a nightclub in Durban, but nothing after that. We could have made inquiries if we had felt moved to do so.

At one time, when we discussed him, Kathleen had said.

"I ought to get in touch with poor George. But then I think he would write back. He would demand a regular correspondence again."

"We four must stick together," I mimicked.

"I can visualize his reproachful limpid orbs," Kathleen said.

Skinny said, “He’s probably gone native. With his coffee concubine and a dozen mahogany kids.”

“Perhaps he’s dead,” Kathleen said.

I did not speak of George’s marriage, nor of any of his confidences in the hotel at Bulawayo. As the years passed we ceased to mention him except in passing, as someone more or less dead so far as we were concerned.

Kathleen was excited about George’s turning up. She had forgotten her impatience with him in former days; she said,

“It was so wonderful to see old George. He seems to need a friend, feels neglected, out of touch with things.”

“He needs mothering, I suppose.”

Kathleen didn’t notice the malice. She declared, “That’s exactly the case with George. It always has been, I can see it now.”

She seemed ready to come to any rapid new and happy conclusion about George. In the course of the afternoon he had told her of his wartime night club in Durban, his game-shooting expeditions since. It was clear he had not mentioned Matilda. He had put on weight, Kathleen told me, but he could carry it.

I was curious to see this version of George, but I was leaving for Scotland next day and did not see him till September of that year, just before my death.

While I was in Scotland I gathered from Kathleen’s letters that she was seeing George very frequently, finding enjoyable company in him, looking after him. “You’ll be surprised to see how he has developed.” Apparently he would hang round Kathleen in her shop most days, “it makes him feel useful” as she maternally expressed it. He had an old relative in Kent whom he visited at weekends; this old lady lived a few miles from Kathleen's aunt, which made it easy for them to travel down together on Saturdays, and go for long country walks.

"You'll see such a difference in George," Kathleen said on my return to London in September. I was to meet him that night, a Saturday. Kathleen's aunt was abroad, the maid on holiday, and I was to keep Kathleen company in the empty house.

George had left London for Kent a few days earlier. "He's actually helping with the harvest down there!" Kathleen told me lovingly.

Kathleen and I planned to travel down together, but on that Saturday she was unexpectedly delayed in London on some business. It was arranged that I should go ahead of her in the early afternoon to see to the provisions for our party; Kathleen had invited George to dinner at her aunt's house that night.

"I should be with you by seven," she said. "Sure you won't mind the empty house? I hate arriving at empty houses, myself."

I said no, I liked an empty house.

So I did, when I got there. I had never found the house more likeable. A large Georgian vicarage in about eight acres, most of the rooms shut and sheeted, there being only one servant. I discovered that I wouldn't need to go shopping, Kathleen's aunt had left many and delicate supplies with notes attached to them: "Eat this up please do, see also fridge" and "A treat for three hungry people, see also 2 bttles beaune for yr party on back kn table". It was like a treasure hunt as I followed clue after clue through the cool silent domestic quarters. A house in which there are no people – but with all the signs of tenancy – can be a most tranquil good place. People take up space in a house out of proportion to their size. On my previous visits I had seen the rooms overflowing, as it seemed, with Kathleen, her aunt, and the little fat maid-servant; they were always on the move. As I wandered through that part of the house which was in use, opening windows to let in the pale yellow air of September, I was not conscious that I, Needle, was taking up any space at all, I might have been a ghost.

The only thing to be fetched was the milk. I waited till after four when the milking should be done, then set off for the farm which lay across two fields at the back of the orchard. There, when the byre-man was handing me the bottle, I saw George.

"Hallo, George," I said.

"Needle! What are you doing here?" he said.

"Fetching milk," I said.

"So am I. Well, it's good to see you, I must say."

As we paid the farm-hand, George said, "I'll walk back with you part of the way. But I mustn't stop, my old cousin's without any milk for her tea. How's Kathleen?"

"She was kept in London. She's coming on later, about seven, she expects."

We had reached the end of the first field. George's way led to the left and on to the main road.

"We'll see you tonight, then?" I said.

"Yes, and talk about old times."

"Grand," I said.

But George got over the stile with me.

"Look here," he said. "I'd like to talk to you, Needle."

"We'll talk tonight, George. Better not keep your cousin waiting for the milk." I found myself speaking to him almost as if he were a child.

"No, I want to talk to you alone. This is a good opportunity."

We began to cross the second field. I had been hoping to have the house to myself for a couple more hours and I was rather petulant.

"See," he said suddenly, "that haystack."

"Yes," I said absently.

"Let's sit there and talk. I'd like to see you up on a haystack again. I still keep that photo. Remember that time when –"

"I found the needle," I said very quickly, to get it over.

But I was glad to rest. The stack had been broken up, but we managed to find a nest in it. I buried my bottle of milk in the hay for coolness. George placed his carefully at the foot of the stack.

"My old cousin is terribly vague, poor soul. A bit hazy in her head. She hasn't the least sense of time. If I tell her I've only been gone ten minutes she'll believe it."

I giggled, and looked at him. His face had grown much larger, his lips full, wide, and with a ripe colour that is strange in a man. His brown eyes were abounding as before with some inarticulate plea.

"So you're going to marry Skinny after all these years?"

"I really don't know, George."

"You played him up properly."

"It isn't for you to judge. I have my own reasons for what I do."

"Don't get sharp," he said, "I was only funning." To prove it, he lifted a tuft of hay and brushed my face with it.

"D'you know," he said next, "I didn't think you and Skinny treated me very decently in Rhodesia."

"Well, we were busy, George. And we were younger then, we had a lot to do and see. After all, we could see you any other time, George."

"A touch of selfishness," he said.

"I'll have to be getting along, George." I made to get down from the stack.

He pulled me back. "Wait, I've got something to tell you."

"OK, George, tell me."

"First promise not to tell Kathleen. She wants it kept a secret so that she can tell you herself."

"All right. Promise."

"I'm going to marry Kathleen."

"But you're already married."

Sometimes I heard news of Matilda from the one Rhodesian family with whom I still kept up. They referred to her as "George's Dark Lady" and of course they did not know he was married to her. She had apparently made a good thing out of George, they said, for she minced around all tarted up, never did a stroke of work and was always unsettling the respectable coloured girls in their neighbourhood. According to accounts, she was a living example of the folly of behaving as George did.

"I married Matilda in the Congo," George was saying.

"It would still be bigamy," I said.

He was furious when I used that word bigamy. He lifted

a handful of hay as if he would throw it in my face, but controlling himself meanwhile he fanned it at me playfully.

"I'm not sure that the Congo marriage was valid," he continued. "Anyway, as far as I'm concerned, it isn't."

"You can't do a thing like that," I said.

"I need Kathleen. She's been decent to me. I think we were always meant for each other, me and Kathleen."

"I'll have to be going," I said.

But he put his knee over my ankles, so that I couldn't move. I sat still and gazed into space.

He tickled my face with a wisp of hay.

"Smile up, Needle," he said; "let's talk like old times."

"Well?"

"No one knows about my marriage to Matilda except you and me."

"And Matilda," I said.

"She'll hold her tongue so long as she gets her payments. My uncle left an annuity for the purpose, his lawyers see to it."

"Let me go, George."

"You promised to keep it a secret," he said, "you promised."

"Yes, I promised."

"And now that you're going to marry Skinny, we'll be properly coupled off as we should have been years ago. We should have been – but youth! – our youth got in the way, didn't it?"

"Life got in the way," I said.

"But everything's going to be all right now. You'll keep my secret, won't you? You promised." He had released my feet. I edged a little farther from him.

I said, "If Kathleen intends to marry you, I shall tell her that you're already married."

"You wouldn't do a dirty trick like that, Needle? You're going to be happy with Skinny, you wouldn't stand in the way of my –"

"I must, Kathleen's my best friend," I said swiftly.

He looked as if he would murder me and he did. He stuffed hay into my mouth until it could hold no more, kneeling on my body to keep it still, holding both my wrists tight in his huge left hand. I saw the red full lines of his mouth and the white slit of his teeth last thing on earth. Not another soul passed by as he pressed my body into the stack, as he made a deep nest for me, tearing up the hay to make a groove the length of my corpse, and finally pulling the warm dry stuff in a mound over this concealment, so natural-looking in a broken haystack. Then George climbed down, took up his bottle of milk and went his way. I suppose that was why he looked so unwell when I stood, nearly five years later, by the barrow in the Portobello Road and said in easy tones, "Hallo, George!"

The Haystack Murder was one of the notorious crimes of that year.

My friends said, "A girl who had everything to live for."

After a search that lasted twenty hours, when my body was found, the evening papers said, "'Needle' is found: in haystack!"

Kathleen, speaking from that Catholic point of view which takes some getting used to, said, "She was at Confession only the day before she died – wasn't she lucky?"

The poor byre-hand who sold us the milk was grilled for hour after hour by the local police, and later by Scotland Yard.

So was George. He admitted walking as far as the haystack with me, but he denied lingering there.

"You hadn't seen your friend for ten years?" the Inspector asked him.

"That's right," said George.

"And you didn't stop to have a chat?"

"No. We'd arranged to meet later at dinner. My cousin was waiting for the milk, I couldn't stop."

The old soul, his cousin, swore that he hadn't been gone more than ten minutes in all, and she believed it to the day of her death a few months later. There was the microscopic evidence of hay on George's jacket, of course, but the same evidence was on every man's jacket in the district that fine harvest year. Unfortunately, the byre-man's hands were even brawnier and mightier than George's. The marks on my wrists had been done by such hands, so the laboratory charts indicated when my post-mortem was all completed. But the wrist-marks weren't enough to pin down the crime to either man. If I hadn't been wearing my long-sleeved cardigan, it was said, the bruises might have matched up properly with someone's fingers.

Kathleen, to prove that George had absolutely no motive, told the police that she was engaged to him. George thought this a little foolish. They checked up on his life in Africa, right back to his living with Matilda. But the marriage didn't come out – who would think of looking up registers in the Congo? Not that this would have proved any motive for murder. All the same, George was relieved when the inquiries were over without the marriage to Matilda being disclosed. He was able to have his nervous breakdown at the same time as Kathleen had hers, and they recovered together and got married, long after the police had shifted their inquiries to an Air Force camp five miles from Kathleen's aunt's home. Only a lot of excitement and drinks came of those investigations. The Haystack Murder was one of the unsolved crimes that year.

Shortly afterwards the byre-hand emigrated to Canada to start afresh, with the help of Skinny who felt sorry for him.

After seeing George taken away home by Kathleen that Saturday in the Portobello Road, I thought that perhaps I might be seeing more of him in similar circumstances. The next Saturday I looked out for him, and at last there he was, without Kathleen, half-worried, half-hopeful.

I dashed his hopes. I said, "Hallo, George!"

He looked in my direction, rooted in the midst of the flowing market-mongers in that convivial street. I thought to myself, "He looks as if he had a mouthful of hay." It was the new bristly maize-coloured beard and moustache surrounding his great mouth which suggested the thought, gay and lyrical as life.

"Hallo, George!" I said again.

I might have been inspired to say more on that agreeable morning, but he didn't wait. He was away down a side street and along another street and down one more, zigzag, as far and as devious as he could take himself from the Portobello Road.

Nevertheless he was back again next week. Poor Kathleen had brought him in her car. She left it at the top of the street, and got out with him, holding him tight by the arm. It grieved me to see Kathleen ignoring the spread of scintillations on the stalls. I had myself seen a charming Battersea box quite to her taste, also a pair of enamelled silver earrings. But she took no notice of these wares, clinging close to George, and, poor Kathleen – I hate to say how she looked.

And George was haggard. His eyes seemed to have got smaller as if he had been recently in pain. He advanced up the road with Kathleen on his arm, letting himself lurch from side to side with his wife bobbing beside him, as the crowds asserted their rights of way.

"Oh, George!" I said. "You don't look at all well, George."

"Look!" said George. "Over there by the hardware barrow. That's Needle."

Kathleen was crying. "Come back home, dear," she said.

"Oh, you don't look well, George!" I said.

They took him to a nursing home. He was fairly quiet, except on Saturday mornings when they had a hard time of it to keep him indoors and away from the Portobello Road.

But a couple of months later he did escape. It was a Monday.

They searched for him in the Portobello Road, but actually he had gone off to Kent to the village near the scene of the Haystack Murder. There he went to the police and gave himself up, but they could tell from the way he was talking that there was something wrong with the man.

"I saw Needle in the Portobello Road three Saturdays running," he explained, "and they put me in a private ward but I got away while the nurses were seeing to the new patient. You remember the murder of Needle – well, I did it. Now you know the truth, and that will keep bloody Needle's mouth shut."

Dozens of poor mad fellows confess to every murder. The police obtained an ambulance to take him back to the nursing home. He wasn't there long. Kathleen gave up her shop and devoted herself to looking after him at home. But she found that the Saturday mornings were a strain. He insisted on going to see me in the Portobello Road and would come back to insist that he'd murdered Needle. Once he tried to tell her something about Matilda, but Kathleen was so kind and solicitous, I don't think he had the courage to remember what he had to say.

Skinny had always been rather reserved with George since the murder. But he was kind to Kathleen. It was he who persuaded them to emigrate to Canada so that George should be well out of reach of the Portobello Road.

George has recovered somewhat in Canada but of course he will never be the old George again, as Kathleen writes to Skinny. "That Haystack tragedy did for George," she writes. "I feel sorrier for George sometimes than I am for poor Needle. But I do often have Masses said for Needle's soul."

I doubt if George will ever see me again in the Portobello Road. He broods much over the crumpled snapshot he took of us on the haystack. Kathleen does not like the photograph, I don't wonder. For my part, I consider it quite a jolly snap, but I don't think we were any of us so lovely as we look in it, gazing blatantly over the ripe cornfields, Skinny with his humorous expression, I secure in my difference from the rest, Kathleen with her head prettily perched on her hand, each reflecting fearlessly in the face of George's camera the glory of the world, as if it would never pass.

THE BLACK MADONNA

When the Black Madonna was installed in the Church of the Sacred Heart the Bishop himself came to consecrate it. His long purple train was upheld by the two curliest of the choir. The day was favoured suddenly with thin October sunlight as he crossed the courtyard from the presbytery to the church, as the procession followed him chanting the Litany of the Saints: five priests in vestments of white heavy silk interwoven with glinting threads, four lay officials with straight red robes, then the confraternities and the tangled columns of the Mothers' Union.

The new town of Whitney Clay had a large proportion of Roman Catholics, especially among the nurses at the new hospital; and at the paper mills, too, there were many Catholics, drawn inland from Liverpool by the new housing estate; likewise, with the canning factories.

The Black Madonna had been given to the church by a recent convert. It was carved out of bog oak.

"They found the wood in the bog. Had been there hundreds of years. They sent for the sculptor right away by phone. He went over to Ireland and carved it there and then. You see, he had to do it while it was still wet."

"Looks a bit like contemporary art."

"Nah, that's not contemporary art, it's old-fashioned. If you'd ever seen contemporary work you'd *know* it was old-fashioned."

"Looks like contemp –"

"It's old-*fashioned*. Else how'd it get sanctioned to be put up?"

"It's not so nice as the Immaculate Conception at Lourdes. That lifts you up."

Everyone got used, eventually, to the Black Madonna with her square hands and straight carved draperies. There was a movement to dress it up in vestments, or at least a lace veil.

"She looks a bit gloomy, Father, don't you think?"

"No," said the priest, "I think it looks fine. If you start dressing it up in cloth you'll spoil the line."

Sometimes people came from London especially to see the Black Madonna, and these were not Catholics; they were, said the priest, probably no religion at all, poor souls, though gifted with faculties. They came, as if to a museum, to see the line of the Black Madonna which must not be spoiled by vestments.

The new town of Whitney Clay had swallowed up the old village. One or two cottages with double dormer windows, an inn called "The Tyger", a Methodist chapel and three small shops represented the village; the three shops were already threatened by the Council; the Methodists were fighting to keep their chapel. Only the double dormer cottages and the inn were protected by the Nation and so had to be suffered by the Town Planning Committee.

The town was laid out like geometry in squares, arcs (to allow for the by-pass) and isosceles triangles, breaking off, at one point, to skirt the old village which, from the aerial view, looked like a merry doodle on the page.

Manders Road was one side of a parallelogram of green-bordered streets. It was named after one of the founders of the canning concern, Manders' Figs in Syrup, and it comprised a row of shops and a long high block of flats named Cripps House after the late Sir Stafford Cripps who had laid the foundation stone. In flat twenty-two on the fifth floor of Cripps House lived Raymond and Lou Parker. Raymond Parker was a foreman at the motor works, and was on the management committee. He had been married for fifteen years to Lou, who was thirty-seven at the time that the miraculous powers of the Black Madonna came to be talked of.

Of the twenty-five couples who lived in Cripps House five were Catholics. All, except Raymond and Lou Parker, had children. A sixth family had recently been moved by the Council into one of the six-roomed houses because of the seven children besides the grandfather.

Raymond and Lou were counted lucky to have obtained their three-roomed flat although they had no children. People with children had priority; but their name had been on the waiting list for years, and some said Raymond had a pull with one of the Councillors who was a director of the motor works.

The Parkers were among the few tenants of Cripps House who owned a motorcar. They did not, like most of their neighbours, have a television receiver, for being childless they had been able to afford to expand themselves in the way of taste, so that their habits differed slightly and their amusements considerably, from those of their neighbours. The Parkers went to the pictures only when the *Observer* had praised the film; they considered television not their sort of thing; they adhered to their religion; they voted Labour; they believed that the twentieth century was the best so far; they assented to the doctrine of original sin; they frequently applied the word "Victorian" to ideas and people they did not like – for instance, when a local Town Councillor resigned his office Raymond said, "He had to go. He's Victorian. And far too young for the job"; and Lou said Jane Austen's books were too Victorian; and anyone who opposed the abolition of capital punishment was Victorian. Raymond took the *Reader's Digest*, a magazine called *Motoring* and the *Catholic Herald*. Lou took the *Queen*, *Woman's Own* and *Life*. Their daily paper was the *News Chronicle*. They read two books apiece each week. Raymond preferred travel books; Lou liked novels.

For the first five years of their married life they had been worried about not having children. Both had submitted themselves to medical tests as a result of which Lou had a course of injections. These were unsuccessful. It had been a disappointment since both came from large sprawling Catholic families. None of their married brothers and sisters had less than three children. One of Lou's sisters, now widowed, had eight; they sent her a pound a week.

Their flat in Cripps House had three rooms and a kitchen. All round them their neighbours were saving up to buy houses. A council flat, once obtained, was a mere platform in space to further the progress of the rocket. This ambition was not shared by Raymond and Lou; they were not only content, they were delighted, with these civic chambers, and indeed took something of an aristocratic view of them, not without a self-conscious feeling of being free, in this particular, from the prejudices of that middle class to which they as good as belonged. "One day," said Lou, "it will be the thing to live in a council flat."

They were eclectic as to their friends. Here, it is true, they differed slightly from each other. Raymond was for inviting the Ackleys to meet the Farrells. Mr Ackley was an accountant at the Electricity Board. Mr and Mrs Farrell were respectively a sorter at Manders' Figs in Syrup and an usherette at the Odeon.

"After all," argued Raymond, "they're all Catholics."

"Ah well," said Lou, "but now, their interests are different. The Farrells wouldn't know what the Ackleys were talking about. The Ackleys like politics. The Farrells like to tell jokes. I'm not a snob, only sensible."

"Oh, please yourself." For no one could call Lou a snob, and everyone knew she was sensible.

Their choice of acquaintance was wide by reason of their active church membership: that is to say, they were members of various guilds and confraternities. Raymond was a sidesman, and he also organized the weekly football lottery in aid of the Church Decoration Fund. Lou felt rather out of things when the Mothers' Union met and had special Masses, for the Mothers' Union was the only group she did not qualify for. Having been a nurse before her marriage she was, however, a member of the Nurses' Guild.

Thus, most of their Catholic friends came from different departments of life. Others, connected with the motor works where Raymond was a foreman, were of different social grades to which Lou was more alive than Raymond. He let her have her way, as a rule, when it came to a question of which would mix with which.

A dozen Jamaicans were taken on at the motor works. Two came into Raymond's department. He invited them to the flat one evening to have coffee. They were unmarried, very polite and black. The quiet one was called Henry Pierce and the talkative one, Oxford St John. Lou, to Raymond's surprise and pleasure, decided that all their acquaintance, from top to bottom, must meet Henry and Oxford. All along he had known she was not a snob, only sensible, but he had rather feared she would consider the mixing of their new black and their old white friends not sensible.

"I'm glad you like Henry and Oxford," he said. "I'm glad we're able to introduce them to so many people." For the dark pair had, within a month, spent nine evenings at Cripps House; they had met accountants, teachers, packers and sorters. Only Tina Farrell, the usherette, had not seemed to understand the quality of these occasions: "Quite nice chaps, them darkies, when you get to know them."

"You mean Jamaicans," said Lou. "Why shouldn't they be nice? They're no different from anyone else."

"Yes, yes, that's what I mean," said Tina.

"We're all equal," stated Lou. "Don't forget there are black Bishops."

"Jesus, I never said we were the equal of a Bishop," Tina said, very bewildered.

"Well, don't call them darkies."

Sometimes, on summer Sunday afternoons Raymond and Lou took their friends for a run in their car, ending up at a riverside roadhouse. The first time they turned up with Oxford and Henry they felt defiant; but there were no objections, there was no trouble at all. Soon the dark pair ceased to be a novelty. Oxford St John took up with a pretty red-haired bookkeeper, and Henry Pierce, missing his companion, spent more of his time at the Parkers' flat. Lou and Raymond had planned to spend their two weeks' summer holiday in London. "Poor Henry," said Lou. "He'll miss us."

Once you brought him out he was not so quiet as you thought at first. Henry was twenty-four, desirous of knowledge in all fields, shining very much in eyes, skin, teeth, which made him seem all the more eager. He called out the maternal in Lou, and to some extent the avuncular in Raymond. Lou used to love him when he read out lines from his favourite poems which he had copied into an exercise book.

> Haste thee, nymph, and bring with thee
> Jest and youthful jollity,
> Sport that . . .

Lou would interrupt: "You should say jest, jollity – not yest, yollity."

"Jest," he said carefully. "And laughter holding both his sides," he continued. "*Laughter* – hear that, Lou? – *laughter*. That's what the human race was made for. Those folks that go round gloomy, Lou, they . . ."

Lou loved this talk. Raymond puffed his pipe benignly. After Henry had gone Raymond would say what a pity it was such an intelligent young fellow had lapsed. For Henry had been brought up in a Roman Catholic mission. He had, however, abandoned religion. He was fond of saying, "The superstition of today is the science of yesterday."

"I can't allow," Raymond would say, "that the Catholic Faith is superstition. I can't allow that."

"He'll return to the Church one day" – this was Lou's contribution, whether Henry was present or not. If she said it in front of Henry he would give her an angry look. These were the only occasions when Henry lost his cheerfulness and grew quiet again.

Raymond and Lou prayed for Henry, that he might regain his faith. Lou said her rosary three times a week before the Black Madonna.

"He'll miss us when we go on our holidays."

Raymond telephoned to the hotel in London. "Have you a single room for a young gentleman accompanying Mr and Mrs Parker?" He added, "A coloured gentleman." To his pleasure a room was available, and to his relief there was no objection to Henry's colour.

They enjoyed their London holiday, but it was somewhat marred by a visit to that widowed sister of Lou's to whom she allowed a pound a week towards the rearing of her eight children. Lou had not seen her sister Elizabeth for nine years.

They went to her one day towards the end of their holiday. Henry sat at the back of the car beside a large suitcase stuffed with old clothes for Elizabeth. Raymond at the wheel kept saying, "Poor Elizabeth – eight kids," which irritated Lou, though she kept her peace.

Outside the underground station at Victoria Park, where they stopped to ask the way, Lou felt a strange sense of panic. Elizabeth lived in a very downward quarter of Bethnal Green, and in the past nine years since she had seen her Lou's memory of the shabby ground-floor rooms with their peeling walls and bare boards, had made a kinder nest for itself. Sending off the postal order to her sister each week she had gradually come to picture the habitation at Bethnal Green in an almost monastic light; it would be bare but well-scrubbed, spotless, and shining with Brasso and holy poverty. The floor-boards gleamed. Elizabeth was grey-haired, lined, but neat. The children were well behaved, sitting down betimes to their broth in two rows along an almost refectory table. It was not till they had reached Victoria Park that Lou felt the full force of the fact that everything would be different from what she had imagined. "It may have gone down since I was last there," she said to Raymond who had never visited Elizabeth before.

"What's gone down?"

"Poor Elizabeth's place."

Lou had not taken much notice of Elizabeth's dull little monthly letters, almost illiterate, for Elizabeth, as she herself always said, was not much of a scholar.

> James is at another job I hope that's the finish of the bother I had my blood pressure there was a Health visitor very nice. Also the assistance they sent my Dinner all the time and for the kids at home they call it meals on Wheels. I pray to the Almighty that James is well out of his bother he never lets on at sixteen their all the same never open his mouth but Gods eyes are not shut. Thanks for P.O. you will be rewarded your affect sister Elizabeth.

Lou tried to piece together in her mind the gist of nine years' such letters. James was the eldest; she supposed he had been in trouble.

"I ought to have asked Elizabeth about young James," said Lou. "She wrote to me last year that he was in a bother, there was talk of him being sent away, but I didn't take it in at the time, I was busy."

"You can't take everything on your shoulders," said Raymond. "You do very well by Elizabeth." They had pulled up outside the house where Elizabeth lived on the ground floor. Lou looked at the chipped paint, the dirty windows and torn grey-white curtains and was reminded with startling clarity of her hopeless childhood in Liverpool from which, miraculously, hope had lifted her, and had come true, for the nuns had got her that job; and she had trained as a nurse among white-painted beds, and white shining walls, and tiles, hot water everywhere and Dettol without stint. When she had first married she had wanted all white-painted furniture that you could wash and liberate from germs; but Raymond had been for oak, he did not understand the pleasure of hygiene and new enamel paint, for his upbringing had been orderly, he had been accustomed to a lounge suite and autumn tints in the front room all his life. And now Lou stood and looked at the outside of Elizabeth's place and felt she had gone right back.

On the way back to the hotel Lou chattered with relief that it was over. "Poor Elizabeth, she hasn't had much of a chance. I liked little Francis, what did you think of little Francis, Ray?"

Raymond did not like being called Ray, but he made no

objection for he knew that Lou had been under a strain. Elizabeth had not been very pleasant. She had expressed admiration for Lou's hat, bag, gloves and shoes which were all navy blue, but she had used an accusing tone. The house had been smelly and dirty. "I'll show you round," Elizabeth had said in a tone of mock refinement, and they were forced to push through a dark narrow passage behind her skinny form till they came to the big room where the children slept. A row of old iron beds each with a tumble of dark blanket rugs, no sheets. Raymond was indignant at the sight and hoped that Lou was not feeling upset. He knew very well Elizabeth had a decent living income from a number of public sources, and was simply a slut, one of those who would not help themselves.

"Ever thought of taking a job, Elizabeth?" he had said, and immediately realized his stupidity. But Elizabeth took her advantage. "What d'you mean? *I'm* not going to leave my kids in no nursery. *I'm* not going to send them to no home. What kids need these days is a good home life and that's what they get." And she added, "God's eyes are not shut," in a tone which was meant for him, Raymond, to get at him for doing well in life.

Raymond distributed half-crowns to the younger children and deposited on the table half-crowns for those who were out playing in the street.

"Goin" already?" said Elizabeth in her tone of reproach. But she kept eyeing Henry with interest, and the reproachful tone was more or less a routine affair.

"You from the States?" Elizabeth said to Henry.

Henry sat on the edge of his sticky chair and answered,

no, from Jamaica, while Raymond winked at him to cheer him.

"During the war there was a lot of boys like you from the States," Elizabeth said, giving him a sideways look.

Henry held out his hand to the second youngest child, a girl of seven, and said, "Come talk to me."

The child said nothing, only dipped into the box of sweets which Lou had brought.

"Come talk," said Henry.

Elizabeth laughed. "If she does talk you'll be sorry you ever asked. She's got a tongue in her head, that one. You should hear her cheeking up to the teachers." Elizabeth's bones jerked with laughter among her loose clothes. There was a lopsided double bed in the corner, and beside it a table cluttered with mugs, tins, a comb and brush, a number of hair curlers, a framed photograph of the Sacred Heart, and also Raymond noticed what he thought erroneously to be a box of contraceptives. He decided to say nothing to Lou about this; he was quite sure she must have observed other things which he had not; possibly things of a more distressing nature.

Lou's chatter on the way back to the hotel had a touch of hysteria. "Raymond, dear," she said in her most chirpy West End voice, "I simply *had* to give the poor dear *all* my next week's housekeeping money. We shall have to starve, darling, when we get home. That's *simply* what we shall have to do."

"OK," said Raymond.

"I ask you," Lou shrieked, "what else could I do, what *could* I do?"

"Nothing at all," said Raymond, "but what you've done."

"My own *sister*, my dear," said Lou; "and did you see the

way she had her hair bleached? – All streaky, and she used to have a lovely head of hair."

"I wonder if she tries to raise herself?" said Raymond. "With all those children she could surely get better accommodation if only she –"

"That sort," said Henry, leaning forward from the back of the car, "never moves. It's the slum mentality, man. Take some folks I've seen back home –"

"There's no comparison," Lou snapped suddenly, "this is quite a different case."

Raymond glanced at her in surprise; Henry sat back, offended. Lou was thinking wildly, what a cheek *him* talking like a snob. At least Elizabeth's white.

Their prayers for the return of faith to Henry Pierce were so far answered in that he took a tubercular turn which was followed by a religious one. He was sent off to a sanatorium in Wales with a promise from Lou and Raymond to visit him before Christmas. Meantime, they applied themselves to Our Lady for the restoration of Henry's health.

Oxford St John, whose love affair with the red-haired girl had come to grief, now frequented their flat, but he could never quite replace Henry in their affections. Oxford was older and less refined than Henry. He would stand in front of the glass in their kitchen and tell himself, "Man, you just a big black bugger." He kept referring to himself as black, which of course he was, Lou thought, but it was not the thing to say. He stood in the doorway with his arms and smile thrown wide: "I am black but comely, O ye daughters of Jerusalem." And once, when Raymond was out, Oxford brought the conversation round to that question of being black *all over*, which made Lou very uncomfortable and she kept looking at the clock and dropped stitches in her knitting.

Three times a week when she went to the black Our Lady with her rosary to ask for the health of Henry Pierce, she asked also that Oxford St John would get another job in another town, for she did not like to make objections, telling her feelings to Raymond; there were no objections to make that you could put your finger on. She could not very well complain that Oxford was common; Raymond despised snobbery, and so did she, it was a very delicate question. She was amazed when, within three weeks, Oxford announced that he was thinking of looking for a job in Manchester.

Lou said to Raymond, "Do you know, there's something in what they say about the bog-oak statue in the church."

"There may be," said Raymond. "People say so."

Lou could not tell him how she had petitioned the removal of Oxford St John. But when she got a letter from Henry Pierce to say he was improving, she told Raymond, "You see, we asked for Henry to get back the Faith, and so he did. Now we ask for his recovery and he's improving."

"He's having good treatment at the sanatorium," Raymond said. But he added, "Of course we'll have to keep up the prayers." He himself, though not a rosary man, knelt before the Black Madonna every Saturday evening after Benediction to pray for Henry Pierce.

Whenever they saw Oxford he was talking of leaving Whitney Clay. Raymond said, "He's making a big mistake going to Manchester. A big place can be very lonely. I hope he'll change his mind."

"He won't," said Lou, so impressed was she now by the powers of the Black Madonna. She was good and tired of Oxford St John with his feet up on her cushions, and calling himself a nigger.

"We'll miss him," said Raymond, "he's such a cheery big soul."

"We will," said Lou. She was reading the parish magazine, which she seldom did, although she was one of the voluntary workers who sent them out, addressing hundreds of wrappers every month. She had vaguely noticed, in previous numbers, various references to the Black Madonna, how she had granted this or that favour. Lou had heard that people sometimes came from neighbouring parishes to pray at the Church of the Sacred Heart because of the statue. Some said they came from all over England, but whether this was to admire the art-work or to pray, Lou was not sure. She gave her attention to the article in the parish magazine:

> While not wishing to make excessive claims . . . many prayers answered and requests granted to the Faithful in an exceptional way . . . two remarkable cures effected, but medical evidence is, of course, still in reserve, a certain lapse of time being necessary to ascertain permanency of cure. The first of these cases was a child of twelve suffering from leukaemia . . . The second . . . While not desiring to create a *cultus* where none is due, we must remember it is always our duty to honour Our Blessed Lady, the dispenser of all graces, to whom we owe . . .
>
> Another aspect of the information received by the Father Rector concerning our "Black Madonna" is one

pertaining to childless couples of which three cases have come to his notice. In each case the couple claim to have offered constant devotion to the "Black Madonna", and in two of the cases specific requests were made for the favour of a child. In *all* cases the prayers were answered. The proud parents . . . It should be the loving duty of every parishioner to make a special thanksgiving . . . The Father Rector will be grateful for any further information . . .

"Look, Raymond," said Lou. "Read this."

They decided to put in for a baby to the Black Madonna.

The following Saturday, when they drove to the church for Benediction Lou jangled her rosary. Raymond pulled up outside the church. "Look here, Lou," he said, "do you want a baby in any case?" – for he partly thought she was only putting the Black Madonna to the test – "Do you want a child, after all these years?"

This was a new thought to Lou. She considered her neat flat and tidy routine, the entertaining with her good coffee cups, the weekly papers and the library books, the tastes which they would not have been able to cultivate had they had a family of children. She thought of her nice young looks which everyone envied, and her freedom of movement.

"Perhaps we should try," she said. "God won't give us a child if we aren't meant to have one."

"We have to make some decisions for ourselves," he said. "And to tell you the truth if *you* don't want a child, *I* don't."

"There's no harm in praying for one," she said.

"You have to be careful what you pray for," he said. "You mustn't tempt Providence."

She thought of her relatives, and Raymond's, all married with children. She thought of her sister Elizabeth with her eight, and remembered that one who cheeked up to the teachers, so pretty and sulky and shabby, and she remembered the fat baby Francis sucking his dummy and clutching Elizabeth's bony neck.

"I don't see why I shouldn't have a baby," said Lou.

Oxford St John departed at the end of the month. He promised to write, but they were not surprised when weeks passed and they had no word. "I don't suppose we shall ever hear from him again," said Lou. Raymond thought he detected satisfaction in her voice, and would have thought she was getting snobbish as women do as they get older, losing sight of their ideals, had she not gone on to speak of Henry Pierce. Henry had written to say he was nearly cured, but had been advised to return to the West Indies.

"We must go and see him," said Lou. "We promised. What about the Sunday after next?"

"OK," said Raymond.

It was the Saturday before that Sunday when Lou had her first sick turn. She struggled out of bed to attend Benediction, but had to leave suddenly during the service was sick behind the church in the presbytery yard. Raymond took her home, though she protested against cutting out her rosary to the Black Madonna.

"After only six weeks!" she said, and she could hardly tell whether her sickness was due to excitement or nature.

"Only six weeks ago," she said – and her voice had a touch of its old Liverpool – "did we go to that Black Madonna and the prayer's answered, see."

Raymond looked at her in awe as he held the bowl for her sickness. "Are you sure?" he said.

She was well enough next day to go to visit Henry in the sanatorium. He was fatter and, she thought, a little coarser: and tough in his manner, as if once having been nearly disembodied he was not going to let it happen again. He was leaving the country very soon. He promised to come and see them before he left. Lou barely skimmed through his next letter before handing it over to Raymond.

Their visitors, now, were ordinary white ones. "Not so colourful," Raymond said, "as Henry and Oxford were." Then he looked embarrassed lest he should seem to be making a joke about the word coloured.

"Do you miss the niggers?" said Tina Farrell, and Lou forgot to correct her.

Lou gave up most of her church work in order to sew and knit for the baby. Raymond gave up the *Reader's Digest*. He applied for promotion and got it; he became a departmental manager. The flat was now a waiting-room for next summer, after the baby was born, when they would put down the money for a house. They hoped for one of the new houses on a building site on the outskirts of the town.

"We shall need a garden," Lou explained to her friends. "I'll join the Mothers' Union," she thought. Meantime the spare bedroom was turned into a nursery. Raymond made a cot, regardless that some of the neighbours complained of the hammering. Lou prepared a cradle, trimmed it with frills.

She wrote to her relatives; she wrote to Elizabeth, sent her five pounds, and gave notice that there would be no further weekly payments, seeing that they would now need every penny.

"She doesn't require it, anyway," said Raymond. "The Welfare State looks after people like Elizabeth." And he told Lou about the contraceptives he thought he had seen on the table by the double bed. Lou became very excited about this. "How did you know they were contraceptives? What did they look like? Why didn't you tell me before? What a cheek, calling herself a Catholic, do you think she has a man, then?"

Raymond was sorry he had mentioned the subject.

"Don't worry, dear, don't upset yourself, dear."

"And she told me she goes to Mass every Sunday, and all the kids go excepting James. No wonder he's got into trouble with an example like that. I might have known, with her peroxide hair. A pound a week I've been sending up to now, that's fifty-two pounds a year. I would never have done it, calling herself a Catholic with birth control by her bedside."

"Don't upset yourself, dear."

Lou prayed to the Black Madonna three times a week for a safe delivery and a healthy child. She gave her story to the Father Rector who announced it in the next parish magazine. "Another case has come to light of the kindly favour of our 'Black Madonna' towards a childless couple . . ." Lou recited her rosary before the statue until it was difficult for her to kneel, and, when she stood, could not see her feet. The Mother of God with her black bog-oaken drapery, her high black cheekbones and square hands looked more virginal than ever to Lou as she stood counting her beads in front of her stomach.

She said to Raymond, "If it's a girl we must have Mary as one of the names. But not the first name, it's too ordinary."

"Please yourself, dear," said Raymond. The doctor had told him it might be a difficult birth.

"Thomas, if it's a boy," she said, "after my uncle. But if it's a girl I'd like something fancy for a first name."

He thought, Lou's slipping, she didn't used to say that word, fancy.

"What about Dawn?" she said. "I like the sound of Dawn. Then Mary for a second name. Dawn Mary Parker, it sounds sweet."

"Dawn! That's not a Christian name," he said. Then he told her, "Just as you please, dear."

"Or Thomas Parker," she said.

She had decided to go into the maternity wing of the hospital like everyone else. But near the time she let Raymond change her mind, since he kept saying, "At your age, dear, it might be more difficult than for the younger women. Better book a private ward, we'll manage the expense."

In fact, it was a very easy birth, a girl. Raymond was allowed in to see Lou in the late afternoon. She was half asleep. "The nurse will take you to see the baby in the nursery ward," she told him. "She's lovely, but terribly red."

"They're always red at birth," said Raymond.

He met the nurse in the corridor. "Any chance of seeing the baby? My wife said . . ."

She looked flustered. "I'll get the Sister," she said.

"Oh, I don't want to give any trouble, only my wife said –"

"That's all right. Wait here, Mr Parker."

The Sister appeared, a tall grave woman. Raymond thought her to be short-sighted for she seemed to look at him fairly closely before she bade him follow her.

The baby was round and very red, with dark curly hair.

"Fancy her having hair. I thought they were born bald," said Raymond.

"They sometimes have hair at birth," said the Sister.

"She's very red in colour." Raymond began comparing his child with those in the other cots. "Far more so than the others."

"Oh, that will wear off."

Next day he found Lou in a half-stupor. She had been given a strong sedative following an attack of screaming hysteria. He sat by her bed, bewildered. Presently a nurse beckoned him from the door. "Will you have a word with Matron?"

"Your wife is upset about her baby," said the matron. "You see, the colour. She's a beautiful baby, perfect. It's a question of the colour."

"I noticed the baby was red," said Raymond, "but the nurse said –"

"Oh, the red will go. It changes, you know. But the baby will certainly be brown, if not indeed black, as indeed we think she will be. A beautiful healthy child."

"Black?" said Raymond.

"Yes, indeed we think so, indeed I must say, certainly so," said the matron. "We did not expect your wife to take it so badly when we told her. We've had plenty of dark babies here, but most of the mothers expect it."

"There must be a mix-up. You must have mixed up the babies," said Raymond.

"There's no question of mix-up," said the matron sharply. "We'll soon settle that. We've had some of *that* before."

"But neither of us are dark," said Raymond. "You've seen my wife. You see me –"

"That's something you must work out for yourselves. I'd have a word with the doctor if I were you. But whatever conclusion you come to, please don't upset your wife at this stage. She has already refused to feed the child, says it isn't hers, which is ridiculous."

"Was it Oxford St John?" said Raymond.

"Raymond, the doctor told you not to come here upsetting me. I'm feeling terrible."

"Was it Oxford St John?"

"Clear out of here, you swine, saying things like that."

He demanded to be taken to see the baby, as he had done every day for a week. The nurses were gathered round it, neglecting the squalling whites in the other cots for the sight of their darling black. She was indeed quite black, with a woolly crop and tiny negroid nostrils. She had been baptised that morning, though not in her parents' presence. One of the nurses had stood as godmother.

The nurses dispersed in a flurry as Raymond approached. He looked hard at the baby. It looked back with its black button eyes. He saw the name-tab round its neck, "Dawn Mary Parker."

He got hold of a nurse in the corridor. "Look here, you just take that name Parker off that child's neck. The name's not Parker, it isn't my child."

The nurse said, "Get away, we're busy."

"There's just a *chance*," said the doctor to Raymond, "that if there's ever been black blood in your family or your wife's, it's coming out now. It's a very long chance. I've never known it happen in my experience, but I've heard of cases, I could read them up."

"There's nothing like that in my family," said Raymond. He thought of Lou, the obscure Liverpool antecedents. The parents had died before he had met Lou.

"It could be several generations back," said the doctor.

Raymond went home, avoiding the neighbours who would stop him to inquire after Lou. He rather regretted smashing up the cot in his first fury. That was something low coming out in him. But again, when he thought of the tiny black hands of the baby with their pink fingernails he did not regret smashing the cot.

He was successful in tracing the whereabouts of Oxford St John. Even before he heard the result of Oxford's blood test he said to Lou, "Write and ask your relations if there's been any black blood in the family."

"Write and ask *yours*," she said.

She refused to look at the black baby. The nurses fussed round it all day, and came to report its progress to Lou.

"Pull yourself together, Mrs Parker, she's a lovely child."

"You must care for your infant," said the priest.

"You don't know what I'm suffering," Lou said.

"In the name of God," said the priest, "if you're a Catholic Christian you've got to expect to suffer."

"I can't go against my nature," said Lou. "I can't be expected to –"

Raymond said to her one day in the following week, "The blood tests are all right, the doctor says."

"What do you mean, all right?"

"Oxford's blood and the baby's don't tally, and –"

"Oh, shut up," she said. "The baby's black and your blood tests can't make it white."

"No," he said. He had fallen out with his mother, through his inquiries whether there had been coloured blood in his family. "The doctor says," he said, "that these black mixtures sometimes occur in seaport towns. It might have been generations back."

"One thing," said Lou. "I'm not going to take that child back to the flat."

"You'll have to," he said.

Elizabeth wrote her a letter which Raymond intercepted:

"Dear Lou Raymond is asking if we have any blacks in the family well thats funny you have a coloured God is not asleep. There was that Flinn cousin Tommy at Liverpool he was very dark they put it down to the past a nigro off a ship that would be before our late Mothers Time God rest her soul she would turn in her grave you shoud have kept up your bit to me whats a pound a Week to you. It was on our fathers side the colour and Mary Flinn you remember at the dairy was dark remember her hare was like nigro hare it must be back in the olden days the nigro some ansester but it is only nature. I thank the almighty it has missed my kids and your hubby must think it was that nigro you was showing off when you came to my place. I wish you all the best as a widow with kids you shoud send my money as per usual your affec sister Elizabeth."

"I gather from Elizabeth," said Raymond to Lou, "that there *was* some element of colour in your family. Of course, you couldn't be expected to know about it. I do think, though, that some kind of record should be kept."

"Oh, shut *up*," said Lou. "The baby's black and nothing can make it white."

Two days before Lou left the hospital she had a visitor, although she had given instructions that no one except Raymond should be let in to see her. This lapse she attributed to the nasty curiosity of the nurses, for it was Henry Pierce come to say goodbye before embarkation. He stayed less than five minutes.

"Why, Mrs Parker, your visitor didn't stay long," said the nurse.

"No, I soon got rid of him. I thought I made it clear to you that I didn't want to see anyone. You shouldn't have let him in."

"Oh, sorry, Mrs Parker, but the young gentleman looked so upset when we told him so. He said he was going abroad and it was his last chance, he might never see you again. He said, "How's the baby?", and we said, 'Tip-top.'"

"I know what's in your mind," said Lou. "But it isn't true. I've got the blood tests."

"Oh, Mrs Parker, I wouldn't suggest for a minute . . ."

"She must have went with one of they niggers that used to come."

Lou could never be sure if that was what she heard from the doorways and landings as she climbed the stairs of Cripps House, the neighbours hushing their conversation as she approached.

"I can't take to the child. Try as I do, I simply can't even like it."

"Nor me," said Raymond. "Mind you, if it was anyone else's child I would think it was all right. It's just the thought of it being mine, and people thinking it isn't."

"That's just it," she said.

One of Raymond's colleagues had asked him that day how his friends Oxford and Henry were getting on. Raymond had to look twice before he decided that the question was innocent. But one never knew . . . Already Lou and Raymond had approached the adoption society. It was now only a matter of waiting for word.

"If that child was mine," said Tina Farrell, "I'd never part with her. I wish we could afford to adopt another. She's the loveliest little darkie in the world."

"You wouldn't think so," said Lou, "if she really was yours. Imagine it for yourself, waking up to find you've had a black baby that everyone thinks has a nigger for its father."

"It *would* be a shock," Tina said, and tittered.

"We've got the blood tests," said Lou quickly.

Raymond got a transfer to London. They got word about the adoption very soon.

"We've done the right thing," said Lou. "Even the priest had to agree with that, considering how strongly we felt against keeping the child."

"Oh, he said it was a good thing?"

"No, not a *good* thing. In fact he said it would have been a good thing if we could have kept the baby. But failing that, we did the *right* thing. Apparently, there's a difference."

THE THING ABOUT POLICE STATIONS

In the first place the boy did not wish to go to the police station to inquire for his aunt's little spotted dog. He was sorry she had lost the dog, but he didn't like police stations.

"I've got a thing about police stations," he explained.

"Your generation has things about everything," she said, "and the only way to conquer your thing about police stations is to go into one."

He felt sure this was a fallacy. He was eighteen. He had already met a girl who had failed to get over her thing about post offices. But his aunt was upset about the dog, and so he went.

It was a dark afternoon in the dead of January. He took a long long time to come to the end of the icy zig-zag lanes which led across the countryside to the police station. The lanes crossed land which had been quarried and abandoned about twenty years ago. Nature had never quite reclaimed itself here. In summer, it was true, when they were covered with tall tough grass and off-white patches of ladies' lace, those gaping pits had an appearance of normality. But in winter they were black thorny wounds in the earth. He feared them greatly and secretly, and always walked stealthily there, so that he would not be noticed by these terrible quarries.

His aunt always made light of that walk along the quarry lanes: "Only a five minutes' walk."

He didn't know what she meant by five minutes. Anyhow, the sky was dark by the time he reached the police station, the afternoon was gone.

He entered, and saw two uniformed men sitting behind a high counter. One of them was writing in a book. For a long long time neither of them took any notice of his presence, and he wondered if he ought to cough, or say something. Should he say, "Excuse me, it's about a little white dog with black spots?" Or should he say, "May I speak to the officer in charge?" He remembered that when he was a schoolboy one of his teachers used often to say, "Discretion is the better part of valour." He kept his peace and waited.

The policeman who was not writing in the book was resting his elbows on the counter, he was resting his chin in his hands and his eyes on mystical space. He was big-featured and broody, like a displaced Viking.

Behind the men was a door, the top half of which was frosted glass. Someone was behind it. The young man could see the shadow moving.

At length, a loud voice came from behind this door, "No. 292 this way! No. 292 this way!"

Immediately the Viking straightened up. The other policeman threw down his pen. They lifted the end-flap of the counter and together approached the boy.

"No. 292 this way," said the Viking to the youth. "No. 292 this way," the other repeated.

He was surprised. Clearly they expected him to follow them and he was about to open his mouth to protest when the adage "Discretion is the better part of valour" seized his brain together with "Speech is silver but silence is golden." So he said nothing. But as he was offended by the tone of their address, he did not move. The Viking took him by the wrist and pulled him into the inner room, the other policeman following.

There were now three policemen. They sat on plain hard chairs on three sides of a table, while the young man stood on the fourth side, being watched by them.

After a long long time the third policeman, the one who had first called "No. 292 this way," made a note on some papers. Then he looked up and addressed the youth in his loud voice:

"There has been an unspeakable crime. Guilty or Not Guilty?"

He remembered "Nothing venture, nothing win" and spoke up.

"What crime?" he said.

"Use your logic, please," the policeman said. "We cannot speak about a crime which is unspeakable. Guilty or Not Guilty?"

"I demand a proper trial," said the boy. This was foolish, for what he should have said was, "I think there has been some misunderstanding". But he did not think of this in the stress of the moment, and in fact he felt a little proud of himself for thinking to demand a proper trial.

The Viking jumped to his feet immediately. "No. 292 for trial!" he shouted. A door at the far end of the room opened and three more policemen entered. They put handcuffs on the prisoner and led him away along a lot of corridors. After walking for at least half an hour they came to a cell. The boy was locked in.

All that night he thought to himself that his aunt would surely come in the morning and clear up the misunderstanding. He fancied she must already have applied for him at the police station, but evidently had found it closed.

In the morning a policeman unlocked his cell.

"Crust and water for 292," he said, thrusting a crust of bread and a mug of water into the prisoner's hands. The policeman disappeared before the boy could speak to him.

Some hours later the head policeman arrived, carrying some papers. He was very suave in his manner. Quickly, before he could speak, the young man put in, "I wish to see my aunt. Has she been inquiring for me?"

He bowed. "There *was* a lady," he said, "about a spotted dog."

"That's my aunt. Did she inquire for me?"

The chief of police bowed. "I believe so. But we explained that you preferred to stand your trial."

"There's been a misunderstanding."

"It will be cleared up at the trial. I have come to tell you that the trial will take place in three months' time. We detain you till then."

"That's irregular," the youth said smartly. "There's a Habeas Corpus Act –"

The policeman bowed. "It is obsolete," he said.

And so, for three months the young man of eighteen watched the sky above the roof behind the high window, dreadfully barred. The walls of his cell were pinky-grey, and there were hundreds of rats. The aunt said later, when he told her of the rats, that this couldn't be. The police are nothing if not hygienic in their habitat," she said. Maybe so, but still there were hundreds of rats.

Needless to say the boy was found guilty at the trial. His aunt, who had in the meantime found her little dog, gave evidence to the effect that he was incapable of an unspeakable crime, being incapable of almost everything. But the Prosecution pointed out that a) her evidence was suspect as she was a blood relation and b) it was impossible to admit evidence in connection with a crime too unspeakable to speak about. The judge had a square face with double-lens glasses. All the jury were policemen with double lenses. The youth wondered afterwards if he should have shouted out in Court, "I am innocent of the unspeakable crime," but perhaps they wouldn't have believed him.

He was sent away to the salt mines of somewhere for three months. Since his return the aunt kept on saying, "It could all have been avoided if you had only handled the situation with aplomb." Anyway, that is what happened, and her nephew still has a thing about police stations.

A HUNDRED AND ELEVEN YEARS WITHOUT A CHAUFFEUR

Grandmothers, great-grandfathers and all antecedents. Don't forget they lived ordinary lives, had pains, went to work, talked, busied themselves, had sex – full days and full nights as long as all that lasted. I see no reason to drool over them. They did not drool over us. They thought, if they wanted and could, of the future, the generations to come, but only in the most general terms, obviously, in the nature of things.

When they wrote memoirs and letters, we know that is not the whole story. When they left only their photographs and a few imputed sayings and habits, still less have we got the whole story. We have their birth and marriage records and their tombstones in some country churchyard, as in the case of my forebears.

When it came to producing photographs for my biographer, Joe, there was little to go on. I hadn't looked them over for at least twenty years. They had been tucked into a drawer in a spare bedroom together with a tiny musical box that still played a tinkly tune when wound up, a few old reels of black cotton, a tin box of Venus pencils (unused, a very useful find). There was also a piece of stone from an excavation of antiquity, but which? Other items.

I took out the photographs and spread them out on a table. Is that all? I could have sworn there had been more. In fact, I knew there had been more. Where were they all? Who on earth could have gone off with my old fusty photos, what use would anyone have had for them?

I looked at the photographs one by one, to make sure I wasn't dreaming. People, even one's friends, do go off with things. But their main objects of acquisition are books. Guests go off with books out of the guest-room, but not photos, not old photos of dull people of modest means.

Gladys was there, an aunt on my maternal side married to my mother's brother Jim. Jim was sitting with a hand on his knee, a watch-chain across his belly, while Gladys stood beside him, one hand on his shoulder. Beside Gladys was a photographer's prop in the form of a pillar surmounted by a bunch of flowers. Date, *circa* 1880.

Next, Mary-Ann, Nancy, Maud and my great grandmother Sarah Rowbottom, who lived to 105, and here shows that possibility already at sixty-five. They are wearing their best frocks, tight corseted waists, prominent busts, as breasts were called, lots of rows of lace and always a locket hanging round their neck with God knows whose photos, whose locks of hair, enclosed in those small breast-warmed cases. Mary-Ann, who was the first to get married, wore a dark brooch. Their hair was done up, all in order. Lower middle class of those days, aspiring. They were corn dealers and managed quite well.

They lie in Vicarage Road churchyard, Watford, every one, they are marked by two stones: Deeply Mourned.

I explained them one by one to Joe, and added what I knew of family lore.

Next came my mother, born 111 years back, dead these twenty-seven years. And a cousin whose name I can't recall but who, I know, was very ambitious. Alas, she never achieved her ambition, which was to own a Rolls Royce with a chauffeur to drive her from shop to shop, as was possible in those days. This cousin – what was her name? – oh, well, she became a Mrs Henderson, wife of an accountant, and got as far as Paris on the Golden Arrow one year. No Rolls, no chauffeur. But Mrs Henderson always said that she wanted one.

Now where was that other photo of Mrs Henderson, one that I remembered well because it was so uncharacteristically informal, where she was standing over her sewing machine? She was slightly bent, in profile, slim-waisted and handsome. Someone with a camera had caught her examining the bobbin of her machine, her beloved treadle-operated Singer. Something was wrong with the machine and Mrs Henderson – what *was* her name? – was looking intently at it. An enchanting photograph. It was gone. Someone had removed it.

The same with a few others I now remembered. My paternal grandmother from a Jewish family in Lithuania, very blonde and Polish looking, her hair piled and plaited, not at all Jewish to look at, unlike my grandfather with his lovely smile inside his beard; he was so like my father, who, however, was always clean shaven. My grandmother Henrietta's beautiful photograph was missing. I remembered her so well in the photograph, never having known her in the flesh. I remember the large space between the eyes which I have inherited. Blue eyes. Where has she gone?

I thought of all the people who had slept in this room and others who had been within easy access of it. Some dozens of friends over the years. Who would have an interest in those meaningless photographs? Sometimes, because I am a writer, journalists have been known to snaffle a photograph of myself without permission, but these old Victorian and Edwardian pictures, without even artistic merit . . . ?

I concentrated on the bundle of photographs that were left to me. They weren't a bad selection, enough to illustrate my long-ago origins and in some cases my memories. I gave them to Joe and put away the rest. I had other things to think of.

Damian de Dogherty – you mention Damian de Dogherty – Oh, my God, I haven't thought of him for five years. Before that he saw to it that I thought of him every month, if not every day. I lived in Paris at the time.

According to his spin, or rather, one of his spins, the family were Huguenots originating from Ireland, taking refuge in France; members of the family were later in the service of Maria Theresa of Austria who conferred on them a princedom. Being modest people they accepted to be merely barons and he, the last survivor of the family, was Baron Damian de Dogherty. Damian was, I must say, a lot of fun. That is, he was fun at the dinner table and of diminishing fun elsewhere. He was a positive bore on the beach where he would leave whatever companion he was with (he was two ways) and take his good slinky body after strange gods such as arose from the glittering sea.

One of Damian's many curious characteristics was his

habit of suddenly falling asleep. I believe it is called narcolepsy. It might be at a quiet meeting of friends sitting round a table drinking in a mild way, it might be in a library while he was taking notes from a book (he loved to study), or sitting beside you on a sofa. Suddenly, he would be gone into sleep. It was quite a healthy sleep, and eventually his friends gave up being alarmed. I always, vaguely in my mind, explained this trait as a reaction to reality; all in a moment, I felt, something would cause him to face an unacceptable truth, and he just tuned out. I still think I was right, there. His narcosis was partly, at least, psychological.

In my early acquaintance with Damian I took his story at its charming face value. I addressed him on the envelopes of my letters as Baron de Dogherty, strange as it sounded. His name was not to be found in any of the reference books for the titles and old families of Europe, although he claimed that it was to be found somewhere. This information, unsought, went unchecked so far as I was concerned. I had other things to do. According to those who had known him some years before, he had been married to a rich Peruvian girl. They had gone their separate ways. It was said she was a talented photographer, still practising in Paris. I took in this fact vaguely; only afterwards did I have some reason to bring it to mind.

I tried to get to his real personality but after a while I realized that there was none. He was, in fact, pure fake.

To a considerable extent I think Damian believed his own stories. He was trying to write an autobiography, for which reason, I think, he rang me or dropped in frequently.

"I've come to the bit when my aunt, la Comtesse

Clémentine de Vevey came to visit me at school in Switzerland."

"I believe you went to school in Salt Lake City," I said, having been so informed by one of his schoolmates.

"Oh, that was earlier."

In my role of his literary adviser I suggested that he should turn his autobiography into a novel. He adopted this suggestion.

Another strange fact: everybody liked to be with Damian while he was alive; he was greatly sought after for weekends, dinner parties and simple picnics in the country; however, in spite of his decided popularity, when he died he was not mourned in any sort of proportion to the force of his attractiveness in life. He was not grieved over at all. He was here, he made us smile, nobody believed a word he said, then he was gone.

Shortly after his death I was in a bookshop in Ghent, rummaging through some old prints. I came across a pile of photographs, all in quite ornate frames. People would buy these, the owner was explaining to me, precisely for the frames. "But personally," he said, "I also find the photographs very attractive, very nostalgic."

I found myself looking at my hard-working grandmother, my greataunts Nancy and Sally. There was Mary-Ann. And Sarah Rowbottom, stout and bold. And Gladys with a regal sash across her bosom.

But these were not the original faded sepia images. They were blacker and whiter, with an attempt at a sort of golden-brown haze.

"Where did these come from?" I said.

"I bought them in England," said the owner. "They were in a house sale."

There was something wrong with my grandmother. My God, she was wearing a tiara and round her neck was the unmistakable Order of the Golden Fleece, an ornate necklace with a ram's skin hanging from it. The same sort of thing with my great-aunt Nancy. Gone was her ebony locket and in place was a medal that was later identified as the Order of the Black Eagle, a Prussian order exclusive to royal families. My humble relatives, one by one, had been exalted with Orders and Garters, ropes of pearls (my grandmother Henrietta had seven strands), bejewelled tiaras. My great-uncle Jim had the Manchurian Order of the Dragon on his breast.

"Who were these people?" I inquired.

"Oh they are the noble relations of the late Baron de Dogherty," said the owner. "These photographs were on the walls of his study. No great interest except for the frames. He was very well connected, of course, so perhaps historians . . ."

I bought the pictures without the frames for a price which was too high, although, according to the owner, it was too low; the usual thing.

On examination by a photographic expert, and comparison with the photos that had not been stolen, it was plain they had been re-photographed with those fake ensignia, about which Damian had been a real expert, tricked in. He had also learned something from his marriage to that Peruvian photographer; it had not been a total loss. But this was what he had lived for: the Order of Henry the Lion, the Order of the Starry Cross, even the Order of the Red Flag . . .

I love these fake pictures, all of them. But my favourite is that of my mother's cousin, slim Mrs Henderson, in profile, stooping, not to examine her sewing machine, but to enter her superimposed Rolls. And standing by the door of the car is the superimposed chauffeur, her dream of a lifetime come true.

THE HANGING JUDGE

"The passing of sentence," wrote one of the newspapers, "obviously tried the elderly judge. In fact, he looked as if he had seen a ghost." This was not the only comment that drew attention to Sir Sullivan Stanley's expression under his wig and that deadly black cap required by British law at the time. It was the autumn following the lovely summer of 1947. The yellow and brown leaves scuttled merrily along the paths in the park.

It had been Justice Stanley's lot to condemn to death several men in the course of his career – no women, incidentally, but that was due to the extreme rarity of women murderers. Certainly, no one would have suggested that Sullivan Stanley would hesitate in the case of a woman to pronounce the words, like a tolling bell, "that you be taken from this place . . . and that you be there hanged by the neck until you be dead". (And, almost as an afterthought, "May the Lord have mercy on your soul.")

The man in the dock was in his thirties, good-looking, as respectable a person in appearance as might be found briskly crossing the street outside the Old Bailey where the trial was taking place. He was George Forrester, perpetrator of what were known to the radio-listening and newspaper-reading public of those days as "the mud-river murders".

Sir Sullivan Stanley's facial expression throughout the trial had been no different from his expression at any other time or in any other trial. He invariably gave the impression that he was irritated by the accused – especially in one notable case where a man had pleaded guilty and refused to be persuaded by his own counsel or anybody else that "guilty" and "not guilty" were mere technicalities, that in fact to plead guilty dispensed more or less with the trial. In no previous case, then, had the press remarked on this expression. Sir Sullivan had loose, spaniel-like jowls and looked the age he was and as annoyed as he was. But "something seemed to come over the Justice," wrote another reporter. "He was plainly shaken, not so much when he heard the foreman of the jury pronounce the word 'guilty' as when he put on the black cap which had been lying before him. Can it be possible," speculated this reporter, "that Judge Stanley is beginning to doubt the wisdom of capital punishment?"

Sullivan Stanley was not beginning to doubt anything of the kind. The reason for the peculiar expression on his face as he passed judgment on that autumn afternoon in 1947 was that, for the first time in some years, he had an erection as he spoke; he had an involuntary orgasm.

It was said that a man who was hanged automatically had an erection at the moment of the drop. Justice Stanley pondered this piece of information. He wondered if it was true. However that might be, he could find no connection with his own experience at passing sentence. But whenever, throughout the months and years to come, he thought about this case, he felt an inexplicable excitement.

The murderer, George Forrester, had stayed, as everyone knew, at the Rosemary Lawns Hotel in north London. It was there he had met the last of his victims, and the discovery of her body and the clues he furnished led to the other bodies. During the course of the trial, Justice Stanley had by way of a working scruple deliberately gone to look at the hotel from the outside. It was small, private, moderately priced, refined, and did not seem to deserve the two policemen who stood outside the entrance during the trial to keep the press and other intrusive elements from bothering those few remaining guests who had not packed up and fled as soon as the mud-river murder case hit the headlines.

In court, the manager gave evidence. A man of good presence, aged thirty-five, direct and frank, he impressed Justice Stanley in inverse proportion to the contempt the judge felt for George Forrester, the man at the bar. Justice Stanley usually despised the accused on some account or other quite distinct from the facts of the case. This time, it was the bright brown, almost orange, Harris tweed coat that the prisoner wore, in addition to his rusty-brown little moustache.

In 1947 George Forrester managed to murder three women in one year. Before that, he had no criminal record whatsoever. He was a commercial traveller in fishing tackle and gear, and apparently, according to his frightened and helpless wife, was in the habit of going off fishing in rivers throughout the country, wherever he happened to be at the end of a working week. His victims, three in all, were discovered shot in the head among reedy marshes where he had been seen wearing waders, plying his rod.

The three victims had in common that they were large, overweight women, widowed and middle-aged. George Forrester met them all in medium-priced genteel hotels where the guests had a fixed arrangement. His object was to rob the women of their jewellery and the contents of their handbags, and this he did in all three cases. The last case, that of Mrs Emily Crathie, was the one for which he was tried before Justice Stanley. An interesting feature of the case was that George Forrester claimed to have had sex with Mrs Crathie before bringing her to her muddy death among the reeds, although the forensic evidence argued against any sexual activity.

George Forrester admitted that he had offered Mrs Crathie "a day out fishing". She occupied the next table to his at the Rosemary Lawns Hotel. This had been noticed by the manager and his wife and also by some of the other permanent clients. Her sudden absence was also noticed and, after a few days, reported to the police, no relatives being known.

In Mrs Crathie's case the killer had been obliged to transport her body, minus her considerable diamond solitaire ring and other possessions, from his car to a part of a river in Norfolk where the reeds and banks were thicker than at the equally tranquil spot where he had killed her by pistol shot in the back of the head. The other two women had been killed and concealed in much the same way, but in the case of Mrs Crathie it was a mystery, never to be explained by the investigative brains of England, how George Forrester, a slight man, had managed to convey massive Mrs Crathie from her death place to his car and from his car to her grave among the reeds.

The hue and cry for the three missing women was afoot when George presented himself at a Norfolk police station with a mud-stained size-42 full bra, claiming he had fished it up when trying out his tackle on some water stretch of the county. The police interrogated George Forrester who, according to psychological explanations, had "wanted" to be caught and, in fact, thus *was* caught. The specimen of bra had been purchased by George himself from a nearby ladies' garments store, and, curiously, he had got Mrs Crathie's measurement right.

Justice Stanley listened to all this, back in 1947, summed up, took the verdict, passed judgment – death by hanging – and experienced an inexplicable orgasm. He remembered it frequently from that day onwards.

Sir Sullivan Stanley (he had been knighted) was in his mid-fifties at the time of George Forrester's trial. The death penalty in England was afterwards abolished, and so there was no further call for Sir Sullivan to experience another such orgasm. Lady Stanley was some years older than her husband, just past her sixties. She was known everywhere as a good lady full of charitable activities such as prison visiting, the governing of schools, the organizing of soup kitchens. She had borne one son, now a lawyer in private practice. Sex in her life was a thing of the past; in fact, her recurring bouts of rheumatism prevented her from sharing anyone's bed.

At that time, Sir Sullivan frequented a lady who was known to the legal profession and who occasionally kept an afternoon for him. Lady Stanley suspected nothing of her existence, nor did she need to know. The affair, if it could be called that, between Sir Sullivan and Mary Spike, the lady in question, was something of an animated cartoon. She induced a mild sensation in the Justice; nothing more. Lady Stanley did not think for a moment that her husband could have another woman. She felt he was too pompous to take off his trousers in another person's house, and in this she was almost right.

After the death of Lady Stanley, Sir Sullivan, approaching his seventies, now visited Mary Spike occasionally, but just for the visit. The unusual circumstances of his sexual experience on the sentencing of George Forrester had really taken him by surprise.

He often thought back on the day when he had that orgasm in court. What happened to that gratuitous orgasm? Where was it now? It was like a butterfly fluttering away into the summer, always eluding the net. It even occurred to him that he might achieve one orgasm more before he died, by hanging himself. But it was problematic whether the phenomenon of an erection would amount to the sensation of an orgasm in a man whose neck was on the point of breaking, if not already broken. Besides, the secretly distraught judge mused, a suicide would look so bad in the *Times* obituary. Not to be thought of.

When Sir Sullivan retired he stayed for a while with his son in Hampstead. But this didn't work well. He decided to go and live in a residential hotel, and it was with great excitement that he discovered that the Rosemary Lawns Hotel was still functioning. Memories of the trial of George Forrester came back to him ever more vividly.

The Rosemary Lawns Hotel sparkled with new paint the day the judge went to seek a room there. The "Lawns" referred evidently to a tennis court, adjacent to the hotel, and an equal-sized stretch of flower-bordered lawn on the other side of a gravel path. It was early autumn, and the leaves scuttled along the tree-lined street. Some schoolgirls were chirpily playing tennis.

Sir Sullivan asked for the manager. A short figure came out of the back office. His white hair and slightly thickened appearance at first, and only for a moment, concealed the fact that this was probably the very man, the actual proprietor of the hotel, who had given evidence in court all those years ago.

"Are you Mr Roger Cook?" inquired the Justice.

"Yes, indeed, sir."

"Good afternoon. I'm Sir Sullivan Stanley."

"The Judge! Sir Sullivan, you don't show your years."

"Yes, I'm the Judge himself. I have been here before, you know. At the time of the trial, when I came to case the joint, if I may use a vulgarism."

"Sir Sullivan," said Roger Cook, "it was a very hard time for us. All the permanent clients left. We thought of changing the name of the hotel, but we sat it out. We were especially grateful to you for that reference to Rosemary Lawns Hotel in your summing up."

"What was that?" said Sir Sullivan.

"You said we were a perfectly respectable place, clean and cosy. That it was no reflection on the establishment that the accused and his unfortunate victim happened to have taken up their abode at Rosemary Lawns. I recall the very words," said Roger Cook. "We always quoted them to the press when we gave interviews in those tragic weeks."

"Well, I congratulate you on the appearance of the place. I am glad to see the tennis court is being used."

"We rent out the court on certain days to a private school," said Roger Cook.

"Well, I'll be direct," said Sir Sullivan Stanley. "I'm looking for a comfortable place for my retirement. A fairly large room, bath and television. And, of course, a dining-room. If you don't have the dining-room any more, I'm afraid it's no good. To me, the dining-room is essential."

"But of course, Sir Sullivan, we have the same dining-room. Nothing's changed except the decoration. Come with me. It would be an honour to have you here."

He led the way to the dining-room, where the tables were laid for dinner with pink cloths. On one table stood a bottle of Milk of Magnesia, but that alone was not enough evidence against the quality of the dinner. Roger Cook showed Sir Sullivan the menu: mulligatawny soup followed by breast of lamb, peas and potatoes. Cheese (if required – extra charge according to choice), and strawberry or vanilla ice cream. Coffee or decaffeinated, as desired. Tea on request.

Sir Sullivan said, "Which of those tables did George Forrester occupy?"

"The third on the right under the window if I'm not mistaken. And poor Mrs Crathie's was the next table to his, second on the right. Of course, we hold receptions, and so on. We use the supplementary dining-room."

"The table by the window looks delightful," said Sir Sullivan with an air of decided nonchalance. "Nice outlook."

The proprietor, somewhat puzzled that the old Judge would actually prefer to sit in the murderer's chair, nevertheless made haste to assure the Judge that that particular table was not occupied by permanent *pensionnaires* at that moment.

So Sir Sullivan Stanley made an agreeable arrangement with the hotel and moved in the following Monday. He came down to dinner at quarter to eight to find the dining-room three-quarters full and some of the diners already nearing the end of the meal.

A middle-aged woman with a long neck sat at the table next to his. She had reached the coffee stage.

"Good evening," said the Justice.

She responded with a kind of extra warmth, as if she approved of this gentleman, it being somewhat of a lottery who one got at the next table.

The waiter brought Sir Sullivan's soup.

The Justice turned to his neighbour, "Are you by any chance," he said, "Mrs Crathie?"

"No, my name is Mrs Morton. Do I resemble a friend of yours?"

"No – no friend. Just a person."

Sir Sullivan felt happy in her company. There was a small fire at the end of the dining-room. Cosy. He thought of the schoolgirls who had been playing tennis outside, so encouraging to look at. He thought then of Mary Spike, his part-time mistress of so many years ago, and remembered how one afternoon when he had failed to come up to scratch she had cruelly laughed at him. "What an antique pendant you've got there. Talk about hanging judge! You're the hanging judge!"

Justice Stanley, seated at the late George Forrester's table, where the man had once sat wearing that bright brown Harris tweed coat, looked at and partook of his mulligatawny soup. Then he looked across at Mrs Morton with the greatest surprise – transfixed in a dreamy joy, as if he had seen a welcome ghost.

Mrs Morton sipped her coffee and looked at him.

ACKNOWLEDGEMENTS

"The Go-Away Bird", "You Should Have Seen the Mess", "Come Along, Marjorie" and "The Black Madonna" first published by Macmillan 1958. Copyright © Muriel Spark, 1958.

"The Curtain Blown by the Breeze" first published in the *London Magazine* 1954. Copyright © Muriel Spark, 1954.

"Bang-Bang You're Dead", "The Fathers' Daughters", "The Dark Glasses" first published by Macmillan 1961 in *Voices at Play*. Copyright © Muriel Spark, 1961.

"The Seraph and the Zambesi" first published in the *Observer* 1951. Copyright © Muriel Spark, 1951.

"The Pawnbroker's Wife" first published in the *Norseman* in 1953. Copyright © Muriel Spark, 1953.

"The Snobs" first published in *Harpers & Queen* 1998. Copyright © Muriel Spark, 1998.

"A Member of the Family" first published in the *Lady* 1958. Copyright © Muriel Spark, 1958.

"The Fortune-Teller" first published in the *New Yorker* 1983. Copyright © Muriel Spark, 1983.

"Open to the Public" first published by Constable 1989. Copyright © Muriel Spark, 1989.

A NOTE ON THE TYPE

Goudy Old Style was designed by Frederic W. Goudy in 1915. It is a graceful, slightly eccentric typeface, and is prized by book designers for its elegance and readability.

Inspired by William Morris' Arts and Crafts movement, Frederic Goudy designed over ninety typefaces throughout his career, and is one of the most influential American type designers of the twentieth century.